Sc

Stephen O'Donnell

Ringwood Publishing
Glasgow

First published in Great Britain in 2014 by
Ringwood Publishing
7 Kirklee Quadrant, Glasgow G12 0TS
www.ringwoodpublishing.com
e-mail   mail@ringwoodpublishing.com

ISBN 978-1-901514-13-1

British Library Cataloguing-in Publication Data
A catalogue record for this book is available from the British
Library

Typeset in Times New Roman 11
Printed and bound in the UK
by Lonsdale Direct Solutions

Acknowledgements

Thanks to: Cliff, Tony, Gregor and of course Lizzy

Thanks also to everyone at Ringwood Publishing for helping to get this book published, especially my Editor, Lynsey Smith

About the Author   Stephen O'Donnell

Stephen O'Donnell was born and lives in Glasgow. His first novel, Paradise Road, was published by Ringwood in 2012. He is currently working on a third book.

Praise for Paradise Road

"A spectacular debut novel packed with social insight but all captured in real world dialogue that flows superbly" **Bella Caledonia**

"O'Donnell has been compared to Irvine Welsh much, and one can really see why" **The Irish World**

"Gritty and often hard hitting... an enjoyable journey of self-discovery" **FourFourTwo magazine**

"O'Donnell relays some great anecdotes and experiences" **The Irish Post**

"Paradise Road is a fantastic read. The short, sharp chapters make it easy to devour and the affinity most Celtic fans will feel with Kevin McGarry is palpable." **Etims.net**

"Provides a subtly impassioned reminder of how much more enjoyable the matchday experience was before the gentrification of football" **When Saturday Comes**

"A bold, biting and thoughtful novel, Paradise Road will strike a chord with many - and not just those of a Celtic persuasion. An excellent and entertaining read." **TheCelticWiki.com**

Dedication

To my daughter Anna Catherine.
You won't be reading this for a long time, babygirl.

O wad some power the giftie gie us

To see oursels as ithers see us

It wad frae mony a blunder free us

An' foolish notion

What airs in dress an' gait wad lea'e us

An' ev'n devotion

Robert Burns

(who could never have conceived of television)

PART 1

1. THE CANAL

'Canal capital of Scotland' the sign reads as you drive into Kirkintilloch, although some witty young urchin has scored out the 'C' at the beginning. The place has changed a lot in recent times, almost beyond recognition in fact, since the dimly remembered days of my formative years, although I've seen enough pictures and family photographs and heard enough highly elaborate stories in my time to suggest that the transformation and growth of the town has been more or less continuous over the decades, going back as far as living memory can testify and beyond. The canal itself has undergone something of a facelift recently and is looking relatively presentable these days, I'm pleased to note, compared to the sickly, green, weed- and junk-infested eyesore that I seem to remember growing up. This town is still my nominal home, although it's been over five years since I was back here, and as we drive up to the parental home on our way in from the airport, it's as if my senses are being assaulted from every angle by the strange familiarity of it all; the sights, the sounds, the smells, the general ambience of the place. The question, what the Christ am I doing here, is one that occurs to me readily enough.

— You'll need to take Lenka up to see the Antonine Wall, my father ventures as we tour through the town centre.

— What is that, Peter, what is this wall? Lenka immediately asks me in her soft Czech accent.

— Kirkie's one and only tourist attraction, I inform her. — If you don't count the canal, that is. I wouldny get your hopes up though, honey, there isny much to see.

— Oh, the Roman wall? Yes you can show me this afternoon. I want to get to know everything about your town, my wife tells me. She's showing an endearing interest in my background and upbringing, a result of her natural intellectual curiosity, but I cany help thinking that on this occasion it's only going to lead to a crushing sense of disappointment.

— That shouldny take too long, I reply.

— Come on, Peter, where's your manners? You need to be a good host, the old boy admonishes me, although I sense from his tone and his wry smile that he's probably sharing at least part of my scepticism. Like I say, it's sweet of Lenka to take an interest in where I'm from, I've lived in her home town for the last five and a half years after all, but her enthusiasm is also unnerving me slightly, because it's no gony take her too long before she realises that Kirkie, unlike Prague, wasny too heavily influenced by the Renaissance. I wouldny exactly describe the place as much ay a cultural epicentre, although mind you, it could have been worse. At least I didny grow up in Airdrie.

— Už jsem ti vysvětlil, I explain to Lenka in her own language. *I've told you already,* — I'll be catching up on my sleep this afternoon.

The car pulls into the driveway of the familiar old Fitzpatrick home and we begin to debus. As we arrive I can see my mother's wee face, all smiles and curiosity, poking through the living-room curtains at us. When she opens the door the rucksack over my shoulder provokes her to burst into song: Happy Wanderer, The Traveller Returns, I love to go a-wandering … followed by a bear-hug. I think Lenka was expecting a more formal, cheek-to-cheek, Continental-style greeting, but she's treated to a full embrace as well. It's only the second time my parents have met Lenka, the first was the occasion of our marriage out in Prague last year, but already they've started treating her like the daughter they never had. We're ushered into the living-room where early afternoon tea has been prepared in advance of our arrival, and as I take our gear up to the bedroom, Lenka is already being interrogated on our recent journey, our plans for the future, as well as married life in general, while at the same time being force-fed from a selection of shortbread, tea cakes and empire biscuits. When I'm finally able to sit down, I notice that she's been taking an unnervingly keen interest in a display of family photographs that are arranged on the mantelpiece, which show a vaguely familiar looking child in various poses and outfits, none of them particularly flattering.

— Just as well I got better looking as I got older, I indicate.

— Poor Peter was an only child, my wife laments with more than a trace of irony in her voice.

— Aye, one ay him was enough, my mother acknowledges.

We spend some time with the mater and pater engaged in this perfunctory idle chit-chat for a while. It's no that I'm no pleased to see them, quite the opposite in fact, but it seems that almost as soon as I'm seated and comfortable I find masel struggling to keep my eyelids apart. The much pressed upon Lenka seems to be bearing up well though, but eventually I notice her trying to stifle back a yawn as well, and if she's feeling anything like me, she must be about to nod off, so I decide I better try and rescue her. We abandon the traditional Caledonian vein-clogging selection and heart-attack inducing assortment of confectionery that's been put in front of us and leave the rest of the catching up for a later occasion so we can head up to my old room to try and grab some sleep. The two ay us have been on the go since 5am Central European Time this morning, and as soon as Lenka manages to climb over our luggage into my newly made up bed, she pretty much crashes out.

At least she had the good sense no to tank hersel up wi coffee, because although I'm lying alongside her, I find that I cany shut my eyes now, despite the fact that I've had about three hours sleep in the last day and a half and I'm feeling completely exhausted. My mother was asking us all about our plans, and although I effectively managed to swerve most of her inquiries for the time being, the recent caffeine injection

4

has started to kick in and they now seem to be reoccurring to me all at once, questions and dilemmas and partially considered solutions flashing in front of my racing mind and preventing me from sleeping. Just why have we come back here, and now that we're here, what the hell do we intend to do wi oursels? Can I honestly see masel going back to work in the financial services sector again, given that one of the main reasons I moved abroad was to get away from my job in the first place, and particularly considering everything that has happened to the industry in the intervening years? I've persuaded myself that it's time to do a bit ay growing up, and that seemed to mean coming home and trying to resume some form of gainful employment. Teaching English was only ever a stop-gap occupation, it was the one job any native speaking ex-pat out in Prague could secure, and although I took it semi-seriously and ended up as a director of the language school that employed me, I never really saw masel as being in it for the duration. When the global financial crisis hit and the work gradually started to dry up, that's when I took the decision to walk away voluntarily and in the process maybe save somebody else's job.

I had a look around for some other work, but to be honest there didny seem to be anything that really appealed or was worthwhile, and I found masel drifting back into the old routine of hanging out wi my mates and staggering home at four in the morning, which is fine when you've nae responsibilities and you're basically just in town for an extended holiday, but no really the done thing once you've settled down and got married. I'd taken up writing, and had a few articles published in English language newspapers and magazines, including a new, British-based football webzine that was looking for occasional pieces about the Central and Eastern European scene. But overall living by the pen seemed to me to be a hand to mouth existence, and I didny want to burden my new wife wi the uncertainties and insecurities that would inevitably be involved wi that sort ay lifestyle. There were a few decent, semi-permanent jobs available that I could have accepted, but the problem in general seemed to be that, despite the increased value of the local currency in comparison to Sterling, the exact same jobs back home were always better paid. I found myself at a bit ay a loose end, so eventually I talked it over wi Lenka and to my surprise she seemed keen to come back here, even though it would mean having to give up a job she enjoyed, leaving behind her friends and family and exchanging it all for an uncertain future in a foreign country. She was an EU citizen though and married to a Scot, so it wasny as if she was gony be left in the precarious position of an asylum seeker or an economic migrant.

I'm wide awake now so I decide to abandon any immediate thoughts of rest and I head back downstairs to see what's left of the cakes and biscuits we were being treated to, as if my arteries haveny taken enough punishment already, and maybe have a shot at trying to overfeed masel to sleep.

— Your pal, what's his name, Mark Sullivan, has been on the phone looking for you, my dad informs me, as I put away another Caramel Wafer. It's all the excuse I need. I knew that Sully would be trying to get in touch wi me as soon as I stepped off the plane, although to be honest I was hoping for some sort ay grace period, a few hours maybe to shrug off the jet-lag, before throwing masel head-first back into everything that the old Kirkie lifestyle had to offer. Clearly there's been a change ay plan already. I make a quick call to Sully on his mobile phone, throw on a pair ay jogging bottoms and some trainers and wait for the boy himself to come round and pick me up. When he arrives I head out, leaving Lenka dead to the world up in the bedroom. She'll no be awake for hours, she was up aw last night saying her goodbyes to half ay Prague and then doing all her last minute packing into the wee small hours, before our 5am crack-of-sparrows alarm call.

— Good to see you, Fitzy, Sully greets me, all smiles, as I climb into his motor. — How does it feel to be back in Kirkie?

— Pretty surreal so far, to be honest, Mark, I tell him. Sully has been an occasional visitor to Prague in the last couple ay years, his most recent trip was just a few months ago when I told him of my tentative plans to come home, since when he's been in regular contact, demanding constant updates to my itinerary and all the details of my intended schedule. I think he's genuinely pleased and surprised that I've finally managed to make a decision, and as a result here I am, sitting next to him in his car as we speed up to Gallowhill thegether. I'm feeling acutely conscious, as we negotiate our way through the all too familiar townscape, that it's almost as if I was never away fae this place and that the last five years of my life might never have happened for all that things have changed around here, and I know that this awareness is only gony become more pronounced once we arrive at our destination.

— I can imagine, he replies. — Are you ready for a culture shock?

— I'm ready, aye. I may have been away for a while, Sully, but I'm still a Kirkie boy. It's good to be back, I do my best to assure him. — What's the score here? I ask, as we pull up to Lenzie Moss.

— Looks like we're gettin beat, Sully indicates as we get out the car and survey the scene. Across the Moss I can make out several figures kicking a ball about an open field, some of them in Celtic strips, a few in Rangers gear, and one poor bastard in a Partick Thistle shirt. As we arrive the ball is fired between the posts and into the back of the net-free goal, causing some of the Rangers boys to roar in celebration.

— Looks like the Catholics are missing my strong influence in midfield, I tell Sully. We leave the car and stroll across the Moss to where the match is being played. This Catholics versus Protestants game, or Tims v Huns to use the local vernacular, has been a semi-regular fixture up on the Moss since long before I departed the scene here. It's good to see that it's still going strong and that old habits die hard, even though there are maybe a few less recognisable and considerably younger faces involved now than would otherwise have been the case if it was all the old troops still playing.

My arrival seems to have attracted the attention of one or two vaguely more familiar faces who were involved in the game, and for a moment the play stops as a few boys come over to say hello.

— The rumours are true, Francis Reid observes wryly.

— Seems like it, Franny, aye.

— What brings you back to this neck ay the woods, Peter?

— Can you no get Celtic TV over in Czechoslovakia?

— Are you still in wi that wee Prague bird, Fitzy?

— I married her, Tambo, so aye. I try to fire back rapid answers to these as well as quite a few other questions, as I find myself overwhelmed wi inquiries. — What's the score? I eventually ask.

— That's 4 – 3 to them, Franny informs us.

— Looks like the Tims are missing my influence in the middle ay the park, I repeat my earlier assertion.

— You're no wrang, we should be fuckin oot ay sight by noo, Robert Skelton remarks, taking the opportunity from the break in play to exchange his sweat-stained version of the current Rangers jersey for an earlier equivalent. Skelton seems to have virtually doubled in size since the last time I saw him, morphing into a bona fide fat bastard of late, to the extent that I'm finding it difficult to drag my eyes away from the unexpected sight of his beer gut and man tits, as he throws his shirt away. I'm wondering if it might be possible to measure the passage of time according to the inflation of his waistline, like you do wi trees, because more than anything else I've seen since I came home, Skelly's appearance forces me to consider that over half a decade has elapsed since I was last running about here, and we're no all as young as we used to be.

— How many ay they strips have you got, Skelly? I inquire, trying to keep the level of sarcasm in my voice to a minimum.

— I've got them aw, mate, he boasts, as he retrieves the dry shirt from his Rangers kit-bag.

— Who do you think kitted oot hawf this team? One of his mates points out.

— I seen you come prepared yoursel, Fitzy, Franny observes, checking out my Kappa Trax and Reeboks.

— Aye, I heard there was a game on.

— Sully? You gony help us oot here, mate?

— Aye, we need to keep the numbers even but. Who's coming aff? It seems the break in play is over, but there's still some reorganisation required, if me and Sully are gony be accommodated into the game.

— Nae cunt's coming aff. John, you go back on their side, pal, Franny instructs one of the younger boys. Young John doesny seem to be too pleased about the idea of switching sides but Franny encourages him, — Mon, mate, it'll no be long before it's next goal wins. Skelly! You take the boy here, we'll have Sully and Fitzy. John, ask him to gie you wan ay his Rangers taps, Franny cany help taking the mince out the lad.

The game resumes with tackles flying in, outrageous shots being attempted, and mazy dribbles being performed all over the bumpy pitch. The scores are soon level at five each and it's not long before 'next goal wins' is declared, just as Franny predicted, and you can tell neither team wants to lose it at this stage. I'm playing on the right and, given my modest ability, it's no surprising that I'm on the end of some abrupt and forthright Glaswegian directives, as I struggle to pick up the pace ay the game.

— Intae him, Fitzy! Franny encourages me and I pluck up

the courage to steam into a tackle. The challenge leaves my opponent floundering in the mud and I'm particularly pleased to note that, as a result of my zealous intervention, the boy's light blue jersey has now been stained a shitey shade ay brown. It seems I've managed to win the ball as well and it's out for a shy.

— Huns' baw! Skelly shouts and naebidy's gony argue. But from the throw-in a young Celtic kid nips in and picks up the ball. The lad neatly steps away from a sliding tackle and rolls it out to the wing for me to run onto.

— Brilliant! Comes a shout from a hooped jersey. I control the pass with a delicate first touch, which isny as easy as it sounds on this pitch because I think it would be easier to demonstrate the fine art of ball technique and close control if we were playing this game on the surface ay the moon. I manage to swing over a ball into the imaginary penalty-box but a defender heads my cross away, meaning that the Tims have won a corner-kick.

— C'mon the Hoops! Big Albert shouts in encouragement as he jogs across to take the corner. He's clearly knackered and his 70s style hooped replica shirt is dripping wi sweat.

— Heid this yin away, boys, the Rangers troops encourage one another, the tension clearly etched on every wan ay their ugly pusses.

Albert floats in the corner and the ball is heading in my direction. I try to get some sort of contact on it and glance the ball towards goal but a defender has nipped in ahead of me and he nods it away. Only as far as the edge of the box however, where Franny Reid has strategically positioned himself. The defender has got height on his clearance but not distance, and as it falls out of the sky, Franny adjusts his body position and swings his left foot at the ball. He's struck a stinging volley which nearly takes my head off as it whizzes past me. It's a sweet, sweet connection he's made, and as I duck out the way,

I'm aware that the shot not only has power and pace behind it, but seems to be on target as well. The ball hits the crossbar with a dull thud and bounces down over the line, into the back of the non-existent net. It's 6–5 to the Tims. The Lenzie Celts have won the day and Franny is tearing across the Moss in celebration, doing a half-decent impression of Marco Tardelli.

By the time we make it to the pub we've just about managed to find him again.

*

— You mairrit noo, Fitzy, aye? Big Melly asks me, as he returns from the bar and takes a big, heavy swig from the pint of fizzy, watered down pish that he's bought himself.

— I am, Melly, I confirm. — It's coming up on our anniversary in fact.

— Is she Czech, aye? Tooncey seems keen to probe. — I could tell you a few things aboot Czech birds by the way.

— Aye, but Peter didny find this yin on the internet, Toonce, Gerry McCourt correctly points out.

— Still, she must be a bit ay looker if she's Czech, Franny reasons.

— She's the one wi the looks, right enough, I try to answer.

— No hawf! She's a pure darling, so she is. Come on, Peter, blow your ain trumpet here, Sully encourages me.

— How do you know that, Mark, have you met her, aye?

— Aye, I've met her, I've been over to Prague a few times now. She's a gorgeous looking girl, man, honestly.

— We'll no be seeing much ay you then, Peter, if that's you married now, Gerry states.

— That's right, it was nice knowing you boys. I'll see yous again in another five years, no doubt.

— Aye that's him under the thumb for sure, Sully affirms. — It's always the case wi a bird like that. Do you know, he even had to wait until his missus fell asleep before he could come oot tae see his pals that he's no seen in Christ knows how long, he lambasts me.

— He's no the ainly yin that's under the thumb, look at that shower, Gerry notes with some disdain, indicating Franny Reid and Michael McGuire who are on the point of leaving the pub after no more than a solitary pint each, along wi most ay the remaining Rangers boys.

— Haw! I'm steyin and I've got a burd, fat Skelly reminds us, — I'm the wan that wears the fuckin troosers in oor hoos!

— I'm taken an aw, Sully adds.

— It's only you that's no gettin a ride, Ger, Melly tells Gerry, although I'm no sure if he's including himself in his quickfire survey, because I pity the poor lassie who has big Melly coming home to her every night ay her life.

There's about half a dozen or so of us left that have decided to stay on and make a night ay it. We order up some more beers and I give them some more of my Prague stories, and in turn they're giein me some ay their Kirkie stories and telling me all about what I've apparently been missing out on for the last five or six years. I'm genuinely quite flattered by the interest they seem to be showing in where I've been and what I've been doing wi masel lately, and how pleased they apparently are to be in ma company again. At first I suspected that their greetings and their enquiries were just an excuse, a reason no to go home but to linger a while longer in the pub, because I don't think they need much persuading, these boys, but my reservations are gradually being swept aside on a torrent of cheap alcohol and rekindled friendships.

We order up some food and some more beer and settle back to watch the Sunday evening Spanish game on the plasma screen telly – Athletic Bilbao versus Atletico Madrid. During the course of the ninety minutes I become gradually and steadily aware that the copious amount of drink which has been free flowing in my direction for several hours now is slowly and irresistibly beginning to assume command ay my brain. Or to put it another way, as they generally prefer to say around here, I'm starting tae get a taste fir the pish. This leads me once more to reflect on my recent decision to return home, and for the first time I'm maybe beginning to relish the prospect of reacquainting myself with everything that West of Scotland life has to offer. Although at the same time I'm no so bladdered that I don't appreciate that this is the sort ay thing that tends to happen when you start to see things fae a swally assisted perspective.

Bilbao give the Madridistas a good humping, although it's nothing compared to the total thrashing that Barcelona subsequently dish out to some lesser Spanish Nou Camp cannon fodder. Fuck me, I've watched enough football in ma day, but what a side they look! It appears we've pretty much lasted the duration, and the end of the one-sided Catalonian goalfest seems to indicate that we've more or less made it through to closing time. We're on the point of finishing up when big Melly, who we thought had well and truly disappeared about four hours ago, staggers back into the pub looking to rejoin us.

— Fucks sakes, I thought we'd seen the last ay that cunt, Sully remarks.

Melly takes some time to regain his bearings before remembering where we were sitting and lurching over towards us.

— Still here, aye? he observes sarcastically in our direction.

— Still here, Melly, I thought you'd went home, ya cunt, Gerry tells him.

Melly ignores the remark and instead trains his focus on me. — Fuckin great to see you, Fitzy, he slurs. — Tell old Garra, I was asking for him an aw.

— I'll pass on your regards, Melly, next time I see him.

— Tell him to get back here. Where the fuck is he? Melly wonders aloud. — Tell the boy to get back here.

— I think Garra's pretty happy where he is the now, Melly. I don't think he has any plans to come home anytime soon, and I've nae plans to go back so you'll need to go out to Prague and tell him yoursel, I explain curtly. I've just been chatting wi the boys about Kevin McGarry, the only other Kirkie lad we still know in the Czech Republic, and I'm no in the mood to go over it aw again for Melly's benefit.

— Aye, I might dae that, Melly considers.

Some of the boys seem to have taken Melly's belated reappearance as the signal to finally call it a night. Naebidy's in a fit state to drive so Gerry and Tambo and wee Mickey Doyle make phone calls and wander off into the night, after much backslapping and handshaking and promises no to be strangers now that we're aw well and truly properly reacquainted. Me and Sully decide to hoof it round to the train station to see if we can find a taxi, and we have Melly in tow as well, because a taxi seems to be his plan an aw. He's pished as a bastard, the boy's obviously been knocking them back in some other establishment for the last good few hours, and he starts giein a few ay the old Celtic songs a good airing, as we're walking up the street to the station: *Hail! Hail! The Celts are here! What the hell do we care? What the hell do we care? Hail! Hail!*

— Gie it a rest, Melly, eh? It's a fuckin residential area, Sully warns him.

— Away to fuck, man. `Mon, Fitzy, sing! *O father why are you so sad on this bright Easter morn.* Sing, Fitzy, c'mon!

— Shush, mate, come on, nae sectarianism, eh? I urge.

14

— Sectarianism? Did you say sectarianism, Fitzy? Melly slurs. — It's no a sectarian song, he looks at me pleadingly.

— I know, you're right, Melly, it's no. But there's a time and a place, sure? I don't think the brainwashed residents ay Lenzie will want to argue the point at this time ay night, dae you? Singing Irish rebel songs at the back ay eleven o'clock on a Sunday night? It cany be the best idea you've ever had, can it, mate? I suggest.

Melly seems to find my description of the good denizens of Lenzie as being brainwashed hysterically funny.

— They are fuckin brainwashed an aw, Fitzy, he congratulates me on my insight.

— See that Rangers game the other night, that European game? Did you hear whit that Dougie Donnelly bastart was saying? "And anyone wi an interest in the well-being of Scottish football is sure to be cheering on Rangers in this evening's Champions League qualifier". I'm like that, Aye, do you fuckin hink so? I'd rather cheer you on, Doogie, while you shag ma wee sister up the arse, than cheer on they cunts in a fuckin Champions League qualifier. You no think, Fitzy? You're the same, are you no?

— Erm, well I don't have a wee sister, Melly, but I can see what you're saying.

— Can you see what I'm saying though, Fitzy, aye? Sully? Can you see what I'm saying, mate?

— I can see what you're saying, Melly, Sully repeats my bland acceptance of the point Melly's making.

— Aye. Too fuckin right. Did you see the game, Fitzy? The Huns got pumped in the end.

— I just seen the goals, mate, I've been out the country, mind? Dougie Donnelly isny exactly top ay the bill in the Czech Republic.

— Oh aye, so you have. Do you agree wi me but? I'm no fuckin cheerin they cunts on, no matter who it is they're playin.

— I just said, I agree wi you, Melly. You're no listening.

It pains me to admit, but if you strip away the drunken overstatement, as well as the partisan prejudices in Melly's assertions, then broadly speaking I'm forced to agree with much of what he's saying, which I suppose is a fairly damning indictment in itself of just what a low ebb Donnelly and many of his colleagues in the mainstream media have come to. Allowing Rangers to pay off their considerable debts to the bank with ill-gotten loot from the Champions League would, I believe, be contrary to the principles of sporting integrity and financial fair-play. And now that they've failed to qualify, the high risk cheque book strategy is gony have to be reassessed, because sooner or later the penny will drop and they'll have to start living within their means again, like the rest ay the clubs in Scotland finally seem to have learned how to do.

Throw in the rumours and suspicions of tax avoidance and improperly registered players, and you can see why I'm no gony be lending Rangers ma support any time soon. Because contrary to Donnelly's alleged contention, I think it will be better for Scottish football in the long run now that Rangers haveny qualified. We might be able to operate on a level playing-field once more, with clubs in general following the model that Celtic seem to have adopted, of living within their means and at least trying to keep their finances in order to the extent that they can. And if Rangers' lack of success on the European front has the added effect of putting a check on their recklessness, and the club's overweening arrogance, then that might be an added benefit for the Scottish game as well. Who knows, it might even persuade the media to start taking their responsibilities more seriously and adopt a more even-handed approach on issues such as impartiality, although I'll no be holding my breath on that score.

I may have been out the country for most of the last six years, but modern technology means that I can still keep in touch, and from what I can gather, it seems to me that not much has changed around here recently and the coverage of Scottish football in the mainstream media is every bit as desperate as it ever was.

This is something you begin to appreciate if you live abroad for any length ay time. You gain a wider sense of perspective and you realise that there are alternative ways of operating and things don't necessarily have to be the way they have always appeared. The Czechs are just as interested in football as we are, and their media is equally competitive and every bit as vital and energetic as it is here. But they don't descend to the ridiculous depths of Dougie Donnelly and inane phone-in shows, their coverage is far more sophisticated and intelligent, yet just as informative, and without being remote or distant in any way. I've decided that there's going to be one or two organisations who will be receiving a letter from me in the next week or so, making precisely that point and suggesting solutions as well as possibly offering my services. I'm looking for work after all, and what better route back into gainful employment can there be than exploiting the obvious gap in the market for more honest and intelligent coverage of our national game in the mainstream media? It's no so much a gap in actual fact, more like a yawning chasm, because if a drunken half-wit like Melly can convince me, after his fashion, that he has a stronger case and is on a higher moral and intellectual plane than large sections ay the press in this country, then it's a decent shout that there'll be a fair size percentage of the population that could reasonably claim the same.

Melly is sauntering down the middle ay the road, still singing his songs, when a battered old car comes screeching round the corner and stops right in front ay him.

A guy opens the door and gets out the car. — Was that you singing that shite? he immediately confronts Melly. Melly's looking totally non-plussed, there's not even a hint ay the merest surprise in his reaction, and instead he accepts the question as a challenge. He smiles at the boy, claps his hands and resumes his singing: *Soldiers are we, whose lives are pledged to Ireland, Some have come* ... he shouts in the guy's face. I may have been out the country for a while, but I've seen enough of the rivalry involved in Glasgow's footballing allegiances to know when violence, fuelled by alcohol, is about to rear its ugly, wart-scarred and plook-infested head.

— Mon, mate, he's had a few beers, I attempt to intervene, doing my best to try and sound conciliatory, but I'm wasting my breath. The boy sticks a dull yin on Melly, who staggers back momentarily. But Melly's a big lad, who knows how to handle hissel, I'll gie him that, and as the assailant moves in to deliver a coup-de-grace to his inebriated opponent, Melly boots him in the shin and the boy crumples. It's Melly who issues the final blow of the remarkably brief confrontation, kicking his erstwhile adversary in the baws, then again in the face, bursting his nose as his head hits the tar-mac with a sickening thud.

— Let's go, boys, Melly urges us as he climbs into the driver's seat of the guy's car, which is still parked in the middle ay the road, with the door open and the keys in the ignition.

— I'm no going anywhere wi you, the state you're in, Sully asserts. — Get oot the fuckin motor, Melly, come on. We need to fuckin scarper here.

— Mon! He's coming roon. Get a fuckin move on, in the motor! Melly directs us again.

Now I'm a big fan ay the Rolling Stones, no as much as Sully mind, or one or two others, but I've been to a few gigs and I've built up quite a nice wee collection of CDs and videos over the years. The honest truth is though, I've long since reconciled masel to the fact that I'm no much ay a Street Fighting Man even at the best ay times, and I certainly don't fancy being stuck out here on my own wi this boy in his irate condition, caused by a combination of religious prejudice, a broken nose and being minus one motor. Christ knows how many ay his bigoted mates are about to show up, and I'm fucked if I'm gony hang about and wait for the Polis to appear and sort aw this oot. I don't mind admitting that the abruptness and severity of the violence has panicked me slightly and I have a powerful compulsion to be anywhere else but my present location right now. So against my better judgment I slip into the passenger's seat of the car alongside Melly.

— Just drive us roon the taxi rank, Melly, it's just up the road, I urge. — Haud on, wait for Sully!

Too late. Melly takes off before Sully has the chance to climb into the back seat of the car.

— You've left Sully! Stop the fuckin motor! I shout but Melly doesny seem to be caring.

— He'll be awright, he can take care ay hissel.

— Stop the fuckin car and drop us off, mate. I need to go back and check on Sully.

— I'm tellin you, he's fine, I'll drop you aff in a minute. I know where we're gaun, Melly puts his foot down.

— Who was that guy? I ask.

— I've nae idea but he's gony be needin a new motor in a minute.

— What are you saying? He's already minus the motor, come on, mate, let's dump the thing fir fucks sakes.

— We're gony dump it, just a minute, Melly tells me as we speed down the Kirkie Road thegether.

— Jesus Christ, look at this shite! I pick up a box that was lying on the dashboard but has fallen into my lap with Melly's wayward driving.

— Here, let me see that.

— You just keep your eyes on the road, pal! I affirm. —
My God, can you believe this shite, what was it we were just
saying about sectarian songs, Melly? The box contains various
cassettes and CDs, onto which a varied host of bigoted hymns
have been recorded. I rummage through the tapes and just
about every Hun anthem imaginable has been burned onto
some disc or other. Most of the vile ditties I've never even
heard ay, although it's clear from the titles exactly what the
broader themes are that we're dealing wi, and I reel off a few
ay the names, — The Billy Boys, The Famine Song, No Pope
of Rome, The Sash et cetera, it's the usual bigoted fare …
But look, what's this, 'The Tims are shagging weans.' Jesus
fuckin Christ, can you believe this shite? This cunt's fuckin no
real! I announce, noticing to my surprise that I appear to have
slipped back into the vernacular, perhaps because I've been
confronted with such a peculiarly West of Scotland situation.

— Fling that doon there, Melly tells me, — it's gaun in the
Canal wi everything else.

— Whit you talking aboot, mate? Take us hame fir fuck's
sakes. The way I'm talking by this stage, it's almost as if I was
never away. Maybe Glaswegian really is the best and most
appropriate form of self-expression, given an imminent threat
to one's person, or it could just be that I instinctively realise,
this is the only language that Melly understands. — Either
that or let us oot the fuckin motor. Come on tae fuck, Melly,
gie yoursel a shake, pal, I continue. For a brief but acutely
unpleasant moment I have a vision of my erstwhile chauffeur
speeding off the end ay the bridge and ploughing straight into
the Canal, wi the pair ay us still strapped in our seats like the
crazed fan in the Eminem song. But instead Melly comes over
the bridge and pulls off the road, driving the short distance
down to the footpath by the side of the water.

— Push! he tells me as we exit the vehicle.

— I'm no fuckin pushin anything, I'm away to get a taxi, mate, see you later. I climb back up to the road and watch from the bridge, as Melly pushes the car slowly but inexorably into the Canal. With a gentle splash and a soft gurgle, it disappears under the murky water like a dead sailor being consigned to the sea.

I leave Melly where he stands and check the deserted road in both directions before crossing over and jogging down the iron staircase to the East Side for a taxi.

When I arrive back at chez Fitzpatrick I find my mother still up and about, but there's no sign of Lenka or the old man.

— Did you have a good time with your pals? My mother greets me.

— Erm, aye. It was good to see them again. Most ay them anyway, I tell her hesitantly while trying to get my thoughts in order.

— Are you pleased to be back in Scotland?

— It's great, mum, yeah, it's like I was never away.

— You must have been having a good time anyway, we tried to call you but your phone was switched off.

My phone. Christ, I've still no configured the thing yet. I was hoping that I wouldny need it immediately and I could take things easy for a few days following my return. So much for that idea. I decide to have a look for the memory card and phone Sully to see if he's awright. — Hang on a second, mum, I need to find the thing … No that's right, I explain, — I've no set it up for this country yet. Here it's here … Where did yous go anyway? I ask while inserting the SIM card and hurriedly trying to reassemble the device.

— We went out for dinner. She's a lovely girl, Lenka. I'm telling you, boy, you better be careful wi a lassie like that. You better gie her the attention she deserves, and no just be running aboot wi your pals the whole time.

— Come on, it's my first day back, mum, I stress. — You seen what happened, I couldny sleep and Mark had been trying to get a haud ay us aw morning. It was a good opportunity for you and Lenka to get to know one another again anyway, you've no seen her since the wedding, have you?

— I'm just tellin you, Peter, my mother warns me again, sounding remarkably serious for this time ay night, — you better gie her the attention she deserves. A lassie like that will no staun for anything less.

— We're married, mum. Lenka's no high maintenance, she's had plenty ay opportunity to run off wi somebody else if she wanted to by now, I reply half-jokingly, although at the same time appreciating the sincerity and good sense of my mother's advice. — Where is she anyway? I ask.

— She's up the stair in the room I made up for yous. I'm sure she'll be asleep by now.

— OK, well I'll try no to disturb her. Goodnight, mum.

— Night night, son.

I head up the stair and into the discreet surroundings of the upstairs bathroom so I can call Sully. He reassures me that he's home safe and that there were no further problems, the boy Melly battered simply staggered off into the night, holding his bleeding nose. I don't mention the car in the Canal episode, for fear of being overheard, but I assure him that I'll fill him in soon enough on everything that happened during my brief but remarkable detour on the way home.

— Some first night back for you, was it no? What did I tell you about a culture shock, eh? Sully laughs.

— You wereny wrong, mate, I reflect. — Mair like shell-shock than culture shock. This place never fails to disappoint, does it?

— I'll speak to you soon, Peter, Sully tells me and hangs up.

I switch off the phone and take a pish. I wash my hands and splash some water on my face and head for the bedroom, where I find to my surprise that Lenka isny asleep after all. Instead, as I open the door, I catch her in a semi state of undress and my eyes light up at the sight of her.

— I thought it was your father, she chastises me with an unfamiliar coyness.

— Nobody's going to disturb us in here, I assure her. — Did you have a nice time?

— Nice time, yes, she smiles. I suspect I'm no the only one who's had a few drinks here, I think Lenka must have been knocking back a few vinos herself. I move in and hold her, kiss her, running my hands over her nakedness, with my mother's recent admonition still ringing in my ears: you better gie this lassie the attention she deserves.

— Where did you go? she eventually asks me.

— I went out with my friends. Sorry, darling, I thought you were sleeping.

— Yes I was.

— I didn't want to disturb you, I explain, — and we have plenty of time to do other things together. We make ourselves comfortable in the wee bed and, mindful once again of my mother's wise advice, it's not long before I'm giving her my full, undivided and complete attention. All of which and more, she deserves.

*

Peter Fitzpatrick
67 Park Avenue
Kirkintilloch
Glasgow G66 7ER
tel.: 0141 776 1888
email: pfitzy@hotmail.com

Gus McGregor
Commissioning Editor
The Scottish Broadcasting Company
Digital Media Avenue
Specific Key
Glasgow

Dear Gus,

Following our recent telephone conversation, I am writing to you with regard to my programme idea 'The Scottish Football Debate', which I believe would, if commissioned, be an excellent addition to your network's schedule.

As we discussed on the phone, I believe the current media environment in Scotland is somewhat stale and unimaginative, particularly when it comes to the coverage of sport, and especially football, our national game. My programme, which I would host, would offer a fresh and lively alternative to the rather staid and jejune phone-in shows which currently dominate the genre, and would provide a much needed injection of vitality, energy and intelligence in a popular format. This would allow the SBC to reposition itself and gain a competitive edge over its commercial rivals, as well as reinvigorating the whole culture of sports related broadcasting in Scotland, which ultimately would go on to benefit our national game at all levels.

I admit that my motivation for proposing this project is chiefly ambition. I have recently returned to live in the West of Scotland after spending several years working abroad as an English teacher in the Czech Republic, with little financial reward, having previously given up a well-paid job in the financial services sector here in Glasgow. I am looking to resume gainful employment in a sector that matches my talents and goals such as the media. After all, in an information age such as ours, the people who control the flow and supply of that information are potentially all-powerful, and the prospect of working in this challenging environment excites and enthuses me.

I'm attaching a detailed programme outline as well as a recent copy of my CV, and I look forward to hearing from you at your earliest convenience.

Yours Sincerely,

Peter Fitzpatrick B.A. M.Sc

---

*

2. SMASH AND GRAB

— Do they dae hospitality here? I hear myself wondering aloud, as we trudge across the muddy, rain-soaked pathways that lead up to Adamslie Park's old-fashioned, brickwork turnstiles.

— Don't think so, Peter, no, Mr. Sullivan laughs in acknowledgment of the irony in my question.

— No unless you count a Scotch pie fae the burger van as hospitality, Sully Junior adds flatly.

— I could murder a pie. Point out the van to us, would you, Mark? I'm calling him 'Mark', rather than 'Sully', or 'Sally', or 'Shagger', or 'Numbnuts', or some other equally inappropriate moniker in deference to his father, who's accompanying us on this afternoon's excursion.

— Do you fancy a pie, Peter, right enough? Here. To my mild embarrassment I realise that Mr. Sullivan has apparently taken my last statement at face value and is starting to fish into his pocket for some change. The haste that he displays in his desire to be generous reminds me of the time, I could only have been about four or five year old, when I asked my late, great Uncle Willie, God rest him, if I could have a second ice lolly. I was only trying it on wi the old boy, but suddenly and unexpectedly, and without the admonishment that I'd have expected from my absent parents, old Willie dug into the deep pockets of his overcoat, turned on his heels and headed back to the shop to buy us a second 'Rocket'. Now, whenever Willie's name comes up in conversation, it's usually accompanied by the sardonic addendum: 'he bought Peter two ice lollies.'

— Erm, I could go wan right enough, Mr. Sullivan, I'm pretty hungry, I offer hesitantly. — But you're OK, I don't think I'll risk it.

— Cany say I blame you, the old man considers, — they're

notorious, they pies, sure they are, Mark?

— My God, Fitzy, I swear, keep away fae them. Mind that time doon here, dad, when we seen a guy feeding his dug a pie?

We're attending a Rob Roy home fixture at Adamslie Park, Kirkintilloch. The Rabs as they're affectionately known, or the Sheesh Kebabs, the Smash n' Grabs etc., etc., etc., play in the Stagecoach League West Premier Division and this afternoon's opponents are the mighty Shotts Bon Accord.

We pay our way in, five pound at the gate.

— Fifteen sheets for the three ay us? I think they've got a cheek, considering the standard of football on display, Sully notes.

— This is the only football a lot ay folk can afford to watch these days, his father correctly informs us.

— That's right, Mr. Sullivan, I mind no so long ago it used to be six pound to get into the Jungle, I point out, recalling the days of the famous old terrace at Celtic Park.

— Aye, and the standard wasny much better, Sully quips in reply. He's being facetious of course, although there's a grain of truth in what he's saying because the late eighties and early nineties wereny exactly Celtic's glory years. I'm no sure we ever sank to the level of the Juniors though, and in fact the centenary double winning team of `88 were noted for the excellent football that they played at times. It was during that period that I first caught the Celtic bug, I used to love going to the games in those days, and over the next three or four seasons I was a fairly frequent attender at Celtic Park. I've no been back as regular since that time to be honest, but then the Jungle's been knocked down now and it doesny cost six pound to get in any more. It's a shame really, you can say what you like about the hazards and the health risks of the old standing room only areas, but teams used to shite themselves running out in front ay the Jungle and the atmosphere and the gloomy humour of the terraces is something that's pretty much been lost to the game. It's rare to experience that same kind ay buzz going to watch football now, even in the new, modernised Celtic Park, despite its creature comforts and the splendour of its architecture.

We're supposed to be meeting Martin Coyle in the main stand, so we weave our way around the puddles and the intermittent groups of fellow and rival supporters we encounter along the way, until we reach the roofed enclosure.

— How's Czechoslovakia, Peter? I recognise the voice even before I see the face. Coyler is standing up the back ay the stand, on the top concrete step, and beaming away at us in his familiar, smiley way.

— It's great, Martin, aye. Good to see you, mate, I beam back. It occurs to me that I probably should explain to Coyler that the Czechoslovak state was dissolved in 1993, and that I've been living in a country called the Czech Republic for the last six years or so, but I decide that this probably isny the time or the place for a lesson in central European geopolitics in the post-Cold War era.

— Who's playing the day? Sully inquires, pointing at the team sheet which has been pinned to a nearby pylon. He's looking at me as he says this, but I'm staring blankly straight back at him, as if to say: are you seriously expecting me to gie you chapter and verse on the current Rabs set up?

— I'm a wee bit out ay touch wi the squad these days, Sully, which I thought you might appreciate seeing as how I've been out the country a fair bit recently, I eventually tell him.

—There's the team the now, Mr Sullivan informs us, as a booming voice reads out the starting line-ups over the loudspeaker. Although the announcement is loud, it's also crackly and indistinct and sounds as though it's being

28

transmitted fae a warzone somewhere. By the end I still cany name a single player on either side, despite the fact that I can almost feel my eardrums starting to bleed.

— That you back in Scotland for good, Peter, aye? Coyler's keen to find out more from me.

— Looks like it, Martin, I reply. — Are you still going to see the Rabs every spare Saturday? I ask as the game kicks off.

— I like to come down now and then, he tells me. — No every fortnight though, just the odd occasion.

— Place hasny changed much, has it? I observe, casting an eye over the facilities and the general surroundings.

— No really, no, Coyler looks round the stadium in confirmation, with a smile that leaves me wondering if he wasny just thinking the same thing himself. — Although I suppose that's part ay the charm, he adds.

— It's aw part ay the mystique, aye, I acknowledge, recognising the tongue-in-cheek tone in Coyler's statement. I can see what he means though, because despite my urbane, university educated, citizen of the world aspirations, I can still recognise, this is what it's all about at the end ay the day. Standing up the back ay the main stand at your local ground, watching the fitba and catching up wi your pals that you've no seen in God knows how long. The fitba, the game, at the end ay the day … it doesn't seem to have taken me too long to reacquire the standard clichés of everyday Scottish football parlance and I must admit, even after my lengthy central European sojourn, I can still feel strangely at home here. Unlike Coyler though, it's been years since I stood on the terraces of old Adamslie and watched Rob Roy trying to run, fight, tackle, shoot their way to the summit of junior football. The dilapidated old stand on the opposite side ay the pitch has been torn down, ending the neglect and disrepair of more recent years, and a row of flats has sprung up on the spare land out the back, but apart from that, many of the familiar old certainties and traditions still prevail at the ground. When I was growing up my uncle John used to rope my dad into taking us down here on a semi-regular basis, and I can still clearly see masel and my cousins, along wi Sully, Coyler, Paul Mills and aw the old troops, running aboot the terraces and the grass verges like a bunch ay wee scallies, collecting the ginger bottles so we could take them back to the shop for the ten pence refund. Now, just as then, rival fans are sharing a few words and a few jokes wi one another, offering bets on early goalscorers as well as the final outcome, and there's a boy wandering about with a bucket so you can throw in your spare change in a desperate attempt to try and stand in the way ay progress and save the local hospital. The hospital where I was born in fact. Some woman wi political ambitions and deep held beliefs has had the idea to stand in the upcoming elections on an independent ticket in a bid to ensure that the hospital doesny close. It's a good cause and one that I agree wi, but I doubt I'll be voting for the girl. My politics are already firmly and resolutely established, in my own mind at least - unless and until someone comes forward and promises that they're gony reverse every last one ay the policies and principles of Thatcherism, and set about establishing a Socialist utopia in Scotland instead, then I'll remain suitably non-plussed and apathetic towards all forms of democratic politics, including the kind of crusading, single issue interventions we're talking about here. I realise that nain ay this looks as though it's likely to happen anytime soon, but still, I remain an optimist so you never know. It used to be a sheet they carried around back in the day, so you could toss in your spare change for some local charity, but I think they're expecting a few notes thrown into the mix these days, so it's a bucket they use instead. I'm no earning just now, but seeing as Mr. Sullivan paid me in the gate, I throw a fiver into the guy's pail safe in the knowledge that it'll no blow away in the wind. *Plus ça change*, as my dad might say.

— What about yourself, Mr. Sullivan, do you still keep up

to date wi how Rob Roy's getting on? I continue wi ma line of inquiries.

— No so much now, Peter, I suppose like Martin says, I still come to the odd game or two, or have a wee shoofty at the paper to check the results and that, you know? But that's about it.

— He can still rattle off the team fae '62, sure you can da? Sully Junior informs us. — Naw you're awright, we believe you, he cuts his dad off before the old man has the chance to show off his knowledge and his powers of recollection.

— Can still rattle them off, aye, Mr. Sullivan asserts instead, smiling proudly. It seems the years haveny diminished his memory of the most famous side in the Rabs' history, the team that won the Scottish Junior Cup in 1962.

— Was Alec Ferguson's brother no in that side? Coyler asks.

— He was indeed aye, Martin Ferguson. It was on the back ay that season that he earned a move to Partick Thistle. '62 was the end ay the road for that team though, they were too good for Rob Roy and the squad was broken up after that.

— Was there no a whiff of anti-Catholic bias about the club in they days?

— There was mair than a whiff! But you never know, son, these are things that are nigh on impossible to prove, Mr. Sullivan responds to my question which, with a wary glance at my two friends, I've thrown into the mix like a hand grenade. — It never bothered me one way or the other whether they were prejudiced or no, the old man seems happy to elaborate. — I'd have seen that as mair their problem than mines if it was true, Peter, know what I mean? I just used to come to watch the games, that was the only thing that ever interested me. It's fair to say though that there was certainly a perception ay that in they days, aye. But I mean, what can you dae? There was that much ay it about when I was your age, he reflects. — Looking back now, it was disgraceful the extent that the bigotry seemed to pervade everything that went on back then. It was shocking, although as I say, nain ay it ever bothered me at the time. Maybe it should have, but whenever I came across any ay that nonsense, I just used to let it go by me, because you accepted it back then. You knew it went on and there wasny much you could dae aboot it. Like I say though, that was probably just me, maybe if I'd hud a wee bit mair ambition about me it might have annoyed me a bit more.

I can see where Mr. Sullivan's attitude comes from, because for years there were only two options available to Catholics in the West of Scotland; either accept the bigotry and discrimination and get on wi your life, or try and challenge it, be seen to stand up for yourself and gie it back in whatever form. By far the majority, it seems to me, were either too powerless or too good-natured or too plastered to dae anything other than just reluctantly and whimsically shrug their shoulders and accept it, while at the same time trying to be above it all and no be like that themselves. Although I must admit that Mr. Sullivan's phlegmatic indifference to the problem grates slightly on my modern ears. But these were the days long before the invention of such concepts as political correctness and a liberal elite media finally taking a stand against the idea of racism in sport and society. Back then the anti-Catholic bigotry was rampant, unchecked and all-pervasive to the extent that the Tories, who held the Orange vote, were the majority party in Scotland at the time, which surely has to tell you something considering that, as more recent years have shown, this is a country which isny prepared to indulge Tories and their ilk in any way whatsoever.

— There's a few ex-Celtic players that have played for Rob Roy, Sully Senior eventually informs us, perhaps still reflecting on the historical allegations of anti-Catholicism at the club, but trying to change the subject at the same time.

— Who?

— Stevie Chalmers, he had a spell here, Andy Lynch ...

— Did you no play wi these yourself, Mr Sullivan? Coyler wonders.

— No, son, the old man laughs, — St. Flannan's boys' guild was about as far as I made it in football.

— Anybody else? I ask. — Do you know any other players that went on to make a name fir themsels?

— Chic Charnley used to get a game here a few year ago, before he was tempted away by a better offer, but that was when his career was winding down. Cany mind now where he went, but he wasny here long.

— Kevin McGarry played wi Rob Roy, that's one we know about at least.

— Did Garra used to play wi these as well, Coyler? I interject. — My God, that's right so he did, I'd forgotten aw about that.

— Aye, he did. No for long though, I'm no surprised you don't remember it, Sully tells me.

— Could you no have persuaded Garra to come back wi you fae Prague, Fitzy? Coyler asks me.

— Still missing your, mate, Martin, aye? I feel pretty bad about what happened, depriving you of your buddy like that. It was his decision you know, no mines.

This is a wee bit ay a touchy subject, because the last time I saw wee Coyler was when he drove over to Prague to take in the Champions League fixture that Celtic were playing there at the time. There were four of them in fact that came over to visit me and see the game at the same time, but there were only three in the car on the journey home, because one of them never went back. I helped to persuade ex-Rob Roy starlet and one time teenage prodigy Kevin McGarry to stay for the duration, although at the time I think Garra's mind was already made up and, as I was trying to explain to big Melly in the pub the other night, he's still living in Prague to this day. No doubt Coyler was a wee bit surprised when his mate never went home, because they were best buddies, those two, and I felt quite guilty that I'd robbed Coyler of his pal. I mind at the time me and Garra had a few laughs about them getting lost on the road home, after they drove back all the way to London without him.

— No missin him so much, naw, Coyler reassures me. — Just that he used to play wi this team, like I says, and it looks like they could use him the day. He has a knack, does Coyler, of no making anyone feel uncomfortable for long, as he correctly draws attention to the struggling start that the local team has made to this afternoon's fixture. The play has already been whirling from end to end for a good half an hour or so by the time Rob Roy concede the first goal of the game and find themselves deservedly behind. — Are you still in touch wi Garra, Fitzy? Coyler continues after a suitably long pause. Clearly he's still itching wi curiosity about his erstwhile friend and he's decided to press me for more information.

— Aye, I see him aw the time, Martin, I reply. — He's still loving his football, he's a coach now. He trains this gang ay under seventeens at one of the city's biggest clubs. It must have been a bit ay a shock when he telt you he was staying in Prague and no going back in the car wi yous to London.

— It was an aw. But it was what he wanted to dae, so you have to go with that, do you no? He was a fitba player hissel, so he cany have any regrets, if that's what he's still daein.

— You're right, Martin, he was injured out ay football at a young age, so I think he's pleased that he's still involved in the game, I add.

— While playing for Rob Roy.

— That's right, it's aw coming back to me now! I laugh. —

Shame, he was a right good wee player, was Garra. There's no many ay the Kirkie boys left, it seems.

— No many ay us left now, Peter, just the hard core, Coyler acknowledges with a broad smile on his face that can't disguise an accompanying hint of regret in his voice.

Half-time arrives wi the Rabs, after an initial setback, having levelled the game up at one each, although it seems we've managed to blether our way through most of the first forty-five minutes. The players are jogging off the field, but Coyler clearly isny finished yet, and he's still keen to gie me the third degree.

— What about yoursel, Fitzy, where are you gony be staying these days? he asks me.

— Me and Lenka have started looking for a place, Martin, but I really need to sort masel out wi a job first, I reply, hoping that we might avoid switching onto this particular subject and that the abruptness of my answer might have the desired effect of steering the conversation in another direction.

— You still wi Lenka, aye? he asks as a couple ay kids are showing off their skills and kicking a ball about on the park during the interval. — What you gony dae wi yoursel, now you're back in Scotland?

— Still thegether, aye.

— How long's that you've been back now, Peter? Mr. Sullivan asks.

— How long is it, Sully? About three weeks, Mr. Sullivan.

— Aye, three weeks the morra since you were back, Sully confirms.

— So what you gony dae wi yoursel, now you're back in Kirkie? Coyler persists. — You're no still gony be sitting aboot at a loose end in three months or three years time, are you?

— That's what I've been trying to figure out since I got

home, Martin, I concede. — I'm no a hundred percent sure yet, that's the honest answer, although there's a few ideas that I'm still kicking about, I suggest, plausibly enough. — And as a last resort I could always pick up from where I left off before I moved away, and go back into financial services.

— That might no be as easy as you think, Peter, Sully tells me. — There's a global recession hit the economy since you've been out the country. I hate to tell you, but you might find that things areny quite the same as they once were in that particular sector.

— I'm aware ay that, Sully. But I still have a few contacts, guys that told me to gie them a shout if I was ever back in Scotland again and looking for work. You're right, I'd rather no go back there if I could possibly avoid it, but I could maybe get on the phone to a few folk in the meantime, just to see what the score is on the jobs front.

The prospect of working in financial services again is filling me wi dread even as the words escape my mouth, and I'm acutely aware once more of why I was so keen to avoid being drawn into a discussion on this.

— I would stay away fae that scene if I was you, Peter. You've been there and done that, and you can see now what a shoddy racket it is. Banks giein people loans they couldny fuckin afford, it's ruined the fuckin country, man.

— You're right, but I was never involved in the lending side ay things, Mark, I point out. — That was never ma line. I can see what you're saying though because the banks were basically running a total fuckin scam ay the first order. It was no surprise to me whatsoever when the whole thing came down about their ears, I'm only surprised that they managed to stretch it out for the length ay time that they did. I was sure the whole shithouse would go up in flames long before the crash eventually came.

— A bit like Rangers?

— A wee bit like them, aye, I reflect. — My God, what's the story there, Sully? I'm away for a few years, I come back and the Huns are up to their neck in debt, what's that aw about? I'm no sure I can believe some ay the stuff I've been hearing recently.

— Don't get me started on them, Peter, honestly.

— No come on, I want to hear it, Mark, what's the latest? Just gie us the long and the short ay it.

— They're deep in financial bother, mate, that's it in a nutshell. It's been bubbling away under the surface for a good while already - behind the scenes, under the radar, the empire has slowly been crumbling away for years now. They're totally Donald Ducked, Peter, honestly, and any day now it's aw about to go doon the plughole, believe me. I'm no kiddin, Rangers could literally be just weeks away fae insolvency.

— Really? I'm sceptical about that, I have to say. I wonder how much ay this 'the Huns are scoobied' idea is just wishful thinking on the part ay mickey-taking Celtic fans. Surely we'd have heard more about it otherwise.

— You'd have thought so, would you no? I believed it was aw pie in the sky as well at first, but it turns out it's aw true, just nae cunt's willing to report it.

— I'm no sure about that, Mark, come on. Financial problems maybe, but insolvency? I must admit, I'd be amazed if that's how it turns out in the end. I guess we'll find out in a few weeks or months time, as you say.

— The economy's fucked, man, and Rangers are going the same way, just you wait and see. If it can happen to RBS, it can happen to a relative financial minnow like Glasgow Rangers FC.

— RBS, what a shoor ay fuckin rogues, man.

— Tell me aboot it, I know. And the Huns were part ay the same mentality, living on credit for years and no caring how

37

they were ever gony pay back the money they owed.

— You're right, Sully, this is what I'm talking about. The banks were running their own wee racket, convincing people they could buy into the celebrity lifestyle and impress folk by spending money which wasny really theirs, because aw they'd done was go up the high street and take out a loan, which they were never gony be in a position to redeem. They were chuckin money at folk, and now these financial institutions have aw been fuckin nationalised! How fuckin scandalous is that?

— It was drastic, Peter, here I'll gie you an example. You mind Tambo? Thomas Boyle? The boy's oot ay work, right? He fuckin stays at home wi his maw and da, nae job, nae dole money, he'll no even go doon the broo office to sign on because he's that fed up wi it … honestly, nae fuckin source ay income whitsoever. He takes this ten pound cheque that he got fae his birthday aff his oul gran one year down to his local branch, and the cunts'll no let him oot the bank until he's taken out a loan. Tambo's like that to them, No way, man, I cany afford it, yous would just be throwing good money after bad … A fuckin mortgage they tried tae offer him, Peter. The boy's totally skint, the maist rooked cunt you could hope to meet, and there's the Bank ay Scotland trying to flog him a fuckin mortgage on a hoos. Seriously, they must have been looking at their computer screens, staring right in the face at every detail of the financial train wreck that was Tambo's lifestyle at the time and wondering how this bastard was ever gony pay them back a single fuckin penny they loaned him. And yet it was Tambo himsel who had to tell them to get to fuck, he didny want their fuckin money. I swear, Fitzy, nae wunner the economy went tits up, man, can you fuckin believe that shite?

— Language, Mark, please! There's weans here. Who taught you to talk like that? Mr. Sullivan admonishes his impassioned son.

— Aye, I wonder, Sully Junior checks himself. — You see what I'm saying, Peter? I know that it wasny exactly your line, but there's an example. It was pure madness what these banks were up tae.

— I wasny aware ay that incident, Mark, but I can easily believe it, yes, I tell him. — It's exactly the kind ay thing that I was talking about, a perfect example of the unsustainable attitude that was so prevalent when I was working as a mortgage adviser. You're right, retail banking wasny ma line, but I seen that sort ay thing going on aw the time, only on a much larger scale. One thing's for sure though, they'll no be offering Tambo any mortgages or loans like that again anytime soon.

— Did you see it aw coming, Peter, aye? Is that how you got out and left the country when you did?

— That wasny the main reason, Coyler, no, I could never have predicted the scale ay the collapse. But there were certain things that went on that I couldny get ma heid round at the time. In a lot ay ways, there's some aspects that make a lot more sense now that everything's come to a grinding halt, because it was so unsustainable. It would have made a lot less sense to me if things had just been allowed to carry on the way they were wi nae consequences. Now the lessons can hopefully be learned at least.

— How did you ever get involved in that line ay work anyway, Fitzy? It seems a bit like you were wasting your talents there, if you ask me.

— It was just a job that I fell into at the time, Mark, to be honest. You know how there's guys that join the army just because they don't know what else to dae wi themsels? I remember thinking when I started out there that I was a bit like that an aw. I was working in a bar for six months after I left Uni, so full time employment wi a reputable firm seemed to me at the time to be a bit ay an advancement. I enjoyed it as well, don't get me wrong, it wasny aw bad, but I was never a capitalistic true believer like some ay ma colleagues. And as soon as I'd earned a few quid, I was out ay there and off to do a bit ay travelling, while I could afford it and I still had the chance.

— It seems a strange choice ay career though, Peter, you could ay done anything wi the qualifications you had.

— Well that wasny really my experience at the time, Coyler, I reflect. — I blame Duncan Campbell, it was him that pointed us in the direction of the vacancy when it was first advertised and then he gied us some good advice wi the whole interview process. There were over a hundred applicants for three positions and I landed one ay them, so I must have been doing something right. I don't suppose you know what Duncan's up to these days, do you? I might need to gie the boy a shout again just to see if there's anything still happening in his world.

— I think he's probably been declared bankrupt by now, Sully considers.

— Aye, I thought I seen him on the news after the crash, jumping out the top storey ay Canary Wharf, Coyler adds.

— You could be right, Mark, although I wouldny be so sure. He was a financial adviser the last I heard, and he had a number ay wealthy clients. The rich haveny been as badly affected by the recession as everyone else, so there's a fair chance he could still be doing quite well for himsel. I might go round to his old house sometime and see if I can find out what he's been up to lately. Hopefully he'll have one or two bright ideas up his sleeve for me because the way things are looking, I might need something to fall back on.

— As a last resort, eh? Aye, fair enough.

— A last resort aye, that's right. My real plan is to get involved in the media, I drop my bombshell.

— Is that so, Peter? What branch ay the media are you looking at? You gony be a reporter, old Mr. Sullivan pricks up his ears at ma latest revelation.

— No quite, Mr. Sullivan, no, I have this idea for a television programme discussing matters relating to Scottish football. Last week I wrote a letter to the broadcasters saying what I imagined the programme was gony be about an that, I explain to my increasingly agog audience. There's a curious note of bashfulness and almost apology in my voice which I'm trying hard to disguise, almost certainly unsuccessfully, because I know how I'd react if somebody else announced their similar such intentions to me.

— What, you gony become a fuckin media pundit like Jim Shite? Sully the younger eventually chastises me. — Pontificating on the travails ay the Scottish game, trying to make yoursel look good while castigating the hard work and honest efforts ay other people. Come on, Fitzy, gie yoursel a shake, man. You're better than that.

— Mark's right, Peter. I'd stay well clear ay that lark if I was you, Coyler concurs. — Sully's putting a website thegether wi Armie, you should help him oot wi that, if you want to have something to say about Celtic or the state ay the game or whitever. The mainstream media are fucked, man, the internet bampots are taking over the show now, is that no right, Sully?

— Too right, wee man.

— You're starting up a website? I ask Sully.

— Looking into it, aye.

— Wi Andrew Armstrong? I might ay known he'd be behind your wee scheme. Does he no stay doon in London now?

— He does aye, but by the magic ay the internet, it doesny matter where you stay these days. There's another guy living in Canada that's gony contribute. We're gony be doing podcasts and radio shows, and taking a more in-depth look at this whole Rangers situation. If you want to get involved in broadcasting, why don't you help us out? We could use your fearsome talents, because we need another man or two, and the more articulate and intelligent the better. You'd be brilliant at it, Fitzy, seriously, and to be honest I've been trying to figure out for a while now a way of asking you, if you want to come and help us out.

— In-depth, eh? See that sounds like what I'm looking to do wi this programme idea as well.

— Fuck that, come and work for us. Your talents will be put to better use online.

— It's a career I'm looking for Mark, no just a hobby, I reply, trying no to sound too embarrassed by Sully's obvious attempts to try and flatter me. — I've got a wife to look after now, I remind him. — As I says to you earlier, we're looking to find a place in the town. It's no just Tambo and Coyler that stay at home wi their parents, I currently find masel in the exact same boat, and on top ay that, I've been earning buttons for the last few years. It's a brilliant idea, mate, but I need to try and sort masel out wi something a bit more serious the now, know what I mean? I cany just fart aboot for the next six years.

— What age are you now?

— I'm fuckin thirty-one year old.

— You're getting on a bit, ya old cunt.

— I am. What age are you?

— Thirty-three.

— Well you cany exactly talk then, can you?

— Fuckin tell me aboot it.

— Are your maw and da chasing you oot the house, Fitzy? Coyler gleefully accuses me.

— They're fine, Martin honestly, I answer, — they're no giein me any gyp, at least no as much as I was expecting

42

anyway, but they're a wee bit set in their ways, you know? They want me to go and dae what's expected of me, especially now I'm a married man and of course they're dead right, but it's aw starting to get a wee bit tedious, even after just a few weeks. On the one hand they're telling me I need to grow up and be responsible, and on the other they're treating me like a fuckin wean. I'm no complaining, they've been brilliant wi us so far, but I just need a wee while to sort masel out, and this programme idea is something I feel I could dae a good job wi.

— Fair enough, Sully considers, — I'm just saying though, Peter, the mainstream media? I was in the car the other night and I found masel listening to that fuckin phone-in show, the one that used to be dead popular, mind? I swear, the level ay shite that these bastards talk, in amongst the inane jingles and the screaming adverts, you just would no begin to believe. I'm tellin you, after fifteen minutes ay that pish you want to go home and fuckin hang yoursel wi a rope. It's murder, Fitzy seriously, you're no tellin me that's who you want to throw in your lot wi, are you?

— No, I don't Sully, and I'll tell you why. When I was abroad, I seen these shows done properly. In the country I've just come from the level ay debate and the seriousness that the media bring to their discussions ay these issues would put the people you're talking about to shame. As I told you already, I want to go more in-depth and that's gony be my pitch if they call me in for an interview. A football discussion show that's intelligent and serious and treats its audience wi respect. I'm pretty optimistic that they'll be interested in the idea, because it'll only improve standards. Scotland is a football daft country and yet there areny too many shows in the media that are ready to treat fans wi a degree of respect for their intelligence. It's what the country's fuckin crying out for Sully, and if they call me in to discuss it then I'm confident I'll be able to convince them that commissioning ma wee project would be in everyone's best interests. If they can do it in other countries, then why not here in Scotland? That's my reasoning, doesny sound too much to ask, does it?

— That's fine in theory, but you wouldny believe the mind-melting shite that goes on in the media these days, Peter. You might think it would be in their interests to go ahead and commission a show like that, and you're dead right, mate, the country's crying out for it and I would love to see a programme like that on the telly. But just wait until they've finished wi your brilliant idea - it'll no be in anyone's interests by then, I promise you. You've reminded me of a story Armie once told me when he was doing his social anthropology degree at Edinburgh University. You know what anthropologists do, don't you? They go off to some remote desert island somewhere and observe how people in primitive conditions organise their societies and live their lives, right? I'm talking about folk who've never heard ay the internet or Nectar points or telephone banking or any ay the other attractions of modern day life. The scientists study how these people run their lives, and what they do to survive, so they can write it all up and publish their conclusions in academic journals. The joke wi Armie was about some anthropologist fae Polynesia or somewhere, coming over here and setting up to study the goings on in a tabloid newspaper or a commercial broadcaster. The poor bastard ended up fucking chuckin himsel in the river, wi a two ton weight tied roon his ankles.

— I know what you're saying Sully, I cany help laughing at his anecdote, — but that's why I approached the SBC wi the proposal. We're no talking about redtops or commercial radio stations here, this is the national broadcaster I'm trying to get on board wi this idea. Their output is supposed to be a wee bit more highbrow, so that's why I'm confident this is the kind ay show that will sit well in their schedule and appeal to their high-cultured sensibilities. I just need the bastards to gie me an interview, that's all.

— They're supposed to be highbrow and mair intelligent, you're right, but no necessarily when it comes to the area you're talking about. The SBC like to think they can slum it wi the tabloids and aw the other cunts wi their coverage of football. Any attempt to break away and dae something even vaguely different or original, never mind groundbreaking or intelligent, would be seen as an outright declaration of war on their rivals, and they've just no got the stomach for it. I wish you good luck and aw the best wi it, Fitzy, but I cany see it happening, mate. These people are aw way too far up their ain arses to gie you the time ay day, you'd be far better off signing up wi the internet bampots if you've got something you want to say about Celtic and Scottish football. Get yoursel sorted out and settled back in again, then come and gie us a hand wi the website. It's a part-time thing we're doing, I'll still be working my usual hours at the day job, and you can contribute as much or as little as you want. Like I say we could definitely put your talents to good use. You should stick wi someone who's gony appreciate your contribution, and no just try and use you to their own advantage, which is what these media types will surely do, if they ever end up getting their paws on your brilliant idea.

— You might be right, Sully, we'll see what they say, I reflect. He's done a pretty good job of talking me down from my bright, overvalued idea, has Sully. Not with cynicism, but with a healthy dose of worldly-wise realism that I maybe needed, because I'm starting to become aware that perhaps I've been a bit naïve when it comes to understanding the machinations of the mainstream media in Scotland. It could well be that Sully is a hundred percent correct in terms of my programme idea being taken seriously. Still, the letter's in the post now, so we'll see what they say.

At some point during the second half ay the game that's been raging in front of us while we've been blethering away, Mr Sullivan introduces us to the captain of the 1977 Rob Roy side that made it all the way to the Junior Cup final, who he's been chatting to and seems to know quite well.

— Looks like the move is going ahead, those flats over there are just the first, he points across the field. — This whole area's gony be built on and the ground's been sold to a property developer, Sully Senior updates us with this new, hot off the press, insider information.

— It's finally happening then?

— Looks like it. Gony be the end for Adamslie Park, it seems.

There follows more nostalgic chat and local reminiscing with comparisons being drawn with modern junior football and the game as it was played in yesteryear. I must admit though, I'm reasonably impressed with the standard of football on display here the day, which comes more to the fore during the second half, despite the deteriorating weather. There areny too many Messis or Ronaldinhos running about, but there's plenty of good honest endeavour and the occasional suggestion of something better, a wee flash of quality or a hint of talent that all too infrequently lights up and interrupts the ordinary, more mundane fare. There are some obvious lulls in the game as well, and compared to the full time guys I would say that the lack ay fitness is a telling factor, but most of the time both sides are at least trying to play some decent stuff. Particularly the home team because, from a goal down in the early stages, the Rabs come storming back towards the end and score three late goals to win the match convincingly and restore some local Kirkie pride.

— Smash and grab right enough, I observe in the immediate aftermath of the contest.

— That puts Rob Roy back up amongst the early pacesetters, Coyler informs us.

— Fancy a pint? Sully asks me as we're making our way towards the exits.

— Aye, sounds no a bad idea. Do you know anywhere that

does Czech lager?

Sully looks at me quizzically, as if I'd just answered him in Czech rather than merely expressed a preference for a beer from that country.

— You're no turning into a bevvy snob in your old age, are you, Fitzy? he chastises me. I'm on the point of explaining to Sully the vast difference between proper Czech lager and the fizzy, Scottish, pish-oot-the-Clyde that he seems to enjoy, and how after years of drinking the real thing I could never in a million years reacquire a taste for Tennents Lager, but I decide to save my indignation at least for the pub.

— Must be, aye, I tell him instead.

— I'll sort you out, mate, don't worry, he assures me eventually.

*

Peter Fitzpatrick
44, Park Avenue
Kirkintilloch
Glasgow
G66 7ER

Dear Peter,

Many thanks for your letter with regard to 'The Scottish Football Debate', and for your follow-up calls. Apologies for the delay in responding. The Commissioning Editors have discussed your proposal at some length, but unfortunately we do not feel able to pursue the project at this stage. Regrettably in the current economic climate budgets are already stretched thin as it is, and we need to be one hundred per cent sure of the feasibility of a new venture before we can even consider taking it further.

We did however like your idea and wish you every success pursuing the project with another broadcaster.

Best wishes,

Gus McGregor (Commissioning Editor)

*

3. WELCOME TO THE BIGOTDOME

I drop Lenka off at the jeweller's on the way over to Hillhead. She'll be having a more sedate Saturday afternoon than me anyway, that's for sure, designing necklaces and other trinkets, but hopefully it'll keep her out ay trouble for a few hours at least. In many ways she's been fortunate to have been able to make such a seamless transition from the job she was doing at home in the Czech Republic; it seems that Pauline Campbell, Duncan's aunt, was very impressed wi her credentials, and Lenka seems happy enough because she's added the design element to her job description now, instead ay the purely customer facing sales position that she held in Prague, where personally I believe she was wasting her talents. She's included a creative dimension in her new role, which will hopefully allow her to express more of her personality in her work. I'm sounding a wee bit arty-farty now, I know, it's fuckin jewellery we're talking about, but apparently some women quite like it.

I on the other hand, being male, am interested in football. That would be the perception anyway, although as far as I can tell there are almost as many women who follow Celtic these days as men. It's great to see, but in truth most sensible people, regardless of gender, will be avoiding the mayhem that I'm about to witness the day. I really should be steering well clear ay this nonsense myself in actual fact, but what can you do? I called Duncan Campbell looking for a job and instead I got a ticket to Ibrox Park. It's been years since I was at one of these fixtures and I must admit, I'm intrigued to find out for myself to what extent things have changed in recent times, and in particular it will be interesting to gauge any perceived alteration in the general mood due to Rangers' gathering financial problems.

So far there's been very few signs on the field that the club has been adversely affected by their apparently straitened circumstances, they still have an assortment of multi-million pound players representing them, assembled from all corners of the footballing world, but I'm keen to see if I can detect any change of attitude amongst the fans and in the general atmosphere at the game, now that the beast seems to have been wounded, or whether, as perhaps seems more likely, it'll be a case of the same old story of hubris and bigotry and ninety minutes of non-stop sectarian abuse coming at you fae every corner ay this ground.

I park the car up on Oldfield Avenue not far from my old digs and stroll down to Byres Road. I'm trying to keep my allegiances well disguised, because although this is the West End and a nice part ay town, there are still likely to be a fair number ay heidcases and bampots going about the place, especially on a day like this when the fixture card dictates that we're gony be outnumbered when it comes to folk wandering the streets wearing football scarves and replica strips. I don't even have the luxury of safety in numbers, not yet anyway, there's still a good few hundred yards to go before I reach the comfort and relative security of the International Bar, the home and spiritual headquarters of the Glasgow University Celtic Supporters Club.

I reach Hillhead Underground station, and immediately, as if to confirm my concerns, I'm confronted by a mingling crowd of the blue uniform brigade, waiting on their pals, mixed in with the steady flow of West End bargain hunters, coffee shoppers and jakey-looking student types. The Rangers boys are hanging about in some numbers, shouting at one another, geeing themselves up, getting in the mood for the game and I involuntarily find myself rechecking my scarf, ensuring that it's safely hidden away, deep in my pocket, and that my jacket is securely zipped up to my chin, concealing my colours – at this stage in the proceedings the garment has the dual purpose of protecting me both from the vagaries of the Glasgow late autumn weather as well as the instinctive prejudices of this crowd ay hoodlums. The merest flash of green and white could have serious repercussions for me right now, but at the same time I'm no about to back away or take a detour round them in any way. It's the little victories that count, I've always felt, like years ago when I was still at school, I went to Ibrox to see Rangers play Tottenham in a preseason friendly; Celtic socks on my feet the entire time. Like I say, never underestimate the importance of the little victories. 'Mony a mickle maks a muckle' as Mr. McCallum, my former History teacher at the time used to say, giving us the benefit of his homespun Highland wisdom. 'Many small things go to make a large one.' How right the old boy was, I'm able to reflect sanguinely, as I meander my way through the midst of the Rangers fans.

It's only after I've crossed the road and am just about to reach the safety of the IB that a chorus of 'The Billy Boys' starts up behind me. The dulcet strains of 'We're up to our knees in Fenian blood' is left ringing in my ears, puncturing the otherwise sedate ambience of the West End. It seems these boys have fewer scruples than me when it comes to disguising their allegiances, they don't seem to care who hears them or what Joe Public makes of their anachronistic views ay the world. They've been led to believe, after decades of practising this kind of overt bigotry with complete impunity, that they can get away with just about anything on the streets of Glasgow on a day like this, and the sad fact is that they're probably right.

— Fuckin sectarian arseholes, I mutter under my breath, glancing in the direction of a couple of supporters in Celtic scarves who are obviously less reticent than me when it comes to showing their colours.

— You said it, Fitzy, a voice at my side quietly informs me. It seems that I was more vocal in my indignation than I had originally intended. — What are they like, eh? The guy next to me continues to vent his displeasure at the cacophonous Hun chorus that's still wafting over towards us, and it takes a wee while before the light of recognition goes on in my head and I realise that I'm in conversation with James Allen, or big Albert as he's less formally known due to a corruption of his surname, another ex-Glasgow University Kirkie boy like myself, who I was kicking a ball about Lenzie Moss with as recently as a few weeks ago.

— Alright, Albert, how's it going? That's right, I'm just glad that I'm a Celtic supporter, that's all I can say, I reflect smugly. I'm reminded of the prescribed admonition that there are decent supporters on the other side too, and that there's always gony be a minority of arseholes who attach themselves to every club's fanbase. This is undoubtedly true and in that regard Celtic are certainly no exception, but I'm afraid in ma experience, when it comes to Rangers fans, it's the majority who spoil it.

— That's it, Fitzy, spot on, mate, Allen tells me. — You fuckin wouldny want to be one, would you?

It seems that broadly speaking big Jamesie and I are in agreement as to the relative differences and the cultural dichotomy which exists between Glasgow's footballing duopoly, as well as the fortunate circumstances of our status within it. Although I also realise that there's no reason why I should be immune to the febrile environment that's currently engulfing the city and I'm probably getting caught up in things myself here. It's Derby Day in Glasgow once more and both sides seem to be getting into the swing ay things. Despite repeated dire warnings of the potential consequences for the club, Rangers are once again warming up and giving vent to their limited and explicitly sectarian repertoire, while Celtic are preparing to don the cloak of righteous indignation and are readying their songbook of defiance.

— You made it in time then, Albert? I ask. He's a few years younger than me, is James, and if memory serves me right he has a bit of a reputation for sleeping in before these big games and no making it out in time for the early kick-offs. I usually don't have any such problems, the trick is to stay at home and have a quiet, relaxing evening before a game like this, instead ay running about the town steaming drunk until the early hours ay the morning. But that's something that a fair percentage of the boys on this bus don't seem to have grasped yet.

— Wouldny catch me missing this, Fitzy, he points out. — You going on this bus the day?

— I am, aye, if I can find Matty Docherty. Do you know where he is? I might need you to help me out here, mate, I've no been on this bus in years.

— C'mon I'll take you over to him, Albert offers. — Are you supposed to be meeting him here, aye?

— That was the idea, I confirm, — but I'm no even sure I'll recognise him now.

I used to travel wi this supporters' club occasionally when I was a student here, although that was a fair few years ago now. Incredibly, I find that I'm able to recognise a few of the old faces from back in the day, some are former students like myself who have obviously stuck wi the same crowd, while others seem to be local characters, the familiarity of their appearance still recognisable across an extra decade or so of the Glasgow highlife and the incalculable emotional variables involved in following Celtic. Needless to say there's not a flicker of recognition in any of their eyes at my sudden and unexpected reappearance.

— Don't think Matty's here yet, Albert tells me as we take a look around.

The pub still isny open, due to a cunning manipulation of the fixtures and schedules, so we find ourselves disbarred from the ritual of the pre-match drink. The bus that's due to take us to the ground is sitting in the car park opposite, but there's no sign of any human activity around it yet, so my fellow Celtic supporters are having to hang about in the rain outside the pub for a while, greeting and acknowledging one another - the fellow pilgrims and other acquaintances who are slowly beginning to roll up. Albert offers me a cigarette which I decline despite the cold and the strengthening wind. At last there seems to be some movement around the bus and I eventually head across the road and climb aboard. I meet Matt Docherty who was apparently looking out for me and we're briefly reacquainted, but it's obvious he's too busy attending to the needs and problems of his various associates for a full catch-up.

The bus quickly fills up revealing the eclectic membership mix that's been thrown together in this supporters' club, a decent cross-section of society, this is the Glasgow Uni bus after all. In addition to the student element, there's also the graduate contingent as well, who remain unwilling or unable to let go of their past associations and have retained their memberships – they're probably still drinking in the Beer Bar, most ay them, and playing snooker in the GU – as well as a handful of college professors and various other studious looking academic types. There's a couple of priests too and an assortment of Westenders, including the odd Irish businessman, no doubt there's a few millionaires amongst them, interspersed with the local boys from slightly further afield, the Partick, Kelvinside and Maryhill crowd.

All the while, ushering everybody aboard and counting the heads is Matt, aided and abetted by his mate Tom McParland. These two boys founded this supporters' club after they graduated nearly twenty years ago now, in order that they could stay in touch with their Celtic supporting mates from the Uni and expand their reach into the local community. They had about a dozen members when they started out back in the early days of the glory-starved Liam Brady era, but times have changed and they now have over three hundred and fifty signed up Tims on their books. The pair of them more or less run this club from top to bottom although, to keep it in touch with its roots, a couple of serving students are always given the largely ceremonial positions on the club's committee structure – treasurer, club secretary etc. – which basically, as far as I can make out, has as much to do with organising the bevvy sessions and the nights out as well as various other miscellaneous social activities as it has wi keeping the club's accounts in order.

There's a monthly newsletter as well, which has expanded over the years from the usual match reports and previews to include other articles and opinion pieces on wider issues. It has a nice balance between the comedic stuff, which these days inevitably involves laughing at the Huns and their intractable financial problems, as well as the vaguely more serious content which examines various issues facing the game and affecting the wider society, anything loosely connected to Scottish football and Celtic, such as sectarianism, football finances, the hypocrisy and double standards of certain sections of the media, the apparent decline in standards in the Scottish game, etc. etc. There's usually no shortage of topics that are up for discussion, with the opinion pieces and the comedy element often overlapping considerably, especially in regard to football finances, which in these sections is analysed properly and forensically in a manner that would put the agenda driven nonsense of some ay the more established outlets to shame. In many ways I wanted the programme that I wrote to the SBC about to reflect similar standards and have the same kind of independent voice, because there's certainly an audience for this kind of analysis. Sadly though, it's dawned on me all too inevitably, just as Sully had suggested back on the terraces of old Adamslie, that my bright idea to try and reinvigorate the coverage of football in this country was nothing more than a pipedream.

It's a pity really because it seems that I've returned home at a strange time for the game here, with Rangers up to their neck in debt, and accusations of tax avoidance and illegal registration of players hanging in the air as well. It'll be interesting to see how it all plays out, because there's been further allegations and revelations even in the relatively short time since I've been home. Of particular concern, from a Hun point of view, is the fact that this time they're having to deal wi people outside the traditional, bigoted set of the West of Scotland establishment, such as the tax authorities and the Met Police. Sully and his partners Andrew Armstrong and Duncan Campbell are gony be all over this story on their website too, and there's a growing feeling which seems to suggest that, due to the nefarious way they've been conducting their affairs in recent years, Rangers really could be one of the first high profile footballing casualties of the credit crunch and its repercussions after all. The mainstream media still don't seem to want to go near any of this, certainly not in any detail or with any serious analysis, I think quite a lot of them are terrified by the prospect of the Rangers monster which they helped to create being about to keel over, and the news coming out of Ibrox is constantly being massaged by expensive PR firms. But they'll have to face up to reality eventually, because this isny a story that's about to go away any time soon.

This is a drugs and alcohol free bus, unlike some buses I've been on, and at this time of the morning drugs and alcohol are the last thing on my mind. It's only a twenty minute or so ride round to Ibrox, so hopefully I'll be able to survive the trip without flaking out or needing to get my fix. There's no even time on this journey for a game of cards, or to get into the swing ay things with a wee song or two, or even just to have a read ay the paper and it's not long before we've made our way out of the car park, through the West End and over the Squinty Bridge. Pretty soon we're pulling off the motorway and nearing our destination, and as we approach the Bigotdome a strange, barely perceptible sense of foreboding seems to have fallen over the bus. Don't get me wrong, we're looking forward to the game, Celtic have a decent enough record at this ground in recent years, and we're confidently anticipating a repeat scoreline from our last visit here the day, but the proverbial shadow seems to have been cast over us, which probably has more to do with what goes on off the field and in the stands during these games, as the realisation hits home of just what we're letting ourselves in for here. I'm guessing that a lot ay folk on this bus, like myself, are from an Irish, Catholic background but whether we are or no, we'll all be treated the same in this hell hole.

The stadium itself impresses you, with its angles and its architecture, as all stadiums do in appreciation of the fact that it's a place where people come to watch football. As we enter the ground the atmosphere hits you immediately, like a low blow in boxing, and we find ourselves locked in a face-off with the other three sides of the ground, a confrontation that will last the entire length of the game. Anti-bigotry and anti-sectarian legislation has existed in this country for some time now, but it doesny seem to matter here, this place is immune, a law unto itself. Even after all these years Ibrox Park still remains a twilight zone, a black hole where the laws of human civilization appear to break down and are flung into reverse, the closer you approach the place. In addition, long cherished and hard fought for laws governing freedom of religious expression traditionally don't apply here, it's not so long ago that a football player would receive an automatic red card if he blessed himself on this pitch. In fact this influence extended even further, because a player could be sent from the field at any ground in the West of Scotland for making the sign of the cross, such was the malevolent influence Ibrox held over the hearts and minds of the wider Scottish game. On the other hand, just to complete the role reversal analogy, tens of thousands of people here can and will be dishing out all the sectarian abuse that their tiny minds can conceive of, in full view of the police and the football authorities, and beamed into millions of living rooms all across the world, with complete impunity, and in flagrant breach of the laws of the land.

The football is underway now, initially as an afterthought to the vile abuse that's being directed at our end, but the atmosphere is just background noise now as concentration becomes centred on the play. Rangers have come charging out the blocks, that's just how they deal with their nerves it seems,

57

because as the game settles down Celtic start to dominate. We find ourselves a goal to the good after half an hour or so, which we enjoy and inevitably we spend most of the half-time interval exalting in the score-line, much to the chagrin of our increasingly deflated rivals. In the second half Celtic seem keen to go for a killer second, but Rangers are fired up too, they've clearly had a rocket up their arses at half-time and they score an equaliser midway through the period. The game ends all square which is a wee bit frustrating, Celtic were by far the better team in the first half although Rangers maybe shaded the second, so we'll take a draw. It's not nearly as disappointing as a defeat, and there doesny seem to have been any major refereeing controversy over the ninety minutes either, which is a major fucking bonus as well.

After the final whistle we head back round to our pub on the bus, eager to discuss the game we've just seen over a few afternoon pints and settling in to watch the English matches on the ubiquitous giant television screens. Unlike before the game, when we had to stand out in the cold, the pub is now a lively haven of football fuelled fraternisation, and doubtless it'll remain so for much of the rest ay the day. As far as detecting any alteration in the mood or the environment at Ibrox due to Rangers' off-field issues, I can safely say that, as suspected, nothing seems to have changed at all and I perceived absolutely no difference in the atmosphere whatsoever. I even had the dubious privilege of being able to experience The Famine Song for the first time in all its unseemly glory. This relatively recent addition to the Hun repertoire, much discussed recently on social media, exhorted us, "the Famine's over, why don't you go home." Presumably to remind us where "home" was, a huge banner was unveiled of a bus heading in the direction of Stranraer. Maybe it's just me, it could be that I really am just having a sense of humour failure here, but as big Albert reminded us only a few hours ago, you wouldny want to be one, and I'm sticking wi that. Clearly, it was naïve of me to expect any financial problems to reveal themselves in a reassessment of values, and in many ways, I suppose, I should have learnt my lesson after the callow expectations I had regarding my recent attempts to try and infiltrate the media with some highbrow football coverage. That was another bright idea which never sailed.

4. THE CALL SHEET

— Is this the best you can do for me, I asked Duncan Campbell, as he handed me the script that I was to work from.

Apparently so.

He was always touted as a bit ay a high-flyer, was Duncan, wi his golf and his snowboarding and his self-made man aspirations. I doubt he ever imagined himself chasing up people who'd been mis-sold Payment Protection Insurance, but there you go, it's a rough old world out there.

I've been touted as a bit ay a high-flyer myself on the odd occasion and yet here I am working off Duncan Campbell's call sheet. I've managed to clear the house for an hour or so, persuading my mother to take Lenka out for a few hours to avail her of the *fin de siècle* shopping opportunities and the café culture of Kirkie Main Street. I've sent my wife and parents out into the street under the pretext of needing some peace and quiet to get stuck into this job, but really and truly, in the deep recesses of my mind, I know that it probably has more to do with avoiding the painful humiliation of being overheard.

I'm suitably psyched up now so, telephone in hand, I decide to take it from the top and call the first number on the list.

— Good evening sir, I'm calling on behalf of Barr Mason Carruthers Solicitors in Glasgow. We are aware that you have received a payment from us for mis-sold Payment Protection Insurance. As an ongoing service to our customers, we always follow up to see if there are any other areas where we may be of assistance to you. Can I have a moment to get some basic information from you? Thank you. Do you have a mortgage, sir? You do, who is it with, may I ask? I see, what is the remaining term and balance? OK, very good and may I know, what interest rate do you pay? That's great, yes, that is a decent rate. And what kind of product is involved? Product. For example SVR, fixed tracker et cetera. OK, well don't worry, it's not important. Do you have any debt related issues that we may be able to assist you with? That's quite a list! Sorry, I assure you sir, I meant no offence. Let me just ask you one more thing before you go, do you have any protection policies that you pay a monthly premium for? Life insurance or critical illness cover, income protection, private medical insurance, buildings and contents, that sort of thing?

That's a bit annoying – allowing me to get that far into the conversation before hanging up. It would be far better if they just cut me off at the start, then I could quickly put a line through their name and move on. Oh well, I'm no sure what else I was expecting, I probably fucked that call up in actual fact, but I'm sure I'll get the hang of it with a bit ay practice. Let's see, who's next?

— Comment t'appelles-tu?

— Je m'appelle Lenka.

— Bon, et quel âge as-tu?

— J'ai hmmm, j'ai vingt … vingt-six années?

— Ans. Not années, the old boy is trying to teach my missus some basic French. — There's a difference between ans and années, he instructs her. — An refers merely to the period of time … whereas année describes …, he explains in his inimitable, professorial manner that used to embarrass the hell out of me at school.

— Sorry, I don't understand?

— Don't worry about it just now, he waves away her incomprehension. — I'm just trying to gauge your standard at the moment. Alors, dis-moi, où habites-tu?

— J'habite Kirkintilloch.

— Tres bien! Kirkintilloch! Tu aimes bien cette ville-ci, tu la connais bien?

— Yes, I like. I'm sorry, connais?

— Do you know it well, tu la connais bien?

— Bien? Non, parce que je suis ici only six weeks.

— Depuis seulement six semaines.

— Oui, je viens de Prague.

— Prague? Magnifique! But the French wouldn't say it like that, he explains patiently.

It was never much fun having your dad as the French teacher at school. Your mates, whose usual inclination would have been to rip the shit out of any teacher they came across, in typical schoolboy fashion, generally tried to be a wee bit more deferential towards Mr. Fitzpatrick, in your presence at least. But occasionally I'd have to listen to an injudicious teenage tirade, gallusly and deliberately delivered in my presence, the like of which I'd have been quite happy to indulge and perhaps even elaborate on myself, if it had been directed at certain other members of staff. But when it's your dad that's in the firing line, and the invective seems to have been issued more as a challenge to yourself, rather than the usual harmless, puerile tomfoolery, then some decision-making is called for. Do you, option one: attempt to defend the family honour and provoke an immediate confrontation with the perpetrator(s)? Or option two: kid on that the joke or the abuse has gone unheard and ignore it completely? Or finally option three: pretend that you find it all hysterically funny as well and laugh like a drain along wi every cunt else? There was of course a fourth option as well: none of the above. Because it's not as straightforward a choice as it seems. Your best bet might be to endure it all in toe-curling silence, perhaps making a mental note and planning your revenge on those responsible as and when the opportunity presented itself. Like I say, not an easy situation at the best ay times. And then there was the problem of having to call your dad 'sir'.

— I know you're only doing your job, mate, an angry English voice asserts, but what sort of a job do you call that, eh? Ringing people up and annoying the hell out of them with this crap. Where's your self-respect? I appreciate you're only doing your job, I know, but I'm fuckin glad it's not my job, that's all I can say. You'd be better off on the fuckin dole, mate.

I suppose I should have hung up on the guy really, reversing the trend of the last ninety minutes or so, but in this line ay work, I'm already beginning to appreciate, you look for any diversion or source of amusement, anything that distracts you from the tedious monotony of it all.

— Well, sir, you must have done some business with us in the past, because every name on my call sheet here represents a client that we've successfully made a claim for in the past. As I've explained, this is a follow-up call purely as a matter of courtesy, to see if there's any other way we can be of assistance to you. Have you made a successful claim in the recent past?

— Er, yeah that's right, I have. You got us three and a half grand.

— There you go, sir, you see. Would you like me to arrange an appointment for you with Mr. Campbell, so that we can ascertain if there's anything more we can do for you at this stage?

— No I would not, fuck off!

*

The old man likes to keep his language skills ticking over by reading the French papers on the internet in the mornings. Le Monde, Le Figaro; to a large extent the Parisian press represents his window on what's going on in the world,

63

which he prefers to view from an alternative, less cluttered, non-British perspective. His habit has the added advantage of connecting him with advances in modern technology, because as far as I can tell he has no other discernible use for the internet or computers in general. It wasny until the dawn of the twenty-first century that he finally bought a VCR, just as the equipment was becoming obsolete, and it'll probably be the next century again before he figures out how to work the thing properly.

French and Spanish he finds easy enough however, although it looks like he's having a few problems with the intricacies and complexities of the Czech language.

— I'm familiar with Russian, he tells Lenka, as they sit over their cappuccinos in a Main Street coffee house, — but I never got to grips with it properly, I must admit. Too many inflections and other variables, I just didn't have the patience for it at the time. From what Peter has told me, I understand Czech is quite similar? he asks. It's true, I did draw the comparison between Czech and Russian when he was showing an interest, and initially I think he was slightly incredulous that I'd managed to get to grips with such a complicated language. Understandably enough, because I have to concede, I found Czech fairly bewildering at first. But thankfully, after my early struggles with a Teach Yourself textbook, it wasny long before I had a patient girlfriend and ultimately wife who was prepared to help me along the way, correcting and encouraging me without complaining too much or losing her patience wi me.

My first girlfriend in Prague, the lovely Martina, just used to laugh out loud at me whenever I was brave enough to attempt a basic Czech phrase. The problem seemed to be that she just wasny used to hearing non-native speakers struggle with the complexities of her language. It's not a problem we encounter in this country, as we're used to hearing people from all over the world using English as a lingua franca, however imperfectly they understand the language. Do I laugh at you

64

when you try to speak English? I eventually had to ask her, as frustration got the better of me. It was only then that I think the penny finally dropped wi the girl, and she finally stopped teasing me. Of course Lenka's understanding of Czech's grammatical pitfalls and weird complexities, like Martina's before her, is based on her native instincts for the language, and therefore her knowledge didn't always lend itself well to protracted explanations to slow foreigners. It wasny always easy for her to make it clear why I was saying something wrong, but as a language teacher myself, I had a decent grasp of how grammar and syntax work, and the importance of such things as making your verbs agree. From there it was just a question ay practice. And more practice. And more practice after that, until eventually I was able to achieve a degree of fluency. It's a great feeling when you realise that perhaps for the first time, you've just succeeded in conducting a conversation in a second language, instinctively and coherently, and you've managed to follow what's been said without having to repeat it over in your head several times, and to make yourself understood as well.

— Yes, it's true. Learning English is much easier, Lenka acknowledges.

— Well you say that, my father counters, — and it's true the basics of English are quite easy to grasp, with there being no genders or cases or complex inflections of the kind that Peter has obviously had to struggle with. It's fortunate that English is the universal language because the basics are quite easy to grasp, but to learn to speak English properly and without mistakes is very difficult. It's easy to get your message across in English, but far harder to speak it with complete understanding of the various tenses and aspects for example. English fulfils the old cliché, a minute to learn, and a lifetime to master.

— Yes, it's true, Lenka nods dutifully as my father imparts his wisdom.

— So Peter really mastered Czech? The old boy wonders aloud.

— Yes, he speaks very well.

— He's a bright boy. I hope to Christ he's no gony be sitting at home, running a one man call centre for any longer that he has to. What a waste.

— Hello, Mrs. Forsyth?

— She's no in.

— I'll call back later, thank you.

— Who's calling?

— I'm calling about her Payment Protection Insurance, in the past Mrs Forsyth has …

— I'd rather you didny bother in that case.

Hangs up.

I'd rather no bother either, mate.

— Do you think we've given Peter long enough? My mother asks. She's finished her trip to the department store and has returned laden wi messages and bags of shopping to join the coffee shop intellectuals.

— What's that, about two hours now? My dad puts down his crossword puzzle.

— Two and a half.

— I think it might be safe to head home.

— I can call him, Lenka offers.

— Maybe it's too soon, he might still be hard at it. Let's give him a wee while longer.

— You're a United fan, mate? Yeah I have been down, I was at Old Trafford a few years ago for Mark Hughes' testimonial. Aw it was brilliant, mate, honestly, some stadium! Yeah, well there's always been a great relationship between the two clubs and their supporters. Liverpool as well, you're right, we get on wi everyone, mate! Aye, it was a brilliant night out, me and ma pals had the sense to make sure we had it all booked up, so we had a ticket for the bus back up the road. There were hunners ay Celtic fans sleeping in the station but some sneaky fuckers must have taken our seats on the bus because the coach company had to go and find a minibus to get us back up to Glasgow. Aye that's right, we had return tickets. All right, mate, nice talking to you too. Sure I cany interest you in some Payment Protection Insurance? No bother. Alright, pal, take care. Mon the Hoops! Too right, buddy. Cheerio.

Nice guy. I was maybe being a wee bit overfriendly there, but I cany be too harsh on masel, I'm fuckin losing the will to live here. That's still nought for about forty-five. Forty-five, Jeezo, is that aw the calls I've made? It feels like about a hunner and forty-five.

— Yes, you see a lot of people think that the Romans never went any further than Hadrian's Wall, but if that was the case, then why did they go to the trouble of constructing another wall this far North? It's well fortified as well, so there must have been some sort of strategic ...

The phone rings, interrupting my old man's local history dissertation.

— I got one, dad!

— What's that, son?

— I got Duncan an appointment!

— What is it? I hear my mum's voice in the background.

67

— He got an appointment for his friend, the mortgage adviser. There seems to be a tumult of general excitement in the background.

— That's great, son, well done. Keep at it! My mother shouts.

— Thanks, OK. I just wanted to let you know.

— Good work, son. You keep it up. Where are you?

— I'm on my way down just now, I'm nearly there in fact.

— Oh right, is that you across the street? We can see you from where we are.

I hang up the phone and hurry across the main road.

— Hi.

— Hiya. You made a sale then.

— No quite a sale, but I arranged an appointment at least. Is he talking about the Antonine Wall again?

*

— Well that's no bad, if you've secured us two appointments, Fitzy, Duncan Campbell reassures me warmly. — That's a hit rate of just under one in two hundred, which is better than I was expecting, he nods his approval.

— No bad, eh? I hope you can close them, I tell him. — I'd hate to think that I've wasted the last week. That's seven days ay ma life I'm never gony get back, Duncan, I hope you appreciate that.

We're sitting in a swanky, slightly pretentious city centre hostelry. The pub affects a sophisticated, upmarket air presumably in order that its vain and aspirational clientele might assume that just by drinking here they've somehow managed to rise above their station. In fact it's a bit of a shithole really, for the most part frequented by arseholes, of both genders. One of the main factors that convinced me to leave Prague was the recent appearance of places like this in the city, which are gradually replacing many of the effortlessly cool bars and other venues that sprung up in the immediate aftermath of the overthrow of Communism, tapping into the city's post-revolutionary chic. At least in Prague you still have something of a choice, whereas in parts of Glasgow these bars appear to be everywhere now. I'm expecting the pub to be busier considering the post work Friday night hour, but it seems to be a pretty sparse crowd in the night so maybe there's hope for humanity after all.

— You've no wasted anything, Fitzy, the two appointments are booked already, I'll be round to seal the deal in the next few days. Nice work, mate, Duncan congratulates me again.

— You sound surprised. I told you, I've done this before. Or something similar anyway. Did you no have faith in ma powers ay persuasion?

— I did have faith in you, you're a salesman, I know that. But still it's no easy, is it? I'm sure you found that yoursel, this line ay work requires a fair bit ay patience.

— You're no wrong, mate. To be honest, Duncan, I think that's the last two appointments I'll be hooking you up wi, because as you correctly point out, you need the fuckin patience ay a saint for this, and I don't think I could look at another call sheet again.

— It's beneath you, I know.

— It's no that. There's folk out ay work, I know that fine well, but …

— You can say it, Fitzy, it's beneath you. It doesny make you a bad person. A man ay your calibre shouldny be working off a call sheet. I warned you at the start, but you insisted.

— Well, I gied it ma best shot, mate. But I'm done wi it, I'm sorry.

— So I guess you'll be looking for work then?

— Could well be, aye. How, what else you got?

— There's a bank that's looking for mortgage control advisers. They're wanting someone wi experience in financial services and I told ma man there that you might be interested.

— Mortgage control adviser ..., I repeated the industry jargon over in my head, trying to filter through the inane job title and searching my memory banks for details and ideas of what the position might involve.

— What's that, like credit control for mortgage customers?

— Pretty much, you're phoning up people who've hit arrears and arranging repayment plans wi them, Duncan clarifies.

— What happens if they cany stick to the agreement? You send round the bailiffs?

— No necessarily. You pass it over to a rep who goes round to their house and assesses their ability to meet their commitments. They might take a statement of means, measure up their incomings and outgoings and determine how much they can afford to pay back. Of course litigation is a last resort but that wouldny be your responsibility, you'd just be the first point of contact in the office.

— This credit crunch is fuckin no real, man. While folk are being put out ay work in almost every other sector, I suppose this is the one area where jobs are being created.

— It's a nightmare, I know. But you might no find anything, Peter, if you're holding out for your ideal job, he warns me.

— How did you fare during the whole credit crunch? I ask.

— It was a struggle, man, to be honest, but I was fortunate. I had connections down South with two or three wealthy clients who are still minted. The London elite haveny been as badly affected by the crash as ordinary cunts. That's what saved me because I was able to hold onto them while everyone else was jumping ship. Survived by the seat ay my pants, so I did.

— That's what we figured, is it no, Sully? I nod to my sidekick.

— We had a hunch, aye, Sully confirms.

— So are you interested in the mortgage control job?

— Aye, send me the details. I'll apply at least.

— Top man. Right, let's change the subject, who wants to score some gear?

— Where are you gony score anything in here, mate? I look at Duncan dubiously, before casting my eyes involuntarily around the pub in an awkwardly nonchalant manner.

— That boy there, Duncan indicates a guy who has just arrived in the pub surrounded by an entourage of friends, or perhaps more likely, colleagues.

— Is that no Dougie Laird? Sully immediately asks.

— It is, aye.

— Who?

— Sports reporter for the SBC, Sully explains to me. — You're telling me he's the boy who you score your gear aff, Duncan?

— It has been known. I used to do his finances when he was a freelancer. Guy's a total fuckin cokeheid, I'm tellin you, he always used to score us a wee gramme or two after I'd been through his books. You up for it, boys? Duncan asks us.

— It's no really ma scene these days, Dunc, I explain, — but don't let me stop yous.

— What you gony do, Duncan? Sully asks. — Stroll up to the boy in the pub and say to him, Hi there, mate, do you mind me, I used to do your tax returns, any chance you could score us some ay the white powder? Look, he's on a works night out, they're aw fuckin here. There's that Mackay cunt and that Moira McGhee lassie.

— Who are you talking about? I ask, confused. I seem to the only one here who doesny know every other fucker in the pub.

— The entire SBC sports department, by the looks ay things, Sully explains to me. — They must be on a works night out. Because I've been out the country for the last five or six years, I'm no as familiar with Scotland's television presenting fraternity as I might have been a few years ago. Seems like quite a party they're having, there's a whole gang ay these media types that's suddenly descended on the place, disturbing in an instant the pub's relative tranquility and transforming it instead into a rowdy, showy den of loudmouths, wannabes and wankers – the sort ay clientèle it was apparently designed for.

— Aye, they're aw here, Duncan confirms. — I used to gie a few ay them a bit ay financial advice in fact, although no any more. They're aw fuckin cokeheids, I'll no be embarrassing Dougie, that's for sure, even if they clock what I'm after. I think I'll go and say hello anyway, and see if I can pop the question.

— Duncan, how many ay this crowd do you know? I ask as he's about to stand up.

— Quite a few ay them, he nods. — Most in fact. Why?

— Is Gus McGregor there by any chance? It's a serious question I'm asking, but half of me is also wondering if I'm gony catch Duncan out, kidding on that he knows folk and exaggerating how well networked he is.

— Aye, that's him at the bar, he shatters my cynicism. —

What do you want wi him?

— I wrote to him recently looking for work.

— Did you, aye? Fair play to you. Well, I'm away to say hello and see if I can sniff out any Class As. Shouldny be too hard wi these boys.

Twenty minutes or so later Sully retakes his seat at our table, after just snorting two fat lines ay cocaine aff the toilet seat in the pub's spacious amenities for the disabled. He hands Duncan back the rolled up tenner that he's just used to hoover the drug up his nostrils.

— That doesny look the least bit suspicious, Dougie Laird has joined us and he comments sarcastically. — Bet that note is covered in more than a few traces of illegal substances.

— Don't think so, mate, that'd be a waste, Sully observes with a throaty sniff. — It aw went up ma nose! The boys laugh. It wouldny surprise me if they were aw fuckin wasted awready.

— So, Fitzy, I heard you had a bit ay a run-in wi big Melly, Duncan accosts me with what I perceive to be a drug-fuelled fire in his eyes.

— You hear about that? I ask incredulously. — Aye I did, right enough.

— Word gets aboot, Sully observes.

— So I see. You're right, Duncan, we did have a bit ay a strange encounter. Some reintroduction to Scotland, I'm no kiddin. On my first night back in the country as well, I point out.

— Were yous singing a few ay they Irish rebel songs, aye?

— I wasny! I protest. — It was Melly that was singing, I was the one trying to persuade the boy to tone it down.

— I heard you left Sully stranded in the street, Duncan

73

laughs.

— It wasny Fitzy's fault, Sully takes up the baton on my behalf and starts explaining all the details to Duncan of how he managed to make his way home after Melly and I abandoned him to his fate on my first day back in the country. He tells the story from the top, recounting every detail of the incident, including Melly's impassioned protest, which I was in expressed agreement wi at the time, that the rebel songs he was shoutin out in the middle ay the street in the middle ay the night wereny explicitly sectarian.

— At that point me and Melly were still on the same page, Duncan, I eventually interrupt. — It was what happened next that I couldny quite get ma heid round.

I suppose it shows the poverty of the argument on the other side of the great Irish rebel songs debate, that I still instinctively feel more sympathy towards a clueless halfwit like Melly's drunken ramblings on the subject, over the more established view emanating chiefly fae certain sections ay the media, that compares these occasionally beautiful but always heartfelt, emotional ballads wi the inane sectarian chanting of unreconstructed bigots, which the likes ay Skelly and Toonce and a few ay their teammates in blue jerseys on that initial afternoon will be well-versed in. This is what a lot ay people cany accept when it comes to some ay the football songs of Celtic and Rangers; the Rangers songs are racist and illegal, whereas the political songs sung by some Celtic fans are by contrast merely controversial, and should therefore at least be tolerated. It's more than just a point of pedantry. In a free and fair society, the racist nonsense is rightly proscribed, while there's no valid argument why the singing of the so-called rebel songs shouldny be perfectly permissible, given the proper time and place of course. As long as they're no been yelled oot in the middle ay a leafy East Dunbartonshire suburb at a time when the sensible, hard-working, nine to five majority are expecting to be getting their eight hours a night.

That's the point I was trying to impress on Melly. I'm aware that it's all too easy for someone in ma position to fall into the trap of the lazy-minded, whose thinking on any relevant subject amounts to little more than, Celtic good, Rangers bad. But like I say, it's a free country and under more normal circumstances, you cany go around banning things just because you maybe don't like them. There's nothing wrong wi a wee dose ay controversy sometimes, it can be healthy in moderation, but unfortunately there are people in Scotland who just cany grasp this particular Old Firm nettle. Instead they try to equate both sets of songs with each other, claiming that there's no difference between them and that the two sides are as bad as one other. If you cany sing 'we're up to our knees in Fenian blood' then 'The boys of the old brigade' will have to go as well. To be honest, these are the kind ay people I was glad to see the back of when I left the country, the bigotry apologists and appeasers as well as other media vested interests, who use twisted and convoluted logic to attempt to justify their position, passing off their views over national radio and television as if they were some sort of received wisdom on the subject.

It's a form of cultural oppression of course and what's particularly ironic and subversive about it is that they try to cloak their arguments in the rhetoric of anti-sectarianism and decency, and consequently even the good old Celtic songs are lumped in wi the kind ay nonsense that the boy who Melly battered that night had on his cassettes. Ultimately though, these people only end up making themselves look and sound ridiculous. Like I say, Melly's absolutely right to insist that the rebel songs areny sectarian and I'm sorry, but if you come out second best to big Melly, in any argument on any subject, then I think it's fair to say that you've lost all claim to credibility.

— Here, I've got a better Melly story, Sully eventually informs us with growing enthusiasm, — one you'll no have heard before, Peter, because it happened when you were away. Listen to this …

The bold Melly had apparently been shagging his next door neighbour Angela for the best part of six or seven months already. It wasny as cosy an arrangement as it sounds however, there were a number of unusual contributing factors to the situation, no the least of which from Melly's point of view, was who was in charge and setting the terms of the relationship. Initially he'd been quite happy to allow Angela to dictate the agenda, but once they started seeing each other on a semi-regular basis, Melly's initial surprise and flummoxed satisfaction at the turn of events was starting to be replaced by a weird, masculine confusion and sense of frustration. It was Angela who would decide where and when they would meet; she was never backward about coming forward; and their sexual encounters were always designed around satisfying her peccadillos and preferences rather than his. To Melly's rather muddled thinking, this represented a role reversal of the gender stereotypes, a feeling that was further confirmed by Angela's frequent boasts about her other liaisons and dalliances, which Melly was unable to convincingly reciprocate with tales of his own exploits.

Nominally, Angela was in a steady relationship with her long-term boyfriend Malky, but because of Malky's alcohol and other problems, for the most part he tended to leave Angela to her own devices and rarely showed any physical affection towards her or paid her any romantic attention. Whether he was aware that Angela was seeking and finding these comforts elsewhere, Melly wasny sure. Angela herself seemed convinced of her partner's complete ignorance. Despite the unstable and, to most people perhaps, somewhat bizarre nature of their relationship, Angela always referred to Malcolm affectionately as 'ma Malky or 'big Malc' or some other equally vomit inducing term of endearment, which invariably, as if to complete the topsy-turvy sexual analogies, got on Melly's tits.

For the most part though, despite the gender confusion and other issues, Melly was getting what he was after. The first time he pulled her was at Hogmanay. After excessive neighbourly celebrations to usher in the New Year, Malky had retired to his kennel around two in the morning and crashed out. Both Angela and Melly were also in a state of insobriety that was appropriate for the season, and it wasny long before they had collapsed into a drunken embrace and were shagging on the couch. That was their first encounter, but from there they were able to arrange their covert meetings around Malcolm's bouts of heavy drinking. Frequently it would simply be a case of Angela popping next door once Malcolm's lights were well and truly out. Once he had woken up and heard his girlfriend's voice in Melly's house, but the situation was convincingly explained away by the fact that Angela and Melly were enjoying a post-coital reefer at the back door at the time. What could be more neighbourly than to share a bit ay weed with the next door's missus, when supplies were running low?

That close call had provoked Angela into displaying a bit more caution and for a time she refused to visit Melly when Malky was at home. A perfect opportunity though presented itself on the night of a recent Scotland match. Malky's planned itinerary was to go drinking in the afternoon, then on to the bookies in the early evening and finally back to the pub to watch the game and make a proper night of it. Melly wasn't interested in Scotland games and when he was invited next door he fully intended to spend several hours in Angela's company trying to satisfy her voracious sexual appetite. After an hour or so in bed, they decided to move into the bath. Bath shagging was overrated in Melly's eyes; as far as he was concerned, there was too much friction and not enough oil to keep those moving parts well-greased. But still, Angela demanded it, so eventually they adjourned to the bathroom. Things were just warming up, Angela actually had her gums around Melly's plums at the time, when suddenly and unexpectedly, Malky's keys were heard rattling in the front door.

Angela's head snapped up and Melly's cock deflated in an instant, as Malky entered the house and started running up the stairs!

— Angela, darling, I've won! he was shouting. — Angela, where are you? I've won. I've won fifty grand! On the Irish lottery, in the bookies, I've won fifty grand!

— Is she no in, Malky? Melly heard another voice belonging to one of Malky's drinking buddies inquire.

— Aye she's in, where are you, Angela? C'mon, hen, aw the boys are here, I've won, I've won!

— Fifty fuckin grand! Angela exclaimed excitedly, — I'm in here, Malky.

— What the fuck, you cany let him in here, Melly protested.

— Oh shite! Realisation dawned on Angela too late, it seemed, — He'll kill me if he sees you here, away and hide somewhere, she instructed Melly.

— There's naewhere to go! he pointed out.

— You in the bathroom, Angela doll? Open up, I've won fifty grand on the lottery.

— Erm, that's magic, Malky, I'll be right out, darling.

— Open the door, Angela, eh? I've been bevvying aw afternoon, I need a fuckin pish.

— Just go oot the back the now, Malky, eh? I'll be oot in a wee minute, she tried to divert him.

— I've no got a wee minute, I'm fuckin burstin here! When you've been putting away the swally like I have this afternoon, you cany just haud on a wee minute. Open the fuckin door, would ye?

— Hey, Malky, whose claithes are these? Melly could hear the voice of another of Malcolm's henchmen inquire from the bedroom.

At this point Melly scarpered. Realising he was totally Donald Ducked, he ran out the bathroom, down the stair, past the rest ay Malcolm's entourage and out into the street wearing nothing so much as a bath towel, before diving into his own house and barricading the doors.

Angela also wrapped herself in a towel and prepared herself for the expected onslaught. But it never came. Malky somehow seemed paralysed by what he'd just seen, and it took a while for Angela to realise that Melly had banged the door against her boyfriend's head as he rapidly departed the scene. Malky wasny just staggering about because he was drunk, but he was in a concussed state of semi-consciousness as well.

— Call an ambulance, somebidy, Malky's no well! Most of Malky's mates seemed as dumbstruck and useless as he was, but eventually the emergency services arrived to stretcher him out.

— You're fuckin dumped! Fifty grand aw tae masel! Were the last words he uttered before they drove him away.

— He'd pished hissel an aw by the way! Sully gleefully concluded his anecdote.

Even in my relatively sober state, I find Sully's new Melly story shocking, but also hysterically funny, so God knows how it must appear to these boys in their drug induced delirium. They were certainly enjoying the narration anyway. I kind ay get the impression that the soiled trousers bit at the end might have been a coked-up elaboration on Sully's part, although the whole thing could be total make-believe, it wouldny surprise me. But it was some story anyway.

— Stone me, where were we, is it ma round? What you having boys? Laird eventually offers.

— Is that Gus McGregor, Dougie? I ask, indicating the man that Duncan had previously pointed out. — Is he your boss?

— That's him, aye.

— Fitzy wrote to him looking for work, Duncan explains.

— Did you? Mon over and I'll introduce you, Laird suggests. — What's your name again? Fitz? Fitzy?

— Peter.

— Do you want to say hello as well, Duncan? Mon over.

— No, I better no. He's still no forgiven me for telling him to go large on Northern Rock a few years ago. I better just avoid the man, if you don't mind, Dougie, Duncan considers.

— Suit yoursel. Come on over, Fitz. Were you looking for work right enough? That's the best way to get into the media by the way. Just huckle wan ay the Gaelic mafia when they're in an emotional and vulnerable state. That's how half the programmes on the telly get commissioned, you know. This is where most ay the editorial policy making goes on an aw, doon the pub wi a few bevvies in you and a few fat lines up your conch. I'm only pullin yir leg, mate, c'mon over and I'll introduce you.

McGregor, it seemed, was totally steamboats.

— Do you know how many proposals cross my desk in a given day, he berates me, — I'm sorry if I can't be expected to remember them all. What did you say it was called again?

— The Scottish Football Debate.

— It rings a bell, give me a call at the office tomorrow, best not make it too early, and we can discuss your idea.

— I'll do that, Mr. McGregor, thank you very much.

That seemed easy enough. Don't get me wrong, I hadny just been offered a five year contract, but I was expecting the whole process of even getting these people to listen to me to be a weird Kafkaesque procedure, nightmarishly long and unfeasibly complicated, but it turns out that Laird was more or less correct, and all you have to do to at least get yourself noticed in this business is to huckle some poor pished bastard on a night out in a bar. It's not what you know, it's who you know in the media, Laird was at pains to assure me, so I was glad that I'd run into him. All I ever wanted was the chance to discuss my idea and I had a strange feeling that maybe I'd already accomplished the hardest part and my potential career in television might be back on track. At the very least, it seemed, I had managed to get my foot in the door.

Or so I hoped anyway.

PART 2

5. BUMPY PITCH

— Hi, Peter, nice to see you again, McGregor offered me his hand. — This is David Henderson, one of my Exec Producers.

— Hi.

— Nice to meet you, Peter.

— Good to meet you.

Hearty handshakes all round.

— So you're a friend of Duncan Campbell's? McGregor asked me, offering me a seat in the fashionable West End pub that he had chosen as the location for our proposed conversation. I was suddenly aware of how long it had been since I was involved in a serious, work-related situation of this kind, and although it had already been impressed on me that this was explicitly not a job interview, and not to be treated as such, I knew they would effectively be trying to size me up in a similar sort of way and the language and dialogue of the discussion would have to be tempered accordingly. It seemed appropriate to remind myself of the number one job interview rule; if in doubt, fake it.

— I am indeed, Duncan and I have known each other for years. We more or less grew up on the same street in fact, I acknowledged, trying to force the sound of nervelessness and relaxation into my voice.

— Great lad, Duncan. And a damn fine accountant, he helped me out on a number of occasions with the old tax returns.

— He's very good at what he does.

— Yes, just a shame about the credit crunch really. I think it hit him quite badly, didn't it? But I hope he doesn't blame himself, there's no way he could have seen what was coming.

It was all tied up in the sub-prime mortgage market in the United States, and from there the effect seemed to spread like an earthquake across the entire financial world. We were all affected you know, not just industry people like Duncan, although as I say, I think it hit him harder than most. He went out of business, didn't he?

— I'm not sure what happened exactly as I was out of the country. He's back on his feet now though.

— Well that's good to hear. Just don't expect me to accept any more of his financial advice, will you? Still, that's all in the past now. And it's always a pleasure to help out an old friend in need. Or in this case a friend of a friend.

— Well, I appreciate it, thank you.

— So. What are we drinking?

— I could go a Staropramen, if they have them.

— One Staropramen coming up. David?

— The usual, thanks, Gus.

— OK, hold the fort. I'll be right back.

— Staropramen, huh? Henderson challenged me after McGregor made his way to the bar. — This might be the last drink the SBC ever buys you, so you might as well make it a fancy one, I suppose.

— I lived in the Czech Republic for five years so I kind of acquired a taste for proper lager over there, David, I explained. — In Prague Staropramen is actually the working man's drink. It's brewed locally, which makes it very inexpensive, and you can get a big half-litre glass for less than a pound. It's only over here that it's seen as a fancy, imported foreign lager.

— Yeah, Gus mentioned something about that. You speak the language, don't you? It must be hard to keep it up though, surely? I've virtually forgotten all my schoolboy Spanish.

84

— Well it's tricky David, you're right, I answered, trying to play for time until the big man returned. Despite the fancy title that he'd been bestowed with, I knew that no matter how much I impressed Henderson with my blethering skills and my capacity for bullshit, ultimately he would have very little input and certainly not the final say in whether my programme idea was going to be taken seriously or not. — The language is no longer all around me like it was over there, I continued. — But my wife is Czech and I still speak it to her, although of course she wants to improve her language skills as well now that we're back in an English-speaking country. So it's not easy. Henderson seemed to react to this news about Lenka as though someone had just pished in his Bovril. I couldn't tell if he was genuinely impressed or had merely been pricked with envy at the revelation of my circumstances, but I decided that I was happy either way. For some reason that wasn't readily apparent, I was reminded of the French footballing philosopher Arsene Wenger's enigmatic observation that everyone always has a prettier wife at home. Henderson might well have been married to Claudia Schiffer's younger, better-looking sister for all I knew, but somehow I doubted it.

— So it's not just the beer then? You have a fancy, imported foreign wife as well, do you? He eventually smirked at me, making little effort to disguise his discomfort just as McGregor returned with the drinks in time to rescue his colleague.

— So, Peter, first things first, your idea, the big man resumed his seat. — Perhaps I should start by saying that you've done tremendously well already just to get as far as you have with it. There's your spritzer, David, and there's your fancy foreign beer, Peter.

— We were just saying …, Henderson cut in.

— Proper Czech lager, I don't drink anything else, I explained briefly, choking back a guffaw as he accepted his white wine and soda.

— Good man. So, Peter, as I was saying, you've done incredibly well so far just in getting to this stage, McGregor resumed. — Most new programme ideas don't make it beyond the proposal form, they're usually dismissed pretty swiftly and summarily as being either too impractical, beyond the scope of our budget or more often than not just too plain wacky. Honestly, you should see some of the shite we're obliged to wade through on a daily basis. It would bring a tear to your eye, and not just in laughter! he announced in what I assumed was a good-natured attempt to try and relax me now that the preliminaries were clearly over and he was getting down to business. I was tempted to offer him my thoughts on some of the shite they actually did commission at this juncture, but I managed to restrain myself. — So the fact that we've agreed to take the meeting and are even sitting here just now is a very positive sign, the big man continued. — If I can just sum up briefly how we managed to arrive at our present position; you huckled me on a night out, when I was in a particularly vulnerable and emotional state, for which congratulations are surely in order. Never underestimate the importance of timing in this business, and I think we've established this is a gift you already possess, so well done. Not only that, you then followed up our initial discussion with a very well-argued, articulate and passionate email, outlining the idea. That in turn was followed by the twenty minute or so telephone call which we had last week, when we went over the idea and you fleshed out some more of the detail for me in your own words. And I have to say, Peter, at every stage so far I've been very impressed with what I've been hearing. Your passion and enthusiasm for the project come through very clearly. As I say, that's why we've invited you to this very informal meeting. I've asked David along here tonight as well so that you can have the opportunity to convince us that it's in all our interests to proceed with the idea and take things to the next step, which would be to go ahead and commission a pilot episode of your programme. I should repeat, you've done well just to make it this far with your proposal, but perhaps this would be the appropriate point to warn you that this is the stage when a lot of good, solid ideas tend to come a cropper and run into difficulties. Difficulties which the owner of the idea himself could never have foreseen. I don't want to put you off or discourage you in any way, but at the same time I wouldn't want you getting your hopes up just yet. There are a number of factors which still have to be taken into consideration, most of which, as I mentioned, you can't possibly be expected to have anticipated. So just give us your best shot, don't try and second guess what it is you think we want to hear from you. For the next few minutes you'll have our complete and undivided attention. This is your big moment, so please, if you wouldn't mind, in your own time and your own words, I'd ask you to run through a brief summary of your idea again for us if you will, from the top, 'The Scottish Football Debate', what's it all about? What's the big idea?

— Well basically, the idea is for a programme called 'The Scottish Football Debate' as you say, Gus, I began tentatively. That was quite a preamble that McGregor had given us, and while I was appreciative of the fact that he had skipped any more of the small talk and moved straight on to the business in hand, all the time he was speaking I was hoping that his next subordinate clause would be his last, and that he'd hurry up and finish, so that I could launch masel on him and blurt out everything that I wanted to say. But now that it was finally my turn to speak, I found that I was a bit tongue-tied. — Erm, I should say first of all, thanks very much for taking the meeting guys, I really appreciate it. Taking the meeting, is that really how these people spoke? In attempting to imitate their pompous jargon, I wondered if I hadny made a fool ay masel straight off the bat. No sign of a response though from either tweedledum or tweedledee, so there was nothing else for it except to plough on manfully. — Yeah, so it's called 'The Scottish Football Debate', I offered, — and basically, well, the title, I imagine, should be pretty self-explanatory really. We debate the hot topical issues of the day, as they arise, in and around what is, after all, our national game. But here's the difference Gus, because as you've previously mentioned, similar shows of this nature have been done before, ad infinitum, but the unique thing about this programme, its USP if you like, is that it introduces a more cerebral approach to every aspect of the material that it deals with. I'm not saying that we should become remote or inaccessible figures, intellectualising football in our ivory towers. No, because we still need to acknowledge the distinctive humour and accessibility that defines our sporting culture, I cleared my throat and continued. — It has to have a cutting edge though, that's the thing. We treat our audience with respect, we credit them with an equal level of intelligence as ourselves and we talk about the issues that they want to hear discussed in a more frank and forthright manner than perhaps they're used to hearing in many other outlets. And we're able to do this because we treat the subject seriously. In the grand scheme of things football is only relatively important of course, but in terms of a diversion from the mundane details and duties of everyday life, then what a diversion! So we treat it seriously, we discuss the things that people want to hear about and we have the wider well-being of Scottish football very much at the forefront of our minds, informing and motivating us every stretch of the way. That has to be the key point here, guys. I know this may have sounded naïve just a few years ago, especially amongst some of the embittered old media hacks that we're used to hearing from in this country, offering us their inane pontifications on the state of our game, and other such subjects, et cetera et cetera ... I realised in the middle of this sentiment that I was beginning to lose track of where the original sentence had begun, — which by the way I know we're not! I interrupted myself. — I must stress that, this is an embittered old hack free zone! This is a programme for a new and different media environment, appropriate to the modern age, and I believe that a fresh approach is what's needed. So we won't be riddled with self-serving agendas, we won't be doggedly returning to the same old narratives, we won't necessarily be concerned first and foremost with our own self-advancement because we're not on a mission here to indulge our own egos or hob-nob with the rich and famous, which invariably in my experience turns out to be a bit of a disappointment anyway. Do you follow what I'm saying? We have an eye on our rivals, but we won't let our competitors dictate their terms to us, because we're the avant-garde here, leading the way potentially into a new era, with the future of our country very much up for grabs over the next few years. As I say, it may sound slightly naïve in that sense, because my proposal means that we should be looking to make a more positive contribution. We have to have an eye on the future, because these are the early years of a new century, a new millennium indeed, and I firmly believe anyway that today's naïvety is tomorrow's political dogma. You can see that throughout history, can't you, whether it's with civil rights, equal opportunities, universal suffrage, freeing the slaves ... you name it. Sorry, I'm digressing. My point is this; can we in the media complement the growth and development of football in this country for the coming decades? That's the important question. We're used to the press calling for the governing bodies to take various actions to improve Scottish football, so I just want us to ask one another this one question - what can we in the media ourselves be doing in this regard? After all, in an information age, the people who control the flow and supply of that information, namely the communications industries, are potentially all powerful, and with that power and influence needs to come some responsibility, I ended my argument with a rhetorical flourish. That final line was pre-rehearsed of course and I was glad that I'd managed to work it in, although to be honest I was struggling not to throw up after the cheesefest that I'd just delivered. I mean really, freeing the fucking slaves? What the fuck was I on about? I know when you're nervous and the butterflies are flapping away that you can find it difficult to shut up once you've opened your mouth, but still, I'm glad nobody I know was around to hear some of that nonsense, because I don't think they'd have recognised me from some of the garbage I was spouting. At least I hope they wouldny, because there was an undeniable element to it that was deliberate, and measured, and calculated to strike a chord with the high ranking members of the liberal elite who were somehow, and for some reason that I still couldny quite grasp, sitting opposite me in this pretentious West end pub and were my exclusive and captive audience for just so much time as I could manage to keep them here.

McGregor sat back in his chair, seemingly oblivious to the toe-curling that was going on under my end ay the table.

— OK, good, he reflected. — Questions, David? Whatever he thought of my closing lines, or some of the verbal diarrhoea that had come before it, McGregor wasn't giving anything away at this stage. I was totally unaware of how my pitch had been received, but I certainly wasny going to be allowed to sit around worrying about it for long.

— Erm yes, one or two points, Henderson pondered. — I'm intrigued, where did the idea for this programme come from originally?

— Well, I'm familiar with the format David obviously, that's not particularly new … More toe-curling … — But the idea for a more accessible, maybe more sophisticated level of content came from watching similar shows in the Czech Republic. I lived there for a number of years as I mentioned earlier, and at first I couldn't speak the language. So I used to watch the football shows merely for the football itself, because I wasn't understanding anything that was being said. But gradually, as I developed a decent grasp of the lingo, it slowly dawned on me that they seemed to be talking a great deal of sense on these shows. There was very little of the clichés and the inane banter that I was expecting, so it was a revelatory, weird kind of experience for me. As I improved my language skills, I found that not only could I understand an increasing amount of what was being discussed, but I was also surprised to discover that they were talking much more about things that I wanted to hear. The partisan, agenda-driven, Machiavellian stuff seemed to me to be wholly absent, and they appeared to be treating their audience with a degree of respect for their intelligence. I couldn't tell you what a relief that was to me Gus, after a lifetime of listening to the phone-in roasters on Radio Kelvin.

— Now now, McGregor cautioned, — we mustn't criticise the opposition, that's not the proper form. Let's stick to the positives, shall we? How can your idea work for us?

— So I'm not allowed to have a go at the BBC either? I joked.

— I'm afraid not, no. Not at this stage anyway.

— Shame, I had both barrels lined up for some of our competitors, I assured them. — The point I'm making though, I rallied, — is that I perceived an altogether more intelligent level of debate on most of these shows. There was a freshness about them, a lack of cynicism that was in marked contrast to what I was used to. This is chiefly what I was talking about when I met you in the pub the other week, Gus.

— You'll have to remind me, I'm afraid, as I don't remember very much of that particular conversation. You must have been making some sense otherwise you wouldn't be here, but the exact details of the discussion are regrettably no longer at my disposal, McGregor offered apologetically.

— We were talking about the fact that the Nationalists are on the verge of winning an outright majority at Holyrood, in a political system that was specifically designed not to allow such an outcome. They could introduce an independence referendum within a few short years, or even, depending on the mandate they receive, push through a split with the rest of the UK in a forthcoming session of parliament. Very soon we Scots might not be able to call ourselves British any more, so we don't have to assume in that slightly arrogant, stand-off-ish manner that there's nothing we can learn from these other countries. The Czechs do things better than us in this particular instance – it's a fact! – So let's see if we can rise to the challenge and do better ourselves. By this stage I had pretty much given up trying not to sound conceited or naff in my various utterances, and I was in fact starting to develop a strange fondness for the kind of indulgent verbiage that was continuing to flow unchecked from my mouth. There was an art to this method of communication, and I was beginning to feel more comfortable with it at last, which may have been just as well because I was hoping to work in the media after all. It was probably no bad thing that I seemed to be gaining an understanding and appreciation of dealing in bullshit. But at the same time I was in earnest now, talking about something I had strong views on, with reasoned arguments to back up my opinions, and I seemed to have finally got into my stride. It's amazing the extent to which the nerves and the toe-curling can go out the window in these circumstances, and I hoped that at last I was managing to convey a bit of genuine enthusiasm in my voice.

— It's not a fact though, is it? It's an opinion, Henderson corrected me, — your opinion.

— No, you're right, David, it is just my opinion, I maybe blurred the distinction between fact and opinion there, thank you for pointing that out to me. But let's look at some facts then, if we can. The Czech Republic has had some remarkable success stories in recent international football tournaments, whereas Scotland by contrast, a football daft country let's not forget, can't even qualify for a major tournament these days. At various points the Czechs have been listed at 2 or 3 in the international rankings, whereas we seem to be in a permanent struggle just to stay in the top 50. And it's not just football by the way. The number one sport in the Czech Republic is ice hockey, and a few years ago the national team won the gold medal at the Winter Olympics, beating the Canadians, the Americans and the Russians along the way. I'm telling you, the whole country went mad. Because of the time difference folk stayed up until the wee small hours to watch the live coverage, and once the Czech team won, the hooters started beeping and blaring right through until sunrise when people were starting to go to their work in the morning. I swear, I never managed a wink of sleep that night. I could go on, couldn't I? I don't need to tell you about the tennis players they produce in such a small country, do I? This doesn't strike me as a coincidence.

— I'm sorry, what doesn't? What's the point you're making? Henderson seemed to be showing a distinct lack of appreciation for the gist of my argument.

— The point I'm making, David, is that a nation which talks more intelligently about sport, performs better at sport, I spelled it out for him.

— So what are you saying? Commission my idea and I'll turn Scotland into a nation of sporting superstars?

— I would never claim to be able to do anything like that, David, or that anything of the sort would follow on from our programme. But who knows, we might just be able to make a difference somewhere along the way, I resorted once more to managementspeak for Henderson's benefit. — Don't you think we should be at least trying to do this? I honestly believe there's a link between the level of debate in the wider sporting culture and sporting success. That's one of the main reasons we should be undertaking this project, in my opinion. It has to be worth our while to at least try, and if we stick one over on our rivals in the process by adding a programme to our schedule that trumps the nonsense that they like to blurt all over the airwaves, then that's the name of the game, surely? And by the way I think there's every chance we will, because it's my firm belief that there's an audience for what we're trying to do here, an audience that's thoroughly fed up with the frankly dreadful bill of fare that for years they've been expected to swallow with shows of this kind.

— You've mentioned the audience a couple of times now, McGregor noted. — How can you convince us that there really is an appetite for another football discussion show, in what is already a heavily saturated market?

I was vaguely aware by this stage that I may have been coming across as an overenthusiastic schoolboy but I didn't care. I was in my element now, relaxed, with toes well and truly uncurled, and desperately trying to emphasise the positive. — At the risk of repeating myself, I think there will be a market for this show, because the purpose of the programme is to reinvigorate the whole genre, Gus. I was glad it was McGregor who had resumed the line of questioning, as I felt he was at least starting to buy into what I was saying, and that consequently I could converse with him in a more forthright and plain-spoken manner than was possible with his underling. — This may be a bit of a diversion, but if you'll allow me just to develop one of the issues we've been discussing. I have a mate who's still over in Prague called Kevin McGarry. He's from the same town as me, Kirkintilloch, and he was a very talented young football player himself. He was on Airdrie's books as a youngster and he represented Scotland at Under 17 level, I believe it was. Anyway, for reasons that I won't go into now, he failed to make the grade as a professional player. He's now out in Prague working for SK Slavia, coaching their Under 16 side. He tells me there's so much respect out there for Scottish football, and that they think it's a tragedy how we've lost our way so badly in the last few years or so. They know, at least the better informed people know, and believe me that's most of them when it comes to football, that it was Scotland, much more than England, that gave the game to the world. The English public schools came up with the rules but it was the Scots who figured out how to play the game properly, and perhaps more importantly, they were able to make their understanding of football more widely available and teach others about the finer arts of the beautiful game too. There was a Scottish guy called Johnny Madden, who played for Celtic in the club's formative years and who, once he retired as a footballer, went over to Prague in the Edwardian era and coached Slavia for over a quarter of a century. He was the first coach they ever had, before Madden they only ever had team captains, never coaches. And he showed them how to play the game in the Scottish style of pass and move, which was the most sophisticated development in the history of football at the time. There was another Scot called John Dick who coached Slavia's rivals Sparta during the inter-war period as well. And of course their tactics and coaching methods became the talk of the coffee houses and kavarnas of Central and Eastern Europe. The Austrian *Wunderteam*, the Hungarian 'Golden Squad' – I'm sorry, I don't know how to say it in Hungarian … – they all grew out of the coffee house culture that persisted after the collapse of the Habsburg Empire, where football was discussed intelligently, intellectually even, in an environment where all sections of society mixed freely. Sadly it was all destroyed by totalitarianism, Hitler's Anschluss in the case of Austria, and Stalin's 1956 invasion ended the dominance of the Hungarians.

— Stalin died in 1953, Henderson informed me.

— Still, his successor then, Khrushchev or whoever it was, it's hardly germane to the argument, is it? Try calling up Radio Kelvin and raising these issues, see how long they let you on the air for, I replied.

— What is the point?

— What is the point? What is the point! What's your point, caller? The point, David, is the one that I was making earlier; namely that if you talk more intelligently about football, you tend to produce more intelligent footballers, who can play the game, read the game and coach the game better. And that's where we come in, I offered, allowing that thought to linger in the air as I waited for some sort of response from either man.

— Why us? McGregor eventually asked.

— Excuse me?

— Why us? he shrugged. — Why are you bringing this idea to the SBC? There are other broadcasters out there, or you could have taken it to an indie? Why us?

— Because I think it will sit well with the SBC's output. Imagine the kudos to be gained if you could play a role in reinvigorating the whole level and standard, not just of sporting debate, but of sport itself. It will reflect well on all of us. An indie, what is that? Sorry, I'm not familiar with all this industry jargon? An independent production company? What, make the show in some disused warehouse somewhere and then have some guy ride over to Specific Key on a bike with a tape? I don't think so. No, the SBC has to own this idea completely.

— It doesn't work like that now, we're end to end digital in our new facility, Henderson informed me.

— OK, so what is it you do now, a thousand gigabyte file transfer? I asked. — Do you get someone to text it to you? It's not really how I see this project progressing guys, I told them flatly, with an emboldened straight face that indicated just how much things had turned around since my first few tentative utterances a mere twenty minutes or so ago. I was feeling strangely pleased with myself by this stage, largely because I'd managed to work in the Johnny Madden anecdote, along with several of the other points that I never thought I'd be able to properly articulate in a meeting of this kind.

— What format do you see the show taking? Henderson asked.

— Nothing too out of the ordinary there, I replied. — It'll be a different discussion for each show. We'll have a couple of regular panellists who will appear every week and a guest from a field appropriate to the particular weekly discussion point; maybe a youth coach one week, or an administrator the next or possibly a fanzine editor sometime, if we can persuade one to come in.

— And it's a themed show every week?

— Yes, it is. We pick one particular topic that might seem particularly current, or we can do specials on youth development for instance, that's always a contentious subject. The point is we dedicate enough time and energy to our subject matter and see if we can make some progress towards a rational conclusion on the issue, rather that skirting over an important topic with nothing more than a few platitudes and well worn clichés.

— Who are the panellists?

— Obviously that would be for the programme makers to determine. I could suggest a few names but the important thing is that we find people who know what they're talking about. I don't want any careerists or people you've nicked from other shows, just to get one over on your competitors. They have to be good people, who can bring a fresh approach and contribute to the level of debate we're hoping to attain.

— And you'll be presenting it?

— I will. And it has to be a live transmission.

— Live? Hold on a wee second, Peter. You've admitted to us that you have no experience at this sort of thing, and yet you're expecting us to let you loose on a live broadcast?

— It needs to be live, how else can we produce an interactive programme that can involve our audience? We want people to participate in the show through emails and social media, we'll have a researcher on set looking at the feed who can put the audience's questions and other bits and pieces to the panel as they scroll through the responses.

— Audience participation is tricky, Gus, this could be a recipe for disaster, Henderson turned to McGregor and voiced his concerns to the big man as if I was no longer in the room. — He freely admits he has absolutely no experience in this field, and he's asking us to give him a live platform from which to spout God only knows whatever agendas or grievances he might have with the world.

— I assure you, David, I have no such intentions, I put in sincerely.

— Even if you don't, you have no experience, Henderson turned back to me.

— How hard can it be? I blurted out, in a somewhat exasperated tone.

— I'm sorry?

— How hard can it be, David? I asked again. — Presenting a television programme, how hard can it be? We're not talking about brain surgery here, are we? As far as I can make out, this job involves reading out loud, and fielding some questions to people in a studio who will hopefully have some grasp of the subject matter. I can do this job, David, and I want to do this job. Honestly, Gus, all I need is for you to give me an opportunity here. My heart sank as I realised that I had started to sound as though I was appealing to their sense of pity, and I'd descended to the level of desperation, which was the one thing I'd been warning myself in advance to avoid at all costs.

— What's the duration? McGregor asked.

— I'm sorry?

— How long will the show last?

— Again that depends on the gap you can find in the schedule, but I would reckon forty minutes might be ideal. We don't want to bore people to death with something any longer than that. This is football we're talking about remember, which is only relatively important in the grand scheme of things. Ideally we don't want our audience having lost the will to live by the time the final credits start rolling.

— I see. Well, it was a pleasure to meet you again, Peter, McGregor suddenly stood up. — We'll get back to you as soon as we can, won't we David?

— We will indeed, Henderson took his cue and got to his feet as well.

— Right, OK, when can I …?

— That was a very interesting and worthwhile discussion, I thought. You've given us plenty to think about.

— Good, well it was nice talking to you both.

— It sure was. Bye.

And with that my two interlocutors departed the scene, leaving me on my own with my thoughts. I was going to leave too, I stood up to go but, realising that I had probably fucked things up with my desperation at the end and my overzealous tone and demeanour throughout, I only made it as far as the bar.

— Another Staropramen please, mate, I ordered. And then I had another, and another, drinking myself slowly into an intoxicated stupor, all the while contemplating the sad turn of events that had brought me to this place and the unfortunate course that my life seemed to be taking. I sat there playing with my technology, fielding a few phone calls and text messages right through to closing time and I ended up steaming drunk on those fancy, chemical-free, foreign lagers. At least the lack of impurities in the alcohol I was drinking meant that, when I woke up the next morning I'd managed to avoid the fragilities of a hangover, although my brain was still scrambled.

6. YES

The theme from 'Ghostbusters' was playing over in my head, rousing me out of my dreamy stupor, as I sat upright in bed and fished about blindly for my mobile phone.

— Hello, is that Peter Fitzpatrick?

— Yes, speaking.

— Hi, Peter, it's Gus McGregor here from the Scottish Broadcasting Company.

— Hello, Gus, I croaked. — Good to hear from you.

— No problem. I thought I would give you a call to discuss how our meeting went the other night. Are you free to talk? I haven't called too early, have I?

— Of course. I mean, of course not, you haven't called too early, I cleared my throat again. — Yes, I'm free. I had no idea what time it was, but there was a Lenka sized gap in the bed beside me, where my wife had already silently departed for her work while I slept.

— OK, good. Well, the first thing to say is that overall we felt that the meeting went very positively, McGregor informed me. — We were impressed by everything you had to say about 'The Scottish Football Debate', and we continue to like the idea. So, on that basis …, his articulation at this point seemed to be painfully slow, — we'd like to go ahead and commission a pilot episode of the programme, with a format very much along the lines of what we were discussing in the 'Highlander' the other night.

— That's erm, that's very good news, Gus.

— Yes, well, commissioning a pilot would be the next logical step in developing the project so, provided you're still keen on the idea, we'd look to start putting things in place to make that happen as soon as possible.

— Yes, absolutely, I'm still keen on the idea, I was already out of bed and standing up by now, very much wide awake. — So where do we go from here? I asked.

— The next thing would be for you to come in and meet a couple of people who potentially you're going to be working with. I've recruited a Producer, for this one episode, and she's come up with a couple of names, who seem to fit the criteria of what would be suitable for the show.

— Names? Who are we talking about?

— Martin Dodds, the former Rangers player. He's been with us for a while now, doing a bit of radio and television work. I've spoken to him briefly and he's very keen to get involved.

— Did he not used to be a pundit on Radio Kelvin? I asked, because I dimly seemed to remember his name and it was associated in my mind with some commercial phone-in show during my pre-Prague days.

— He did indeed, but he left them some time ago, and he's been working with us for six months or so now. Very much the modern Rangers man, Doddsy, you'll like him. He fits in with your idea that Scottish football maybe needs to shed some of its baggage and shape up for the challenges of the future. Martin sees himself as representing the new Rangers going forward, much more tolerant and receptive to new ideas, and not just stuck in the old certainties of the past.

— Sorry, representing Rangers?

— Yes. It sounds strange, I know, but that's what a lot of these ex-Rangers players see themselves as doing. They represent the club's interests in and through the media. In the past a lot of outlets have been quite happy to let them do that in whatever way they saw fit, usually with the steady guidance of an expensive, by-the-hour PR firm looking over their shoulders. We'll let him know that he needs to move on from that to the extent that he can, and we'll emphasise again the need to buy into the modernity concept, which, as I understand it, he's very keen to do. So he should fit in with what the show is all about.

— OK, I announced cautiously, sitting back down at my desk. McGregor hadn't quite thrown a damp squib on my enthusiasm but he'd immediately raised some concerns, particularly in regard to using cast-offs from other programmes, which was something I'd warned against in the pub the other night. But still, this was all coming at me very fast and I felt it was important to keep an open mind. — Who else is involved at this stage? I asked.

— I'm speaking to Davie Keane and his agent this afternoon.

— Davie Keane?

— Yes. The former Celtic captain. He's a bit suspicious of the media, but we've done some things with him in the past, and again from initial conversations, I believe that the breaking new ground angle is one that we can sell to him.

— Davie Keane?

— Yes.

— Wow!

— I know, it certainly would be a bit of a coup if we could persuade him to get involved. As I say, it's not finalised yet but I'm optimistic at this stage that he'll be joining us, for the pilot at least.

— That would be fantastic, he was a bit of a hero of mine growing up, I don't mind telling you.

— I think he was a lot of people's hero, not just Celtic fans but Scotland fans too. If we can tie him down then I think it will demonstrate that we mean business, and that this programme isn't just another version of the same type of show, regurgitated into a new format, but it offers a new take on a familiar genre. He'll bring a bit of charisma and presence, and the very fact that he's agreed to do the pilot will prove to people that we're serious about taking this forward.

— This sounds terrific, Gus. I don't really know what to say.

— Don't worry. Although I should just remind you once again, Peter, that we're still only talking about a pilot at this stage. I've recruited a Producer to make a pilot. These people have agreed to come in and do a pilot, McGregor emphasised. — If we decide to go ahead and commission a series, then we have to address the issue of pinning these guys down contractually. And of agreeing a contract with yourself as well of course. I forgot to ask you the other night, do you have an agent?

— Do I have an agent? I repeated out loud, more for my own benefit than McGregor's. It wasn't a question that I'd ever been asked before. — No I don't, I'm sorry.

— Are you planning on appointing one to represent you in any future negotiations?

— To be honest, that's not something I've really thought about at this stage, you've just sprung that one on me, Gus. How do you go about finding an agent anyway? What do you do, just look one up in Yellow Pages?

— I wouldn't try that, no. OK look, let's not worry about that yet. But it's something you should think about, if we were to go ahead and commission the programme.

— I'll bear it in mind.

— It shouldn't be a problem, agents around here are ten a penny. I'm sure someone will sort you out with one who has represented people in your position before.

— Fine. So what's the next thing for me to do, where do we go from here?

— I need you to come in and meet the Producer. Ideally we want to progress things quite quickly from here. Are you free tomorrow morning?

— I am.

— Right, come in about 10 a.m. then and meet Helen. She's already fully briefed and is very excited about the show. You can have a very informal chat about every aspect of what you're going to be working on, and maybe I'll arrange for you to meet one or two other people who'll be involved as well. We'll require a complete production team for the pilot. Helen is going to act as our Producer-Director, but we'll need a Floor Manager, a sound man and a full camera crew. Oh, and the bigwigs will be coming down too, the Head of Sport, the Head of Programmes, the Head of Editorial Content as well as myself and David Henderson, who you've already met. And hopefully we'll get Doddsy and Davie down to say hello as well.

— Quite a gathering then?

— You could say that, yes. And if it all goes smoothly tomorrow with Helen, which I'm sure it will, we'll bring you back in the following afternoon to run through the pilot.

— OK, well, that's great news Gus, thanks for arranging all this.

— No problem. Do you have any questions?

— Erm, I have quite a few questions but to be honest I can't think what they are right now. I'll go away and try to get my head together, and hopefully all my queries will be answered by this time tomorrow.

— Right, I'll let you sleep on it then and we'll see each other in the morning, he told me, although I wasny sure if I'd be getting much sleep the night. — See you around ten o'clock then.

— Looking forward to it, Gus, thanks. See you tomorrow.

*

— Peter, this is Helen, McGregor introduced me.

— Hi, I offered shyly.

— Helen, Peter.

— Nice to meet you, Peter.

— Good to meet you.

— Helen's a big Celtic fan so I'm sure you'll get along, McGregor informed me, although to be honest I was so nervous I was barely able to offer a smile in her direction, never mind engage in any witty, Fenian banter wi the woman.

— Cool, I nodded diffidently.

— Right, let's get you two seated over here, and then I'll leave you to it, McGregor instructed us. The foyer of the SBC building didn't appear to be much of a meeting room, but apparently this was where a lot of the organisation's business was conducted, particularly with outsiders and potential new people such as myself. Helen and I sat down on our plastic seats next to the coffee and sweets stall beside a couple of garish posters advertising some of the company's radio and television shows and featuring huge, smiley close-up photographs of some of their better known presenters. I wanted my show to be commissioned and meet with success, but I also hoped to Christ that I didny end up one day with my ugly mug featured on one of these cardboard placards wearing a cheesy, corporate smile.

— Maybe I'll end up on one of these boards, I told Helen. It seemed that I still hadny got the nerves out my system.

— Who knows? Let's hope so anyway, she smiled. She looked kind and accommodating, on the threshold perhaps of middle age, and ready to take pity on me in a motherly sort of way, which was just as well because if she'd been anything other than gentle with me at this stage, if she'd breathed on me too hard or looked at me the wrong way, then I think I would have ran away. — Shall we talk about the show? she suggested. I glanced over at McGregor as he flashed his badge and disappeared past the security men and into the main building.

— OK, I shrugged.

— Good. So I've been fully briefed by Gus and David, and from what I can understand, we could sum up your idea as being 'a football discussion show for grown-ups'. Does that sound like a fair summary?

— Yes, that sounds pretty fair.

— Great. I've been wanting to get involved in a show like this for ages, it's long overdue if you ask me. If we can make this work, then I think it could be a huge success.

— That would be great, I gulped. — Sorry, I'm not really sure what to say to you, Helen. Everybody's sounding like you've already made the decision to commission the show, and yet at the same time I'm being told that we're making a pilot first, and that the decision will be made on that basis. It's great that you're all sounding so positive about it, but I don't really know what's happening. I thought I had to convince you about the show's merits, but you're already telling me how great it is, and how keen you are to get involved. It's all a bit confusing, and I've no idea what to say to persuade you to go ahead and commit yourselves to the idea.

— You don't have to persuade me of anything.

— I don't?

— No. I'm not the one making those decisions.

— You're not?

— No.

— But you'll be involved in the decision making process though, surely?

— Not really, no. I can hopefully have some input as to why I think the idea might work, but other than that I'm as desperate as you are that they'll offer to make the programme. I've been recruited by Gus to produce the pilot, but that's really the extent of my involvement at this stage. If they offer us a commission, then I'll hopefully be involved in working on the series in some capacity; if not then it's back to my day job on the radio. No, I'm in the same boat as you right now, Peter. I've been wanting to move into television for years, so this is my big opportunity too.

— Jesus, I'm sorry. It shows how much I still have to learn about all this.

— Don't worry. It's best to get your mistakes out the way on day one, she smiled, although I wasny sure that I completely agreed with her. Making an arse of yourself almost as soon as you opened your mouth didny exactly seem to me to be the best way to make a good first impression. — As I say, I'll be moving from radio if this goes ahead, so a great deal of all this is new to me too, she added.

— So what are we here to talk about exactly? I coughed and sat up straight, hoping to recover my composure.

— The pilot. To start with anyway.

— Of course. The pilot. How's it going to work, what do I need to do?

— Well, as I understand it, the show involves selecting a different topic for discussion every week, and then settling on that theme, asking the panellists their views, interspersed with highlights of the weekend's games and a report featuring a more in depth look at the relevant issues.

— Yes, although I would like to include some audience

participation as well, if that's possible. We can go to the studio audience and canvass their views, as well as using texts and emails so the public can let us know what they're thinking too. It has to be a proper debate, we want to encourage people to think analytically and intelligently about the matters we're discussing. It shouldn't just be a procession of media orthodoxy that we're hearing. Let's throw it open to the nation so we can hear their thoughts as well. That way we keep it grounded but serious, we don't have any inappropriate pretensions, we just do things a wee bit more perceptively and with maybe a slightly better attitude than people are used to seeing in this type of show, that's all.

— That would have to mean that it was a live broadcast?

— Of course.

— OK, I'll certainly try and make that point to the powers that be.

— I went over all this with Gus and David the other night, I pointed out. — I think it would make the discussion more edgy and exciting if we were transmitting and receiving that kind of instant feedback, which could then inform and enhance the debate we're conducting. David seemed to have his reservations, but hopefully I've convinced them.

— Have you seen some of the emails they get on these shows?

— Yeah, but I'm sure they're usually pretty selective in the messages they read out. We would only use the best points of course, because I honestly believe that there are a lot of people out there who would want to participate in this kind of grown up discussion, as you put it, if we get the tone of the show right. People generally will only start to take the mickey once they think the mickey's being taken out of them, if you see what I mean.

— I'm sure it can be done, Helen smiled. — Let's move

on to the content of the pilot. I've selected a hot topic, which I think we can use as the main theme for tomorrow's show. Did you see any of the games at the weekend?

— I did, yes.

— Well then, the subject I've chosen for us to discuss in the pilot tomorrow will probably come as no surprise to you.

— Referees?

— Exactly right!

— Great, I laughed. — You're right, it's certainly topical. Did you see that decision at Ibrox?

— Honestly, Peter, don't get me started. So, I think we agree, it's a relevant issue.

— Officials and their decisions are always going to be a relevant issue in these parts, it seems, I considered.

— Sadly, you're right, she agreed. — Do you remember the referees' strike last year?

— I do, of course, even though I was out the country.

— Right, well, we'll be using a lot of the material that we have from that dispute for the purposes of this show. Because we're doing a dummy run, as it were, that means we can effectively kid on that some of the things which people were saying during that dispute are what people are saying now, in our programme. Do you follow?

— In our hypothetical discussion?

— Exactly. And, she paused for added emphasis, — I've convinced former referee Campbell Thomson to come in and participate in the show and speak on behalf of the referees, just as he did during last year's strike.

— He'll have his work cut out for him after what happened at the weekend.

— Well, he is a lawyer, so I presume he'll be putting his argumentative skills to good use.

— A lawyer and a referee, huh? How unpopular can one man hope to be?

— Tell me about it, Helen laughed. — Although wait til you meet Doddsy – a media pundit, football agent, ex-Rangers player! I think that even beats Thomson.

— What's Doddsy like? I asked. — Gus told me that he was quite a forward thinking guy, for a Rangers man.

— No, he is, he's lovely. You'll enjoy working with him, I was just taking the mince. Don't tell him I said that by the way.

— I won't, although …, I hesitated, — is there any way we could maybe work it in?

— How do you mean?

— The Mr. Popularity thing, could we use it in the pilot tomorrow? I think it would add a bit of humour, which we need, because we want to keep the show edgy and accessible. Remember, it's not a stuffy, highbrow discussion we're having, of no interest to anyone who isn't a football intellectual.

— We could maybe do something, she considered carefully.

— How would it work anyway? This is something I've been meaning to ask; how much of the show will be scripted?

— Well, I'm letting you in on the trade secrets now of course, she revealed. — I've written a few lines here which will open the show, she rummaged through her folders and produced a sheet of headed notepaper. — Have a read through that and tell me what you think. I took the script from Helen's hand. — Read it out loud, she instructed me.

I glanced over the document and began reading,

— Hello and welcome to the first edition of our brand new programme, 'The Scottish Football Debate' which is a show that, well … it pretty much does what it says on the tin really. Each week we'll be debating the hot topics in Scottish football with an honesty, a boldness and indeed a level of intellectual rigour which you may not have heard before in many other outlets. We'll select a broad theme for every show, relevant to the burning footballing issues of the day, and we'll be discussing it until you're blue in the face hearing about it basically. And we certainly won't be shirking any challenges or bottling any important decisions. I'm sure many of you watching at home who are of a certain age will remember the old Rikki Fulton sketch about the talking dog who refused to discuss either politics or religion. Well, there'll be none of that on this show – there are no taboos, no no-go areas. We'll talk about anything you like, providing of course that it's relevant to the matter in hand. Joining us in the studio every week will be former Rangers and Motherwell defender Martin Dodds and ex-Celtic captain Davie Keane.

— What do you think? she asked me.

— I love it. You've hit the nail right on the head, I enthused.

— You see, I've been paying attention.

— The talking dog, I remember that sketch! My God, I think it's starting to slowly sink in. I'm really gony be doing this, sure I am?

— You are indeed, the pilot anyway. Tomorrow, in front of all the big bosses, so I'm glad it's sinking in. Hopefully you'll have your wits about you.

— Jeezo, I fuckin hope so, Helen. Excuse me, I checked myself. — I like the bit about shirking challenges and bottling decisions. An appropriate metaphor considering we're gony be talking about referees.

— Yes, well, that's not a coincidence. These things don't just write themselves, you know.

— Right enough, I nodded. — No I really like it, Helen,

you've definitely managed to capture the feeling I had for the tone and content of the show.

— Thanks. I had a long chat with Gus about the programme yesterday, and from what I can gather, he seems quite keen on the idea. It's the others you have to worry about, Tom and Hamish and the rest. If we can just get it past the Gaelic mafia then we might be on to something.

— The Gaelic mafia? I've heard that expression before, who are you talking about?

— This place is run by Gaels, don't you know? All the top jobs, all the decision making positions are held by Gaels, Helen confided in me.

— Really, that's a bit of a worry, isn't it? What do Teuchters know about football? I suggested, plausibly enough.

— Listen, forget it. I'm teasing you, just concentrate on what you're doing and on impressing all those who are gony be watching.

— Will there be an audience?

— There will. I've sent out an email inviting people to come along, so there'll be a few dozen in attendance at least.

— Right. I paused to try and think if there was anything else I could or should be asking her. — Did you say that the co-presenters might be coming down to say hello?

— Co-presenters? Please. Call them what they are. You're the presenter, they're the pundits. Don't give them ideas above their station, Helen picked up her mobile phone. — Doddsy should be here by now, I'll see where he is.

— Just Doddsy, what about Davie Keane?

— Davie is still reviewing his options. He'll be in tomorrow, but he hasn't given us his commitment yet. He's still considering a coaching job that he's been offered.

— That's a shame, I remarked because I'd given my old

112

man the impression that I'd be meeting Keane today and possibly working with him in the future. Still, it would only be a twenty-four hour delay, and there's only so much you can absorb in one day, so meeting boyhood idols would have to wait for a later occasion.

— Doddsy ... where are you?... Yes ... we're waiting on you ... yes ... OK hurry up ... yes, now! Bye. Helen snapped her mobile phone closed. — He's on his way, she smiled.

— Right then.

— So, Peter, she reflected, — do you have any ideas for future episodes of the show? What would be the main themes you'd like to see discussed in the weeks ahead?

— I think referees is a good start, I replied. — It's an issue which will always be topical and is never going to go away, as we suggested. But also tactics and game strategy, how formations have evolved over the years and how they're applied in different countries. Money and funding, the affect that finances have had on the game? I suggested cautiously. — Foreign players? Sectarianism? I think we should have a serious look at that. Politics, religion, social issues, anything along these lines. Youth development? I think we should have a proper go at explaining the obvious decline in standards in the Scottish game in the last few years, I've never heard a convincing or adequate explanation for that. You cany just blame it all on kids playing computer games instead of going out and kicking a ball about and working on their basic skills. That doesn't really seem like a sufficient reason to me. We should devote at least one show to that, I think.

— I can see you're really passionate about this.

There was that word again, passion, I'd heard it a number of times now since I started discussing this idea with these media types. I didn't really consider it an appropriate term either in a football context or as here, in relation to strongly held views on a particular topic. Passion, I reckoned, was something that was best left to the bedroom. I also thought Helen was being slightly condescending towards me, but on the other hand I supposed she knew what she was doing and it was far more likely that I was taking it the wrong way, especially given my nervous introduction.

— I guess I have those sort of feelings about it, yes, and hopefully that will come across in the programme, I reflected in my best job interview type manner.

— Here's Doddsy now.

— Is this the boey? The boey wi the great idea?

— Doddsy, this is Peter. Peter, this is Martin Dodds. I recognised him immediately. He was plumper and more red-faced than I recalled from seeing him on the television in the pomp of his playing days. But he had a happy face and an infectious smile and he shook my hand warmly.

— I hear you're looking for an agent, Peter? He nudged me forcefully in the ribs.

— Could well be, aye, I acknowledged, shielding myself from his flailing elbow. — Depends if we get the gig or not.

— You can gie mine a call, he suggested, offering me a business card. — He'll see you right, I promise you. He's straight as an arrow and he's brand new to deal wi an aw. At least wi his clients, he is. But he's tough as old boots when it comes to negotiating wi employers on your behalf. I've done a bit ay agenting masel on the football side ay things, but I just scraped through the exams and I'm no in this boy's league.

— Brilliant, I'll give him a call. Cheers, Doddsy, I thanked my new mate.

— Aye, he's a tough yin awright, and you'll need a tough yin an aw when it comes to dealing wi the contract negotiators they have in this place, I'm no kiddin. I'm tellin you, Peter, you can say whit you like aboot agents but if it wasny for this boey, I'd be way oot ma depth wi these buggers, honestly to

114

ma God. Tell him what they're like, Helen, they're murder, sure they are. The contract negotiators in this place?

— Can we leave that for now, Martin, we only have a limited time, so if you don't mind, let's stick with matters relevant to the show for the time being, Helen suggested sensibly.

— Nae bother, down to business, that's how I like to play it. Here, take this, Peter. I took the agent's card from Doddsy's hand even though it seemed to me that he must be on a commission to find the guy new clients. But even if that was the case, I thought it might no do any harm to share an agent wi a potential colleague, especially if we were gony be working together on the show.

— So, Doddsy, you're a Rangers man, but a modern thinking Rangers man, is that the idea? I eventually asked him.

— That's the idea, Peter, aye. This is the twenty-first century, the brave new world, so we need to be moving into the modern era. That's what the club are saying anyway, and I'm acting wi their full approval, he chuckled. — Fortunately these SBC types seem happy to let me do ma thing here, and I'm only too pleased to oblige. Keeps me oot ay trouble anyroad, he informed me. We chatted away some more about the show for a while, Doddsy seemed like a nice guy and 'no as daft as he looked', as he liked to put it, and Helen was generally on top of things and seemed to know what was happening. Which was just as well because between me and Doddsy, we didny seem to have much ay a clue what was going on. After the informal chat was over I thanked them and wished them all the best and told them I'd see them tomorrow. The plan of action seemed to be – come in mid-morning, run through and practise a few things, have lunch, and then shoot the pilot in the afternoon.

It would be a long, drawn-out twenty-four hours before we met again, because not for the first time that week, I don't think I shut my eyes once that night.

7. THE PILOT

Helen was there to meet me as I entered the lavish, modern SBC building, recently constructed extravagantly and controversially at the taxpayer's expense. The old offices in the city centre that had served the company for decades were no longer considered fit for purpose in an era of devolution and end to end digitisation, and despite swinging cutbacks in other sectors, a new facility for the broadcaster had been considered a necessary and worthwhile disbursement. I was escorted over to reception and issued with a visitor's pass, so for the first time it seemed, we would be vacating the foyer and the surrounding area, and they were gony allow me past the security doors. I pinned the pass to my lapel, after showing it to the guard, and entered the building proper.

The office interior that immediately greeted me was striking and impressive. The building was constructed on three floors and from the spacious open area in the centre I could see recording studios, meeting rooms and other facilities rising up on both sides, flanked by moving staircases and elevators, all dotted with dozens of employees absorbed in their work and lost in their daily duties and routines. The layout was arresting and demanded immediate attention, but there was also an elusive ambience about the place which I found slightly unsettling – a weird, otherworldly impression which no amount of forced modernity or expensive, futuristic architecture could eradicate.

I was ushered up to a first floor meeting room and offered a selection of hot and cold drinks, before Helen told me to sit down and wait with Alison, the research girl. She then left me for a nervous ten minutes before returning with Doddsy and former Celtic captain, in the flesh, Davie Keane.

— Good to meet you, Peter, Keane greeted me, offering his outstretched hand.

— Good to meet you too Davie, I stood up and answered, trying no to sound too much like an anxious schoolboy. I'd met one or two sportsmen before and various, assorted television personalities at one time or another, and I was always struck by how small they appeared to be in real life. Davie Keane was a former rangy Celtic midfielder, but even his six foot stature seemed slightly ordinary and even disappointing up close. I took that as my cue to try and treat the guy normally and if possible avoid the usual boyhood idol, hero worship clichés on our first meeting. We were after all going to be working together, so I was keen no to embarrass either him or myself with any doe-eyed deference or puerile, sycophantic platitudes at this stage.

— How's it going, Peter? Doddsy patted me on the back and pulled up a seat, as I attempted to gather my thoughts. I was still trying to shake off the irking sensation that I was merely an imposter here, who had somehow managed to blag his way in the door, and that I'd be outed as a fraudster and a charlatan at almost any moment.

— No bad, Doddsy, thanks. How's yoursel?

— Aye, no so bad.

Helen, consummate professional that she was, got things started in a businesslike manner.

— OK, now that we're all here, I thought it would be a good idea to have a few practice runs with some of the material, especially seeing as this is going to be the first time that Peter has ever done any television work, she smiled in my direction.

— Nothing to it bud, Doddsy assured me.

— Here's a copy of the script we were working off yesterday, Peter. If you could just read it from the top, Helen instructed me.

— From the top? I repeated, taking the script and glancing over it.

— Yes. Hello and welcome …

— Just relax and you'll be fine, Peter, Keane advised me. — It's as easy as reading out loud.

— In your own time.

— How hard can it be? I wondered aloud. — Right then, I cleared my throat.

— H.....

And my voice failed me.

— Sorry, could I have a glass of water? I asked.

— You've already got one.

— So I do, I gulped down some water from the paper cup that I'd been offered earlier.

— When you're ready, Peter. From the top.

I cleared my throat once more and tried again.

— Hello and welcome to the first edition of our brand new programme, 'The Scottish Football Debate' which is a show that, well … it pretty much does what it says on the tin really, I read. — Each week we'll be debating the hot topics in Scottish football with an honesty, a boldness and indeed a level of intellectual rigour which you may not have heard before in many other outlets. We'll select a broad theme for every show, relevant to the burning footballing issues of the day, and we'll be discussing it until you're blue in the face hearing about it basically, and we certainly won't be shirking any challenges or bottling any important decisions, I'm sure many of you watching at home who are of a certain age will remember the old Rikki Fulton sketch about the talking dog who refused to discuss either politics or religion, well there'll be none of that on this show – there are no taboos, no no-go areas, we'll talk about anything you like provided of course that it's relevant to the matter in hand and we want to hear from you too, this is very much an audience participation show so feel free to get in touch, you can send us your emails to Scot underscore foot underscore deb at sbc dot com, I'll repeat that, Scot underscore foot underscore deb at sbc dot com or if you prefer you can text us your opinions on eight four three six eight and we'll try to read out a few of the more coherent ones anyway. Joining us in the studio every week will be former Rangers and Motherwell defender Martin Dodds and ex-Celtic captain Davie Keane, well Doddsy … did you enjoy your games at the weekend?

— I certainly did, Peter, for sure, there were some cracking games on the card this week …

— Sorry, could we hold it there just a wee minute? Helen immediately intervened.

— How was that? I asked.

— Erm, it was a bit rushed, you were going at a hundred miles an hour by the end. You need to pause in the right places, and maybe include one or two full stops in your delivery. Try to be a bit more relaxed, and slow down! Don't be in so much of a hurry.

— Rushed? Was it? It didn't seem to me to be too quick.

— It was, I assure you. You didn't read it like that yesterday. Now go again, from the top once more, in your own time.

— OK, I'll give it a shot, I took a deep breath and tried again. — Hello and welcome to the first edition of our brand new programme, 'The Scottish Football Debate' which is a show that, well … it pretty much does what it says on the tin really. Deep breath. — Each week, pause, — we'll be debating the hot topics in Scottish football with an honesty, a boldness and indeed a level of intellectual rigour which you may not have heard before in many other outlets, I enunciated. — We will select a broad theme for every show, relevant to the burning footballing issues of the day, and we'll be discussing it until you're blue in the face hearing about it basically. Another deep breath. — And we certainly won't be shirking any challenges or bottling any important decisions. I'm sure many of you watching at home who are of a certain age will remember the old Rikki Fulton sketch about the talking dog who refused to discuss either politics or religion? Exaggerated inflection. — Well. Pause. — There'll be none of that on this programme – there are no taboos, no no-go areas. We'll talk about anything you like, providing of course that it's relevant to the matter in hand. Further pause for reflection. — And we want to hear from you too. This is very much an audience participation show so feel free to get in touch. You can send us your emails to Scot underscore foot underscore deb at sbc dot com, huge wheezy deep breath. — I'll repeat that, Scot underscore foot underscore deb at sbc dot com. Or if you prefer, you can text us your opinions on EIGHT, FOUR, THREE, SIX, EIGHT, and we'll try to read out a few of the more coherent ones anyway. Breath. — Joining us in the studio every week will be former Rangers and Motherwell defender Martin Dodds and ex-Celtic captain Davie Keane. Doddsy, final deep breath, — did you enjoy your games at the weekend, mate?

— I certainly did, Peter, for sure, there were some cracking games on the card this week …

— OK, I think you've probably gone too far the other way there.

— Sounds like a cracking show anyway, Davie offered. — Brand new, right enough.

— A brand new show, eh? I like that. It's gony be brand new an aw! Doddsy agreed.

— And if you could avoid referring to anyone around the table as your 'mate' or 'buddy', that would be a big help. Use people's names, Doddsy wants to be known, he wants people to be aware of who he is and what he does, so tell them, Helen explained to me.

— That's right, Peter, you have to say my name, I'm no wearing a badge here. We need people to know who we are, it should be, Doddsy this, Doddsy that … as often as you like, honestly. You cany say it enough.

— OK.

— Let's move on to some of the links, Helen took charge again. — And remember, not too fast, not too slow. Nice and relaxed.

— Right.

— So obviously Campbell Thomson isn't here yet, but if you want to introduce the panellists, they'll say something in reply. Then introduce Thomson and Alison here will say a few things on his behalf. Once you've done that I'll inform you that the highlights package is ready, which will come through your earpiece on the set, and you'll introduce the link. OK, so, joining us in the studio each week …, she cued me in.

— Joining us in the studio each week will be former Rangers and Motherwell defender Martin Dodds and ex-Celtic captain Davie Keane. Doddsy, did you enjoy your games at the weekend?

— I certainly did, Peter, for sure, there were some cracking games on the card this week.

— Conditions weren't great for playing football, particularly across the West, were they Davie, but there were some high-scoring encounters nonetheless?

— There were. Conditions weren't great, as you say, Peter, but there were some terrific goals scored around the country, as I'm sure we'll see.

— I'm sure we will, but first I'd like to introduce this week's special guest, former grade one referee, Campbell Thomson. Campbell, we saw one or two contentious decisions again this weekend that I'm sure we'll be wanting to talk about in due course. Any early thoughts?

— There's always contentious decisions in football, Peter,

Alison reflected.

— Ready to go to highlights, Helen announced softly.

— You cany keep giein the refs a hard time aboot it! Alison mocked Thomson's voice and intonation.

— Oh yes we can, Campbell, just you wait and see! But first of all, let's have a look at the highlights of all the action from the weekend …

— OK, very good, Helen sounded more conciliatory this time.

— She's putting me off, I accused Alison, to the general humour.

— Just you wait and see what his voice really sounds like, that'll put you off awright.

— Do you want to run through anything else, Peter, before we go to lunch, or are you feeling confident enough now?

— No sure about confident, but I'm sure it'll come. I'm still trying to find my rhythm and get into the swing ay things. Could you just explain what happens with the other link?

— OK, Alison will read out some emails …

— Some genuine emails, Alison pointed out.

— Yes, real emails that we received the previous time we had a discussion about referees on the radio last season, Helen explained.

— How will I know when Alison's about to read them out?

— I'll cue you in and you just take us over to her.

— Right enough.

— And when the emails are done, we'll move on to Dougie Laird's report. Again, a genuine report taken from the crisis last season.

— Sounds easy enough.

— It's a doddle once you get the hang of it, Helen assured me again. — For a bright guy like you, I'm sure you'll sail through it. The trick is to link the show together, to react to what these guys and Campbell will say, pick them up on any points they're making and keep the debate lively and interesting and moving at the right pace.

— I'll do my best.

— We'll go easy on you, Doddsy promised me, — sure we will, Davie?

— Of course, but he's a smart boy, so he'll be fine. And if you want to have a go at us at any time, Peter, feel free. We can handle it, so don't hold back. Just say what's on your mind, if you think we're talking shite, tell us. Chances are, you'll be dead right and that might score you a few brownie points wi the heid honchos upstairs as well.

By the heid honchos I reckoned that Davie must have been referring to the Gaelic mafia that Helen was talking about yesterday, who apparently run the show here. I needed to be careful though because Helen had confided in me and swore me to silence, and besides I was only just in the door and still trying to make a good impression with these people, so I decided it was probably too early for me to be engaging in any office politics at this stage, even in jest. — I've only just met you, Davie, I cany really see me having a go at you, I contented myself with a banal observation instead.

— Well you should, he told me again. — Go on, Peter, honestly, don't be holding back. You'll certainly no be the first to have a go, that's for sure.

— I'll play it by ear and see how we go, Davie, eh? I suggested.

— No bother at all.

— OK then, let's do lunch, Helen announced and we all

rose.

During the break we chatted about a few more details concerning the format, tone and content of the show. We also had a brief discussion about future topics for our weekly debate, and it was decided over our paninis and baked potatoes, in what I took to be our first editorial meeting, that a neutral subject such as the fluctuating fortunes of the national team would make for a suitable first episode.

I asked the lads how they felt about working in the media and whether they could give me any general advice.

— Get an agent! Was Doddsy's first offering. — And a psychiatrist! he followed up.

— How did you find yourself roped into this lark, Davie? Do you enjoy it, aye?

— I do enjoy it, Peter, most aspects anyway. And now you come to mention it, Gus McGregor sold me on the idea for your show, so I hope you're no gony let me down here. I have to be honest though, coaching is my first choice. If a suitable coaching job comes up, then there's a clause in the contract we've drafted that allows me to take it. But in the meantime I promise you, I'm committed to giein this ma undivided attention. Let's just hope we can leave Gus and the rest ay them suitably impressed this afternoon.

— Just be yoursel, that'd be my best advice, Doddsy postulated. — Keep your feet on the grun and take your job seriously. Don't think about being on the telly, or how it's gony affect your lifestyle, or whether you're gony be pulling ony mair ay the wee burds on the back ay having your fizzog on the box on a weekly basis. Let that shite affect your thinkin, and you'll no be hawf as good at your job as you could be. Think you can manage that?

— Well I'm married, Doddsy, so I don't see that as being

a problem.

— Aye, but you're no used to the attention. I've seen hunners ay marriages go doon the tubes within weeks ay some cunt getting their ugly mug on the telly. Is she a looker, your missus?

— Well, I think so.

— Right, well that'll staun you in good stead. If she was an ugly burd then I wouldny be haudin oot much hope for yous, wi aw the competition she's gony be faced wi.

— Don't listen to him, Peter, he's teasing you, Helen assured me.

— I know fine well he is. I'm no doing this for the attention, female or otherwise, I promised them. — Who do you think I am, Frank McAvennie? At this point my assurances seemed to raise a smile in the corner of Davie's mouth.

— Where za burds? he and I both announced in unison and everybody laughed.

— Come on, Peter, I'll take you down to your dressing-room, Helen informed me after lunch, which was another in a long line of sentences I'd heard recently, that I never thought would be aimed in my direction.

I'd been allocated my own room, at least for this afternoon and two women fussed over me as I sat back in the big swivel chair; one applying my make-up, which was needed to dull my face in the bright lights and take the shine off my skin, the other offering me a range of sweaters and shirts to choose from. I was only going to be visible from the waist up on the set so they wereny bothered about my Levis or my trainers. In the end I selected a navy blue shirt which seemed to meet wi the general approval, and it suited my physique as well, they were keen to assure me.

I made my way down to the green room, where I sat and waited for things to get underway alongside Doddsy and

Davie. The Floor Manager, Kirsty, came in and told us to wait until we were called onto the set. Doddsy accosted her about the lack of booze in the room, which was customarily available to guests and regulars alike.

— This is just a pilot! he was reminded emphatically.

— It's a full rehearsal, but, Doddsy whined. — We should be keeping it as authentic as possible!

— That's the only way they can persuade a Rangers man to enter the green room, Peter, if they put booze in there, Davie informed me, and Doddsy was forced to agree.

Helen arrived along with Campbell Thomson, a renowned teetotaller, which seemed to put paid to Doddsy's protests. Helen introduced him to the three of us, and we tried to make pleasant, civilised conversation, although I was suddenly feeling quite tense again and I seemed to have become pretty quiet by this stage. Davie assured the former referee that he'd be giving it to him wi both barrels, regardless of the fact that this episode wasny being broadcast. Thomson muttered words to the effect that he wouldny have expected anything less.

— Davie, Martin, Peter, on set please, Kirsty came in and announced and I strolled out of the green room with my colleagues down to the studio and onto the set. It was a small location with four seats placed around a semi-circular table on a raised metallic platform, and an audience arranged on curved wooden seats that rose up in tiers and gave the whole set the appearance of a miniature Greek amphitheatre. We were surrounded by an array of cameras and, from up in the gods, angled lights illuminated the entire floor. There's no fuckin hiding place now, I couldny help considering as I squeezed into my seat.

I was fitted with an earpiece and I gave Helen the thumbs up when she asked if I could hear her. Kirsty announced to the audience that they would be running through a few rehearsals to camera on the set before the show got properly underway, because we have a new presenter, she explained, referencing me obliquely in a manner that only caused me to shift nervously in my seat once again.

— Could I have a drink of water? I asked, and a runner immediately did what she was paid to do and ran off to find me a drink.

Campbell was welcomed onto the set. He was applauded and fitted with an earpiece.

— A warm welcome also to Davie Keane ... applause ... Martin Dodds ... applause ... and our new presenter, hoping to impress this afternoon, Peter Fitzpatrick ... applause. The clapping gave me a slightly warm, fuzzy feeling - a gentle waterfall of relaxation sent to loosen the knot in my stomach, which only began to tighten again when I saw Gus McGregor and David Henderson sitting in the front row, alongside Hamish Cameron the Head of Sport, and the Head of Television as well, whose name I couldn't remember. For all I knew the Station Controller could be there as well because I didny yet know who most ay these people were. I had a sudden urge just to get up and walk out and go home to my wife, or my mother, or to head straight for the pub, but for whatever reason I did none of those things. I just sat tight like a nervous wee lamb, taking another sip from the cup of water that I'd been brought as we ran through my opening remarks, with me delivering them to camera a few times. There then followed an inordinately long, very quiet period where nothing much seemed to be happening, until Helen's voice came over the earpiece and asked if I was ready.

— Yes, I replied.

— Counting down from ten, Floor Manager Kirsty announced and I realised that I had been having a conversation with myself because nobody else on the panel or in the audience could hear what Helen was saying to me.

— Five, four, Kirsty articulated before completing the

countdown digitally with her fingers, as silence descended on the set. — Cue music, she announced.

I took this to mean that the opening, title sequences were running, so I cleared my throat for the final time, and when the music died away, I began:

PETER: *Hello and welcome to the first edition of our brand new programme, 'The Scottish Football Debate' which is a show that, well ... it pretty much does what it says on the tin really. Each week we'll be debating the hot topics in Scottish football with an honesty, a boldness and indeed a level of intellectual rigour which you may not have heard before in many other outlets. We'll select a broad theme for every show, relevant to the burning footballing issues of the day, and we'll be discussing it until you're blue in the face hearing about it basically. And we certainly won't be shirking any challenges or bottling any important decisions. I'm sure many of you watching at home who are of a certain age will remember the old Rikki Fulton sketch about the talking dog who refused to discuss either politics or religion. Well, there'll be none of that on this show – there are no taboos, no no-go areas. We'll talk about anything you like, providing of course that it's relevant to the matter in hand. And we want to hear from you too. This is very much an audience participation show so feel free to get in touch. You can send us your emails to Scot underscore foot underscore deb at sbc dot com, I'll repeat that, Scot underscore foot underscore deb at sbc dot com. Or if you prefer, you can text us your opinions on eight four three six eight and we'll try to read out a few of the more coherent ones anyway. Joining us in the studio every week will be former Rangers and Motherwell defender Martin Dodds and ex-Celtic captain Davie Keane.*

APPLAUSE

Doddsy, can I start with you? Did you enjoy your games at

the weekend?

DODDSY: *I certainly did, Peter, for sure, there were some terrific games on the card this week.*

PETER: *Conditions weren't great for playing football, particularly across the West, were they, Davie, but there were some high-scoring encounters nonetheless?*

DAVIE: *There were. Conditions wereny great, as you say, Peter, but there were some cracking goals scored around the country, as I'm sure we'll see.*

PETER: *Well, we will in a second, Davie, all in good time, just hold your horses there a wee minute because first I'd like to introduce this week's special guest, former grade one referee, Campbell Thomson.*

APPLAUSE

Campbell, there were some contentious decisions again this weekend that I'm sure we'll be wanting to talk about in due course. Any early thoughts?

THOMSON: *There were indeed, Peter. I'd like to examine on some of them with you, if you don't mind.*

— Highlights are ready to go, Helen sounded like a voice in my head as she spoke softly to me through the earpiece.

PETER: *We'll do that in just a second, Campbell. First of all we're going to have a look at all the action from the weekend. Run VT.*

— Run VT? Another voice, this time one I didn't recognise, protested in my ear. — You're out of date, Peter, this channel is now end to end digital.

— I know but I want to make that my catchphrase, I answered with a smile, once again experiencing the strange sensation of sitting in a crowd of people and, through the miracle of technology, talking to someone who wasn't even there. Although I supposed that the other people around the table and the media insiders in the audience must have been used to it, so I put it down to experience. — How are we doing, is everybody OK? I asked, in a hopeful attempt to sound as if I was maybe starting to feel in charge of the situation at last.

— Great stuff, Peter, yeah, really nice start.

— Can we pull back camera two slightly, I want to be able to get Davie and Doddsy in the same shot, so we can see one while the other's speaking.

— Can you no cut me off like that, Thomson moaned at me.

— Sorry, Campbell?

— If you ask me a question, I expect you to wait for an answer. You said any initial thoughts, and you then cut me off before I had the chance to reply. And keep it specific, I cany answer general questions, if you want to ask me about a particular incident, fine, but I cany talk in general terms.

— Well it was just a brief introduction, Campbell, I wasn't expecting you to say anything too profound straight off the bat like that. It was just to present you formally to the audience, both here and at home watching this on television. Thomson was already getting huffy with me, but despite the fact that this was only a pilot, and it seemed to have started well, I was aware how many high powered individuals were watching and judging me on my performance. So I made a conscious decision to try and sound conciliatory and to give Thomson the benefit ay the doubt, because I was still learning all about how this works. — I'll bear that in mind, Campbell, but go easy on me would you? You know, this is my first experience of anything like this, I reminded him.

— I know you're new here, that's how I'm cutting you some slack. Keep it specific though, always specific. Referees cany think in general terms.

— I'll do my best. Christ, what a huffy cunt this is, I

considered. The Floor Manager was right though, it did seem to me like a decent start and I was pleased to have come through it apparently without fluffing my lines.

— How we doing, Davie, everything OK? I asked. — It didny sound too patronising, did it, me telling you to hold your horses like that? Both Davie and Doddsy had been smiling at the hard time that Thomson was giving me, and I was hoping for a bit of moral support from them.

— Of course not, no. You're doing great, Peter.

— You're a patronising cunt anyway so it was nothin unexpected, Doddsy winked at me.

— Some goal that, was it no? Davie remarked, referring to a stunning strike from a Motherwell forward against Inverness that he was watching on the monitor. — You played wi that boy, Doddsy, did you no?

— I did Davie, aye. He should be playing at a higher level. He was just breaking through at Motherwell when I retired, I thought he'd have a really bright future in the game. I cany believe he's ended up back where he started. A case ay too much too young, it seems to me. Honestly, the number ay talented youngsters round about that age group in Scotland that have fallen by the wayside, you just would no begin to believe.

— You're right, Doddsy, but Motherwell's a decent level though, is it no? I offered cautiously. — It might no be AC Milan but what's wrong wi playing there, it's an SPL club after all, do we no want to believe in our clubs? I wondered aloud, although my intervention was greeted with a stony silence.

— A topic for another day, someone suggested in my ear.

— What sort ay fuckin decision is that, Davie was still glued to the monitor that was feeding through the highlights from the weekend. — I'm glad you're here, Campbell, I hope you're no gony let your mate away wi that. Call it as you see it now, don't forget, call it as you see it.

— Don't worry, I will.

— Clear the set, please. Ready guys, we're back in five, four …

— Keep it going, Peter, you're doing great, Davie Keane encouraged me. I was still finding it hard to believe that I was sat there right next to the guy, but that was just another weird factor in what was turning out to be probably the most surreal day of my life so far.

— … two, one …, Kirsty mouthed.

PETER: *Right then, Campbell, only one place to start, seeing as you're here!*

THOMSON: *I thought you might.*

PETER: *Well, seeing as you're here. Let's take another look at that penalty decision at Ibrox, shall we? Correct call or no?*

THOMSON: *No. It's not a penalty. I think the referee will admit that himself when he sees it again. I can't honestly defend him on this occasion. The only thing I would maybe say in mitigation is that he may well have been unsighted when the challenge came in, but as you can clearly see Armstrong won the ball cleanly and the Rangers player has obviously thrown himself to the floor, because there's very little, if any, physical contact.*

DAVIE: *Can I just ask you though, Campbell? You said he may have been unsighted. That may be an excuse for not seeing a foul, for not giving a penalty when perhaps there was a case for one. But in this instance the referee seems to have seen something that never actually occurred. How can you explain that?*

THOMSON: *I can't. As I've already mentioned, I'm not going to defend the referee on this one, I'm merely suggesting a plausible explanation for his error.*

PETER: *It was a costly mistake as well from Aberdeen's point of view, was it not? In the ninety-first minute, there's no time to come back from that.*

THOMSON: *It was a costly mistake, but that's football. Human error is part of the game and you just have to accept it and get on with it. It's no use talking about conspiracies or refereeing prejudices if that's what you're alluding to, because they don't exist, I assure you.*

PETER: *Conspiracies eh? Well seeing as you raise the subject, Campbell, let's talk about them, can we? Refereeing conspiracies, lads? Discuss!*

DODDSY: *I don't believe in them. I have to agree wi Campbell there. Of course referees are gony make mistakes, but they're honest mistakes. You cany go around calling their integrity into question every time there's a decision you don't agree wi. What about the incident early in the second half that wasny given in Rangers' favour?*

DAVIE: *Here's what I'd say to that. I understand what you're saying about referees making honest mistakes. But I also think it's quite a complacent attitude we're in danger of developing. What about boyhood allegiances or family loyalties? This is a football daft country after all. Are you honestly telling us, Campbell that there's no referees who were maybe interested in football as kids, and maybe feel pressurised into making certain decisions in favour of certain teams?*

THOMSON: *Honestly Davie, believe me. Referees just don't care who wins football matches. They're far more concerned about getting decisions right and being good referees. Yes of course some may have had preferences for one particular team in the days of their youth, but they're told to get over that. If they can't, then they won't make it very far as a referee.*

DAVIE: *I appreciate that, but I just think more can be done to reassure people. That referee on Saturday has well known*

Rangers affiliations, which have been outed in the press, and there he goes giving a ridiculous decision in that team's favour which wins them the match. Don't you think more can be done? As I say, I think it's a rather complacent attitude we're in danger of developing here. I'm sure we all remember the case of the referee who was photographed out jogging in his Rangers top, and then there was his mate who requested Ibrox as the venue for his last appointment before he retired. Can we do more to reassure folk, Campbell, ordinary punters I'm talking about, no just paranoiacs like myself? Because it's hardly appropriate for a referee – someone who has to be a judge – to be conducting himself in that kind ay manner, you must admit.

THOMSON: *That was in the past, Davie, I assure you. None of those things would be allowed to happen now.*

DAVIE: *It was the recent past.*

THOMSON: *Well ...*

PETER: *Are you saying refereeing standards have changed, Campbell, are they evolving? Are they improving?*

THOMSON: *I think they have changed, yes. And yes, things are evolving and improving all the time. I think the main difference now is that in the past the referee was in total charge of the game. Their instructions were to control the game. How they controlled it was up to them, but controlling the game was the primary objective. Now with the advent of increased television coverage, the most important aspect of a referee's task is consistency. Because various different decisions, even in different matches, can be contrasted and compared instantaneously. This means that the referee has no leeway, there's less scope for interpretation or individuality, they're becoming more and more like rules lawyers, because consistency is now the most important thing.*

DAVIE: *Surely the most important thing is getting decisions right, something Mr. Urquhart there conspicuously failed to* do with that penalty decision.

THOMSON: *We're back where we started, aren't we? I can't defend the decision, but it was an honest mistake.*

— Emails.

PETER: *OK. Let's cross over to, Alison. What have the viewers been saying Alison on the texts and on the emails?*

ALISON: *Thank you, Peter, first up this one's from Stephen in Cambuslang. He says refereeing is such a hard job, I can't understand why anyone would want to be one. It's unfair the amount of scrutiny they're under these days. Terry in Gourock says referees cause more misery and heartache than redundancies and marriage break-ups. I'd make a big bonfire and burn the ruddy lot of them. Thanks for that, Terry. Here's one specifically for you, Campbell, Kevin in Dundee asks: a referee and a lawyer, how unpopular does one man want to be? I guess that's a question only you can answer, Campbell.*

DODDSY: *I was wondering the same thing masel.*

PETER: *That's rich coming fae you, Doddsy - a media pundit, football agent, ex-Rangers player!*

LAUGHTER

— Brilliant, well done for managing to work that line in. Report ready.

OK, thanks, Alison, keep those texts and emails coming in. Well, earlier in the week we sent our intrepid reporter, Dougie Laird, over to the referees' college in Largs to find out how young, aspiring refs are put through their paces. Take it away, Dougie.

— Sorry about that, Doddsy, I couldny resist, I apologised after my on-air outburst, as soon as the VT was rolling, metaphorically or otherwise. I couldny believe that Doddsy fell for that line, especially after the way me and Helen had set it up for him yesterday.

— You're doing well, mate, don't let it go to your heid, Doddsy admonished me sourly. Alison and Davie were cracking up, but it wasny just on the set, there was more laughter from the gallery as well, which offered me reassurance, and made me feel, maybe for the first time, a wee bit more comfortable in my surroundings.

— That's him told, a voice echoed in the ether.

— I left Radio Kelvin over less than this, Doddsy finally sounded as though he was maybe starting to see the funny side as well.

— Don't give us that, Doddsy, what was it you told us? You wouldny go back to that crowd, no matter what they offered you, Floor Manager Kirsty reminded him.

— Aye, well I'm beginning to reconsider my options.

— Too late, we've got you under contract.

— And a nice wee contract it is as well, he emphasised gleefully.

— Some good points he's making there, Campbell, Davie was conscientiously listening to Laird's recorded piece as it came through. — Making the correct call, that's what it's all about at the end ay the day. Doesny matter what team it is, how big the crowd is, what the situation in the game is, as long as they get the decisions right, especially the big decisions, then nobody will complain. The opposite will be the case in fact, good refs will earn the recognition they deserve.

— That's the ideal situation, Thomson agreed.

— Your cue is 'something we surely all want to see,' Peter. Back in five, four ...

LAIRD: ... *for the good of Scottish football, which given the present state of our game, is something we surely all want to see.*

PETER: *OK, welcome back, some interesting points raised*

there, Campbell. Dougie mentioned goal-line technology in his piece, is that something you'd be in favour of? Is it something referees would welcome, broadly speaking?

THOMSON: *Broadly speaking, I think they would, if it could be made to work. I'd welcome anything that assists the officials in making the correct decisions.*

PETER: *Doddsy?*

DODDSY: *I'm all for it, yes. Bring it on, the game needs it and not before time. Other sports have it and football could use it as well. It would stop all this talk of contentious decisions. We seen the penalty incident that we've just been talking about - a fourth official could take a look at that on a monitor and relay that information back to the ref in seconds. It wouldny disturb the flow of the game at all.*

PETER: *I guess it begs the question though, Davie, who's in charge of the game.*

DAVIE: *Of course it does. I'm all for the use of technology as well in these instant, matter of fact type decisions, such as, is the ball over the line or not. If you can put a chip in the ball, a light goes on somewhere or a buzzer goes off, the referee is administered wi an electric shock, whatever. As long as it's an instant decision. You can't have it for penalties or other more subjective decisions though. That Aberdeen one might have been clear-cut, but for every obvious decision like that, there's a hundred others that are far more contentious. Then what are you gony do? It's a can ay worms, I'm telling you. The referee thinks it's a penalty, but the fourth official says no. The referee looks at it on a monitor but they still cany decide after they've examined it from a hundred angles. I don't know how many times I've sat in studios and argued wi clever guys, the likes ay Doddsy and Campbell, and we still cany agree over a particular call. So in the end do you go with the ref's decision on the field? Fine, but it was his decision anyway and you've just interrupted the game. What if the ref turns down an appeal and waves play on, when do you stop the game to look at the footage? By the time there's a natural break in play somebody might have scored a goal up the other end, or been red-carded, or broken a leg, then what you gony do? I'm tellin you, it's a can ay worms. We're looking for technology to make decisions less contentious, not more contentious. Nobody has yet explained to me how it's gony work, when you're gony stop the game et cetera. All I hear is people with a vested interest saying that the game needs it, but I remain to be convinced.*

PETER: *People with a vested interest, you mean the television companies?*

DAVIE: *Of course, Peter. They're the ones who are gony be providing the replay pictures and they want to get their claws into the game even more than they already have, so they'll tell you the game needs it until the cows come home. What they really mean is, they want it for their own reasons, which don't necessarily coincide wi what's best for the game.*

PETER: *OK, well that's an interesting point and a good note to end on. Our half hour is almost up. Campbell if I can just finish with you, we're going to ask our guest every week, if they could change Scottish football for the better in one way, what way would that be? What one thing would you change in our national game?*

THOMSON: *I think it would have to be an automatic yellow card for backchat with the referee. I know there are laws and existing sanctions governing dissent already, but I would like to see it made more straightforward. If you speak back to the referee or question his decision, then it's an automatic yellow card. That would soon put an end to the problem of dissent and disrespect to referees.*

PETER: *Is that it? With the state our game's in? You've had a wee while to think about this, Campbell, we did give you prior notice. Nothing about teaching kids how to control the ball better?*

THOMSON: *Well, I'd do that too, but you did say one thing.*

PETER: *I did, right enough, OK. Alison, what are the viewers saying?*

ALISON: *John in Falkirk says, Great show guys, very refreshing and honest, good to see a football show that tackles the big issues head on.*

PETER: *You just made that one up!*

ALISON: *I did indeed, here's another I've just made up. Brian from, wait a minute, Brian doesn't tell us where he's from. Drumnadrochit, that's it. Brian from Drumnadrochit says, Totally agree with Davie about goal-line technology, it's not needed.*

DAVIE: *That's not what I said. I said goal-line technology was fine for matter of fact decisions, if it could be made to work instantly. It becomes problematic if you start looking at fouls or off-sides again on a monitor.*

ALISON: *OK, final one for Doddsy, Alison in Glasgow says, Don't worry, Doddsy, if you're worried you're not unpopular enough already, after the recent departure of Graham George, there's a vacancy for chief executive of the SFA which you could apply for.*

LAUGHTER

DODDSY: *The CV's in the post, don't worry.*

LAUGHTER

PETER: *OK with that, I believe, we have to wrap it up. My thanks go to Doddsy and to Davie and to my special guest Campbell Thomson, and to you at home for watching. I hope you can join us next week, when we're going to be talking about the fluctuating fortunes of our national team. We'll be considering what we can do to produce more quality players in this country and looking at what the future holds for the*

Scotland team. Until then, have a good week and enjoy your football. Good night.

— Roll credits.

SUSTAINED APPLAUSE AND CHEERING

Helen appeared on the set, all smiles, but out of the corner of my eye I could see Gus McGregor also approaching us, flanked by his boss, the Head of Television, whose name I still couldny remember.

— Peter, Helen, could we have a word? he said.

8. COMPLIANCE

— Peter, Helen, could we have a word? The important man whose name I couldn't remember asked. — If you could just wait here for five minutes or so until the audience has cleared. Helen had emerged from the gallery, just off the set, and joined us at the debating table, replacing Thomson who was thanked and excused from the ensuing post-production de-brief.

— What's he gony want to talk about? I whispered to Helen as the studio emptied.

— Not sure at this stage, he'll probably just want to discuss how you think it went, were you happy with the format, that kind of thing.

— How do you think it went then? I returned the question, inviting Davie and Doddsy to offer me their opinions as well.

— You did well, are you sure you haveny done this kind ay thing before? Keane wondered.

— Never, Davie honestly, I've maybe just been watching too much TV.

— You seem like a natural anyway, Peter. Great wee show we could have on our hands, all being well.

— Cheers, Doddsy, I managed to get through it without any major screw-ups anyway, I acknowledged.

— I agree with the boys, it went well, Helen smiled. — Let's hope Malcolm sees it the same way.

— What's his name? Malcolm who? What's his position?

— Malcolm Munroe, he's the Head of Television. And that was Alasdair Ballantyne alongside him, the Head of Editorial Policy. Impress these guys and the show's ours.

— Can I call him Marilyn?

— Probably not the best idea, although you've managed to

pick up on his nickname pretty quickly. That's generally how he's referred to, in certain quarters anyway.

— Have they all got nicknames, the bosses?

— Most of them yes, but I wouldn't start using them just yet, you're still hoping to impress them, remember.

— Right enough. I just need to get it by the Gaelic mafia, then it's in the bag, I joked, causing Doddsy to baulk at my use of insider, SBC vernacular.

— You better no let anybody catch you coming away wi that pal, no if you're wanting them to gie you a job, he warned me, although Davie seemed to see more of the funny side.

— Gie the boy a break, Doddsy. I'll take the Gaelic mafia over the Hun mafia anytime, he mocked his colleague, although I surmised from his tone and his wry smile that he wasn't being entirely facetious.

— What are yous like, the pair ay you? Doddsy lamented.

— What about the cheese factor? I inquired. — I'm glad there was nobody I knew in the audience, because I found that spouting some ay the shite that I was coming away wi was a lot easier than it otherwise might have been, if there had been friends or family watching. Everything I said seemed to be slightly off kilter, a wee bit contrived, if you know what I mean. I was cringing at times at my own choice ay language, because I don't normally talk like that.

— I know where you're coming from, Helen told me. — There's a slightly unreal, rarefied quality about the way we speak to one another in the media, which you're just gony have to get used to, she pointed out. — At least you're aware of the cheese, that's a good sign anyway. The fact that you noticed and are maybe slightly uncomfortable with it puts you streets ahead of most television presenters, who are mostly unselfaware egomaniacs and attention seekers in my experience. Most of them are only involved in this business for their own vainglorious reasons, but you come across well, she informed me. — You seem interested in the subject matter and appear professional in your whole approach, there's no hint of the kind of smug or unctuous narcissism more usually associated with this kind of role. As long as you can cope with the unreality of it all and not be bothered by it, then things like the cheese factor you refer to shouldn't affect you. Like I say, you'll just need to accustom yourself to it, then you'll be fine.

— Spoken like a true radio aficionado, I responded to her compliment somewhat awkwardly.

We chatted away about one or two more technical issues for a while as the last of the audience members and the crew slowly filtered out. A group of Helen's friends and colleagues came over to offer their opinion and she was still saying goodbye to a few of them when Munroe returned. Heid honcho Alasdair had departed the scene, but David Henderson was still in attendance.

— Could we see you in the restaurant upstairs? Munroe inquired. — Do you two have to be anywhere? You don't have to join us if you don't want to, he informed the two pundits.

— I don't mind hanging about if you think my opinions are worth listening to, Malcolm, Davie told him.

— Erm I'm sorry, I have a previous engagement, if you don't mind, Doddsy excused himself. — Good luck, Peter, and gie that agent a ring afore they make you sign anyhin, he advised me, patting me on the back as he left.

— Shall we? Munroe ushered us up to the restaurant, which under no circumstances was to be referred to as the canteen, despite that being exactly what everyone who was on less than a hundred grand a year in this organisation called it. He bought us all a hot drink and sat us down at a long, wooden, school dining-hall style table. — So how do we think it went then? he eventually asked. — Peter? You're the main man here, what are your thoughts? He looked at me initially for my observations.

— Erm, yeah, considering it was my first bash at it, I thought it went OK, I suggested tentatively.

— Definite potential there, Keane offered on my behalf.

— I'm surprised to see you still here, Davie, we've yet to receive your full commitment for the project.

— And we've yet to receive yours, Malcolm, Helen correctly pointed out. — Are you in a position to give us your answer now?

— I'm afraid not, it won't be this evening, no. But, Peter if you can stay a while longer, so we can have a brief tête-a-tête, that might help us in the decision making process.

— I can commit to this, Malcolm. If you go ahead and take this show on wi this young man fronting it up, then you'll get a big thumbs up from me. I've been waiting to see a football show like this for years. You have everything in place here to make it happen, so I hope yous areny gony take fright at the sound of a few straight, honest opinions and drop the ball at this late stage ay the game. Let's sort things out, as soon as we can, and get this show on the telly.

Sitting next to Davie Keane, and hearing these words of praise and encouragement coming from his lips, directed towards my efforts and my work in this way, was a real hairs on the back ay the neck moment for me. It's not hard to see why this guy was such an inspirational leader and captain, right now he was making me feel as though I'd just scored the winning goal in the Cup Final.

— Well thanks for that, Davie, we've one or two things that we still need to sort out here, but we appreciate your feedback.

— See you soon, Peter, all the best, Davie got up to leave. Instinctively, I stood up to shake his hand before sitting back down again, feeling slightly self-conscious. I had to tell masel to keep the feet on the ground and no get too overexcited, because this was a potentially important next half an hour or one point I considered contacting an independent production company, but I quickly dismissed the notion. The SBC must own this project, Malcolm, it can't be a co-production. Just think what would happen if the guy with the tape was held up in traffic. The show might no go out for another week.

— It doesn't quite work like that now, our new facility here employs end to end digital technology. There are no tapes. A co-production or an independent production would be perfectly feasible even for an as-live recording like this.

— I apologise, I'm being slightly glib of course. Forgive me. But I want the SBC to own the project completely and to take responsibility for everything that we say and do. I think this is the kind of show that you should want in your portfolio, an intelligent discussion programme about all matters pertaining to our national game. You will be able to throw down the gauntlet to your rivals with a bold new departure in what is already an incredibly over-crowded and familiar genre. Because we'll be talking sense about sport for a pleasant change, while the rest are still peddling the same old clichés.

— I see. What are your political views?

— Sorry?

— Helen would you excuse us for a few minutes?

— Of course.

Helen departed the scene without further comment. I was left alone with Munroe and Henderson, which on the one hand was concerning, particularly in light of the tone and direction of the last question, but on the other hand I was starting to relish getting down to brass tacks with Munroe in particular. I sensed that he was a different type of interrogator to what I'd been exposed to up until now, there was a bluntness and a directness to his style, which lent him a more aristocratic air in comparison to McGregor's touchy-feely, middle-class

so I had ahead ay me, and I needed to get ma heid on st
here.

— My dad's a big fan ay his, I remarked, after Davi
left.

— Well, we'd certainly like to have him on board.

— Me too.

— So, Peter, our first impression is to agree with y
Munroe had clearly decided it was time to get down to the n
gritty. — I thought the pilot episode went well and you sho\
yourself to be a capable host for this type of programme. I
had a chat with David here, who you know, as well as Alasda
Gus and one or two other colleagues, and I must say that we
all very impressed with your passion and enthusiasm for t
project. One question leaps to mind though … why us? WI
did you bring your idea to the SBC?

There it was again, that word passion. I felt like tellin
him, you're right, Malcolm I'm so passionate about the idea
I want to go home and make love to it right now, I like the
idea so much. Not only did they all seem to use the same
language, these media manager types, but they also seemed to
ask uncannily similar questions. It was only a couple of weeks
ago that Gus McGregor was putting the exact same query to
me over a few Staropramens when I pitched him the idea
Fortunately though I had been lying awake in my bed virtuall
every night since that initial meeting, replaying the intervie\
over and over again in my head and rehearsing my answers.
almost felt like I was giving a well scripted speech rather tha
a spontaneous reply as I responded to Munroe's question.

— You're the national broadcaster, I explained. — I wa
this to be a serious discussion programme for serious peop
I don't really want it being interrupted by adverts for lo
sharks, injury lawyers or price comparison websites. I thou
I would try to aim high all the way with this idea and th
what I feel I've done by bringing it exclusively to you.

approach.

— Your political views? he repeated. — You don't have to go into too much detail, just give me a brief summary.

— Aren't you supposed to suss that out for yourself, Malcolm? Isn't that the purpose of this discussion, so that you can you can figure out where I'm coming from, what my agenda is, how my mind works and so on … , what makes me tick?

— It is yes, but you're a bright young man. You've clearly figured that out already, so I thought you might appreciate it if I cut to the chase. I'm asking you a direct question, what are your politics?

— I'm not really terribly interested in politics to be honest, I shrugged. — You know there's an argument that politics isn't working, and that you shouldn't vote for politicians because it only encourages them. My uncle was a big union man in his time and I would say that my political opinions, such as they are, probably come from the same place, but I don't think my generation is anywhere near as politicised as his, and I'm probably the living embodiment of that.

— What did your uncle do?

— He worked in the yards.

— I see, but what was his trade?

— He was an electrician. He helped to build the ships they sent to the Falklands.

— And how did he feel about that?

— It was his job. Employment in those days was mostly contractual and the work was temporary and intermittent. He had little choice but to accept a job wherever he could find one, but he was pretty ambivalent about the whole war with Argentina. That's why he started to involve himself in things politically, so he could do something about the fact that he

147

loved his work, he loved the camaraderie and the community spirit, but he felt guilty about making weapons of war. And of course once the ships were built, or even just refitted by him and his colleagues, and Maggie Thatcher had won her war and secured her premiership, she started closing down all the yards and disrupting and destroying working-class communities in general, the length and breadth of the country.

— By contrast, I suppose, you've had things pretty easy.

— Well, my working life has certainly been less interesting, yes. I think I take after my father, he's more the academic type.

— What does he do?

— He's a French teacher.

— I see. So would you describe yourself as coming from a working-class background?

— Personally no. I work for a finance company, I used to teach English to foreigners, I've travelled around Europe, I drink decaff cappuccinos in boutique coffee shops; none of these are traditional working-class pursuits. But I would say this: one of the things you notice as you get older is how much these influences are there in your upbringing. My uncle and my grandfather come from archetypal, West of Scotland, working-class backgrounds; as I mentioned my father is more academically-minded, my mother too. She studied at Notre Dame, the teacher training college, but her father was a miner. How else were they going to bring me up, other than in accordance with their own values and ideals and the way they knew best?

— I see. But what about social mobility, don't you want to move up in the world?

— Of course, but that shouldn't mean that I have to forget where I'm from, should it?

— Perhaps not. Tell me about your friends, your peer group.

148

— I have a broad group of friends, from different backgrounds and different sections of the community; guys from the same street as me, guys who went to the same school as me, as well as the people I went to Uni with and the people I work with, not just in Glasgow but in the other cities and countries where I've lived as well.

— And yet you're apolitical?

— I would say I'm not particularly interested in the politics that is currently being practised, rather than being completely apolitical.

— Come off it, someone with your upbringing? Convince me that you're not a radical left-wing firebrand, ready to subvert the political neutrality of this organisation with your liberal, socialist agenda.

I couldn't help laughing at this point. — Liberal and socialist at the same time? You'll need to explain to me how that one works, Malcolm.

— You're not addressing yourself to my concerns. I need you to convince me, set my mind at ease.

— Why? Convince you of what? That I'm some sort of nihilist, that I have no belief system or any views of my own on how the world works? Is that what's required? What if I told was a raving communist, would that preclude me from working here?

— It might.

— You know, when I lived in Prague I went to a rally. The World Bank was having a big meeting there, and I went along to one of the demonstrations that had been organised. Not as a participant, you understand, just as an observer. The demonstrators tried to march up to the conference centre and disrupt the meeting, but of course the police were on hand to prevent them.

— What did you witness?

— A stand-off basically. It was boring, nothing happened.

— But whose side were you on?

— As I say, I was there merely as an observer. I wasn't on anybody's side.

— Emotionally though, you must have had more sympathy for one side over the other.

— Maybe, it's hard to tell. I think the most damning thing I can say is that the question never really occurred to me, until someone else who I was there with asked me the exact same thing.

— And how did you answer?

— I think I said something like, if these protestors are genuinely concerned about poverty then I'm on their side every time. If they're just there for a rammy, then they deserve to get battered.

— And what was your conclusion? Why were they there in your opinion?

— I'm not sure, I left eventually. Like I say, it was boring. But the demonstrators seemed to me at least to have made a good point, and to be drawing the world's attention to an important issue.

— Namely?

— Namely, the inequalities that are inevitably produced within a capitalist-style economy. And the poverty gap that exists not only between the developed and the developing world, but also within the various social strata of Western liberal democracies.

— Sounds to me that you're an authentic left winger, that's pretty bog standard socialist rhetoric you're coming away with.

— Well I'm Scottish, am I not? What else do you expect?

— Sorry, I don't understand.

— Us Scots, we can't help it, can we? We're a good example of a modern democratic country, because everyone here's entitled to their views, but still, Scotland is probably the most instinctively socialist country in Western Europe in my opinion.

— Just a shame we don't have a modern political party that can adequately represent our views, eh?

— Something like that, yes.

— Interesting. What religion are you?

— Come on, Malcolm, what is this?

— It's another direct question.

— It is, but I'm wondering why you're asking it. Apart from anything else, you've seen my CV so you must know what school I went to and I've already been less than subtle with one or two hints that I've dropped. You know the answer to your own question before you've even asked it, surely? For the first time, it seemed, I had put a dent in Munroe's inscrutability.

— I've only had a brief look over your résumé, he conceded diffidently.

— I'm Catholic, yourself?

— Presbyterian.

— Is that going to be an issue between us? Can't we all just be friends?

— We can, and indeed we should. Please don't be offended, I merely want to know what section of the community in Scotland we're representing by employing you. By potentially employing you, I should say, he corrected himself. — And at the same time, I need to know that you're not about to use the platform that we provide you with to intervene in a partisan manner on some of the social issues affecting us all. You see, under normal circumstances we'd be in a position to vet you more gradually, if you were an employee advancing up the career ladder within the organisation for example. But you're not, you're a freelancer, with no experience of working in television before, so we need to know that you're somebody we can trust. We wouldn't allow you to start spouting off about the political situation in Ireland for instance, which is an interesting subject for debate in itself, but would be inappropriate in the forum we're considering giving you access to. Everyone tells me that you're bright and enthusiastic, so I'm assuming you can understand that.

— That's not going to happen, Malcolm, I assured him.

— So, if you wouldn't mind, he continued, — please outline your views to us on the current political situation in Ireland.

For a fleeting moment I almost felt like telling Munroe to stuff his job, find someone else to front the show, because he was delving into territory that was none of his or anyone else's business. But at the same time I could see there was a semblance of perverse logic to what he was saying. This was a serious programme I wanted to help them create, not a vehicle for fronting up an individual's agenda. That was the last thing I wanted the show to be about. It seemed wise to reassure him about my intentions, and anyhow I was quite enjoying the cut and thrust of our conversation by this stage and I felt happy and relaxed enough to allow the discussion to meander in whatever direction Munroe wanted to take it. I was also aware that in part at least his blunt manner was an affectation, which he was using to try and test me, to push my buttons by being deliberately provocative with me. It was up to me not to take the bait but to remain unflustered and try to answer him. I decided that he could ask me anything he wanted, and I would be ready, willing and able to at least try and engage in a discussion with him.

— I support the peace process, I told him truthfully.

— So you believe in what Adams and McGuinness are doing?

— I do, yes, but it's not just them who are doing it, is it? The whole country's on a path to peace. The partition of Ireland was clearly a disaster, but hopefully the agreement that's now in place is going to allow us to deal with the hand that history has dealt us. Shite! I was trying to keep it neutral, but I've gone and used the first person, which I'm sure he'll have noticed, the only question is whether he's gony pick me up on it or no.

— Us? I didn't have to wait long for my answer. — Us? Surely you mean them? The Irish people. You're Scottish, aren't you?

— Every bit as Scottish as you, Malcolm yes, and I wondered if you were going to let me away with that. At first I considered trying to laugh off my mistake as a casual slip of the tongue, but I quickly changed my mind. — Look, Malcolm, I'm proud of my Irish background, it's not something I want to cover up or deny and I don't see why I should have to. Yes, I mean us, all of us. Scotland and Ireland have a lot in common, you know. Glasgow and Belfast are like peas from the same pod, with many similar issues and problems, yet many of the same things going for them as well. They're sibling cities in many ways and at times I think we should be looking out for each other.

— A lot in common, you say? Are you referring to a common enemy, perhaps?

— No, I wouldn't use the word enemy, this isn't the age of William Wallace. But seeing as we're talking about history, then I think we can say yes, both countries seem to have been the subject of unwelcome external interference from South of the border down the centuries.

— And why is that?

— I don't know, like I say, I think it's something that's been there for centuries. Arguably it goes back to the Norman Conquest, if you want to examine it closely, but I'm not sure we want to go down that route here, do we?

— As far back as that? he considered. — Explain.

— OK, I shrugged, — England was conquered by the Normans, who came over the Channel, defeated the Saxons and took control of the country. They established their hegemony, suppressed any and all dissent, and never went away. I would say England is a good example of what happens to a country that is brutally and aggressively conquered by a hostile foreign power, which arrives and sets itself up as the aristocracy, the new ruling-class, and remains there forever. But Scotland was never conquered in this way, and neither was Ireland, I insisted. — These countries always resisted, even when they were executing local leaders and replacing them with their own, ethnically cleansing areas like Ulster or the Highlands, we were never completely subjugated. So yes, I think the Scots and the Irish probably do have a lot more in common with each other than they do with people in England. But again, that's just a personal opinion.

— So you don't like the English then?

— Don't put words into my mouth! I didn't say that, I just think they have their way of doing things and we have ours, which is entirely normal of course.

— Yes, I tend to agree with you. The Normans made England a far more class conscious country, for example. Whatever way you look at it, the conquest was certainly a pivotal moment in the history of these islands.

— It was yes, because England never really recovered from the invasion, and you can still see it in the mentality of the modern British ruling-class today. Duke William came over from Normandy waving the Pope's banner, because he'd persuaded himself that the Saxon king had broken an oath, and had promised him the throne. This ability to convince themselves that they're fully justified in the action they're taking has been a feature of the British mindset ever since, even down to modern times; whether it's Cromwell burning his way across Ireland, or Churchill flattening Dresden, or Thatcher invading the Falklands, or even wee Tony Blair supporting the Americans in their war against Iraq; they can be as brutal as anyone, the Brits, but only after they've utterly persuaded themselves that what they're doing is right and just, regardless of the obvious and overwhelming evidence to the contrary.

— I see, he uttered, smart bastard that he was. I had to hand it to him, I was way off course here. I was supposed to be interviewing for a fucking job, convincing a potential employer of my suitability for the post, and here I was spouting shite about King Harald taking one in the eye for the Anglo-Saxons. Yes, Munroe was a skillful interrogator, a clever cunt who knew how to entice furtive opinions and attitudes from his unsuspecting interlocutors, but I was also a stupid arsehole, because I saw what he was doing, and I did nothing to stop it. I'd fallen for his patter completely, and in doing so I truly believed that I'd blown my chances here. I wished that I could somehow push the rewind button and go back to the start, but there was no way he was going to let me off the hook at this point, — We don't share a common state religion though, do we? he told me.

— Sorry, who doesn't, Malcolm? I asked, feeling suddenly quite flustered.

— Scotland and Ireland, he pointed out.

— I believe we do share the same state religion in fact. Both countries believe in a free and fair society that is diverse, pluralist, democratic and governed by the rule of law. What more do you want? That surely replaces any historical differences we may have had, and I would also include our cousins to the South in that as well, I replied almost in resignation.

— OK, a good answer, he smiled. For a moment, I sensed that perhaps our discussion might be finally coming to an end and that he'd had enough of toying with me. But I was wrong. — So I'm presuming you're in favour of Scottish independence then? he asked me.

— Are you? That's quite a presumption. To be honest, that's not something which has really preoccupied my thoughts recently, while I've been out the country. We're still a good few years away from a potential referendum on that subject.

— It's only two or three years down the road, not as far as you think, and you must have a view on the matter.

— I suppose I would have to put myself in the pro-independence camp, if you were to push me.

— Why?

— I don't know. You seem to think I'm rabidly anti-English, but I'm not in the least. I just believe that the most important question with regard to that issue is this: what self-respecting country wouldn't want to govern its own affairs? The other side will say that we're better off being ruled from Westminster, but my response to that would be: what characteristics do you think the Scottish people are lacking, which would prevent us from running our own affairs in a competent and capable manner?

— It's a fair point, he reflected, perhaps sensing my mental exhaustion by this stage.— And you're married? he asked.

— Yes.

— Happily?

— Happily, yes, I straightbatted it back to him.

— What are your views on homosexuality?

— My views on what? I really should have known that

156

he was far more interested in my sexual orientation than my marital status. I mean, I was applying for a job in the media for fuck's sake, and despite the fact that the SBC was a fully paid up member of the liberal elite, I doubt whether he could have coped with a left-wing, Nationalist, Catholic poofter boy on his hands. Despite my earlier resolution to do my best to answer and humour Munroe, I was approaching the end of my tether with the whole fiasco by this stage, and I was also vaguely aware by now of a curiously liberating sensation that I was starting to lose the plot.

— My views on homosexuality are similar to my views on politics really, Malcolm, in that I don't really waste too much time thinking about it, I answered tersely. — I mean, what is there to think about anyway? I'm pleased if they don't get their heads flushed down the toilet at school anymore to the extent that they used to, and that people are generally a lot more tolerant, if that's any help to you. That's my take on it, although I must admit, the idea of man on man sex leaves me with a slightly unpleasant taste in my mouth, if you'll pardon the expression. Don't get me wrong, I don't have a homophobic bone in my body, I shared a flat with a gay guy at Uni and what people decide to do in the privacy of their own homes, or even in their own rooms in the case of my mate and his dubious collection of nocturnal companions, is entirely their business as far as I'm concerned, I was in full rant mode by now. — One thing I would say though, just as the women's movement has been appropriated by corporations and other vested interest groups, so the baton of the gay agenda seems to have been taken on by the likes of yourselves in the media, precisely because there's such a disproportionately high number of gay people involved in politics, the media and show business, the cultural triumvirate by which we're all ruled in our society. I'm happily married, Malcolm, yes, can we just leave it at that?

— We can indeed. David, any questions?

— Can I ask you about your football allegiances? Henderson, who had been sitting patiently during Munroe's grilling, finally ventured.

— Sure, I sighed, — ask away, mate.

— Now you're from a Celtic supporting background, I think we've established?

— Yes.

— You're a Celtic fan?

— I am.

— Are you a season ticket holder?

— No, not for a long time. I've only been to the odd game since I returned home. I've taken my wife to a couple of matches recently, and I was at Ibrox for a game last season.

— So you went to see Rangers?

— Yeah, against Celtic obviously.

— I see. Have you ever been a season ticket holder?

— Years ago, my first year at Glasgow Uni in fact. I used to go with a group of my friends every fortnight. It was great fun, even though Celtic were terrible at the time.

— I can see it now. A teenage Peter up the back of the old stand, singing all the old rebel songs with a bunch of his pals …

More Tomfoolery. I'd already taken the bait more than once during the course of this conversation, but Henderson wasn't nearly as sharp as his boss and I'd fallen for it already so I wasn't falling for it again. — It wasn't really like that, David, I told him flatly. — I can assure you that I will be a completely impartial arbitrator on any subject we decide to discuss on the show. And besides, I'm assuming I won't be the only person working in the media who supports a team.

— It's a fair point. You mention impartiality, are you capable of complete and utter impartiality and objectivity on every issue that you deal with?

— Of course, completely and absolutely.

— Let me explain to you why I ask. The default position of the SBC on any given matter is neutrality. On any issue, across the whole spectrum, whether it's sport, politics, business, you name it. We like to analyse any questions that arise objectively and to hear both sides of the argument, or even a range of viewpoints. It doesn't mean that we can't hear alternative opinions, some of them maybe even quite radical, but we can't allow our staff or those who we employ on a contractual basis to express extremist views on any topic. And the best way to ensure that this does not occur is not to employ people who hold extremist views in the first place. Do you follow?

— I do, David. And I hope you're able to ascertain that I don't hold any extremist views, I told them both. — In fact, philosophically, I'm quite well disposed to this idea of impartiality, and of being neutral. There's an aspect of my personality which this appeals to greatly. This idea of being a judge, of being a ..., I checked myself. — I almost said of being a referee there. But you know what I mean? The notion that the responsibility for being above the hubbub rests with me, of listening to what other people are saying without revealing my own hand, this is something that I have always found very appealing. Perhaps because, as we've discussed, I don't hold particularly radical or strong views on anything really, if I'm being honest. Apart from one thing of course; I believe that people are entitled to their opinions. And not just to hold an opinion, I should stress, but to express themselves freely, and if they choose, to use the power of persuasion to convince other people of the strength of their argument and the merit of their position. That's one thing I believe very strongly, it's what freedom of speech means as far as I'm concerned, and hopefully that's what this show is going to be all about.

— OK, well that seems a good note to end on, Munroe announced. It seemed that the interview was over at last, as he and Henderson stood up in unison and offered me their hands in turn, — I've enjoyed talking with you, Peter, Munroe offered. — Stand by your phone and we'll let you know what happens next as soon as we can, he told me brusquely and departed, Henderson following on behind, with neither of them offering me so much as a flicker of an indication regarding how they felt the discussion had gone, or what the prospects of offering to commission my programme were.

Helen, who had been observing but not listening to our conversation from a corner of the canteen approached me after the two senior managers had departed the scene.

— How did it go? she asked me, all smiles. It took a wee minute for me to regain my wits and recover my composure and for the tension that had been building up over the previous half an hour or so to finally drain out of me.

— It was like the fucking Spanish Inquisition, Helen, I eventually informed her.

PART 3

9. SHAWLANDS' DINNER

— So, you're gonna be a big TV star? My wife asks me, although I seem to detect more irony and sarcasm in her question than anything approaching genuine admiration. I'm taking her out to dinner in Shawlands to a wee Italian restaurant up the street from our flat. I've decided that we need to sit down and talk everything through, no so much for her benefit, but more for my own. I want it all to sink in as quickly as possible, and by vocalising everything that has happened to me in the last few days, in the presence of somebody who isny necessarily gony be too easily impressed, the hope is that reality will dawn on me, and no a moment too soon, because I need to start focusing on what the fuck happens next, and on addressing the challenges that are sure to lie ahead.

— Don't tease me, I warn her, — but it looks like something could be happening, yeah. They've picked the show up for a year at least, and we're going to be making the first programme in two weeks time, to coincide with the start of the new football season. There's a beginning anyway. I've said it out loud and apparently the world still continues to spin.

— Do you know what to do? Lenka's eyes narrow as she shakes her head at me sceptically. — Working in television, it's not easy, I think. You never did this before, are they going to show you how it works? There must be lots of training for you, no?

— I don't think so, darling, I'll probably just have to pick most of it up as I go along. I'm hoping it's no gony be as difficult as you maybe think.

— What if you make a mistake? she asks. — It won't be easy for you.

— During the transmission you mean? They'll have a chance to do corrections and editing after the recording. This is what they explained to me at the meeting this afternoon, they

162

can't commission a live show. I wanted to do it live, *direkt*, in the presence of a studio audience so that we could have interaction, I explain. — I also wanted to be able to discuss things with the viewers and answer their questions and emails in real time, just like a proper debate. But apparently this is not possible. I always knew it was a bit of a long shot, but this afternoon they formally said no, it can't be a live show. It has to be recorded in the afternoon or early evening and then transmitted at night, probably around 9.30pm.

— Are you ready to order? A pretty waitress smiles at us.

— Yes, I'll have the carbonara with Italian ham, and a bottle of Moretti please.

— For Senora?

— I'm having spaghetti with meatballs, and also a beer.

— Any starter?

— We'll have some bread and olives, thank you.

— Grazie.

— Are you happy about it? Lenka continues after the waitress removes our menus and departs with our order. — Making a recorded show is easier for you, yes?

— It's easier, you're right, but I don't necessarily want it to be easier. When I approached them with the idea I made it clear that this should be a live show, so we can fully involve the audience. That was the whole point, I tried to explain to them. When we made the pilot episode, we pretended it was a live show, so the bosses could see how it would work. I wanted to convince them that this was the best way of approaching it. But they said no, they like the idea, they want to make the programme, they want me to present it, but a live show is impossible.

— Why?

— I don't know, they tried to give me some sort of technical explanation, but I didn't really understand what they were saying at that point. I think I was trying to take in too much information by then, but I'm sure they have good reasons They're television executives after all, and they understand the media much better than me. Although I think that's maybe their problem too, I add, trying not to sound too frustrated. — They're very risk averse, Lenka, this is what's so exasperating, do you understand? They don't want to do anything too radical, anything that would be seen as a departure from the norm. The novelty is in the content and the way we deal with the subject matter, they told me. Audience participation has to be controlled, and they don't feel a live transmission would be the best format for this project, with its anything can happen kind of feel to it.

— You are disappointed, yes?

— I don't know how I feel, honey, I reflect. I'm soaking the bread we've been served in oil and vinegar, which makes it go down well with the olives. — This is all new to me, you know? I continue between mouthfuls. — I don't want to kid on that I'm not excited and pleased and looking forward to what's coming, but at the same time this whole 'getting a glamorous job in the media thing' is a lot more underwhelming than I thought it would be.

— What do you mean? I don't understand.

— It's confusing. I don't think we're going to be making the show that I told them about, the way I wanted it to work, I try to clarify. — I'm not exactly sure what kind of programme I'll end up presenting, the way things are looking.

— Because no audience?

— That's right. No audience means no debate, not in a meaningful way anyway. We record the show on an empty set so there is no way to involve other people at all, there's nobody there even just to laugh and clap. Then when we have completed the recording and everything is finished we go out to dinner or to the pub, we talk about how the show went, and then we return to the studio in time for the broadcast. During the transmission the viewers can send in emails and social interaction, Facebook, that kind of thing so we can maybe answer their questions and talk to them that way. But it's not how I envisioned it.

— Facebook only? This is shite.

— Tell me about it, darling, I smile at her attempted Scottish turn of phrase. — I'm terrified at the prospect of becoming just another media talking head, towing the party line, regurgitating the same old crap to no greater end than maybe being able to pull a few more birds or get a few nice trips on expenses, I rant as Lenka looks at me blankly. — But still, I add, — of course I am excited about it all and looking forward to it. I think it will be interesting.

— Pull birds? she repeats quizzically.

— Sorry, honey, just ignore me, I tell her.

Our dinners arrive and an Italian waiter, who speaks only his native language, sprinkles our plates with parmesan cheese and some exotic spice from a giant pepperpot.

— Dobrou chut', Lenka tells me as she makes a start on her meatballs.

— Bon appetit, I reply.

I tuck into my carbonara and drift away into a daydream as I enjoy my meal. It's a genuinely perplexing situation in which I seem to find masel, for a moment there this afternoon I thought there was a chance that they would accept the concept of the show as I pitched it to them, but I suppose that will teach me to get my hopes up. I only want to do this if I feel that I'm participating in something a wee bit inventive, groundbreaking even, and I was literally panicking during the course of the meeting at the prospect of them turning me into the next Jim White, a company man without a single original idea in his head on any subject you care to mention, although they were at pains to assure me that this wouldny be the case and I eventually calmed down. I feel like I've just been offered a contract to play football professionally, but rather than the offer coming from Celtic, who I was expecting to sign for, instead it's come from Partick Thistle or Rob Roy or somebody slightly less glamourous. Rangers or somebody. Whatever the case though, I'm sure it'll beat working off a call sheet.

— I think it is a better job than making telephone calls for your friend, Lenka seems to read my thoughts exactly.

— Sorry, honey, is it that obvious? I was miles away.

— No, it's OK, I like watching you eat.

— You're right though, they pay me one thousand and five hundred pounds per show, which involves roughly two days work per week. Not a bad deal when you look at it that way, is it?

— Two days only?

— More like one and a half in all likelihood. We'll have an editorial meeting the day before transmission to discuss the important issues, and decide what we're going to talk about on the programme. All the research and booking of guests, etc. is done by other people, I just need to be aware of what's going on. And then on transmission day, we run through the show, practise our discussion a few hours before the recording and then we make the programme. Afterwards we can discuss whether it was a good show, have something to eat or drink, and then when the programme is broadcast, we have to congregate in the green room to answer questions as I was telling you, read about what people are saying online, and so on. That's the format, it's maybe twelve or fourteen hours work per week, maximum. Maybe you should ask Pauline if you can work four days a week at the jeweller's instead of five, so we can spend more time together. Otherwise I think I will be bored a lot.

166

— Maybe she will like this idea, she always wants to pay me less and we are not so busy just now.

— Well, think about it, we can afford it now that I earn a little bit more.

— How did the meeting go with your agent? Lenka asks me.

— Yeah, it was interesting, I laugh.

*

— Peter, good to see you, take a seat, Agent Nimmo shook my hand and offered me a green plastic seat in the foyer of the SBC building. — How much are you wanting for this gig then? he asked me.

— Thanks, Mark, er, I'm not sure really. You tell me, what's the going rate for someone in ma position?

— I can get you two grand a week for the show - that includes my fifteen percent of course – but you'll be looking for add ons, I assume.

— Add ons?

— You don't want to work a two day week, do you? A man of your calibre, it would ruin you, surely? The SBC is a big organisation, I can get you radio work, internet work, do you fancy a blog? Every self-respecting media numpty has got to have a blog these days, how much do you want for yours? he asked. — Shall I tell them you're available for a thousand words a week?

— The thing is, Mark, I'm just finding my feet in this organisation, I pointed out. — I don't want anyone thinking that I'm trying to take over the place. No just amongst this crowd here in fact, but the whole industry. I'm a total novice

167

at this mate, this media business is all new to me, don't forget.

— Worried about taking on more than you can chew, eh?

— More a case ay wanting to ease masel in, if you follow me. I was becoming slightly self-conscious and embarrassed about my apparent lack of ambition in the presence of this self-made man. Ever since Thatcher, the lower-middle classes have been taking over this country. Not the working classes, not even the middle classes with their intellectual pretensions, who Maggie despised almost as much as she hated the urban proletariat, but vulgar, unskilled, uneducated, aspirational lower-middle class cunts like Nimmo here. These bastards are everywhere now. — My main focus in the short term is on the show and making it work, I assured him. — If I'm honest Mark, I'm not particularly interested in doing the whole rent-a-quote media lackey thing, those guys are ten a penny and they tend to …

— Tell you what, Peter, we'll leave that open, he interrupted me. — That's no bother at all, I'll negotiate a few extra options for you, insert a few clauses here and there, and you can come back to it at some point in the future, when you feel you're ready. How's that sound?

— Aye, that sounds about right, cheers, I nodded. — Are you sure about this two grand a show by the way? Seems a bit generous me to me.

— It is generous, but that's what I dae, Peter. That's why I'm here, to fuckin make sure they're generous. Two grand will be a piece ay piss, I might even batter old Catriona up to two and a hawf.

— That'd be great, but are you sure? Doddsy told me that Catriona McConnell has a bit ay a reputation. Is that who you're talking about, the SBC's chief contract negotiator? She's pretty tough to deal wi apparently, a bit ay a fuckin battle axe actually, is what I heard.

— She does have a reputation aye, but no for whit you're thinkin. Fuckin goes like the clappers apparently, he winked at me. — Fat birds like that always dae, cause they're that desperate for it, particularly middle-aged old boots like her. When was the last time you think she got her hole plugged?

— Erm, I don't know, is she not married? I offered, slightly taken aback at the course the conversation was taking. I had a sudden inclination to ask Nimmo, does the same thing no apply to middle-aged auld fat cunts like you, you're no much ay a looker yourself you know, when was the last time *you* had a decent ride, ya fuckin disrespectful bastard! But any natural reticence I possess served me well on this occasion, because I needed to keep the guy on my side, for the time being at least.

— Honestly, Peter, she's a pussy cat really, Nimmo continued, — don't believe a fuckin word Doddsy tells you. I deal wi them aw the time, these contract negotiators, and this yin is aw show, believe me. I'm tellin you, I've seen it aw before a million times, they act like every penny's a prisoner until you start laying it on the line for them. That's when they crumble. Honestly, I'll have her drinking milk oot my lap by the time I'm done wi her, you just wait and see.

— OK, well best ay luck. I shook his hand again and he disappeared into the building and up the stairs to his meeting. I was issued with a pass and I headed up to the canteen, where I picked a secluded spot to have a coffee and read my book for an hour or so while Nimmo was locked in negotiations with Catriona and attempting to negotiate a freelance contract on my behalf as a television presenter with the national broadcaster.

Eventually they came down into the canteen together laughing and joking together like a pair ay teenagers, and they approached me with the contract.

— £1500 per show? I glanced over the document.

— We've been as generous as we could in the present climate, Catriona assured me.

I fixed my gaze on Nimmo and decided to stare him out until such time as he offered me an explanation for his seemingly misplaced confidence of little more than sixty minutes ago. I swear, it was worth the five hundred pound a week shortfall just to see the look on the cunt's face.

— Cutbacks, he eventually lamented sheepishly.

*

— How were your meatballs? I ask Lenka.

— They were good. How was yours?

— Aye, it was delicious, I reply, — this is a nice wee restaurant, don't you think? We should come here more, I suggest. I genuinely prefer these small, secret, off the beaten track type locations, where the food is tasty and the service comes wi a friendly smile, to the fancy, expensive places where the waiters are bowing and scraping in front of you, sycophantically fawning over your every need, and where you can call for the chef to be hung if he hasny cooked the prawns the way you like them.

We're offered coffee and desert but instead I pay up and take Lenka for a slice of cake and a cappuccino over to a nice wee coffee shop across the road.

— Café culture has hit Glasgow at last, I observe, taking in the relaxed, semi-intellectual surroundings of the 'Bean House'. I'm no sure Lenka agrees, unlike the West End where she works, which has very much bought into the whole upmarket new image scene, many of Shawlands cafés and coffee bars seem to have retained an authentic Glaswegian element, while at the same attempting to pursue a more sophisticated, Continental ambience. I'm no sure how this particular establishment achieves this, I cany quite put my finger on it, in fact I might well be talking a load ay pish

170

because they're aw franchise places up here anyway, but for some reason the surroundings just seem to agree wi me and that's probably the most important thing. What this town really could use though is a coffee bar wi an alcohol license, that's open into the wee small hours. If we could just keep the jakeys and the alkies away, then we might be able to consider oursels proper Europeans. On the other hand, I suppose, I could always just move to Edinburgh.

All these random musings seem to have brought an idea, which has been at the back of my mind for some time now, abruptly into my immediate thoughts. — Lenka, honey, how would you like to go to Amsterdam with me for a few days? I ask.

— Amsterdam? When? she queries, flashing that familiar, sceptical look at me once again.

— Next week, I venture. — Celtic are playing in Amsterdam on Wednesday, in a qualifying game for the Champions League. There are direct flights from Glasgow, we could go for a few days, take a boat on the canals, visit some museums and then watch the football before we go home. It would be a nice break for us before my new job starts.

— What about my job? I have to work next week.

— You can take some holiday time. Ask Pauline, or if you like I can ask her for you, because it's short notice. If she says no, we can tell her where to stick her job because you only have to work when you want to now.

— Can we go to the Anne Frank house?

— What? Of course, yes absolutely, we can go to the Anne Frank house. I've always wanted to go as well.

— Ever since I was a small child, I always wanted to go to Amsterdam and visit the Anne Frank house.

— It'll be the first place we go, I assure her.

She almost explodes with delight, and it occurs to me, not for the first time, how simple and easy it is to make this girl happy. All I've done is suggest a souped up trip to a Celtic away game, and here I am fulfilling one of her childhood dreams in the process. I always imagined it would be next to impossible for someone like me to satisfy the whims and the capricious demands of a beautiful girl like this, but with Lenka there are no airs and graces, no affectations or prohibitively expensive tastes. She's a product of her upbringing of course, and of her culture. There is no class system in a communist society, how can there be? There's only us and them, and although consumerism has well and truly taken hold in the Czech Republic in recent years, and there are plenty of posers and golddiggers about these days, Lenka has explicitly rejected this new mindset in a reasonable and natural way.

Thank God for normal people, I cany help thinking. You can say what you like about Communism, which has been roundly rejected as a viable, modern political system, and no doubt for good reason, but as with Catholicism, which also receives a bad press in certain quarters, the people who are brought up in these supposedly flawed belief systems don't seem to have been too traumatically affected by the whole experience in my judgment. In fact, as far as I can see, for the most part they seem to be pretty decent, well-rounded people. That's one of the aspects of Lenka's character which I find appeals to me most, the idea that she's stunningly beautiful and so well-adjusted and grounded at the same time. It isny necessarily a combination that you see every day and I feel lucky just to be sitting here in this coffee shop having a conversation wi the girl, never mind married to her. I hope that's a feeling that doesny go away any time soon.

— How about we go back and watch that film you were talking about? I eventually suggest after we've polished off our cappuccinos and our slices of cheesecake.

Pretty soon we're curled up on the couch with a wee

dram; Becherovka for me, Slivovice for the missus, both of which we've been drinking quite sparingly because they're so damn hard to find over here. But this is a special occasion. So special in fact that the DVD we're watching will have to wait for another occasion, because it's not long before we're completely distracted by each other. I take my wife into the bedroom next door and the evening ends in pretty much the way that I hoped it would.

10. DRUGS AND PROSTITUTES

I'm determined to have a shot at least at forgetting all about career moves and fuckin television programmes for a few days, and to see if I can take my mind off my impending celebrity for a while by soaking up a bit of culture in the beautiful city of Amsterdam. I've no been able to stop thinking about the changes that may or may not be about to happen in my life, and to be honest I need a break from it all because I seem to be wading through treacle at the moment when it comes to the passage of time and counting down the hours until it all kicks off. So I'm hoping that a short break in a famous European city, wandering the streets and taking in the sights, will prove to be the best way to chalk off a few days with my mind on something else. That's what I told Lenka anyway, although she wasny slow in pointing out that, as well as the promised trips to the likes ay the Rijksmuseum and the Concertgebouw, the main reason I suggested that we come here in the first place was to attend a football match. Football is culture, I was keen to stress to her in reply, it reflects the character and identity of a country or a city every bit as much as anything you'll see at a concert or an art gallery. She looked at me dubiously as she processed my answer and I must admit, it's a debatable point. One that I could argue all day in fact, but no matter how persuasive and rational a case I set out, I doubt whether I'd be able to convince my wife.

I point out the Amsterdam Arena to her as we ride in from the airport on one of the city's spacious, double decker commuter trains. We've added a tour of the stadium to our itinerary tomorrow, the day before the match, so I suspect we'll no be the only Hoops fans being shown round Johan Cruyff's old stomping ground. We seem to have beaten the majority of our fellow supporters across the water however, because there were only sparse pockets of green and white clad Glaswegians at the airport, although I expect that to change in the next few days as tens of thousands of football fans, whether wi tickets

174

or not, descend on the town for the all important Champions League qualifier. Broadly speaking, Lenka's happy to be going along wi the football aspect ay the trip, and in return I'll be staring at the Van Gogh masterpieces in the museum the morra and wondering what in God's name could have driven the guy to detach his own ear from his body. Or was it his dick he chopped off, I never can remember?

We arrive at Centraal Station and wander down the Damrak with our luggage in tow looking for our hotel.

— Just think, when I'm a famous television presenter, we'll no have to hobble about here, I tell Lenka. — We'll be driven in a fancy car from the airport straight to the hotel.

— What about your rule? she reminds me. — No television, no programmes. You promised that you wouldn't talk about this.

— Sorry, you're right, I chastise myself for breaking my own guideline so soon into our holiday. Clearly I've not yet managed to complete the mental transition, and I'm still back in Glasgow thinking about bright lights and television studios, so I need to try harder to adjust my mindset, and see if I can stick to what I promised masel.

— That would spoil it anyway, Lenka tells me, — I like to see the streets and the people, it's more interesting. I cany argue, it's an intriguing sensation wandering the streets of a city you don't know much about, checking out its inhabitants, discovering its curious idiosyncrasies, the peculiarities in the layout and the architecture and slowly gaining a feel for the place. Even nearly being knocked off my feet several times by bicyclists teaches you something, as we get a good look at the city close-up. This is something the Celtic players and staff and their entourage of journalists will never get to experience. Straight after arriving at Schiphol the morra, they'll all be bussed straight to their hotel, before flying out again the next night having seen little more of Amsterdam than the inside of a football stadium.

We find our hotel and check in. Up in the room, I take a shower and freshen up and Lenka does the same before we head out and take a tram down to the Leidseplein, where we have a nice alfresco Italian meal. We add a few drinks to our tab and chat for a while with another, older couple who are also in town for the game. The old boy reckons that the new Europa League is about Celtic's standard just now, and he's happy that even in the case of a defeat against Ajax, they're at least guaranteed to be playing European football for the next few months as the losers are relegated into that competition. I don't know whether it's an age thing, if he's right and Celtic end up in the second tier tournament then I'll be there supporting them all the way, but I hope to Christ I never lose the ability to dream that the club I support can win just about any game they take part in. Maybe it's because I lived abroad for a few years and the recent negativity surrounding Scottish football hasny seeped into my bones yet to the extent that it obviously has wi this boy, but I still believe that Celtic can potentially achieve just about anything they want on the football field. It goes without saying that the guy has a point; Ajax are theoretically the stronger team and at some stage we're gony lose a game and the competition will be over for another year, but the day I turn up expecting Celtic to come off second best in any football match will be the day I decide to find another hobby. I swear, no matter what happens, I'll no be pitching up here in twenty years time when I'm this boy's age, thinking that the Europa League will do for Celtic, before a ball's even been kicked. I'll have taken up golf or mountaineering or trainspotting long before then.

We eventually say cheerio to the couple and head back in the direction of the hotel, soaking up the sights for a while on the way and eventually availing ourselves of the convenience of the city's public transport system. There's a theory I've heard, which in my thirty-two years to date on this earth, I've had precious little opportunity to test, that hotel sex is the best sex you'll ever have. We eventually arrive back at the four star luxury of our Damrak lodgings, and quickly set about proving this hypothesis beyond all reasonable doubt.

Suitably satisfied and well rested, I wonder whether Lenka detects the glint in my eye the next morning as we take breakfast in the hotel restaurant. Regardless she's no the type to say anything, and it's not long before we head out into the city, full of fruit juice and croissants, and ready to properly begin our Amsterdam experience. We've tried to simplify things by dividing our schedule along basic boy/girl lines, with hopefully a balance of what might be considered of interest to the two genders on our itinerary. For example, the tour of Ajax's ground and the Heineken experience have been allocated to me, and presumably I'll be allowed to indulge myself to my heart's content on these sections, beer and football generally being considered to fall within the remit of the male sphere of interest, whereas diamonds and looking at pictures, which I think we're going to be doing for most of today's excursion, are assumed to have evened things up for Lenka and the fairer sex. The theory seems sound anyway, we'll need to see how it works out in practice.

First stop is the Amsterdam historical museum, which charts the growth and development of the relatively young city. It turns out that at the time of the Norman invasion, when old William the Conqueror was doing his thing, and the light was going out forever on Anglo-Saxon England, Amsterdam was basically nothing more than a swamp. There was literally nothing there. Then they dammed the River Amstel, hence the name, stuck some poles in the ground, and opened up a few brothels and hash bars. It's an interesting and well presented series of exhibitions in the museum, although I was expecting to see more about windmills and dykes and land reclaimed from the sea. Perhaps they think that sort of stuff is a bit too clichéd, but it's clear enough that the 17th century was the heyday of Amsterdam and the Netherlands in general, with commerce making the city one of the most influential and

177

important trading centres in the world at the time.

It's also clear that the Dutch have a fairly healthy regard for themselves, which is often not altogether a bad thing, as for example we witness in the Johan Cruyff exhibition. Cruyff, or Cruijff to give him his correct Dutch spelling, apparently claims that he considers himself to be just a normal kid from the Dam, but what incredible self-confidence the man possesses, what amazing self-belief! And the Dutch absolutely love him for it. The whole museum leaves you with a decent grasp of the city's history and character and it's immediately apparent to me what the Czechs and the Dutch have in common; they're both relatively small countries with their own language and culture, similar but clearly distinct from those other, sometimes larger and more threatening nations which surround them.

Coming from Scotland I find it all fascinating but also curiously frustrating; I can just about conceive of the notion of being an independent country, with or without the intriguing and wonderful self-confidence that these other small nations often possess, but I cany quite grasp the idea of foreigners turning up in our country and trying to learn our language, mimicking our accent and using the local dialect and vocabulary. I don't know why that should be the case, the fact that I could make a half decent, though far from perfect, stab at the vagaries and complexities of the Czech language is one of the reasons, Lenka has since cited, that she liked me when we first met. Czech and Dutch are not languages that are commonly taught in schools but they are important distinguishing aspects of their respective countries, both of which now have sizeable populations of foreigners dwelling within their borders, whose grasp of the native language varies widely. But it just couldn't work the other way about. I can never imagine myself patiently trying to indulge Lenka as she struggles with the peculiarities and vagaries of Scots grammar and pronunciation, hearing her tentatively trying to articulate about laddies and lassies and roaming in the gloaming. Of course she's already picked up on some Scots slang and dialect, but the notion of this being acquired through some kind of formal language training is too bizarre an idea to contemplate seriously. I'm no sure why this should be the case, the Scots usage of the English language is as different from standard English as Czech is from Slovak for example, and nobody disputes that these are separate languages. If football really is culture, as I would argue, and therefore important beyond a mere sporting context, then where does that leave language? For some reason I'm reminded of the time at a Celtic supporters function a few years ago, when former manager John Barnes was read Burns' 'Address to a Haggis' by a prominent committee member, and then asked what he made of it. It sounds like a conversation between Paul Lambert and Kenny Dalgish, the Englishman quipped in reply.

We take an early lunch, which I linger over, because I'm dreading the prospect of the van Gogh museum. Fortunately though, when we reach the Museumplein, van Gogh is closed for renovation, but the nearby Concertgebouw is offering a free lunchtime concert, so we take that in instead. I'm no really into Mozart and Haydn, I'm more of a Beethoven man myself, but it's pleasant enough listening for half an hour or so I suppose, the attraction of which presumably would have been lost on Mr. van Gogh.

The whole Museumplein fascinates Lenka. She's keen to explore the Rijksmuseum, but after a brief coffee house detour, the main state museum gets relegated to a later part of our schedule because there's also a diamond exhibition and a tour of the processing premises on the square, which seems to be top of Lenka's priorities. Amsterdam means different things to different people, for some it's all about freedom and tolerance, others are interested in drugs and prostitutes, for me Amsterdam is primarily associated with Ajax, its celebrated football team; but for Lenka, as a jeweller, the city is all about diamonds. This is despite the fact that, as the tour guide tells us, most of the world's trading in diamonds these days is focused on nearby Antwerp. But Amsterdam and diamonds are still invariably linked with one another, especially in popular culture.

The tour is interesting and informative and also free, presumably in the belief that at the end, when they show you some of the finished gemstones for sale in the shop, some poor fools with more money than sense are actually going to part with tens of thousands of Euros for a polished bit ay subterranean carbon formed under high temperature and pressure. In fairness, it's slightly more complicated than that, and the exhibition reveals to us the journey that the stones endure, from being dug out of the ground in South Africa to ending up in a diamond ring in a museum shop in Holland. I must admit, I was dreading coming in here, as I assumed it would be one of the more painful compromises to the female leg of our itinerary, but despite my initial cynicism, due in part at least to my instinctive distaste for the ostentatious wealth on display, in the end I actually quite enjoy the tour and I find the whole process of mining, cutting, rounding and polishing the stones pretty interesting. Among the intriguing bits of trivia, I'm surprised to learn that the Koh-i-noor isny just an Indian Restaurant at Charing Cross and that diamonds are in fact so hard that the only thing you can use to cut them with is other diamonds, which surely must get confusing at times. There's Shirley Bassey theme music playing throughout and a section showing clips from various films with diamond related subplots, including Peter Sellers showing us how it's done in The Return of the Pink Panther, and a scene from Diamonds are Forever that I must have seen about a hundred times.

"You wanna ride in the front, Mr Franks?"

"It's a lot smoother ride in the front, Mr Franks."

"I gotta brother!"

I'm managing to take a genuine interest in everything that I'm being told and what's going on, which is made a lot easier by the fact that Lenka isny behaving like a star struck wee lassie in the presence of such serious wealth and doing the whole 'Diamonds are a girl's best friend' routine. She's no materialistic or covetous in any way, but instead I notice that she's taking a very professional interest in everything that's on display, and her insider knowledge and tradecraft seems to be making the whole experience more interesting and less baffling for someone like me, whose previous knowledge of diamonds extends no further that what he's gleaned from a Bond movie. By the time we approach the end of the tour I'm starting to feel a bit peckish, and I'm keen no to linger any longer that is necessary, so in the hope that it will finally entice Lenka to make a move in the direction of a café or some other eating-house, I buy her a diamond necklace from the museum shop. Actually the necklace is made from cut glass, not diamonds, and it cost forty Euros, no forty thousand, but she seems happy enough with it.

By late afternoon, I've finally managed to drag her out the building, and we head over to Leidseplein once more for a meal, taking the opportunity to reflect positively on a pleasant and interesting day, which we round off by becoming stooshingly drunk in the Irish pub across the square.

Day two and I'm hoping the balance is gony be redressed somewhat the day, and we're gony be taking in some of my preferred destinations now that we've gained an extensive knowledge on the processes of cutting, rounding and polishing precious stones. It was fascinating to learn all about the four Cs; carat, cut, clarity and colour I think was the last one, but now I'm looking forward to a change ay scene at last. We have a tour of the Amsterdam Arena lined up for this afternoon, and before that there's a visit to beer heaven in the form of the city's famous Heineken Experience.

First up however, we have a trip to the one place we both agreed from the start had to be visited, namely the Anne Frank House. Most people know the story of how the Frank family hid out in a canal-side house during the Nazi occupation of the city, until they were discovered and deported to concentration camps along wi the rest of Amsterdam's Jewish population, and how the young Anne kept a diary of the whole experience. But moving through the house itself, with its hidden chambers, concealed entrances, moveable bookcases and secret living-quarters, we're subjected to an incredibly moving and thought provoking experience. It certainly takes you out of your bubble of complacency for a while and there's an educational element too, you learn how Anne's father was the only family member to survive the holocaust and that he later edited and published his daughter's diaries; that he travelled to America to meet the president and how from an initial print run of just a few hundred copies in Dutch the diary went on to become one of the bestselling books of all time. In the shop I buy Lenka a translation of the diary in French, a language she's been brushing up on recently with the help of ex-French teacher Mr. Fitzpatrick, and in return she presents me with an edition of the book in Czech.

Lenka seems pensive and distracted and almost in tears after we emerge from the shop with our mutual gifts. I take her across to the nearby Westerkerk, which the guidebook advises us is a suitably quiet and reflective excursion after the horrors of the House. We're informed that the building is the tallest Protestant church in the Netherlands, which invites me to wonder aloud if there's maybe a bigger Catholic one somewhere in the country. Nothing from Lenka in response, and we don't linger. Instead I escort her down to a waiting boat and we take a tour of the Prinsengracht. I'm hoping she's gony start feeling herself again soon because a relaxing tour of the canals in the sunshine is one of Amsterdam's unique attractions, a box which has to be ticked by any self-respecting tourist who visits the city and certainly something that she was eagerly looking forward to enjoying before we arrived. The whole experience seems to be totally passing her by though, not even my quip about the likelihood or otherwise of someone organising a canal tour of Kirkintilloch raises a smile in her.

It's no as daft an idea as it sounds; there's a lot ay history on that canal, industrial history especially. Kirkie was way ahead of Amsterdam when it comes to the Industrial Revolution for example. I can just see us now, steaming through the Hillhead, opening up the bridge, holding up the traffic as our wee puffer scrapes its vulnerable keel over the concealed chassis of Melly's drowned motor, wi the passengers aw wondering what the fuck a clapped out Ford Sierra is doing at the bottom ay the water.

— She was so young, Lenka tearfully reflects and I decide that the best thing I can do is to try and give her some space, and show some respect for her period of withdrawn reflection, so I call a halt to my flippant and somewhat pathetic attempts to try and distract her out of it. Lenka's emotions seem to be directed towards the sad story of the young girl herself, and while it's easy to individualise the tragedy in this way, for me the whole Anne Frank story is more of a scary and shocking indication of the potential within all of us for inhumanity towards our fellow man. The Nazis just took it to extreme, and it's a timely reminder, I suppose, of how lucky I am that I'm able to concern myself with such relatively trivial matters, like the attractions of gainful employment and wondering who some football team are gony sign next. Lenka's still looking like she's in need of some affection and I cautiously offer to put my arm round her, which she responds to, and we sit there on our boat for the best part of an hour in almost perfect silence. In a strange way though I manage to derive some peaceful enjoyment from it, and I suggest that we cancel the rest of the day's activities or at least postpone them for a few hours. Lenka refuses, and by the time we alight at the Heineken Experience, it's a full circuit and a half of the outermost canal that we've completed in the warmth and haze of existential reflection.

I'm hoping to be able to get into my element here finally, seeing as we've arrived at the beer and football leg of our itinerary, with a tour of Ajax's stadium scheduled for later in the day. Lenka tells me that she's feeling better, which I'm relieved to hear, because the Heineken experience is about as different from the Anne Frank House as you could hope to imagine. I'm starting to worry about her becoming bored as well as distracted, but as the whole tour of the brewing facility progresses, she starts giving us chapter and verse on the intricacies of the alcohol fermentation process, the brewing of beer apparently being something they do quite a lot of in her country. This was supposed to be my side ay the blanket, a male compromise for all the diamonds and other nonsense that I've had to put up wi so far, but Lenka has snapped out of her quiet and absorbed phase and she's enjoying this more than me now. She certainly knows a lot more than I do about beer and everything related to how it's produced, it wouldny surprise me if she started lecturing me on the football as well this afternoon, giein us her thoughts on the Ajax tactical system and the mysterious way that Dutch teams like to deploy their full backs.

It's an enjoyable and entertaining tour, and like all the best exhibitions, you learn plenty of stuff along the way as well. There's a whole heap of information about the history of the company, how it grew in the twentieth century under Freddie Heineken, who was apparently a bit of a philanthropist in his day, and a man who looked after his workers. This fits in wi the idea of civic responsibility, which they were so keen to stress was an Amsterdam characteristic in the Historical Museum yesterday. Here's a guy who seems to fit the description and is an example of that doctrine in action, with the way he ensured that his employees were well looked after and his profits were put to good use.

We pass through a section depicting Heineken commercials of the past and present, which we move swiftly beyond and out into a football section, with clips of games and goals involving top European sides on giant screens. I'm confused momentarily, but the ubiquitous advertisements and the smiling Heineken 'e's remind me soon enough that the brewer is a sponsor of the Champions League. There's a facility to search through the archive on a touch screen panel, and I'm immediately looking up and watching just about every goal that Celtic have scored in the revamped competition since its association with Heineken. Lenka's having a shot at the table football, sharing a game with a bunch of young guys from England while I'm overindulging myself on the Hoops' three nil win over Benfica in 2007. Finally we head into the bar and exchange our tokens for a couple of free beers, although presumably the cost is included in the hefty admission fee. There was more beer earlier in the tour, as they described and allowed you to sample the correct way to pour the perfect glass. It's the old trick, serve them up a few not so free beverages, then bus them off to the brand shop while there's still the hint of swally in their system to influence their judgment. Bus isny quite right in actual fact, it's a short trip on the canal over to the gift shop, with a tour guide who informs us on the way that roughly fifty people a year fall into the city's waterways and are never heard from again. Usually guys wi their flies undone apparently, taking a pish in the Herrengracht after a few too many samples of Mr Heineken's product in their system. I tend to prefer lavatories masel, it's just an old habit I acquired when I was very young, but still, it's a salient warning because anyone can drink too much when they're on holiday, last night being a perfect example in my case.

I couldny afford a proper necklace at the diamond museum yesterday, but this time I make up for it by buying Lenka a skimpy, branded top from the Heineken gift shop, which I'm sure she's gony look gorgeous in. Consumer tourism, don't you just love it?

After another couple of beers we take a canal boat up to Centraal Station and head out to the Amsterdam Arena on the train. We seemed to have skipped lunch, because our tour has been internet booked in advance and we're a bit behind schedule, but we make it out to the stadium in time and are greeted outside the club shop by a chap called Markus, who speaks to the various groups of guests in turn in fluent Dutch,

English and Spanish. He takes us deep into the bowels of the stadium, and inside the home dressing room which is much larger and more comfortable than the visitors' equivalent. We pass the photos of Ajax's Dutch international contingent and mementos of other great players and managers of the past, and I'm surprised to learn that the pioneering club of the Dutch style and system of football has on a number of occasions been managed by Englishmen. I cany help wondering, when I see the anglicised names on the plaques in amongst the Van Gaal's and the Rinus Michels's - great English coaches, what the fuck ever happened to them?

We're up near the royal box, patiently waiting for the translation to switch to English so we can learn about the retractable roof and how the grass has to be watered and occasionally bathed in electronic light, at great expense. It makes you wonder, what was the point of the roof in the first place if you have to maintain an artificial environment most of the time? I think some salesman must have done a good job on them, because the problems of the roof seem to outweigh the benefits. Nobody wants to interrupt Markus though as he continues to ply us with an impressive amount of information and data on Ajax's history. It's all very interesting, even the statistical overload doesny seem to dampen Lenka's enthusiasm and curiosity and the other Celtic fans on the tour seem to be absorbing all the facts and figures diligently and quietly, which I suppose for Celtic fans makes a pleasant change. After the tour of the ground we make our way back into town and I take Lenka on a posh ride round the Herengracht to make up for the fact that she wasny really paying attention on the earlier boat trip. It's late and we're pretty drained by the time we head back to our hotel at the end of an exhausting but remarkable day.

Day three is the day of the game; first up though we're at the Rijksmuseum in the morning. Much of the building is still under renovation but enough of the restoration work has been completed to allow the museum to be partially accessible, to gullible tourists like us at any rate. I don't detect too many of the locals queuing up in the rain alongside us, I think the Dutch themselves are happy to wait, holding themselves back for the big reboot. Giant screens attached to the building and facing out onto the square count down the number of 'Night Watches' remaining until the formal reopening of the museum, when the story of their nation's history can be retold in full. I'm afraid me and Lenka areny operating on that sort ay timescale, so we're in wi the foreigners and the day trippers. I must admit, I find the whole history of Holland as it's presented here totally fascinating. Once again, as with the Historical Museum, the main focus falls on the seventeenth century after the Dutch had their reformist revolution, known as the Alteration. There was no violence though, no gruesome sectarian executions, the end of established Catholicism in the Netherlands saw the nuns and priests simply escorted down to the canal banks and put on boats. Where exactly they went after that is anybody's guess, but the new era which followed saw the Dutch republic become one of the most influential countries in the world, largely on the back of their capacity for trade, but there also ensued an extraordinary flourishing of style and culture, especially art. The monarchy had been overthrown and the country was now ruled by burghers, who introduced this Dutch idea of civic responsibility. They also competed with one another to be the patrons and commissioners of renowned painters, because this was the time of Rembrandt, Vermeer and the other famed Dutch masters. You never know what might have happened if the country had remained Catholic, but I'm no sure if the Church would have approved of Rembrandt depicting himself as St. Paul.

What strikes me though is the obvious difference between Dutch Protestantism and the British variety, which I'm obviously more familiar with. In Holland, it helped to bring about and define a new era of cultural expression and self-confidence, whereas in Britain you had the Calvinists and the Puritans, who despised art. This in turn led to a very static culture in Britain, rather than a dynamic one, and you can see that today in areas where staunch Protestantism still thrives; this stagnancy in the culture has resulted in the preservation right down to the present day of attitudes and beliefs that come straight out of the seventeenth century. In many ways it's an admirable achievement, to maintain the same doctrines and principles down the generations over a period of several centuries, but of course the rest of the world has moved on. Back in the day, the whole of Britain shared the same raging, febrile hostility towards Catholicism, but there are only remnant enclaves of that mentality left today. I must admit, I've gained a healthy respect for the reforming zeal of the Dutch Protestants this afternoon. The reforms in the Low Countries were principled, modern and, as always with the Dutch, eminently sensible, and by and large they helped to make Holland the tolerant and liberal country that it is today. At the same time though, I've lost any lingering vestiges of forbearance I may have held towards the bigoted sections of our own society, and I'm determined to evince a less diffident and sanguine attitude towards these issues when we discuss them on the programme, as we surely will, because of course we're talking to no small degree about football here. At the same time it goes without saying that I'll need to sharpen up my own act and cut out the kind of trivial and petty observations that I was making at the Westerkerk yesterday, the like of which West of Scotland Tims like myself have a tendency to indulge in too readily perhaps, but that's a step I feel I can take without too much difficulty.

While we're still in the museum, and trying to appreciate what the whole place is revealing to us, I resolve to be a bit more grown up from now on, no just for the benefit of a television audience, but in the rest of my life as well. We eventually emerge onto the Museumplein once more and have a coffee out on the square. I'm feeling a bit like I used to as a child, whenever I came out the pictures after seeing a great film, emerging into the all too familiar Glasgow rain and wondering what the rest of the world had been up to while I was being transported inside. Lenka and I resolve to come back here, when the place has properly reopened, and experience it all once more.

We take an early dinner in a canalside restaurant and then at last we're off to the football, which comes as a blessed relief after all the tourism we've been doing. We ride out on the train to the Bijlmer Arena again, with one obvious difference from the trip yesterday; this time the place is packed out with Celtic and Ajax fans. There's a few Celtic songs in the air, which is nice to hear and adds to the atmosphere and the sense of occasion. The pockets of Celtic boys are vastly outnumbered, but they're determined to enjoy themselves and for the most part the Ajax fans are happy to leave them to it. I'm relieved there's no hint of trouble in the air because there's quite a naughty element sometimes associated with Dutch supporters these days, and you certainly need to watch out for their plain clothes Polis, because it's a well-attested fact that they're a shower ay cunts. But only occasionally are individual fans intervening here, which is when the banter and laughter breaks out. Lenka and I are looking pretty inconspicuous, we're not in the Celtic end so we try to blend in as we make our way into the now familiar stadium, thanks to yesterday's tour, and take our seats.

The game kicks off and Ajax are immediately on the front foot; the club has a style of play which they're renowned for and they set about imposing their game on Celtic in a manner which assures me that the players are all familiar with their roles and the pattern of play. Celtic cany seem to get out, and when Ajax score after twenty minutes the only surprise seems to be that the opening goal has taken so long in coming. Lenka is clearly sensing my growing frustration and she sympathetically heads off up the stairs to the bar to buy me a beer.

Yes, she buys me a beer.

We have a ten Euro card that we bought yesterday on the tour, and the system they use, ingeniously, involves exchanging credit on the card for plastic cups of beer, so no cash changes hand during the sale. The system seems to work and at half-time, I encourage Lenka to take pictures on her phone of me inside a football stadium with a cup of beer in my hand. Then our friendly Dutch neighbours and fellow patrons offer to take more pictures of the pair ay us drinking alcohol in a football ground, and everybody seems to be having a great time. I imagine myself posting the pictures on social media when I get home, underlining the images with witty captions and observations, such as 'Fan drinks beer inside a football ground, no violence ensues', 'Person consumes alcohol in football stadium, stewards and police nowhere to be seen' and 'Note to SFA: Find out how this system works, see how they do things in other countries, and introduce the policy in Scotland'. My idealistic speculations are only cut short when I remember that I don't use social media, because it's for fuckin twallies.

Instead I have a better idea; the notebook comes out and I start scribbling down my thoughts on the subject. And I don't stop there. Celtic are two nothing down here after forty-five minutes, and the frustrating thing is, the team don't seem to have any coherent game plan. This is a Champions League qualifier we're watching, no a preseason friendly and at the moment it looks like there's only one team that's gony be qualifying for the group stages. I know that I agreed at the start of this holiday, that I was gony relish and enjoy the break for its own sake, immerse myself in the present and no think about what happens when I return home, but I've decided to change my mind, and during the interval I start taking more notes on football related matters. I'm a fan in a fortunate position, one who's going to be able to air his views on national media in a forum where I'm in control of the discussion and I can at least ask the questions that I want to hear answered. So I decide that I better take advantage of the opportunity and get my thoughts down on paper, so the note-taking continues as the football resumes. I'm surprised to see that Celtic have upped their game in the second period, and they set about playing a high tempo brand of half decent football, which the home team struggles to cope with at times. Midway through the half Celtic pull a goal back, a precious away goal as well and one that puts a totally different complexion on the tie. It makes me wonder what's going on here and why we didny have the necessary belief to play like this in the first half.

The problem seems to be that, unlike their opponents, Celtic don't have any default system of play. When they're pushed into a corner or are sparked into action, after getting their arses kicked at half time or whatever, then they're capable of playing some positive and effective football, and imposing their style on their opponents. But there's no set pattern, which they're trying to impose on the other team from the start. It's clear what the Ajax way is, but it's not quite so clear exactly what the modern Celtic method involves. It's another argument for the link between football and culture in my eyes, the Dutch play sensibly, which is what you expect; the Czech teams that I've seen always try to play correctly, again reflecting their character. Scottish teams seem confused as to what they're supposed to be doing, which is inexcusable in many ways because the traditional "Celtic way" of inventive, attacking football was a match for any team and any system in its day. But we don't seem to have adapted that style to the modern game and it's reactive football that we're playing now. Celtic need to discover an effective methodology, a modern variant of the "Celtic way", then learn that style meticulously from every youth level through to the first team, and set about imposing their distinctive approach on every opponent they come up against. That's how you develop a system of play. I'm furiously taking notes at this point, scribbling down my random thoughts as they occur to me … must adapt Celtic way to modern game …

could apply to whole of Scot foot …

TELEVISION!...

in the past teams played their traditional systems and styles against foreign opponents, didn't know any better!... Now we all watch each other on **TELEVISION!**...

teams from different countries familiar with each other's style of play, cross border influences etc ….

adapt Celtic way to the modern game, i.e. trad. "Celtic way" with a modern twist … take it out onto the wider stage, show it off to the world and see how effective it is, cf. Barcelona!! Ajax!! Etc, etc.

So much for my expressed desire to forget all about my impending new career in television, that's well and truly out the window now. Still I did well, we've had a wonderful trip to Amsterdam and for the most part I managed to relax and enjoy myself and stay in the moment for a few days at least, it was only when we found ourselves at the football that I got carried away. Coming here was a great idea, it's been a useful and enjoyable exercise, and who knows? With the scoreline balanced at 2 – 1 after ninety minutes, Celtic might still have a chance of qualifying for the group stages.

We head back to our hotel after the most tiring day of the trip yet. Lenka crawls into our freshly made up bed and crashes out almost immediately. There's no question of any fun and games the night it seems, because she's already asleep and I'm far too tired as well. Anyway, I think we've already managed to nail that theory about hotel sex pretty much, I would suggest, beyond all reasonable doubt.

11. THE FIRST EPISODE

PETER: *Hello and welcome to the first edition of our brand new programme, 'The Scottish Football Debate' which is a show that, well ... it pretty much does what it says on the tin really. Each week we'll be debating the hot topics in Scottish football with an honesty, a boldness and indeed a level of intellectual rigour which you may not have heard before in many other outlets. We'll select a broad theme for every show, relevant to the burning footballing issues of the day, and we'll be discussing it until you're blue in the face hearing about it basically. And we certainly won't be shirking any challenges or bottling any important decisions. I'm sure many of you watching at home who are of a certain age will remember the old Rikki Fulton sketch about the talking dog who refused to discuss either politics or religion. Well, there'll be none of that on this show – there are no taboos, no no-go areas. We'll talk about anything you like, providing of course that it's relevant to the matter in hand. Joining us in the studio every week will be former Rangers and Motherwell defender Martin Dodds and ex-Celtic captain Davie Keane. Gentlemen, good evening.*

DAVIE: *Hi, Peter.*

DODDSY: *Hi, Peter. A brand new show, I like that! Wee bit ay confidence to start off wi, great stuff!*

PETER: *I see what you've done there, Doddsy, a nice Scottish play on words straight off the bat, that's the spirit, but I was meaning brand new in the literal sense of the phrase. I wouldn't presume to make any extravagant claims as to the quality or popularity of the show at this early stage, ultimately it will be for the viewers to decide if we're any good or not. Anyway guys, what are going to talk about this week?*

DAVIE: *Pick a subject, Peter!*

DODDSY: *Only one place to start, it seems to me.*

PETER: *Well OK, now you come to mention it, lads, let's talk about the national team, shall we? For anyone who's been living on Mars for the last week or so, allow me to summarise; Scotland once again failed to qualify for the World Cup in the summer, and the new campaign doesn't seem to have got off to a much better start either, as we've just lost our opening game of the Euro qualifiers to opposition Scotland would have summarily dismissed in the short time since you guys were playing the game, not to mention the heyday of Souness, Dalglish, Johnstone and the rest. In addition, even at this early stage of the season, all our club teams have already been knocked out of European competition. So can somebody please tell me, where did it all go wrong for Scottish football? Davie, you first, mate, can you enlighten us here?*

DAVIE: *I'm afraid the decline of Scottish football is a long, sorry story of arrogance, complacency, neglect, greed, any one of the seven deadly sins in fact you care to mention. It doesny matter, we've been guilty of them all at one time or another, and now it seems that the years we've squandered are finally starting to catch up wi us.*

PETER: *Doddsy, I'm aware there's a tendency in Scotland to see a kind of national narrative accompanying, if not quite the complete demise, then certainly the decline I think was the word Davie used, of our game here. Leaving that aside for a minute, if there are indeed numerous and complicated causes for the general malaise, can we at least try and identify some of those causes in order that hopefully we might be able to do something about them?*

DODDSY: *Can we start wi lust? That's always been ma favourite deadly sin.*

PETER: *You can start wherever you like, Doddsy, the floor is yours.*

DODDSY: *I think the main contributing factor, or at least one of the main yins, is the fact that kids areny playing the*

194

game in the same numbers now as what they used to. When the likes ay me and Davie were growing up there would be weans on every street corner wi a baw, kicking it aboot in their free time. If they couldny afford a baw, then it would be an empty can ay coke, a stone, a pair ay ladies' undies, you name it, it didny matter. Young kids were playing football to all hours ay the day, and hawf the night as well, developing their talent on street corners the length and breadth ay the land. That's where I honed my skills, and fae there I was fortunate enough to be able to progress to playing the game I love professionally.

DAVIE: *You haveny progressed at all, Doddsy, you're still chasing ladies' undies to this day.*

Laughter.

— He has to justify that and expand on it. Ask him about technique, Helen instructs me in my earpiece. — Great start by the way, she adds softly.

PETER: *Is that one reason why modern Scottish players are perhaps technically inferior to their counterparts of yesteryear, the lack of football being played nowadays by youngsters in the parks and on street corners?*

DODDSY: *There's something in that, Peter, I believe, aye. But at times I think we dae oursels a disservice by harping on about technique aw the time. Our game has never been technically that brilliant, it's fair to say. Never. Here, I'll gie you an example; the great Aberdeen team that won the European Cup Winners Cup back in the eighties - Franz Beckenbauer said that they were technically no better than Bielefeld, a team that Bayern Munich had just gubbed five nothing. A few days later Aberdeen went out and knocked his side out the competition. You don't get marks for technical merit in fitba, we're no talking about ice skating here. It was other qualities that Aberdeen used to win that competition, and that's what I feel we need to get back tae.*

PETER: *Davie, do you agree?*

DAVIE: *To an extent, yes. There are important qualities in football other than technical ability, but I disagree that our game has never been about technique. It's always been one ay the first things they test you out on as a youngster, when you go for a trial or an assessment. It's technique that young lads are developing when they kick a ball about on street corners. When I was a kid playing wi Celtic boys club the first thing the coaches did was throw you a ball and see if you could control it. If you couldny trap the ball you were sent away. The basics remain the same at any level ay the game. But Doddsy's right when he refers to other qualities, which we used to have in abundance, but sadly we don't seem to possess them to the same extent that we used to.*

— I want to hear more about the seven deadly sins, what is it that we're doing wrong in our game?

PETER: *I'll ask you about those qualities in a minute, Davie, but first I'd like you to expand for us what you were saying at the top of the show. What are the faults that have crept into our game since you made the breakthrough at Celtic as a young lad?*

DAVIE: *Where do you want me to start? I mentioned a number ay faults.*

— That's up to him, tell him. Only help him out if he needs it.

PETER: *Whichever one you feel most strongly about. You mentioned greed, I assume you were referring to the amount of money in the game. Has the game been undermined by finances, do you think?*

DAVIE: *I think it has yes, without question. Look, I wouldny criticise any player or coach for wanting to make a decent living from the game. There are increased amounts of revenue available to players now and I for one was lucky enough to benefit from that, certainly towards the end of my playing days. The guys who were just retiring as I was breaking through from the Youth teams never made a fraction of the money that I earned from the game, and we're talking about great players now. But I believe that it's the culture of money, rather than the money itself, which has fatally undermined the game North ay the border. And it isny immediately clear to me how we retrieve the situation, in the short term anyway.*

PETER: *Are you saying that we might go the way of the Hungarians, and perhaps we'll never return to the era of our glory days?*

DAVIE: *Possibly, although I'm not sure we were ever as good as the Hungarians of the fifties.*

PETER: *True enough. And we don't have Khrushchev about to send in the tanks. A lot of people think it was Stalin who ordered the invasion of Hungary in 1956, but in fact it was Khrushchev.*

DODDSY: *Is that right?*

PETER: *It is as a matter of fact. Stalin had been dead three years by then.*

— Interesting point about money, get it back and expand, my earpiece informs me.

PETER: *Anyway, that was an interesting point you made, Davie, about the culture of money. Can you give us an example to illustrate what you're telling us?*

I glance at the monitor and notice that Davie is in full profile, a talking head about to share his wisdom with the watching nation, so I take the opportunity to send a silent, gestured signal to the gallery to tell them to stop holding my hand so much and talking me through every question and answer. And if I want to show off how erudite I am, and that I know something about a subject other than football, I feel that I'm perfectly entitled, even if it's only a few short weeks since I was convinced it was Stalin right enough that sent the tanks into Hungary. Still, that's something the audience will never know.

DAVIE: *I think we suffer in a financial sense, particularly in comparison to our English neighbours. We can't compete with them off the park in terms of revenue. On the park I think we've proved down the decades, in the historical matches we used to play against England, that we were able to match them all the way. And if you look at the results between Scotland and England that's exactly what we did, right up to the point when the fixture was discontinued. Even with a smaller population we were able to compete in footballing terms, but now that financial considerations have become so predominant off the park, our football has become a mini-me version of the English game, derided for its lack ay quality, smaller stadiums and its relatively meagre resources. And we seem to have just accepted our new found inferiority; we've lost our defiance, our fighting spirit, our distinctiveness and our character. As I say, instead of a worthy and respected rival, we're just a poor man's version of the English game now.*

PETER: *And I suppose, because we're constantly after a slice from their banquet, that's where the greed comes in, undermining our own way of doing things.*

— Nice metaphor, Peter, I'm congratulated. I check again that I'm off camera before sending out a 'see, I know what I'm doing here' sideways glance in the direction of the gallery.

DAVIE: *I think that has a lot to do wi it, Peter, yes. Just like the English, we've made our game all about money. But whereas in England money is the secret of their success, because they're rolling in it, up here it's our greatest weakness, because we've barely got two bob bits to rub thegether. In copying the English and introducing the culture of money into our game, we've made the fatal mistake of making our football all about our greatest weakness, ignoring and fatally undermining our strengths at the same time.*

PETER: *Doddsy, would you agree? The culture of money,*

rather than the money itself has contributed to our downfall.

DODDSY: *Erm, yes and no. I can see where Davie's coming from, but I don't really see how you separate the two. I must admit, I love the money in the game. I've benefitted from it enormously, like Davie has, I'm honest enough to admit that as well. I still point to the fact that kids areny playing the game in the same numbers as what they used to. The pool has shrunk and there's less talent to choose from. The youngsters are aw playing computer games now, that's how there's an obesity crisis in this country.*

DAVIE: *I think you can separate the two, Doddsy; we have a culture of money in our game up here, just no the actual money to justify it. That cany be right. But I'd agree wi your second point, participation levels are an issue all right, but they're no the main problem. Don't they have computer games in Spain?*

PETER: *Well, I feel that brings us back to the perennial issue of technique, doesn't it? Our players are simply technically deficient in comparison to footballers from other countries such as Spain. Is that not the case?*

DAVIE: *As I stated earlier, you need to have players who are technically proficient, that's an absolute necessity. But this leads us back to the point we were making about other virtues. We play Northern European football in this country, which is fast and dynamic and has an element of trial and error about it. If we try and copy the way they play in Spain, then we'll step away from our natural game and we'll lose. Certainly against Spain we will anyway, because unsurprisingly they play the Spanish way far better than we ever will. The most important thing for any national team is to find a talented bunch of players and then get them to play in a way they believe in and they're comfortable with. That's where you get that clash, that competition from, between the way the best players in one country play against the best players of another country; the two sets of players then fight it out using the style of football*

199

they've learned and been brought up with, and the best team will win in a natural and normal way. That's what European and international football is all about. Collectively and individually you have to believe in your own methodology, and then have the confidence to go and inflict it on the opposition in a way that they might no be used to, and they struggle to cope with.

PETER: *Just so we don't misunderstand you, Davie, you're not saying technique isn't important, you're saying we suffer from some form of inferiority complex regarding our players' level of technique, and that lack of confidence undermines their other qualities?*

DAVIE: *Look, do you know what they say in Brazil when they lose? They say Brazilians cany defend. It's just contrary to their natural instincts, and players from other countries understand this side of the game far better than they do. Almost every defeat Brazil suffer is accompanied by much wailing and gnashing of teeth, lamenting the fact that the old failures have reared their ugly head once again, and nobody ever does anything about it. Sound familiar? Just goes to show, even the strongest countries have their inferiority complexes. In Scotland our failings are all attributed to a lack of technique, but it's a gross oversimplification. We produce skilful and technically adept players just as Brazil produce great defenders, one just moved to Barcelona for gazillions of pounds during the summer. I say again though, that's not the problem; the problem stems from a lack ay confidence in our own methodology.*

DODDSY: *That's dead right, what Davie's saying is one hundred percent correct; that there are other qualities in football that can overcome technique.*

— Don't forget our strengths, you were going to bring it back to talk about them. We're focusing too much on the negatives here.

PETER: *That can complement, rather than overcome technique, is I believe the point Davie was making.*

— Actually you need to take us to the highlights package, we can bring it back to a discussion about our strengths after the interlude.

DAVIE: *Exactly.*

PETER: *OK, we've talked enough about our weaknesses, or our perceived weaknesses, what about our strengths? We'll be talking about them shortly, but first it's time to hide behind the couch once more, because we're going to have a look at the highlights from the Lithuania game at the weekend. Run VT.*

— VT? This is the twenty-first century you know.

— Sorry, I thought I'd told yous already, it's my catchphrase, I explain, amid much guffawing and shaking of heads in the gallery and on the set.

As the highlights are being shown Davie and Doddsy are watching and commenting on the game, lamenting the litany of shoddy defending and poor finishing from the Scots. It occurs to me, not for the first time, how much the media can potentially benefit from sporting failure. I mean, we've devoted a whole show to this fiasco, but if Scotland had won the game, I'm no sure what we'd be talking about right now. We certainly wouldny have been presented with such an obvious topic, and one so urgently needing addressed. Aw this heartfelt, emotional discussion makes for great television, but in our case the difference is, we want to intervene and help the national game, that's our mission on this show, delusional and naïve as it may appear to some. Certain other outlets want to wallow in all this misery and defeat, because it makes their audiences more vulnerable to suggestion. If they can convince people that their way of doing things will provide a road to recovery or a viable alternative to erroneous practices, then pressure will be exerted on the relevant authorities and the people and organisations making these suggestions will become relevant, and subsequently will find themselves in a better position to be able to influence policy and wield power. That's basically how the media works in this country, it seems to me, whether we're talking about sport or politics or any other sphere. It goes way beyond mere commercial considerations, these foreign media moguls are already aw billionaires anyway. The bottom line is important but ultimately power and influence is their primary concern, and if you set that against the fluctuating fortunes of the national football team of a small semi-state off the North-west coast of Europe, then there's only gony be one winner. Unfortunately that's the reality of what we're up against here, but it also gives us an angle because our agenda is to be positive and show faith in our Scottish methodology, as Davie alluded to, and hopefully people will respond to that.

— All yours, Peter.

PETER: *It's alright children, you can come out now and open your eyes again, it's all over. Doddsy, it's for other shows perhaps to pour over the individual errors and the specific failings that led to this defeat, we needn't go over it all again here. But I'd like to focus more generally on the other qualities you were mentioning earlier, the other virtues, which you were implying we instinctively possess in Scotland. Based on the evidence of what we've just seen, what are those qualities and how can they serve us going forward?*

DODDSY: *We're no arrogant. Arrogance is a weakness in sport as well as in life, but we're fortunate that on the whole we don't succumb to it.*

PETER: *You're right, nobody likes arrogance but you can go too far the other way though, can't you? We were talking a minute ago about lack of self-belief in our own methods, that's a danger as well, is it not? Sometimes it can do you good to strut your stuff a wee bit, surely.*

DODDSY: *In Scotland we call that gallusness, Peter. Be*

gallus but don't be arrogant, strut your stuff but don't lose your heid in the clouds. Football here is in the tradition ay the working man's game so always respect that, even if you're no from a working-class background yourself. Remember that these are the guys who made Scottish fitba great, your Johnstones, your Dalglishes, your Jim Baxters. They were aw gallus but they were down tae earth at the same time, that's the secret.

DAVIE: *It's about making your arrogance appealing to other people. Whether it's the French flair at rugby, or the way the Dutch play football or the swagger of the West Indian cricketers in their pomp. That's all arrogance, but the viewing public love it. This is something in England they struggle to come to terms with at times, they don't know how to make their arrogance attractive to other people. But we do, as Doddsy said, and we give it a name. Think of the gallus way that Celtic destroyed Inter Milan when they won the European Cup. It changed European football forever. That's a great strength in our game.*

PETER: *Davie, do the media allow us to emphasise this point about the working-class roots of Scottish football?*

DAVIE: *Are we allowed to talk about this, Peter?*

PETER: *Yes!*

DAVIE: *Oh good, just checking, because there are other shows where this would never even be brought up.*

PETER: *Thanks for pointing that out to our audience, Davie!*

DAVIE: *Haha yes, well it's worth pointing out. The answer to your question is no, not in a meaningful way. The media don't emphasise this aspect of our football any more, they pander to the working man, but they don't share his concerns. We hear clichés like 'up and at em', and 'get in their faces', but that was never what Scottish football was about in the first place, not at the top level anyway. Large sections of the media would rather not emphasise this aspect of our football at all, in fact more the opposite I would say. They want to drag our football onto their turf so that they can redefine it in terms that conform more readily to their own agendas. If you look at the coverage of football and cricket on Sky Sports for example, it's exactly the same. They give both sports the same treatment even though football and cricket come from very different traditions and have their own unique history and character. The fact that the media have been very successful at these practices hasn't been reflected in success on the field; rather the opposite in fact, and to my mind it has contributed to the disastrous decline of our game.*

— That's a topic for another show, four minutes isn't nearly enough to do a subject like that justice. Get it back to other reasons for the declining standards.

PETER: *Interesting point, Davie, it's a complicated issue. But I'm sure you're right in saying that the increased power and role of the media in sport has reshaped the very nature of sport itself, and not always in a positive way. We'll certainly want to talk about that more maybe in the weeks and months ahead but we don't have a lot of time left. Can we briefly come up with some other reasons for the apparent decline in Scottish football and, if possible in the time we have remaining tonight, determine what are the strengths and virtues that we possess, and are we optimistic that those strengths can be used to restore the fortunes of our game? Doddsy?*

DODDSY: *It's related to what Davie was saying about the media, but I reckon there's too much football on the television now. That's a problem for us. We watch football from Germany, Spain, Italy, England and inevitably we see aw these great players, aw these great sides and we try and copy them. But it's unrealistic to think that our teams can knock the ball about like Barcelona, that only leads to the kind of inferiority complex we were talking about earlier. When I was playing in a big European game wi Rangers, we never studied too much about the other teams' tactics. The manager maybe said a few words to us, but basically we just went and played the way we always played and left the opposition to deal wi it. Now we're much more familiar with foreign football because it's on the telly every night, so we try and figure out how to neutralise it. And since these teams are seen as better than us, our game's become more defensive, because we lack the confidence to play our natural game.*

PETER: *Davie?*

DAVIE: *Brilliant point. It's true to say that we've lost our defiance, always a key part of our game, particularly in those struggles against England we were talking about earlier and against other big countries. Against smaller countries we've always had a problem, because how do you play wi defiance against Iran or Costa Rica? The answer is you go and do a professional job on them, inflict your natural game on them and see how they cope.*

PETER: *So to conclude, are we optimistic or pessimistic for the future of our game? And what about the Scotland manager, he's coming under a lot of pressure now. I'm not sure we want to be associated with these kind of witch-hunts on this show, but can he be a part of a better future for our game?*

DODDSY: *He's coming under pressure but he's got friends in the media so that'll help him. He won't lose his job because of this result, but we all know it's a results business and there needs to be an improvement. Overall I would say that I was pessimistic, because the problems we've been discussing are deep-rooted in our game now and you cany just wave a magic wand and make them go away.*

DAVIE: *I don't want to say too much about the manager because he's an honest guy and he's doing his best. But we need to think our way out of the current malaise, because answers areny just gony jump up and make themselves apparent to us, when the problems are so deep-rooted, as Doddsy says. We need people in charge who can analyse what the problems are and come up with solutions that can answer those challenges. I'm no sure this guy has the capability to do that, although it shouldny be his sole responsibility. It needs to come from the top and the manager needs help behind the scenes wi that aspect. Unfortunately his bosses are all bottom line financial people, rather than football people, and that feeds back into the problems we were mentioning earlier. Overall though I would say I was probably more optimistic than Doddsy, because we're a football mad country and the key strengths in our game haveny gone away. We just need to rediscover them and if we do, you'll be surprised how quickly things can fall into place, and a bad series of results can be turned round in a relatively short period of time, even with the players we currently have at our disposal.*

PETER: *OK, well on that note, I think we'll have to leave it there for this week. I hope you've all enjoyed the show, it's been a very entertaining and enjoyable discussion. My thanks to the boys, Davie and Doddsy, for their insight and expertise. We'll be back again next week with another illuminating discussion on a key aspect of our national game. I hope you can tune in then. In the meantime, keep enjoying your football and we'll see you again soon. Goodnight.*

— Roll credits, and … we're clear.

— Just one or two pick-ups, if you could remain in your seats please, gentlemen. Thank you.

— That was terrific everyone, well done.

— Wow! That was half an hour? It felt like about ten minutes to me, I confess jubilantly.

12. REFEREES POST MORTEM

— Didny think it would take very long afore we seen you again, Campbell, Doddsy slaps Thomson on the back as the former referee climbs into a low seat in the dingy, city-centre hostelry. The pub is well chosen for its isolation and hidden entrances, the dim lighting and effortless sophistication of the place only adding to my perception of it as a secret hideaway for media types and other minor celebrities. The reality though is probably more mundane. Despite its Charing Cross location, the pub is not well sign-posted in a deliberate attempt to avoid any unwelcome overspill or accidental association with the studentsville carnage of Sauchiehall Street, just the other side ay the motorway. — We should book him a regular slot every Monday, Helen, Doddsy suggests. — He could come in for every show and tell us how the refs have cocked up aw the major decisions again this week.

— I'm just happy to help, Thomson shrugs, — I must admit, I didny think it would be too long before you were on the phone tae me again, inviting me in to dae a real show this time, and no just a pilot or whatever it is you call it.

— And whose fault is that? Doddsy wonders. — Come on, Campbell, we're aff the air noo, you can drop aw that blaming the media nonsense. How are the media to blame this time for aw the mistakes we seen at the weekend? You were at it again the night wi that shite, you're no gony carry that on in here, are you?

— I wasny blaming the media, Martin, you should have been listening to what I was saying, brother, Thomson points out. — The coverage is far more intrusive these days than it ever was in the past, and mistakes are easy to highlight. That's aw I was trying to bring to your attention. But like I say, I'm happy to help. I'm part ay the media masel now, in my own small way, and if I think a referee has made a mistake, there's nae chance I'm gony go public and try to defend his decision.

I hope you're starting to gain an appreciation noo of the way that I like to play it, how I try to balance up any justified criticisms wi defending particular officials. I see it as my role to stick up for the refereeing fraternity, despite the occasional error, because if I don't dae it, who else is gony?

— Well you certainly done a grand job ay that the night, Campbell, I chip in, leaving his last question unanswered.

— Aye, no thanks to yous. Like I says, you need to gie us a bit ay leeway here. Hopefully yous'll dae that, once you gain a better understanding of the way I like to play it, he repeats his earlier assertion, the awkwardness of his turn ay phrase only jarring on me even more the second time.

— The way that you like to play it? Are you sure your name's no Alistair Campbell Thomson? I remark amid much guffawing and shaking of heads. You don't like to gang up on a guy but already Thomson is starting to stick out like a sore thumb here, with his attempts to sound media savvy, in the company of a bunch of industry insiders, not appearing too convincing or being particularly well received. He's being more than a touch presumptuous as well. Despite the apparent inevitability of more refereeing howlers in the weeks and months ahead, there's nothing to indicate Thomson will ever be asked back on the programme, in which case we'll never have the opportunity to gain a deeper understanding of exactly what he means by 'the way that he likes to play it', in his quest to defend the indefensible in support of referees.

— That reminds me, where's that Davie Keane bastard? I want a word wi that cunt. Thomson's outburst is greeted with mystified silence, not so much at Davie's continued absence, which I think is starting to puzzle quite a few ay us, so much as his glaringly obvious lack ay respect for a legend of the Scottish game, no to mention a good friend of everyone who works on the show. True, I think Davie probably laid it on pretty thick during the recording tonight, haranguing Thomson in a more persistent and sustained manner than we had rehearsed only a few weeks ago during the pilot, not just about the individual errors which had once again decided a tight and important game in Rangers' favour this weekend, but also about the broader mentality within refereeing. He had berated Thomson about officials who had previously been season ticket holders at Ibrox being put in charge of Rangers' games and then awarding baffling decisions in that club's favour, recent examples of which had all been well-attested and documented, if not regularly commented upon in the mainstream media. Thomson was becoming more and more uncomfortable, and was left groping around for a suitable riposte as Davie continued his assault, claiming that referees and officials not only needed to be impartial, they needed to be seen to be impartial too, something which these episodes demonstrated they had singularly failed to do in recent times, at least as far as he was concerned anyway. Davie's attack on the flawed and complacent culture within refereeing in Scotland concluded when he pointed out that he had heard rumours of retired referees attending various Rangers supporters' functions and boasting to their audience about their exploits with regard to dubious decisions they'd given in the club's favour. Thomson had managed to rally by this point and seemed determined to recover his composure, but the ex-ref was once more left tongue-tied and floundering when Davie co-opted Doddsy into his allegation, the ex-Gers' defender quite sanguinely admitting that he had regularly attended such events.

— I'm sure Davie will be along soon, Helen remarks as many of the rest ay us stare into our drinks, or regard the ceiling with apparent fascination, or otherwise find oursels indulging in an exercise of gaze-avoidance syndrome, as we vainly try to kid on that we haveny heard what Thomson said.

— Cheers darling, Thomson tells Lenka as she returns from the bar with a tray of drinks. — Bit ay awright there, he nudges me, inspecting Lenka's arse as she continues to unload the glasses from the tray. — I'm sure I seen her the other day on the side ay a building somewhere, advertising underwear.

— I think I'd know about it if you had, Campbell mate, I tell him, as with perfect dramatic timing Lenka hands me my drink last of all and returns my change, before planting a kiss on my cheek and taking her seat next to me, holding my hand.

— Oh sorry, brother, I thought she was the sound lassie.

— Haha! Put your foot in it there, Tommo, Doddsy laughs at him. — Cheers, Lenka sweetheart, he raises his glass to her.

— I see, it's like that is it? Thomson regards me scornfully. — You've no had your face on the telly five fuckin minutes and already you've picked yoursel up a nice wee dolly bird. Congratulations, pal, some ay us areny that shallow, you know.

— We've been married nearly two years now, Campbell, I tell him flatly.

— Have you, aye?

— Keep digging, Campbell, keep digging bud, Doddsy mocks him gleefully. — Never mind advertising underwear on the side ay buildings, he adds, — I'm sure I seen your wife recently on the side ay a box ay Sugar Puffs, Tommo.

— Aye, yis are aw so fuckin funny, Thomson laments, once the laughter has finally died away.

— Looks like you're all enjoying yourselves anyway, Gus McGregor arrives and pulls up a chair at our table. — If I could just interrupt, maybe I should kick things off? After acknowledging the customary greetings, McGregor is keen to get started on the evening's formal business. — How do we think the show went tonight then? Helen, any thoughts? he asks initially.

— It went remarkably well once again, it seemed to me, Helen coughs, quickly recovering her professionalism after the ineptness of Thomson's various interventions. — I had the strange feeling in fact, that I'd seen this particular show somewhere before, she suggests.

— You may well have. The audience haven't though, that's the only thing that matters. What about the presenter, how did he see it?

— I think it went really smoothly, I nod, smiling diffidently at being referred to in the third person in this way. — The fact that we'd gamed out a lot of the discussion a few weeks earlier obviously helped, I add, un-selfconsciously adopting some the jargon I'd heard flying about the office in recent weeks. — At least it helped me, I cany speak for anybody else.

— Campbell was a bit unhappy about some of the things Davie Keane was saying, Helen reminds us, bringing Thomson's presence to McGregor's attention in a calculated manner. Her words are accompanied by an unambiguous gesture in the boss' direction, signalled discreetly from beyond Campbell's eyeline.

— I'm sorry, Campbell, should you still be here? Gus immediately picks up on Helen's unsubtle gesticulations and wastes no time in quickly latching onto the mood music. — This is a contracted employees only discussion, he informs the ref.

— I was under the impression that I could hang about.

— Not for the de-brief, I'm afraid.

— What? I was told this would aw be very informal. I'm enjoying masel here, this is a celebration for me too, you know. I far prefer the real thing to that pilot malarkey. I was hoping I could stick around for a while, maybe see what's what, and take it fae there. We're aw enjoying oursels, sure we are, troops?

— Aw the women here are taken, Campbell, Doddsy correctly informs him.

— Aye, but once I've had a few more whiskies …

— Goodbye, Campbell, thanks for your contribution this evening, McGregor dismisses him.

— My God, it's no hard to see why referees aren't always the most popular people in the world, is it? Helen observes, once the former whistler has finally buggered off.

— Speaking of Davie Keane, I have some bad news, Gus resumes the discussion. — Davie won't be continuing with us on the show, I'm afraid. Tonight was his last appearance on The Scottish Football Debate.

Stunned looks all round.

— Why not? What's happened? I eventually manage to articulate my shock and disappointment.

— It seems he's received a better offer. He's accepted a post as technical director with Celtic football club. Apparently he's been given carte blanche to restructure the club's entire youth development system from the bottom up. It was always in his contract that he could leave if he was offered a coaching role, and this position has only recently become available. We had to iron out one or two of the details, as our lawyers pointed out that it wasn't exactly a coaching role he was being offered, strictly speaking. But we certainly didn't want to stand in his way and it's all been resolved very amicably, just in the last few minutes in fact. That's why I was late. Davie has asked me to pass on his best regards to everyone and he wishes us all the very best with the show going forward, McGregor concluded.

My initial horror and disbelief at the news of Davie's departure was quickly replaced with a strange sense of euphoria. From what I knew of the man in the short time since I'd met him, it seemed that Davie had landed himself the perfect job, not to mention it being the ideal appointment for Celtic as well. The club's youth structure was clearly in need of an overhaul and it occurred to me just how much Davie would relish and look forward to the task.

— That's great, I heard myself saying. — I mean, it's great for Davie, I'm sure he'll do a brilliant job.

— I'm sure he will, McGregor agreed. — I'm sorry, I didn't mean to put a damper on things. We've still got a tremendous show on our hands here, obviously one or two things will need to be tweaked with regard to how we take things forward and we'll have meetings about that over the coming days. In the meantime though let's enjoy our evening, and once the dust has settled on tonight, we can start working towards another great programme again next week.

The news seemed to be accepted fairly quickly and almost stoically, as perhaps the sort of thing that happens all too frequently in the media. Questions were being fired in McGregor's direction about replacements and alterations to the show's dynamic, all of which were batted back with the unruffled confidence of an industry professional, revealing nothing, but asking for patience and promising that answers to all legitimate inquiries would soon be provided.

It was only a matter of a few minutes after I first learnt of Davie's departure that my mobile phone pinged with a text message from the man himself:

Expect you'll have heard by now, will give you a call 2moro and we can have a chat

My initial instinct was to call him back on the spot. For a moment though I hesitated, because I hadny known Davie that long, and I didny want to be too presumptuous. But I managed to pluck up the courage, and after stepping outside onto the street, I pressed the call button on the phone.

— Hello?

— Hi, Davie, it's Peter, I hope you don't mind, I just thought I'd give you a quick call.

— Gus has arrived then and given you the news?

213

— He has, just there the now.

— Sorry I couldny come down masel, but I've got stuff that needs to be sorted out the night.

— No, that's fine, I thought I'd give you a wee call though, just to make sure it wasny a wind-up. Is it the Celtic technical director's job right enough? I suppose you couldny really turn that down, could you?

— It's more than just a technical role, Peter. I'll no just be sitting up in the directors' box every fortnight, taking notes and making polite suggestions. It's restructuring the whole set-up behind the scenes at the club, from scouting and youth development to player recruitment and helping the manager. It's the job I've wanted for some time now, and I only got the chance to go in and speak to them about it there this week. I have all these ideas that are bursting out ay my head that I'm dying to put into practice, I don't just want to bring Celtic in line with what's going on at some of the top European sides, I want us to develop a strategy that leads the way for other big clubs in our position. I'm gony try and implement the kind ay policies that suit our particular circumstances, so that in the fullness ay time we can hopefully make up for the financial shortfall that exists between us and some of the other big European clubs, who play in leagues that are better resourced than ours. Financial fair play is here to stay, so we need to figure out what else we can do to combat the gap in funding that's developed in recent years, in order to give ourselves the best chance of competing at the highest possible level. Obviously I cany do that and work on The Scottish Football Debate at the same time.

— Of course no, that'll be a full-time job by the sound ay it. I think it's brilliant, Davie, it sounds like the ideal job for you, and the perfect appointment for Celtic as well. You're wasted on this show anyway, I'm glad you're putting your talents to better use.

— Hey listen, it's a great wee show you've put thegether down there. It's just bad timing fae ma point of view, but it's your baby, so stick with it. You'll probably outgrow it yoursel soon, but by then you'll have your foot in the door and you'll know what to do, he tells me, which sounds strange to my ears, given that I'm so new to the role. But already I know that Davie is the kind ay guy who means what he says and he's no just trying to flatter me.

— Can we still get you back on as a guest sometime? You can come in and tell us how things are progressing in your new role, we could even do a whole programme about what you're up to, taking in the European dimension and financial fair play.

— Of course, aye, if you can persuade Gus and the rest to invite me back in. But here, I was thinking, why don't we do it the other way about? Ask Gus or Helen or somebody if you can bring a camera crew into Celtic Park or the training ground up at Lennoxtown. You can follow us around for a few days and we'll try and give you an idea of exactly what it is we're hoping to do up here.

— That sounds like a great idea, are you sure the Celtic directors would be happy to let us do that? A lot ay that long-term strategy stuff at football clubs is usually kept behind closed doors, is it no?

— You're forgetting, I'm the boss here now. Never mind the directors or the board, if I say it's OK, then it's OK. We'll no be giein away any state secrets anyway, and it'll be a good thing for you as well, to get you out the studio for a change. Do you like the idea?

— I do, it sounds brilliant. I've just newly arrived on the scene here though, I need to get my feet under the table, but maybe in a few months time, if I can pitch it to Gus and the others and they like the sound ay the idea …

— I'll see if I can help you persuade them, he promises, — hopefully I might still have some clout over there. And I'll need a few months here as well, so just whenever you think the time's right, make a few discreet inquiries.

— I'll float it wi one or two people over the next few weeks and see what they say.

— Don't forget to mention that it I'm agreeable to the whole idea. If you want to impress them, tell them it was your baby and you persuaded me to go along wi it.

— I might dae that, Davie, I laughed.

— Nice one, I'm sure the programme's gony go from strength to strength. The first few weeks ratings wereny just a flash in the pan, you know. You're onto something here, so keep at it.

— Hopefully, aye. Right, well I'll see you later, Davie. I must admit, I was shocked a few minutes ago when I heard the news, but you've definitely reassured me that you're no just running out on us. I think it's a brilliant job you've landed, and I wish you the best ay luck wi it.

— I'll see you again soon, Peter, and we can talk about that proposal sometime. I'll be back in over the next few days, so we can have a chat then.

— I'll look forward to that. You know, I'm gony be hassling you for tickets now, don't you?

— Aye, I fully expect it! Don't worry, it's nothing I'm no used tae. Here, I meant to ask you, has Gus said anything about the future format ay the show?

— Nothing concrete, he's just stonewalled all our questions, saying there'll be meetings over the next few days about it.

— I'm sure there will, there'll be a lot ay jockeying for position, I imagine, now that I've stepped aside and created a vacancy. You need to be aware, this is an opportunity for you. Have a word wi that agent ay yours and see if he can get them to renegotiate your package. You can be sure as fuck that

Doddsy will be in there already. He's in a strong position now, but so are you, regardless of who else they bring in.

— Mark? Yeah, it's Doddsy, a nearby voice emerged onto the street. — Your client, Martin Dodds! It seemed that Davie's prediction was accurate; Doddsy was already on the phone to Mark Nimmo, taking stock and exploring his options within the shifting dynamic of the programme's new pecking order.

— I better go, Davie, that's a great suggestion about Lennoxtown, we'll need to follow that up, and best ay luck again in your new role. I expect to see Celtic winning the Champions League in the next five years now.

— We'll dae our best for Celtic, Peter, I can promise you that. Then it's just a case ay seeing how far our best takes us. Right I'll see you soon, mate, keep that show going, you're the only sensible wan left! he told me and hung up.

— Tell Catriona to stick it up her arse! Doddsy was arguing in the background.

— Is that Mark Nimmo? I ask him. — Here, can I have a quick word?

— Beat it! Go on, scram! he tells me. — Yes, Mark, sorry about that, I certainly think that's the case, aye. We can pit the fuckin squeeze on them noo, sure we fuckin can ...

— He's away, right enough, I announce to the room after I leave Doddsy to his scheming and return from my phone call with Davie.

— We have to see it as an opportunity, people. The show has made a strong start, and it will go on, believe you me! McGregor assures us. — No small thanks to this chap here! He slaps me on the back as I retake my seat.

His gesture surprises me and Robbie's glass to the mouth signal confirms what I already suspected, that McGregor is in fact three sheets to the wind already. All those lengthy, high-powered meetings with company lawyers have clearly taken

217

their toll on his sobriety by this stage of the evening.

— I take it you're pleased with my contribution so far then, Gus, and happy overall with the way the show's been going?

— Don't you worry about this, Peter. Davie's departure is an opportunity, not a setback. The show's going well yes, and it's not about to crumble because one guy has left, regardless of how charismatic and authoritative that individual was. The show must go on, I'm sure yous have all heard that expression before? Well, it's true. Onwards and upwards!

— Right enough. Do you think I might even be able to put in for a pay rise now that Davie's left? I suggest, as Doddsy rejoins us.

— You might. They can only tell you to get lost. In fact leave it to me, I'll put a word in for you. I think there's a good chance we might be able to have another look at certain aspects of your package.

— Well, I feel a bit embarrassed trying to take advantage of a situation like this, but I've been advised it would be worthwhile to give it a try.

— Absolutely give it a try, don't be shy. You have to know your own worth in this business! McGregor encouraged me. — Listen, Peter, it wouldny be a case ay you exploiting the situation to your advantage anyway. And even if it was, there's no point in feeling squeamish about things like that. You deserve a renegotiation on the basis of what you've done, regardless of the alterations that will be needed now that Davie has left. OK, it might be a bit early under normal circumstances to start battering down Catriona's door, but even this early, you're already showing that you're a valued asset to this organisation. You're aware of that, are you not?

— No really no, I considered, unsure of the extent to which McGregor's judgment and demeanour was being influenced by alcohol. — I'm enjoying what I'm doing, I told him, —

and it seems to be going quite well, but what do you mean by valued asset, Gus? How can I be a valued asset, when I've only just been in the door here for a month or so?

— The media is all about presentation, Peter, McGregor seemed keen to elaborate. — In an organisation such as this, the simple matter of whether or not your face fits may well count for more than any other consideration you care to mention. You're projecting the company's image and objectives in the most immediate and effective way possible; you're speaking to people directly while they're sitting in their own living-rooms.

— And my face fits, does it?

— It would appear so.

— Why? I don't get it, what have I done right? I'm still new to all this, you know? I'm still terrified before every recording, I struggle to remember people's names at times, the jargon confuses the hell out ay me, and I've still no idea what useful thing a Floor Manager does.

— A Floor Manager's job is to make sure that the studio is arranged properly and that the crew are ... fuck, I don't know what they're supposed to do either, McGregor declares.

— You see what I'm getting at though? Don't get me wrong, it's great to be appreciated, but it would be nice to know what it is that I'm doing right exactly, so that I can maybe do it more often.

— You're seen as a happy medium.

— What, like Derren Brown on E? What the fuck does that mean, Gus?

— Football is our national game, but it's very much rooted in the urban working-class. The SBC, by contrast, is not, he offered. — This presents a challenge for us when it comes to covering football. How do all these middle-class, privately educated careerists like myself give the national game the

219

attention and level of analytical detail that it deserves? We don't want to be seen as out of our depth, do we? That's why we've hired guys like Doddsy and Davie, so that we can cover football in the way that football people understand. But that creates tensions within our organisation because some people, who shall remain nameless, think that we're dumbing down by employing people like this. That's what I mean by a happy medium. It's thought that you have a foot in both camps, as it were. You can speak to the urban population in a way that they can understand and relate to. But you're an articulate and intelligent young man, who the posh boys can tolerate as well.

— That's absolutely terrible, Gus, I told him. — Jesus Christ, I've heard ay back-handed compliments in ma time but that fuckin takes the biscuit, mate, honestly. I have to tell you, I really don't know what to make of that Gus.

— It is terrible, you're right, but it's the way it is. My advice to you is to run with it, you've come this far just by being yourself, so carry on doing what you're doing. Everything's falling into place quite nicely for you just now.

— So if Davie Keane is seen as dumbing down, I guess that means that you're not too perturbed by his departure after all?

— We were sorry to see him leave, but we'll cope. As I said before, the show must go on. Let's be honest, all that working-class hero baloney doesn't tend to go down terribly well around here, does it? Let's face it, Davie was never going to be much of an SBC man, was he? You can see that surely?

— Well he should be! I mean, the man's a legend, what more are you looking for?

— Someone such as yourself, Peter, not to put too fine a point on it. You could very well be an SBC man, in which case, you can have a long and highly rewarding career here. Anyway, let's change the subject, shall we? That's all for the future.

— A couple of us are going into the town to make a night of it, Helen informs me. — Do you want to come, Peter?

— Erm, what about the green room?

— Robbie and Alison will head back and respond to the viewers' reaction and enquiries tonight. It doesn't take all of us.

— I better check wi Lenka, I spot my wife at the bar attracting the good-natured attention of a couple ay young guys. — I think we'll probably just head home if the green room's taken care of, I reply, anticipating Lenka's ambivalence to the idea of a midweek night on the town.

The evening appears to be breaking up, so I thank Gus for the revealing chat, make my excuses and say my goodbyes, before Lenka and I head back to Shawlands in a taxi. She's talking to me in Czech but I keep interrupting her in English, with remarks like, How can they value me more highly than Davie Keane?

— Yes it's true, I like him more too, she teases me. Her playful demeanour has a welcome, mood-altering effect on me and I realise that it's probably time to switch off from work and maybe give my wife some proper attention finally.

— We nearly there yet, driver? I ask.

13. PROGRAMME SIX: RELIGION AND SOCIETY

PETER: *Welcome to another edition of The Scottish Football Debate with me, Peter Fitzpatrick. I'm joined in the studio tonight by my regular sidekick, Doddsy. Davie Keane has left the show to pursue other interests ...*

DODDSY: *Good luck to the boey!*

PETER: *Well indeed, as you may have heard, it's been widely reported, Davie has accepted a job as head of youth development at Celtic and from what I hear, he is going to oversee the restructuring of the whole programme behind the scenes at the club. So we'll need to keep an eye on how he's faring in his new role, and Davie, if you're watching, we look forward to having you back in when the time is right, so you can let us know how you've been getting on. In the meantime we're joined this week by the editor of the online Celtic fanzine 'Tic Talk', Joe Ferris. Welcome, Joe, it's been an interesting week, has it not?*

JOE: *I suppose it has, Peter, yes, although not for Celtic. We've had a very quiet week, there's nothing much happening with our club at all.*

PETER: *Still, with everything that's been going on over the road, you must have been taking at least a passing interest in the UEFA verdict, banning Rangers fans from away grounds in Europe for two matches, for singing what we can now say, without fear of legal recourse, are sectarian songs.*

JOE: *I think everybody's been taking an interest, yes. They say schadenfreude is something that only happens to other people, but beyond that it's not an issue which affects my club. It only affects me personally in that I'm a Catholic person. So if tens of thousands of people are singing about being up to their knees in Fenian blood, or some of the other more unpleasant ditties, then that's something I'm not going to encourage. In a sense, growing up in the West of Scotland, you become inured* to this kind of thing, because you hear it so often and only very rarely will it be commented upon or condemned. I'm glad somebody somewhere has put their hands up and said this isn't acceptable. Obviously this happened in a European game, so it came under the jurisdiction of UEFA. It's just a shame that it took an external body to recognise and rule on such a quintessentially West of Scotland problem. The fact that nothing was done about it by the authorities in this country, I think says a great deal about the nature of the problem, how it was allowed to grow and fester, and probably sums up rather succinctly what's gone wrong with the governance of the game in this country.

PETER: *Doddsy, what are Rangers going to do about this, how are they going to handle it?*

DODDSY: *They have to take it on board. The fans have to realise now, they're only hurting the club. The events of this week have to be seen as a line in the sand. I agree with what Joe was saying, the authorities in this country have maybe turned a blind eye to the sectarianism for too long, and that's allowed a certain element to believe that they can get away with it. It died down for a while, but it seems to be back now and it needs to stop, no just at Rangers, but at Celtic and other clubs too. Because Rangers areny the only ones who are guilty of this.*

PETER: *Well nevertheless, it's Rangers who are in the dock this week so if we can stick with them for now. It's two decades since Rangers signed Maurice Johnstone, and ended the no Catholics need apply signing policy, but it seems that attitudes in certain quarters are as prehistoric as they've always been.*

DODDSY: *I don't disagree, Peter, this is the twenty-first century, you're right. I'm a Rangers man, I'm not ashamed to say, but I'm a modern Rangers man. The club has a great history and tradition but there's certain aspects that we need to set aside. Once again I come back to it, the authorities should have been harder on Rangers years ago, then I'm sure all this would have been sorted out a good while back, and the club wouldny be in the bother they're in just now.*

PETER: *Interesting that you both want to blame the governing bodies for this.*

JOE: *Well, hang on a minute. I think it's a bit too easy for Martin to blame it all on the SFA or whoever, culpable as these people may be. But you can't just blame somebody else for not stopping you from behaving in a way that is willfully and morally wrong on so many levels. There comes a time when you have to accept responsibility for your own actions. Yes, I want to blame the authorities for their indolence and cowardice in tackling the issue, but I want to blame Rangers more. They're the ones who pursued the sectarian signing policy, and consequently or otherwise, a section of their fans have turned into a bunch of retarded bigots. You mentioned Maurice Johnstone, Peter, but I mean, how long does it take? I think in retrospect we can see what a wasted opportunity that signing was for Rangers. That was when they could have said, OK, here's an end to all the nonsense of the past. All those people who were laying wreathes outside Ibrox, all those people who said they'd never go and see Rangers again...*

DODDSY: *That was a tiny minority that said that.*

JOE: *Fine, Doddsy, fine. Then say to them, you're no wanted here any more. Sorry, this is a modern club which is moving away from certain aspects of its past, and those people who can't or won't accept it can no longer be considered Rangers fans. Instead ay that, what did we get? We got two fingers up at Celtic again. You thought Johnstone was gony be your player? Well he's no, he's ours, so there you go. There was no contrition, no humility in the face of acknowledged wrongdoing. Instead it was just, we wereny signing Catholics before, but we've signed one now, so that's the end ay that. And by the way, get it right up you, Celtic.*

PETER: *It was quite a clever move though, was it not?*

In the context of the rivalry and the ending of the old signing policy.

JOE: *In terms of the rivalry, yes. And if Mo Jo still thinks it was the right move for him personally, then good luck to the man. I was angry with him at the time, but that has long since faded away and now I just feel sorry for the guy. You know, Celtic were interested in a player and Rangers nipped in and signed him from under their noses. Fair play to them for that. I'm not sure how much of it was strictly above board because when FIFA were called in, they agreed he was legally Celtic's player, as he'd signed a pre-contract agreement. But that's all water under the bridge now. All I'm saying is, it was a missed opportunity. Two decades later and here we are, Rangers have been censured and sanctioned for the same age-old crime. If they don't learn their lesson now, and there's very little evidence to my eyes at least to suggest that they will, then they're in danger of being kicked out of Europe altogether. Because, if anything, the bigotry is even worse these days than it was back then.*

PETER: *Do you agree with that, Doddsy? Do you think the bigotry is worse now than it was in the past? You grew up a Rangers supporter.*

DODDSY: *Erm, no. I think it was worse in the past and I think a lot of progress has been made in terms of what is and what isny acceptable, despite what happened with the UEFA ruling this week. And I also believe this will be a wake up call for a lot ay people and a good thing for Rangers in the long run.*

JOE: *Well I hope you're right, Doddsy. And I agree with you that a certain amount of progress has been made, and there cany be any going back to the bad old days of fighting on the terraces and that. But in other ways the bigotry is as bad now as it's ever been, you even have people trying to defend it these days with various pseudo-intellectual arguments. Nobody's saying there areny decent Rangers fans out there, quite the opposite, I know fine well that there are. But as always with Rangers fans, it's the majority who spoil it, because it wasny just a few that were singing at the UEFA game the other night.*

— That was your line, was it not? I'm sure I've heard you say that before, you fed him those exact words!

PETER: *You were wanting to get that line in, weren't you, Joe? The majority who spoil it, well done for fitting that in. Will things change at your old club, Doddsy? Can you see this as a seminal moment for Rangers?*

— I cany believe you fed him that line.

DODDSY: *Things will have to change, Peter, and I'm sure they will. I'm confident the fans will realise, they're only hurting the club, and that will bring about a shift in attitude.*

JOE: *The problem is, I don't hear too many people in Martin's camp calling for it to end. The stock answer you hear is that it'll never change, because it's been going on for so long, as if that was some sort of excuse for it all. Well it'll need to change now, otherwise the club will be in more bother, and it won't just be a fine and a ban on travelling fans next time, it'll be something altogether more serious. But unfortunately, as I was just alluding to, I've noticed the emergence recently of a new class of bigot. People with laptops and a decent level of education, who aspire to be taken seriously, and who really should know better. In the past bigotry knew its place and it would rarely be mentioned in polite society; but now these events have forced the issue out into the open and all of a sudden everybody wants to have their say. Prejudice seems to have developed ideas beyond its station, and now we have to listen to people attempting to rationalise and even defend the old attitudes. You know who I'm talking about, the equivocators and the appeasers, the people who claim that one side is as bad as the other, confusing victim and perpetrator for convenience sake. I say victim, but really, I should use another word, maybe target would be more appropriate, because Celtic fans areny victims of this. Catholics in Scotland areny victims of this mentality, it's only when it spills over into something more serious that we can talk about victims, because for the most part these people are just there to be laughed at. They're the real victims, those poor souls who hold these views and display these attitudes, and are three hundred years or so out of their time.*

PETER: *What about Doddsy's point about other clubs? Are Rangers alone with this problem?*

JOE: *They're not completely alone, no, because the problem has infiltrated the entire culture, which is hardly surprising, given that it went unchecked and unpunished for so long. There are those teams who for decades have seen themselves as coming from a similar tradition to Rangers, and they emulate them; and then there are other clubs whose fans define themselves, broadly speaking, as coming from a different tradition, and they oppose them. So you have some clubs who follow Rangers and others who give it back to them, but overall the problem of sectarianism, as it relates to Scottish football at least, is a problem that starts and ends with Rangers, and anyone who thinks differently must have been living on another planet all these years.*

PETER: *Well OK. Lest we forget, there was actually some football played this weekend. Let's have a look at the action, shall we? Run VT.*

— Everybody OK, everything going well? I ask.

— He fuckin talks too much, Doddsy accuses Joe.

— Well this is a debate show, Doddsy, we're no gony rebuke people for having something to say.

— Aye but he's no letting me get a word in, you need to cut him aff at some point if he's interrupting me like that. I mean, who's the guest and who's the regular man here?

— We've been over this, Doddsy, you're the main man but

we let the guests take centre stage for a period, if that's what they want to do. Unlike you, Joe's no gony be back here next week.

— Well said, a voice in the ether concurs with my arbitration.

— I'm not interrupting you, Doddsy, I was very careful no tae, Joe points out. — It's true I have plenty to say on the subject, but if you want to answer back or even cut across me yoursel, then feel free.

— It's going well, just be careful though, Helen warns me in my ear. — we don't want to overstep the mark here. As we stressed in the editorial meeting yesterday, this is new territory we're entering here, and as always, it's wise to dip your feet in the water first before diving right in, particularly with these sensitive and previously taboo subjects. Tell them there's nothing wrong with keeping it lively, just you make sure it doesn't get out of hand.

— There's nothing wrong with keeping it lively lads, just make sure it doesny get out of hand, I repeat my directions verbatim.

— No bother, are we gony talk about the establishment club? Joe enquires.

— I'm gony talk about it. You leave that one to me, you can have your say at the end, Doddsy insists.

— Fine by me, Joe replies. I kind of suspect that Doddsy is maybe falling for Joe's trap here, because I know from speaking to him on the phone and gaming through some of the discussion with him that Joe is just itching to tee off on this subject and now Doddsy has indicated that he's gony give him the excuse he's looking for. It's a fine balancing act from my point of view, this could become very interesting but at the same time, if it does kick off and I don't keep it under control then it becomes bad television, and in those circumstances I'll have failed to do my job properly.

228

— And we're back.

PETER: *Doddsy before we go any further, I'd like to address the idea specifically of anti-Irish racism. Does it still exist in Scotland, are Rangers fans guilty of it? And where does it come from, what have we got against the Irish anyway?*

DODDSY: *We've nothing against the Irish, I love the Irish. But there existed in the past, and maybe there's still remnants ay the same attitude that persists down to the present day, a certain distrust of the immigrant Irish community and the alien religion that they brought with them into Scotland.*

PETER: *But why? Where does it come from? I don't mind telling you, I've experienced anti-Irish racism myself, even in the few short weeks since this programme first went on air, my appointment has created quite a stir in certain quarters, in part clearly because of the things we're talking about, which is great, we want to generate talking points, and even a small amount of controversy is no bad thing at times. But there's also been an aspect to the reaction which I have more trouble with, in that I myself am a very visible representative of the Irish, Catholic community in this high profile role. There's been nothing overt, nothing said to my face, it's all rumours and innuendo, the odd joke and things I've heard on the grapevine as well as comments in the log. For some people watching this programme, that won't be enough to make a proper case and no doubt they'll accuse me of paranoia, but there aren't too many other people from my background in positions such as this. I get the distinct impression at times, it's almost as if my presence in itself is enough to offend some, although I should point out that in any event we're talking about a tiny minority here.*

DODDSY: *You're Scottish, not Irish, how many times have you even been to Ireland?*

PETER: *You're absolutely right, Doddsy, I am Scottish, that's what makes it all the weirder. Although I think the nature of my identity is something for me to determine and decide on personally, but I certainly feel as Scottish as anyone else. Joe, do you have an answer for this, why has anti-Irish racism been around for so long in Scotland and why does it still linger, when other forms of racism are quite rightly considered unacceptable?*

JOE: *Yes it does still exist, and I think the reason it has been such a persistent problem has to do with the fact that there was very little backlash against it when it first appeared. It quickly became the accepted and entrenched attitude in the West of Scotland establishment, because there was no political correctness in the 1920s don't forget, no way for people to challenge the received wisdom of the day. The Irish community, the Catholic community simply had to pull together and stand up for itself, there was no recourse to the external body of public opinion, which probably would have been against them at the time anyway. But hopefully attitudes can change, and I think they are changing, slowly. Rangers are still dragging their heels, claiming rather disingenuously that it's a social problem rather than a football issue, but I think there's an acceptance at the club that things can't go on as they always have done and that there has to be a thawing of some of these hard line, antiquated attitudes, if we're all to move forward together on these questions.*

PETER: *Doddsy? Do you agree?*

DODDSY: *Of course. And Rangers are moving wi the times. They can't just pay lip service to the anti-bigotry agenda, in the modern world they have to mean it too. And I believe they do mean it. They don't want to be stuck in the failings of the past.*

PETER: *Aren't they concerned about isolating their own core supporters though?*

DODDSY: *Quite the opposite, I think, Peter. They want to take their core supporters with them. Rangers have traditionally been seen as the establishment club and if they want to convince their supporters that they remain so, then they have to change with the times, as the accepted views of mainstream society themselves evolve.*

PETER: *So it's a question of practicality, the expedient thing to do rather than the moral one?*

DODDSY: *It's the moral thing to do as well. Everybody's happy.*

JOE: *Sorry, but ... in the words of Graeme Souness, "can I just say something here?"*

Laughter.

PETER: *About Maurice Johnstone?*

DODDSY: *He's a better player than I first thought!*

More laughter.

— Very funny, but there's no need for us to be giving a free plug to the 'Only an Excuse' boys. I'm a bit concerned about the overall direction of this discussion, get it back on course in the final segment, if you can, Helen advises me.

JOE: *No, not about Maurice Johnstone, as the impressionists say - I've talked enough about him already - but about this ludicrous, risible concept of Rangers being the establishment club. If ever it was true, then it was surely nothing more than confirmation that Rangers were bigoted and the establishment in Scotland was bigoted too. I suppose they did have that in common at least. I think the whole idea of there being an establishment club is a ridiculous notion anyway, but if you're going to make a case then surely, in the twenty-first century, there can only be one establishment club in this country and that's Celtic. I mean the first clue is in the name, Celtic, Keltic, the club of the Kelts. Celtic's culture is a blend of the two traditions - down to earth Scottish straightforwardness and easy Irish exuberance, and it's an intoxicating, captivating mix. You see it when Celtic fans travel to other countries. I mean,*

I know we take the mickey out of them, and quite right too at times, but essentially Celtic fans and Scotland fans behave in a pretty similar fashion when they go abroad. They're welcome everywhere because they know how to enjoy themselves and make friends in the process, whereas Rangers fans tend to travel like an imperial army on the rampage, leaving mayhem behind them in their tracks. Do you need me to continue? Look at the values that Celtic chose to define them when they were formed. Even back in the nineteenth century they were a club which represented openness and tolerance and access to all, according to their talents and aptitudes. These are now the accepted values of mainstream Scottish public opinion, and indeed of all mature, modern democracies. Celtic were setting the agenda for the establishment a hundred years before these ideas became fashionable. I could talk about the Labour Party and the former MPs who are in the Celtic boardroom, because if there's one organisation that has represented the establishment in Scotland over a considerable period of time, then surely it has to be the Labour Party. Do I need to go on? Can I stop now? Do you want me to start listing the contributions Celtic have made to Scottish football over the years? This Rangers are the establishment club nonsense has got to end. Rangers in the twenties and thirties became the means by which the Protestant working-class were allowed a share in and given a stake in the anti-Catholic bigotry of the establishment at the time. So if you're serious about ending the bigotry Doddsy, then we have to shoot that particular goose wi both barrels. Let's end all talk about an establishment club.

— Where the hell is this going? Helen sounds concerned in my ear, but I decide to let the boys argue it out in the short time we have left.

DODDSY: *I'm sorry, I cany agree. I don't see it as a bigotry thing at all. And you're no gony convince me that Celtic will ever be seen as the establishment club in Scotland. Because I'm here to tell you, it's never gony happen pal.*

JOE: *You're probably right, Doddsy, it'll never happen. Nor should it, because as I mentioned, the whole idea of an establishment club is ridiculous. Celtic have never tried to lay claim to that particular mantra, but Rangers have. And that's the point because hopefully we've shown that no club should be claiming that they represent the establishment.*

PETER: *Well it's an interesting point, but I'm afraid there we have to leave it because our half hour is up for this week. Join us next time for another intense and lively debate about the issues facing Scottish football. Let the credits roll! Goodnight.*

— Thanks, lads, I enjoyed that, I mention as the monitors are still scrolling through the closing credits. — You got some good points in there, Joe, I wink knowingly in Ferris' direction, but he responds only with a coy smile.

— You know Graeme Souness never actually said that, Doddsy informs Joe. — That was a shameless caricature, that "Can I just say something here, about Maurice Johnstone".

— He's right, it was 'Only an Excuse', I concur.

— I know fine well where it's from, but I bet Souness would have said it somewhere or other. He must have, he talked enough pish in his time. Go on, gie us your best impression Doddsy, Joe suggests.

We're chatting away along similar lines with Doddsy giving us his piss poor impression of Jonathan Watson, a.k.a. Graeme Souness, until the recording is complete and beyond the point where presumably the channel announcers will be doing their thing. When Joe asks me to do my Kenny Dalglish I refuse, reminding him of the line from one ay the Airplane films: "So Doctor, can you give the court your impression of Mr. Striker? Sorry, I don't do impressions, my training is in psychiatry", which gets me off the hook. A few minutes later, after we're off the air and clear, Helen comes down from the gallery and walks onto the set looking like she's just seen a ghost.

— You're not actually expecting us to broadcast that, are you? she looks sternly at the blank faces around the table before finally focusing her eyes on me.

— You're damn right I am, that was brilliant! I tell her.

PART 4

14. THE DIRECTORS' BOX

— Have you ever had a seat in the directors' box before, Sully? Davie Keane asks, as I introduce my old mate to the Celtic legend.

— Can't say that I have, Davie, no, Sully answers. — No wait, that's no quite right in actual fact. One time when I had a tour ay the ground, they let us have a wander up the back here then.

— I'm no sure it really counts if there wasny even a game on at the time.

— No, I suppose no.

— Be a nice wee change for you then.

— I'll tell you a secret, Davie. I've never sat in the directors' box either, this is a first time for me as well, I take the opportunity to point out.

— Is that so, Peter? You surprise me, I thought you were a regular ay the hospitality circuit these days.

— No really. I've indulged in the odd upgrade on a couple of occasions, no thanks to yourself, I remind him of his hospitality towards me and Lenka over the last season or so, since we first met. — And once or twice I've splashed out on a padded seat and a complimentary pie at half time, and sat in one ay the other lounges after the game until I was steaming drunk, but this is the first time I've been in wi the A-listers.

— Let me tell you, the A-listers get the exact same treatment, there's nothing special goes on in here, Davie points out. — A pie and a heated seat, that's aw they can expect an aw. We're no talking corporate hospitality or fancy restaurant food in here.

— Shame, the restaurant's great, I took my wife and my mum and dad for a meal down there one Saturday night to celebrate after they offered me the show, I admit.

— Where is your lovely wife, I thought she liked the football? Davie asks me.

— She does, aye, but she's busy the day at her work.

— What is she does again, jewellery, isn't it?

— Jewellery and accessories.

— Sounds like it's going quite well anyway.

— It appears so. She's certainly good at what she does, and they seem to be getting by, which is no mean feat considering how the economy's still fucked and we're in the grip ay a recession.

— You're no wrong.

— So we're stuck wi Sully the day, I'm afraid.

— Oh right, I see.

— I'll tell you what it is, Davie, Sully shifts nervously in his seat, as if he's about to offer us a scandalous confession. — I'm doing a wee report for this website that I contribute articles to. When Peter mentioned that he might have a spare seat the day, I was quite keen to come along and see what it was like to experience an afternoon at Celtic Park from the point of view ay a hospitality lounge, watching the game from the directors' box and meeting your good self of course, he reveals his intentions to Davie. It was a condition that I insisted upon when I invited Sully along, that he was up front about his intentions from the start. You don't mess guys like Davie Keane about, especially when he's pulling favours for you, and I impressed on Sully that complete honesty fae the get-go was the only way to approach this. If Davie wasny happy wi the idea, then he would have to accept it and that would be the end ay the whole thing. Fortunately though that didny appear to be the case.

— Oh aye, sounds a nice idea, Davie tells him.

— And maybe I could ask you one or two questions along the way, which I could quote in the article? Anonymously of course, Sully suggests.

— Aye, no bother. Ask away, Davie tells him, — I'll do ma best to answer you. What's your first question?

— Erm, well I've no really thought of anything specific to raise with you yet, I must be honest.

— Some fuckin journalist you.

— I know, I should have come more prepared, you're right. I just thought maybe we'd take things as they come, and I could ask you one or two questions over the course ay the afternoon.

— That's no bother at all, Sully. I'll tell you what, I have to go and do some meeting and greeting in a wee minute, unfortunately. I'll show yous to your seats in time for the kick off and you can use the time in between to think ay something to ask me. How does that sound?

— That'd be brilliant, Davie, cheers. Sully thanks him. — Any chance you can sort us out wi a seat next to Rod Stewart? My dad's a big fan.

— I'm no sure where Rod sits these days, or even if he'll be along the day. But if I see him, I'll introduce you, Davie promises.

Davie wanders off to perform his hospitality responsibilities and I chastise Sully for fluffing his lines in front ay his idol. He should have had a question ready for when he was asked, even if it was just a standard introductory effort about how it felt playing for and captaining Celtic in front ay sixty thousand fans every fortnight.

— I cany believe he's sitting there, calling me Sully and everyhin, he responds. — Why did you no introduce us as Mark? That would have sounded a lot less fuckin strange.

— You're acting aw starstruck, mate, what was that shite about your dad being a Rod Stewart fan? He's no, is he?

— I'm no sure the old boy's even heard ay him, Sully admits.

The lounge is busy, but there's a plentiful supply of food and drink so we order up some lunch and wash it all down wi a few beers, while playing the old game, that many a punter must have indulged in before us, of trying to spot the ex-player wandering about or the celebrity figure wi some sort ay connection to the club. On a couple of occasions the tables are turned on me, as besuited Celtic fans approach our table, wi the light of recognition in their eyes, to say a few words about the show and how much they're enjoying it, and so on. Fortunately, that seems to be as far as it goes though wi these punters, because after a year and a half of having ma face on the telly, I've still no fully adjusted to the various trappings and pitfalls of my recently acquired minor celebrity status. I'm in no particular rush for that to change either, I must admit, I've already heard multiple stories from within the SBC about seriously famous people kidding on how much they dislike being recognised in public, when the truth of the matter is that what these people really fear most is the exact opposite, naebidy knowing who they are.

In my case though, I'm genuinely quite happy with my Z list standing, for the time being at any rate, and I have no desire whatsoever for ma public profile to change. At times I can still feel like a bit ay an imposter on the whole media circuit, which may be due to the fact that I haveny developed a huge, brittle ego requiring constant pampering and indulgence, or a habitual taste for cocaine. Of course all this could be hopelessly naïve on my part, and with the show starting to be taken more seriously now and gaining UK wide appreciation and critical acclaim, I might well be saying something totally different in a few months time, once I'm fully integrated into the broader scene and I'm needing my regular fix of public recognition.

Right now though I can honestly say that fame for its own sake is not something I have any interest in at all, and when this circus is all over and the show has run its course, my contract has expired or the whole thing has just come to a natural end, then I'll be quite happy to walk away and find something else to do wi masel in peaceful anonymity. Provided of course that it's in no way whatsoever connected wi financial services.

Sully's asking a few ay the punters how much they paid for their tickets, so he can use the information in his article. It turns out to be quite an expensive commitment, three or four times the price of his season book, and that's before the cost of your food and drink, and there's an initial membership fee you have to cough up as well. It's a brief and incomplete survey but there seems to be quite a range of occupations amongst the clientele, no just your bankers and accountants and financial advisers. I shouldny be surprised, some plumbers and other tradesmen are fuckin minted nowadays, even by respectable middle-class standards, especially if they have the good fortune to be able to work for themselves. Good luck to them, I cany really complain, we're aw fuckin self-employed these days.

Davie returns in time for kick-off and takes us along to our comfy, padded seats for the game. We're having a good look to see if we can make out Coyler and Gerry McCourt in Sully's regular seats, and wi ma eagle eyes I reckon I can just about spot them. Sully waves but he's being a bit optimistic if he thinks they'll be able to pick us out in this crowd, even in the directors' box, because unlike us they don't know exactly where they should be aiming their eyes. It's strange, but I cany help feeling glad that there's a stadium-wide chasm between me and the two Kirkie boys, because I'm no sure I'd know what to say to Coyler and Gerry now. Of all the old pals that I was so warmly reacquainted with back in the day, when I first returned home to this country, Sully is the only one that I'm still in even semi-regular contact wi.

— The show seems to be going well, Peter, ever since I left funnily enough, Davie tells me.

— It is, Davie, aye, although your leaving had nothing to do wi it! I assure him. — We had a big upgrade there at the start ay the second season, so the presentation has certainly improved, I inform him. — We've got dolly cameras and everything now and we go out across the UK, although it's still only on the internet if you're outside Scotland.

— I liked your quip about the Americans in the introduction to the first show of the new season.

— Quip? Oh aye, spur ay the moment thing. And if you believe that, you'll believe anything!

*

PETER: *Hello and welcome to the first show in a brand new season of 'The Scottish Football Debate'. It's been a long summer, not least because there's been little or no football to watch, but also, dare I suggest, because we've been off your screens for a few months. But we're back now and as you can see we have a brand new set and Doddsy, this is a show with an actual budget now, it would seem.*

DODDSY: *We must be doing something right, Peter.*

PETER: *It seems we must, because by the miracle of modern technology, this year the show will be available to viewers not just in Scotland but all across the UK. And in celebration of this fact, I'd like to welcome our very special guest to the show, veteran English sports reporter Nigel Sackville. Welcome, Nigel.*

SACKVILLE: *Thank you, Peter, it's nice to be here.*

PETER: *Doddsy, is there anything you'd like to say straight off the bat to our UK wide viewers?*

241

DODDSY: *It's great to have you with us, and don't worry, you'll get used to ma sense ay humour.*

PETER: *It's the Americans I worry about on that score, Doddsy.*

DODDSY: *The Americans?*

PETER: *Aye, have you no heard? We're going out across the States next week.*

*

— So, did you think of anything to ask me yet, Sully? Davie inquires as the game kicks off. — Who have you been talking to, have you managed to secure yoursel any major scoops so far?

— Well I was wondering what you thought ay the whole hospitality scene here, Davie? Do you think it's a good thing or a bad thing overall?

— It can be a right pain in the arse having to meet so many folk, but I suppose that's part ay the job. No, I'm only kidding you on, they're aw Celtic supporters, so they're great fun.

— There's your scoop, Sully, I point out. — Celtic legend Davie Keane thinks Celtic supporters are a pain in the arse.

— I wouldny say that. I just wish some ay them wereny so fuckin overfriendly at times, Davie laments and the three of us are laughing.

— What would you say are the benefits to the club of having a separate hospitality package available to supporters? Scoop Sullivan continues.

— They're called premium tickets and they're an important source of additional revenue for the club. Fortunately or otherwise, we're no as reliant on television deals as some big clubs in other countries are. Matchday revenue is a much more significant part of our turnover than it is for clubs in England, say. And look around you, the punters seem to enjoy it as well. I'm tellin you, there's a long waiting list for these type ay tickets, so there's obviously a demand there.

— Don't you think it's a bit expensive though?

— It is, but as I say, there are enough people who seem to be able to afford it. What I'd like to see is a return to designated standing areas in the ground so that people who cany afford aw this can come in and see the game, and support their team without burning a hole in their pockets. That would be ma solution, but there's rules and regulations governing that which have to be adhered to.

— What about the whole experience? Sully continues. — Is this a good way to watch football, do you think? I must admit, I quite like having a cash bar here and being able to have something decent to eat before the game, rather than being crammed into a pub or having to grab a burger or a poke ay chips on the way in. But at the same time it doesny seem right somehow. It's aw very enjoyable, I must confess, but there's an unreality about it all, would you no agree? It's no the way football was meant to be watched.

— That's just because you're no used to it, Sully. If you think this is unreal, wait til they put you in a sponsor's box. In there you're about as detached fae reality as you could hope to get. But you're right though, the ordinary fans are the lifeblood ay the club and that has to be remembered at all times. Aw this operates around the fringes, it'll never be the norm. It's just another revenue stream for the club which they're right to take advantage of in the current climate. Lots ay people use the premium seats as an occasional treat, a wee present for their dads on their birthdays or whatever. It's there for that kind ay thing.

— That leads me on to my second question, Davie, if you

don't mind, Sully persists. — There's our pals Martin Coyle and Gerry McCourt over there in the Jock Stein stand. They're no here to cause trouble, they just want to enjoy the game. Do you no think they should be allowed a drink inside the ground an aw? How come it's just us up here that has access to alcohol during a match?

— I think you've got a point, Sully, it's about time that rule was looked at again in my eyes.

— When I was at the Amsterdam Arena at the start ay last season, they gave you a card and you topped it up wi credit, I note. — It's like a voucher system, when you buy your beer, they swipe it off your card. Do you think something along those lines could be implemented here?

— Could be, aye. I'll see if I can get that raised at the next board meeting, Peter. It might be worth taking a look into exactly what they do at Ajax and whether or not it could be a solution here. Of course, it's no just a Celtic thing, it's a Scotland-wide ban, but leave that yin wae me, it might be worth exploring further.

— Right, so if there's another riot like in 1980 we know where to lay the blame, eh, Fitzy? Sully rebukes me. — It's you that's got the fuckin rules changed.

— That was the Huns fault, I point out. — We'll obviously no include them in our new scheme. We'll make an exception for clubs whose supporters don't know how to behave themsels.

— Fair enough, aye, Davie laughs in agreement.

— Besides, when was the last time you saw any real bother at a football match? I offer. — Of course in a crowd ay this size you'll always come across the odd arsehole but you'll find them anywhere, and that's what the police are there to deal wi, should the need arise. Honestly you'll see worse behaviour at a wedding than you will at a football match these days.

— Aye, particularly if it's a Catholic marrying a Protestant,

244

Sully points out. — Hang about wan ay they dos long enough and it's bound to kick aff.

— What are you two, a fuckin double act? Davie laughs again. It seems we're managing to keep the boy amused anyway, so that has to be something.

— Right well that's great, Davie, cheers. I think I have more than enough to be going on wi, Sully eventually tells him.

— No bother at all, Sully, happy to help. Good luck wi the article.

The game's unfolding in front of us with Celtic pressing high up the field against opponents who seem to be playing most of the game from the edge ay their own penalty box.

— So how have you been getting on since you left the show, Davie? I ask, as the action continues. — Any regrets about walking out on us after a few weeks or so? What was it you said to the board when you outlined your ideas for youth development to them?

— You've been dying to ask me that aw day, sure you have? Davie reads me like a book. — How long you been saving up that question, Peter, a year is it now? More?

— Round about that long, aye, I acknowledge Davie's insight. — I was just sorry to see you depart so soon, you left me all on my own in there to deal wi Doddsy and Helen and aw the big media bosses. I could have used your moral support, but instead ay that you threw me to the wolves, mate, I chastise him.

— You seem to be coping awright, he replies. — The last few shows have been terrific, how many's that you've done now in total?

— I think that's forty six programmes all told that we've recorded over the last eighteen months or so. Are you still keeping an eye on them?

— Absolutely, I've seen most ay them, aye, and I've enjoyed them. Honestly, it's great to see such a refreshing alternative on the television for a change, compared to the muck we're used to watching.

— Any particular favourite programmes? I venture.

— Of course I enjoyed the time when you came up to Lennoxtown, that goes without saying, and I thought you talked a lot ay sense about youth development and the difficulties a lot of young players have in making the transition from talented youngsters into first team regulars. I found the one about football in the Highlands very interesting, and I loved the episode back at the start wi the Celtic internet man.

— Joe Ferris?

— Aye, he was great. Did they no insist that you put a Rangers man on there the next week just to balance things up? Most media outlets usually do that.

— No, we have complete editorial independence, mind? We've tried a number ay times to get Rangers people on, but we always run into problems either because their views tend to be quite extreme, or they don't want to deal wi the real issues, or they just don't like the show and refuse to be associated with it, so in the end we just decided to stop wasting our time wi them. We're quite happy to let other outlets gie these people airplay, but we've taken the radical decision that we're no gony indulge some of the more ridiculous nonsense associated wi Rangers in any way whatsoever. We did manage to have a serious, grown-up discussion about sectarianism one week, so it's no been a total write-off, and we've recently tried again to get people on to talk about the whole tax avoidance thing and Rangers ever worsening financial problems, but so far we've drawn a blank. I'm no bothered though because for the more moderate Rangers types, we have Doddsy there week after week, representing that perspective.

— And of course I wasny there for long either, which was

your original intention.

— That's right, so in fact we have to balance it up the other way most weeks, I agree, — but I can offer that viewpoint myself, if needs be. So still no regrets then about leaving, was there no a possibility that you could maybe have done both jobs? The show isny that time consuming, you know, I'm only in there two days a week, and you'd have been the same. We're no like Helen and Alison, who have to worry about presenteeism and sitting at their desks from 9 to 5 every day ay the week. I'm sure it could have been organised so that it didny impact on your commitments wi Celtic.

— I discussed it wi them at the time, Peter, but we agreed that the size and scope ay the project here meant that I needed to gie the task ma full attention. I didny want them thinking I was only in it half-heartedly, because this is a major undertaking I still have on my hands here. Arguably it's a job for two men, but I've been working on my own for the last year and a half. Unfortunately people wi the right qualifications and aptitudes areny easy to find.

— What was your pitch to them? How did you convince them that you were the right man for the job? Did you just say to them, I'm Davie Keane, former Celtic captain, here I am, the position's mine.

— Jesus Christ no, it wasny quite as simple as that. They gied us the fucking third degree, so they did. Quite right as well, you cany just turn up and expect to be handed a job like this, no matter who you are. I knew what was coming as well but fortunately I'd done aw my preparation and I told them everything they needed to hear.

— So what did you tell them? How did you lay out your vision of youth development? You must have said something right, Davie, otherwise we wouldny be sitting here right now.

— I gave it to them from the top, Peter, in minute detail.

*

— Come in, Davie, sit down. How's it going?

— Very well thanks, Mr. Chairman, yourself?

— No so bad, Davie, cany complain certainly, cany complain.

— Lovely day.

— It is, right enough. Doesny make up for the dreadful summer but there you go, that's Scotland for you. You know Derek, our director of football.

— Of course. How's it hanging, Deek?

— Straight as an arrow, Davie, ma friend. Good to see you.

— Straight as an arrow? How come your shots always miss then, Derek? And I'm no talking aboot the fitba here.

— We cany aw be ladies' men like you, Davie.

— What are you saying, Deek? This man's a paragon of moral virtue. Happily married, three lovely children, sure you are, Davie?

— Absolutely, Mr Chairman, don't think I haveny been tempted though. Fortunately my good Catholic upbringing has helped keep me on the straight and narrow over the years.

— I'm sure it has, Davie, I'm sure it has. So, Davie, can I get you anything? Tea or coffee, it's a wee bit early for anything stronger.

— No thanks, Mr Chairman, I'm fine.

— OK, then, well let's get down to the matter in hand, can we? Namely the future direction of youth development at the club. I don't want to sit here talking all morning, Davie, but

248

I could lay spreadsheets out in front of you detailing all the expenditure that the club's incurred over the last number of years, on players wages and on transfer fees and aw the rest ay it. I'm no gony bore you with the detail of that right now but suffice to say, we haven't had the success we'd have liked in recent years with regard to bringing through our own players, or 'rearin wir ain', as they generally like to say in footballing parlance. Needless to say anyway, this is something we'd like to address, no just for financial reasons, but also because, put quite simply, we feel this is the way a big club like Celtic should be operating. It increases the feelgood factor around the place if the fans are able to see one or two boys from the local area, stepping up and making the breakthrough into the first team on a consistent basis. I don't know, can you help us out here, Davie? What are your thoughts?

— Well, my initial thoughts are that we can and should be addressing the very problem you've highlighted, Mr Chairman.

— How do we address it though, Davie, how do we address it?

— I think the main thing we should be looking at is that we need to have a wee bit more faith in our own methodology. That would be a good place to start.

— How do you mean, Davie, how do you mean? More faith in our own methodology? I like the sound ay that, but what do you mean by that exactly?

— Well it's my personal belief that if you grow up in this part ay the world, and you've made it onto the radar of a club like Celtic by the time you're twelve or thirteen years old, then you've already had a fabulous grounding in everything that's gony be required to help you understand the game of football, and the skills and resources you'll need to play the game at a high level. We live in a football mad city, and if a boy has developed a talent for the game by that age then he'll already have gained as valuable a footballing education as you could hope to receive in any other part of the world. I firmly believe that. As a young man, he should have an excellent grasp of how important football is in the wider community, and that'll stand him in good stead. From there we just need to hone and shape the boy's individual talent, allow him to express himself in his own way on the field, and then make him aware of the pitfalls and the other things that can distract the attention of a talented young man, who's inevitably gony play out much of his youth in the high profile glare of the media spotlight.

— I see. Please elaborate, Davie, are there any other thoughts you can share with us on this matter?

— I don't suppose you saw me on television the other night talking about this very subject, did you?

— I did actually, terrific wee show. You were tremendous on it.

— I don't suppose you'll let me continue to work on the programme, should you offer me the position? I really believe in what they're trying to do over there.

— It's possible, but this is a full time position that we're offering here, Davie. There's really enough work for two men in this role, but I don't want to get into any of that just now. This is just an initial wee chat, very informal, to see what your thoughts are and whether we share the same vision. We can leave all those discussions for a future date. There'll be plenty of time for you to hammer all that out with Derek here and the Chief Executive, when he's back from his business trip.

— And Frank too, I'm assuming he'll be involved. I was rather expecting to see him at this meeting.

— We'll consult of course, but the head coach's remit is to oversee all matters pertaining to the first team. Frank wouldn't be involved in a decision like this.

— I see. Middle management, eh?

— This is a PLC now, Davie, it has to be run properly.

— Quite right, Mr. Chairman. Quite right.

*

— Just a second, Davie, I interrupt. I'm surprised to notice that Sully has produced a notebook, seemingly from nowhere, and is writing down everything that Davie has been telling us.

— Sully, put your notebook away, mate, Davie hasny said you can use any ay this. You're here to write about the matchday experience, no the future ay youth development or Davie's role at the club.

— It's awright, Peter. I presume this website ay yours is gony have more than one article on it, Sully? You can do a separate piece on this if you want.

— Can I put your name to it, Davie? Sully inquires.

— That's up to you, mate, but I would suggest you probably don't want to reveal your sources. That way you let everyone know where your information has come from.

— That would work. Maintains the sense ay mystery, I see where you're coming from, Davie. Man in the know kind ay thing? Perfect, thanks very much.

— So what has been happening behind the scenes? I ask. — Has there been a complete restructuring, fae the ground up?

— No, I wouldny describe it as a complete overhaul, we're just trying to continue the young players' formal education, that's the main thing. There's been a few changes of course, but what we want is to see a neat progression through the youth teams into the first team. That's the ultimate aim, to produce players capable of playing in the Champions League.

— So do you try to copy the way the first team plays at every level wi the youth teams, like Barcelona?

— We try to do that yes, but exactly how the first team plays is ultimately the job of the first team coach to determine. I cany interfere in that. But we want to get them playing the Celtic way, and keep it level-headed so they can cope with a wee bit ay the limelight if it comes their way at a young age. 'Keep your feet on the ground and aim for the stars'. That's how I summed it up in the various meetings I've had.

— Very poetic, I comment.

— The Celtic way, huh? What is that exactly? Is it a 4-4-2 or a 4-3-3?

— The exact formation isny so important, Sully, and you can always vary it according to the players you have and the opposition you face. When they sign their first professional contracts at age sixteen, we like to have them playing in the old WM style for at least the first year, because that suits us when it comes to aiding their development.

— How come? The WM, is that no a bit old-fashioned? I ask.

— It wouldn't work in the modern men's game, but don't forget it was the established formation all across the world for decades, and it suits young players who are still developing their skills down to the ground. At that age you don't know your best position, so you have to teach young players every aspect of the game. The WM works perfectly for this; for example one of the central strikers can play as an inside forward, and one of the centre backs can be released to go forward and learn how to play in midfield. Wingers can concentrate on beating their opponent and full backs can learn how to tackle. These are the basics of the game; and in addition you can switch people around into different positions, let the winger operate as a striker for a while, and so on. This is what players should be learning at a young age, no four-four-two or four-three-three.

— So that's how they play in their first year as a professional at the club? Presumably they'll no be playing Stanley Matthews style football aw the way into the first team.

— How no, we could use a few ay his type? But yes, you're dead right, we expect them to progress from there. The system of play at higher levels aims to mimic the first team, so that above all we can produce players that are gony play the game in a manner that suits them individually and collectively. As they gain more experience, they'll become more accustomed to the model of the "Celtic way", which should work to everyone's advantage, seeing as this is Celtic football club after all, and that's who we hope they're gony be playing for.

— Does that mean attacking football then?

— Of course it does, but no in a naïve or a gung-ho fashion. The Celtic way in a modern context, that's the expressed aim of how the team should develop in the coming years. We take that methodology out in to the SPL and hopefully all over the Continent, so we can inflict our vision of how the game should be played on opponents at every level of European competition.

— So is that a 4-4-2 or a 4-3-3?

— Look at this, Sully. Davie fishes around in the pockets of his jacket and produces a diagram. — I scribbled this down recently in one of our meetings. The ideal formation would be a flexible four-four-two. In midfield you have two men holding in the centre, with a winger on one side and a guy who can swing in a cross on the other. He doesny necessarily need to beat a man to put a ball in the box, because he relies on his technique when it comes to striking the ball. In fact this other type of wide man is probably a converted central midfielder, so you can see, if you're playing against a team that has three men in the centre, he can tuck in and match up, so you're no overrun in there, Davie explains, pointing to the arrows and wee figures that he's sketched out in an impromptu fashion on his piece ay paper. — Then look, he continues, the winger pushes forward and becomes an auxiliary striker and one of the strikers, probably the more skillful of the two, drops off to cover the gap on the other side. See what I'm saying? You're rigid four-four-two has now morphed in a flexible and dynamic four-three-three. The coach can then use that alternative formation as he sees fit, depending on the opponent, maybe away from home in a difficult European tie, or as I mentioned, against a team that wants to flood the midfield.

Sully's indulging in some furious notetaking, as Davie baffles him with footballing science. — Can I have that? he asks, pointing at Davie's improvised diagram. I'm mortified at my mate's gallusness, but Davie doesny seem to be caring.

— Aye, sure thing. Here, take it, he offers.

— Thanks. This might turn out to be an important piece of Celtic paraphernalia.

— You never know. Don't worry, it's aw sketched out in my head anyway.

— We have a terrific record at youth team level, Davie, are you hopeful that somewhere down the line the changes you're implementing will translate into more young players advancing through the ranks into the first team?

— Of course I am, aye. As I mentioned, if we don't produce more players that make it all the way into the first team over the coming years then I'll have considered my time spent in this role as a failure. So far it's looking good, we already have young Gallacher and McMahon out there doing their thing, as you can see, but it's still early days. You're right, Peter, we have a good record at youth team level, but we can always improve. Here's a wee exclusive for you, boys, if you're interested; the under 21 league is gony be done away wi soon and replaced with an under 20s league. It's been coming for a while, but now it's definitely gony happen. Everything's already agreed and there's a meeting wi aw the clubs next month. The media don't have the full agenda yet, but it's a done deal and that'll help us wi what we're trying to achieve here as well.

— A scoop for Timsnet? Brilliant! The internet bampots beat the mainstream media to a story yet again! I swear, the lunatics are taking over the asylum here, Sully enthuses.

— How exactly will that relatively minor change help? I ask.

— By the age of 21 you need to be playing first team football, Davie tells me. — Our model involves sending players out on loan, something which we believe should be standard practice for young players. Doesny matter how good they are, it's unlikely they're gony shift an experienced professional who's holding down a first team place at a club like Celtic. That's just one of many reasons why we believe all young players should go out on loan for a full year before returning and then trying to push for a first team place. We need two players for every position, remember, so with a wee bit ay first team football under his belt by the age of twenty-one, twenty-two, a player should be ready to accept that challenge.

— One of the things I've noticed, Davie, Sully probes, — is that young players in Scotland don't seem particularly adept at handling the spotlight and attention that comes their way if they manage to break into the first team of a big club like Celtic or Rangers. Do you have any particular plan or strategy in mind to help them cope wi the burden ay fame and expectation, and for handling the temptations that are presented to them in this country?

— Aye we send them to see the priest, 'Lead us not into temptation'. For years priests used to get into Celtic Park for free, now you know why.

— Is that how you handled it when you were a young player here?

— I'm joking of course, but I think it was maybe easier in my day. I mean you had your McAvennie's and Nicholas' that courted the limelight, but if you wanted to keep a low profile it was easier when I was just coming in. What was it I said earlier? 'Keep your feet on the ground and aim for the stars', that's basically the message we try to get across to the boys. I'm glad you said the burden of fame there, Sully, because it can be a burden rather than a boon at times. What I used to crave was recognition, not fame. I wanted people to see and appreciate that I was a good football player. That was first and foremost in my mind, and that's what we try and transmit to the youngsters. Fame on its own can be a pain in the arse, whether people love you or loathe you. It's obviously better if they love you, don't get me wrong, but there's an important distinction between fame and recognition, and it's very much the latter that we try and encourage the young boys here to be hungry for.

The half time whistle sounds and the players trudge off up the tunnel directly beneath our seats. Sully is still scribbling away furiously in his notebook, having claimed three exclusives at the latest count for Timsnet.com.

— Are you just sitting here, I ask Davie, — or do you have to go and do any more gladhanding?

— I'll just remain here wi you boys for the interval if you don't mind, he tells us.

— No that's great, Davie, keep talking, would you? I've almost got enough material here to keep us going for the rest ay the season.

— I was hoping Billy Connolly might be about, I remark. — I'm a big fan ay his and somebody in the office mentioned that he'd seen the show and quite enjoyed it.

— There's Billy down there, Peter, Davie points out. — Awright Big Yin, he shouts across and Connolly turns in his seat and gives us a cheeky wave and a trademark smile. — And here's Rod Stewart coming over to say a few words the now, Davie notes.

— Eh?

— Hi there, Peter, how's it going? Love the show by the way, I recognise the trademark husky voice, before I see the face, as the ageing rocker moves along our row and sits in the seat right next to me.

— Oh my God, I announce.

— I usually prefer to be known as Rod, not God, he informs me, — although I suppose that depends on who's doing the speaking, don't it?

— Sorry, Rod, aye. You erm have seen the show, did you say?

— Love it, mate. Great work, yeah, Rod opines.

— You haveny fuckin seen his programme at all, Davie cuts in. — You're only here because you thought that Peter's wife might be about, sure you are?

— Well I heard she was a bit of a looker, Rod concedes. — Where is she then?

— Erm, she's at her work. I brought Sully along instead, I point out. Sully, for once, is speechless.

— Don't believe a word he says by the way. Of course I've seen the show. Love it, mate, honestly. We need more shows like that on the box in Scotland, hopefully you'll help Scottish football recover its former glories.

— Well yeah, that'd be nice, I'm struggling to remember the publicity line, which has been at the front of my mind for the purposes of instant regurgitation for the last year and a half, but for some reason is currently beyond my recollection. — Get the public thinking in a different way about the game, that's the motivation, I extemporise.

— Has to be the right idea, Rod agrees. — Well I'm off to see if I can get myself a wee shandy before the second half kicks off. Congratulations and nice meeting you, Peter, he stands up. — Speak to you soon, Davie.

— See you, Rod.

— Nice meeting you too, Rod, I smile.

— And remember, he turns and tells me, just as he's leaving, — it's Rod, not God. Although many a woman in her time might have begged to differ.

— That's fame, lads, Davie Keane informs us. It's not long before the players are jogging out for the second half.

— I've forgotten the score, are we even winning here? A dazed and confused Sully eventually asks me.

— I've nae idea where I am or what day it is, I tell him.

— We're up one nothing, Davie reminds us. — Come on boys, let's be paying more attention to the action in the second half. We need the three points in this one.

15. LIQUID REFRESHMENT

Unusually for me, or for anyone wi a part-time job in television for that matter, I'm up reasonably early the day, in advance of what has to be the most important editorial meeting I think we've ever had on The Scottish Football Debate. Rangers are in the throes of liquidation, and while we've danced around the issues and the implications resulting from the financial collapse of Scotland's self-styled establishment club on many occasions before now, this time we're staring the full story in all its sordid detail straight in the face, because the long-foretold day of reckoning is finally upon us. Despite this I can detect a certain amount of doubt and hesitation in the air at the SBC, as if in a final moment of indecision and uncertainty, a collective breath has been drawn in before we jump off a cliff thegether.

This is perhaps understandable, given the size of the organisation involved and the scope and depravity of the allegations against it, but we cany skirt around the issues any longer and I'm relishing how we're gony approach this now. This is a fast moving story so following our meeting we'll be recording the show this afternoon in advance of transmission later this evening, after which we'll have a few end of season drinks to mark the cessation of domestic on-field hostilities. We'll still be continuing with the show over the summer in order to cover amongst other matters the continuing story with Rangers, the fallout and the impact on Scottish football as well as the forthcoming European Championships which are being held in Poland and the Czech Republic. I'll no be celebrating the night though, if we fuck this show up. It's a huge cross-media event we're dealing wi now and there are genuine issues for us to get our teeth into which, as we've come to expect, have so far been left unresolved in many mainstream outlets.

In short, it's perfectly set up for another brilliant edition of The Scottish Football Debate, or 'Scotball' as the press have rather unkindly christened us. Hopefully their indignation is a sign that we've been getting under their skin and rubbing one or two people up the wrong way with the range and depth of our coverage. Over the last two seasons we've approached our material with a level of seriousness and energetic intelligence that has left many of our rivals trailing in our wake. That seems to have been the secret of our success so far and we're no about to stop now that this story has finally landed in our lap in all its unseemly glory. Because I think that by and large we've done a pretty good job of showing up the tabloid culture which dominates our business as being wholly insufficient for the needs of a modern Scotland in an information age. This is what motivates me. This is why I'm up at this time ay the day, because otherwise I'd be daein what I enjoy best – lying in my bed until a decent hour in the morning.

This is what the boo boys and the naysayers have never been able to grasp. You see the comments in the log every week, a sizeable element of the Rangers support accusing me of being a 'Rangers hater' and an 'enemy of the club'. Ridiculous language like that just makes me laugh. Rangers as far as I can tell are absolutely bang to rights here, nobody's disputing the enormity of the story we're dealing wi now, so naturally I'm gony want to be all over it, because even this far down the line, I still enjoy the job we're doing here and I can still get the same buzz off it as I did way back in the days of our very first episode, when me and Davie and Doddsy were examining the fallout of Scotland's painful defeat against Lithuania. I'm only interested in approaching the whole Rangers story with fairness and professionalism and dedicated journalistic zeal, and if that leads me in the course of my work to disapprove of some of the actions of the club, then I'm entitled to my opinion because at some point we're gony have to start making judgments and reaching a few conclusions about what's been happening here. If anything, I would say I'm a Rangers disapprover rather than a Rangers hater, but it's the actions of the club down the years that have led me to this stance.

I'm up early so I can call Sully and try to catch him before he goes into his work. He's been a useful sounding-board for me over the past two years, has Sully, and our occasional chats have often proved useful in terms of helping me clear my head and get my thoughts in order before an important editorial meeting. Because of the size of this story, I reckon I might benefit from his outsider's, non-media, or 'civilian' perspective, so I fish out my phone and press his speed dial button.

— Sully?

— Hello, he answers.

— How's it going, it's Peter.

— Peter. What took you so long, mate? I was wondering when you might get around to phoning me. What's on your mind?

— Are you at work? Sorry to call you at this time in the morning, Mark, but I was hoping you might have a wee minute so I can pick your brains?

— Sure, go ahead, that's no bother. We've no even started yet, the boss is still on his way over and we cany dae anything until he turns up and lets us in the building.

— I sense that you've probably guessed why I'm calling, mate. We have an important meeting the day and to be honest I'm struggling to get ma heid round everything that's going on wi this liquidation business. I'm telling you, Sully, the place is in meltdown here, obviously we've been building up to this for some time, but now it's finally upon us naebidy really seems to know how to approach this story. I was hoping you might be able to shed some light on it all for me, gie us the benefit ay your usual insight. Help us to see the wood fae the trees, if you can, in your usual inimitable way.

— What are you lot like, eh? Sully laughs. — Like I says, I was wondering how long it was gony take before you called me on this. I should've had a fuckin sweepstake on what time the phone was gony ring, I might have made a few quid. You've got the biggest story in the history ay Scottish football in front ay you but you've nae idea how to handle it, dae you? I can just imagine you boys running around panicking, struggling to grapple wi the implications and the fallout fae aw this. Don't forget though, Peter, your show's different, is it no? You're no just another tabloid hack, are you, so you're no bound by the same restrictions and restraints that they cunts operate under. Just be bold and tell folk the truth, that's aw they want to hear. Doesny matter what team they support, aw folk want you to do is tell them the truth about what's going on, so gie it to them straight, that would be ma advice.

— That's easy for you to say, Sully, but the truth may be too terrible to contemplate, that's the fuckin problem here, I tell him only half-jokingly.

— Doesny matter, Fitzy. You follow the truth wherever it leads you and to hell wi the consequences. Is that no the code? Is that no the most exciting part of what you do? Woodward and Bernstein and aw that? You follow the facts wherever they lead you and whatever the consequences. After that, you just have to deal wi the fallout and the implications, as you say, and ultimately we aw just have to evolve fae there. If the world has changed forever as a result of what you reveal, well then the world will just have to adapt, because one thing's for sure, the earth will still continue to spin no matter what happens in the wacky world of Scottish football.

— I'm no sure Woodward and Bernstein could hold a candle to this story, Sully. I know, I've seen the documentary evidence, the Huns are fucked for all time here.

— Well fuck them then. And make sure you make it personal too, there's nothing wrong wi that. If it falls to you, that you're the boy that's gony dae them in once and for all, then get on wi it. Fuck them fae high heaven! It's their ain doing, Fitzy, no yours, you're just the guy who's gony swing the axe. The

262

mainstream media are too feart or too biased to go the whole hog on this, maybe even understandably from their own selfish side ay things, but from your point ay view you can well and truly nail the bastards for what they've done. If it's fallen to you to be the man who takes the whole Rangers story through to its logical conclusion, then get on wi it. Dae your Panorama thing on them. You've got the resources and the will so that's half the battle and it puts you in an enviable position. Gie them the fuckin treatment, Peter, that's your remit and believe me, folk will thank you for it if you dae.

— It's no just me, Sully, this isny a one man crusade. There's good journalists out there, but they're aw hesitating just now. I'm just keen to steal a march while I can and hopefully be a part ay the whole process.

— Fine. Like I say, get on wi it then.

— So what's my angle? Where dae I start? I inquire.

— Well, you said the truth was too terrible to contemplate. Scratch that fir a start. What's terrible about putting the boot into the Huns if it turns out they've been cheating and tax-dodging aw these years, and as a consequence, either directly or indirectly, they're about to go out ay business? As I say, it's their ain fault they're in this mess, remember, no yours.

— Sorry, 'terrible' is the wrong word, I meant to say incredible or unbelievable, you know what I'm getting at. The potential fallout is mind-blowing.

— It only seems mind-blowing to you and me because we're that close to it aw, but really and truly a football club going down the tubes through their own mismanagement and incompetence doesny amount to a hill ay beans in the grand scheme ay things. It's no gony send Wall Street into meltdoon, is it? Just you make sure that you get your story straight and tell it like it is.

— That's good advice, mate, a wee bit ay perspective, I like that. Where the fuck do I start though?

— Start at the beginning. You say you've seen the documentary evidence?

— I have. And believe me, the evidence is overwhelming and totally convincing. Rangers have made no secret of the fact that they were using these tax loopholes for years to pay players' salaries which they otherwise wouldny have been able to afford, and they've admitted liability in several cases already. But I've also seen the evidence of the dual contracts, and they're bang to rites there as well as far as I can see. Season after season they were fielding players who they'd failed to register properly wi the SFA; and season after season they were winning trophies wi aw these players in the team. The only question seems to me the extent to which they can get away wi it or no.

— That's right. So for ten or twelve years or more, if the allegations are correct, every result involving Rangers would potentially be null and void.

— It's one ay the biggest fuckin stories in the history ay sport, Sully, that's what I mean. This big team, wi a huge fanbase and massive resources is turning up week in, week out, fielding players who are improperly registered and therefore technically ineligible, and whose wages they can only pay through a dodgy tax avoidance scheme; and they're up against these small provincial clubs, who for the most part have learnt their lesson from the financial carnage that has afflicted Scottish football in recent years, and are desperately trying to live within their means …, what fuckin chance have they got?

— There you have it, Peter.

— What is it that makes you most angry about this whole situation though Sully? Is it the cheating? Is it the tax avoidance and the fact that they've artificially increased their player budget, or is it the potential impact on Scottish football and

264

the way the game's been ruined here? What do you reckon?

— I think Rangers' offences are bordering on criminal to be honest wi you Peter, and thanks to the internet bampots we know that the Polis have been chapping on their door recently. But the worst aspect for me is the way I've been feeling all these years. I've been chastising masel aw this time, telling masel no to be paranoid, no to be a bigot, to be reasonable, the media cany aw just be a bunch ay liars, maybe it's me who's no got things in perspective after all. Because I always knew something wasny right wi Rangers, it was a feeling I had deep down that there was something fundamentally no right wi that club, and yet I kept berating masel, because I never knew about aw this scheming that was going on. How could I have? We were right all along though, sure we were, and that uncomfortable, vaguely uneasy feeling we had about Rangers, that something dodgy was going on there … well it wasny just paranoia and it certainly wasny bigotry. They were just fundamentally corrupt, although obviously we couldny put our fingers on it at the time. But we know now, sure we do? They've corrupted sport, all the drama that's played out every week, all the emotional energy that's been spent, to say nothing of the money, it's all turned to ashes because the game wasny straight. We've been cheated, all ay us, Rangers fans too because the titles they won wereny real. They won false trophies whereas their opponents were cheated out ay the genuine ones.

— So now do you feel vindicated for your antipathy and suspicion towards them?

— I do feel vindicated, aye, but that's no the point. We were right no to trust them, but now I'm angry about the way I've been made to feel aw this time, that I was somehow no right in the heid for being suspicious ay the club and for no being able to show any goodwill towards them. I've been made to feel almost dirty, that my feelings were merely a result ay my own prejudices and narrow-mindedness, which somehow, through my own lack ay insight and sense of perspective, I wasny quite able to suppress. And you know what, I was starting to believe the hype masel because it had been coming at me for such a long period ay time. And that of course is no just Rangers' fault, it's their cronies in the mainstream media that are responsible for that as well. That's why your show is so important, Peter. I'm repeating masel now, but you need to fuckin lay it on the line what's been going on between this club and the media aw these years, because nae cunt else will, that's for sure.

— I'll see what I can do. You're right about the corruption though, they've corrupted sport. All those emotions, all that intensity, all that time spent contemplating your team's fluctuating fortunes, the ins and the outs, the pros and the cons, it was aw in vain, wasted time, money and energy, because the game wasny straight. The Huns wereny playing by the same rules as everyone else.

— Course they wereny, that's what I'm trying to tell you, and hopefully it'll start to sink in now across the board. You need to reflect the anger and indignation that people are quite rightly feeling about aw this.

— I'd like to ask you one more thing, Sully, while I've got you on the line. What about this ongoing argument about Rangers history? Most people seem to think that the history died wi the club, yet again we're hearing in some sections that they're still the same club, it's just a new corporate entity that has taken over. What's your take on that, are we just arguing about semantics here, does it really matter if they're still calling themselves 'Rangers' and harking back to the bad old days of Bill Struth and foaming at the mouth religious prejudice?

— This is one of the most important points that remains to be put to bed, Peter, and the answer to your question is yes, it does matter. Whether it's a concern to you and me or not is up to us, but it matters to the tax authorities and the other regulatory bodies, believe me. This is potentially a massive fraud they're trying to perpetrate here, the club has gone bust

266

owing tens of millions of pounds to everyone from Rapid Vienna to Joe the Plumber, and yet they seem to be saying that it's OK just to start up again, having shed all this debt through the liquidation process, and carry on as normal as if nothing had ever happened. We're still called Rangers, we still play in blue jerseys wi the five stars on the shirts representing all their ill-gotten trophies. We might be playing in the third division because we've been liquidated, but guess what, liquidation was really something that happened to somebody else, because we're still the same Rangers. This is fraud, Peter honestly, we've taken advice at the website and the clear legal opinion is that you cannot buy history. The new owner may have bought the old club's assets but he cany buy Rangers' history any more than he can buy Celtic's. These things cany be traded, Man United cannot buy Liverpool's European Cups even if they wanted to. Rangers' history died with the old club and the taxman will have plenty to say about it if they try and convince anyone otherwise. That's the line we're running wi on the website and of course it's another crucial aspect ay this whole story that your colleagues in the media are conveniently ignoring.

— They're no just ignoring it though, are they Sully? Some of these outlets are actively trying to convince people that the opposite is the case, quite explicitly. Certain sections ay the press are stating unequivocally that it's the same Rangers, and the history and traditions have passed to the Newco. They seem to be deliberately feeding misinformation to the Rangers fans, who are desperately trying to grapple wi the financial and legal implications of what's happened to their club. Why are they doing this, do you think? Are they trying to intervene and exert some influence? Because as you suggest, the relevant authorities areny gony be the least bit impressed by the inaccurate, agenda-driven ramblings of a few nutters in the media, sure they're no?

— You'd certainly hope that'd no be the case, Peter, and this is what you have to go after them for. It's fraud that's being perpetrated here, fraud and collusion, by Rangers and their pals in the press, who look like they want to have a hand in the Newco's downfall, just as they did wi the Oldco. Hector the Taxman isny gony allow himself to be bullied by tabloid editors in the West ay Scotland or anywhere else. This is the crux of Rangers problem, they're dealing wi people who cany be scared or intimidated by their antics or who areny necessarily too impressed by their perceived status within society. This is what this club has always feared the most – being subject to the assessment and judgment of fair-minded people, and in particular of course fair-minded people with authority over them. They've no had to deal wi too much ay that down the decades, whether it was wi their infamous sectarian signing policy or anything else. And now of course they're gony be subjected to the full force of the bureaucratic aloofness of Her Majesty's Revenue and Customs. Bring it on.

— Bring it on right enough, I laughed at Sully's rhetorical flourish at the end there.

— Listen, mate, I need to go. The boss is here, I need to put a shift in.

— What you up to?

— We need to gut these flats so the owner can do them up and rent them out again, or sell them or whatever he decides.

— Right, well good luck wi that. And thanks for your thoughts again, Mark, you've been a big help.

— No bother, hope it goes well at the editorial meeting.

— Cheers, aye. I doubt there's ever been one quite like this before, but you've gied us some good pointers anyway, so thanks. Speak to you later.

— Keep the faith, Fitzy, mate! We wereny paranoid enough!

— See you soon, Sully, I laughed, — thanks again.

I hung up the phone and fished out my notebook.

268

PETER: *Good evening and welcome to another edition of The Scottish Football Debate with me, Peter Fitzpatrick. I'm joined in the studio tonight by my regular sidekick, Martin Dodds. Doddsy, there's only one story in town, and consequently only one place we can start the show tonight, and I guess it's the question a lot of Rangers fans and fans of other clubs will be asking as well ... how the hell did it ever come to this?*

DODDSY: *Dear me, I must admit, Peter, I've been asking myself the same thing over and over again. I've been following this story very closely for what seems like a heck of a long time now, but I can honestly say that I never thought I'd see the day when Rangers football club were liquidised.*

PETER: *Well I mean, just where do we start? We've been doing this show for nearly two years now, but this is unquestionably the biggest story we've covered in all that time, and we'll be devoting the entire show to this issue tonight to see if, over the course of the next half an hour or so, we can shed some light on exactly what's happened here. In the meantime I'd like to introduce our studio guest this evening to talk about this huge story in the history of Scottish football, Michael French of the Scotsman. Michael, it's been a long drawn out affair since Rangers entered administration, has the length of the process dulled your senses at all? Can you still get your mind around what's happened to this club?*

FRENCH: *Good evening, Peter, yes I was kind of getting used to the idea that this day might eventually arrive, it has seemed inevitable to me for some time now, although I have to concede Doddsy, I'm still struggling to come to terms with the idea of Rangers being liquidised.*

Laughter.

DODDSY: *Sorry, liquidated. I meant liquidated, sorry.*

PETER: *You know, he's been getting that wrong all afternoon, so he has. I tried to gloss over it, but apparently it didn't go unnoticed.*

DODDSY: *Liquidated, sorry. Hey, dae I look like a financial expert to you? They may as well have been liquidised, Scottish football has been liquidised as far as I can tell, if there's no gony be a Glasgow Rangers any more.*

PETER: *Doddsy, come on, redeem yourself here, mate. How did this happen? I don't want to play the blame game with you, I know we live in a blame culture, and we've always tried to steer clear of that on this show, but we're no talking about Scotland losing a friendly international here, or one of our teams suffering an early exit from Europe. We're talking about one of the biggest clubs in the country going to the wall over unpaid debt to, amongst others, the tax authorities. Her Majesty's Revenue and Customs of all people, just to add a wee dash of irony to this whole mess. I'll repeat my question to you at the start of the show, how did it ever come to this, and who is responsible?*

DODDSY: *Well I think that's all gony come out in the end-up, Peter, once the liquidators have completed their investigations. I nearly said liquidisers there for a minute ...*

PETER: *You did well, carry on, naebidy noticed. Never mind the liquidators though, who at the club do you think is gony carry the can here?*

DODDSY: *Well I think it's clear that the two previous owners of the club are the ones in particular that the liquidators will be looking at. They ran up massive debts when times were good and the banks were allowing them to borrow money left, right and centre; and then when times changed and things became a bit harder, as they inevitably do, the economic winds shifted direction, and they were left with bills that they couldny afford to pay back. And catastrophically, as it turned out, they* started using money that should have been collected as tax to run the day to day overheads at the club.

PETER: *Do you feel the same way, Michael?*

FRENCH: *I do yes, but I think you've only touched the tip of the iceberg there, Doddsy. I mean that's how the club found itself in administration, which at the time we all thought was a day that we'd never see. Now this has happened. There's no doubt, if you're going to start divvying up the blame, that the greatest culpability will have to be borne by the two owners, as you mentioned, one who ran up the debts and the other who came in promising to turn things round but in the end only made matters ten times worse.*

PETER: *You say ten times worse, but is that the case? I'm astonished at the scale of the wrong-doing under the David Murray regime. All these matters are still sub judice of course, but there are allegations of illegal payments to players and other staff, which is effectively a form of tax evasion. Then they used this dual contract system to try and cover their tracks, but only the original contract was registered with the football authorities. So presumably, for a decade or more, Rangers were playing games with improperly registered players. This is unbelievable, isn't it? The sheer scale of it, Michael. We're used to the idea of a smaller club occasionally maybe making a mistake, and fielding an ineligible player in a Cup tie, perhaps because they're poorly administered or can't afford to employ someone to check for these potential oversights, and consequently finding themselves thrown out the competition. But the implications here, if Rangers have been fielding ineligible players for such a length of time in all competitions, go way beyond anything we've ever had to deal with before. I mean, this is off the scale, is it not? This has to be one of the biggest scandals in the history of sport, surely?*

FRENCH; *You would think it was unbelievable yes, but apparently it's true. It's a complicated matter, but for the EBT payments to be legal they had to be discretionary, so they couldn't be included in the players' contracts. But by not including the payments in the contracts that meant they were improperly registered. Rangers tried to keep both the taxman and the football authorities happy, but by coming up with this second contract fudge, they fell foul of both bodies and will now be subject to the judgment of both.*

PETER: *Doddsy, it's the club you love, but where do Rangers and indeed Scottish football go from here?*

DODDSY: *I'm coming round to the idea that the club should start again in the third division, Peter. The assets have been bought and a so-called Newco has been formed that will retain the old Rangers name in one form or another. They should go down to the third division and start again from there. Because if they're back in the SPL, it's gony be humiliation, they're no gony have any players, so there'll be nae chance of winning the League. Can you imagine going to Celtic Park with a bunch of kids in the team, and the abuse they'll be subjected to by the Celtic Park crowd ... No. Far better to start again in the lower Leagues and work your way back up the divisions.*

PETER: *And what about the sanctions and penalties? Should they be applied to the Newco if Rangers are found guilty?*

DODDSY: *No. It's a fresh start. The debt died with the old company and so should the sanctions. We're going down to the third division for goodness sake, what more sanctions do you want?*

PETER: *Does that make sense Michael? Fresh start for everyone.*

FRENCH: *To an extent yes, but what about the history? Does that die with the Oldco as well? Rangers seem to want to carry round the history of the old club with them, they'll play at Ibrox, call themselves Rangers et cetera et cetera, in a sense almost as if nothing has happened. Look, there's two ways of looking at it as far as I can tell. Logic dictates that either it's*

272

a new beginning for everyone, the new club starts again in the third division, they have no ties to the old club so the sanctions are void, the debt is void, the old Rangers are void and a new club takes their place, playing out of Ibrox perhaps, but in no way claiming to be tied to the old club. Or, the alternative argument is to say, the old corporate shell died when Rangers went bust, but the club itself survived. It was bought up along with the assets, they retain the history, the fanbase, everything that we would associate with the old Rangers, in which case of course they are subject to the penalties imposed by the football authorities for the crimes and misdemeanours of previous regimes at the club. In the latter case they might well find themselves flung out the League anyway, or have their license to compete withdrawn by the SFA, and they might also have their ground and training park seized by the liquidators, because they still have a potentially huge tax liability hanging over them, as well as all their other debts of course. It's not an easy choice, I must confess, it's a kind of Scylla and Charybdis scenario, but unfortunately that's just where Rangers find themselves just now.

PETER: *Doddsy, which of those two options would you prefer for Rangers?*

DODDSY: *I honestly wouldn't like to make that call right now, Peter, it's a nightmare scenario. In the end I think Scottish football needs Rangers, and the relevant arbitrators will do well to bear that in mind when they're passing judgment on all of this. Because you don't want to shoot the goose that lays the golden egg.*

PETER: *So it's a financial argument as much as anything else, Michael? The other clubs won't vote Rangers out the League because they need the income that the club generates through ticket sales and television revenue?*

FRENCH: *I think it is a financial argument as much as anything else but let's not make this mistake about voting Rangers out the League. Rangers aren't in the League.*

Rangers have been liquidated. We're talking about whether or not to admit a Newco calling itself Rangers, or Rangers United or Rangers of Glasgow or whatever new name they come up with, into the League or not.

PETER: *The Govan heidbangers, would that work, Doddsy? Can you see them in the top flight next season?*

DODDSY: *Hey, just be careful.*

PETER: *Just be careful, that's your response? Anything else you'd like to add, Doddsy? No? OK, we'll move on because this is what concerns me, I must confess. The immediate future of Newco Rangers is in the hands of the other SPL clubs, most of whom have been regularly beaten by Rangers in the last ten years; a big club, living beyond its means, allegedly cheating the taxman and artificially increasing its player budget, competing week in week out with ineligible players against these smaller provincial clubs who have for years been struggling to live within their means in increasingly difficult economic conditions ... and now potentially these clubs are going to vote a new Rangers back into the Premier League, effectively saying to them yes, come on, come back and beat us again so that we can feed off the scraps from your table. I mean, where's the integrity, where's the self-respect? Indeed, given the proposed scenario I've just illustrated, what is there left for Scottish football at all?*

DODDSY: *Totally agree, that's why Rangers should go down to the third division.*

PETER: *Even though Scottish football needs them?*

DODDSY: *Scottish football needs them, yes. I didn't say the SPL needs them. The smaller clubs in Scotland might benefit by playing Rangers for a few seasons as they progress through the Leagues. Then we'll see how the SPL gets on without them.*

FRENCH: *Not much contrition there, I notice, from the Rangers end.*

PETER: *Can we leave that for now, Michael if you don't mind. I've tried, and honestly, if you're looking for an apology or a wee bit of humility here from Rangers, it's like chasing a fart in the wind to be honest. I'd like to develop this idea that Scottish football needs Rangers. Does it really? In the past when Rangers have been weak, in the early 1980s for example, Scottish football seemed to flourish; Aberdeen won European trophies, Dundee United very nearly emulated them on two occasions, Hearts and Hibs had strong teams, all full of Scottish players. Isn't this a bit of a myth that Scottish football needs a strong Rangers?*

DODDSY: *I was talking primarily financially, Peter. Of course if there's no Rangers in the League then one of those teams that you mention has the chance of finishing at least second. But what's the point of finishing second in a League that's financially crippled, with the individual clubs all struggling just to make ends meet?*

PETER: *Champions League qualification?*

DODDSY: *Och away, Motherwell or Kilmarnock in the Champions League? Sorry, I'm no buying it.*

PETER: *Can we leave aside the financial argument just for a minute? We've talked about the finances of football ad infinitum on other editions of this programme. I'm talking about the possibility of considering a brighter future for our football. Seeing this as an opportunity to ensure that going forward the game up here isn't all about money. It's been said before on this show and I'll say it again because it's worth repeating, the English have made the game down South all about money and that's the source of their strength. But in Scotland it's our greatest weakness, so we need to find something else to make our game revolve around. Can't we take what's happened to Rangers as a salutary lesson, and treat it as an opportunity to refresh and reinvigorate our football, free of the pernicious influence that the iron fist of this club has had on us down the years? There is this notion that Rangers tend to choke up the*

275

culture, Michael, they set the agenda in the mainstream media and elsewhere, and now they're effectively dead, can't we get back to the idea of football for football's sake, of playing the game for the love of it, for the enjoyment and of course for the winning? Am I just a hopeless romantic or is there an opportunity for Scottish football, in the wreckage of Rangers' liquidation, to bring about a change of emphasis in the overall direction of our game?

FRENCH: *I'm not sure I follow you, Peter.*

PETER: *Well I'm not repeating myself, Michael, this show isn't long enough. You don't see anything positive in this situation?*

DODDSY: *I think you're right, Peter. How did you put it, a salutary lesson? I think lessons have to be learned here, no question. You're quite correct when you say that there was an altogether far too cosy relationship at times between the media, or sections of the mainstream media, and the Rangers hierarchy. I know, I was there, on both sides ay the fence, and succulent lamb doesny begin to do it justice. The relationship was far too cosy and subservient at times, and it did infest the culture for the worse I would say. Not least because there was nobody there to warn Rangers when things were getting out of hand. Nobody wanted to bite the hand that fed them.*

PETER: *I find this intriguing, this really gets to the heart of the matter as far as I'm concerned. What you're saying, Doddsy, if I understand you correctly, is that this very idea which Rangers cultivated, that you had to be in with the in crowd, that criticism or even awkward questioning in the press would not be tolerated, this is the attitude which in the end played a part at least in Rangers' demise, because there was nobody there to offer a bit of perspective. Is that correct, nobody wanted to give Caesar the bad news?*

DODDSY: *I think that's fair comment, Peter, yes.*

PETER: *So what do you know? In the end the Laptop Loyal*

helped to kill off Rangers! How ironic is that!?

DODDSY: *I think at the very least the shenanigans of certain sections of the press were a significant factor, Peter, certainly. As I say, I was there, on both sides of the fence.*

PETER: *Extraordinary. Who'd have thunk it, eh? I guess your profession has a lot to answer for, Michael.*

FRENCH: *I don't know why you're looking at me, I was a lone voice in the wilderness, trying to offer an alternative viewpoint, away from the West of Scotland mafia, as they've become known in certain quarters. You're entirely right though, there was a kind of symbiotic relationship between Rangers and sections of the press in Glasgow that was quite frankly unhealthy to say the least, and I've no doubt it was a contributing factor to what went wrong in the end. That's certainly one lesson for my profession that has to be taken from all this, as you say, Peter. You have to be able to stand back and ask questions of power, and that applies as much to the sports related media as it does to media in other spheres, because of course a lot of this was motivated by sheer partisan allegiances. A lot of people just wanted Rangers to keep on winning, and to continue enjoying the situation as it was. But nothing lasts for ever, sadly, and now it seems, it's all over.*

PETER: *I'm interested in the partisan allegiances that you refer to, because of course the bloggers and the internet bampots out there were dismissed as precisely that, weren't they? This catastrophe was predicted years in advance, I remember discussing it with some friends who run a blog a good while ago now, when I first moved back home to this country, long before this show was even conceived of. Not with members of your profession though Michael, but with biased, partisan, nothing better to do with their time internet bloggers, who analysed the figures and did the math, as the Americans say, and predicted this outcome years ago. Yet they were never taken seriously by the mainstream media, who for far too long appeared to just carry on regardless. I guess what I'm asking Michael is, do you sense that, just as the first Gulf War was CNN's war, and the second Gulf War was Al Jazeera's, ownership of the Rangers liquidation story can be claimed in the same way by the internet bloggers? I'm not saying they were there with their cameras in their hotel rooms in Baghdad as the bombs flew over, but metaphorically at least they were there on the ground, tracking this story from the start. Particularly I would have to say, certain websites run by unapologetic Celtic supporters, who were on the case right away, and despite the obvious temptation on their part to indulge in a wee bit of partisan wishful thinking, they appeared to predict and analyse the progress of this huge story with uncanny accuracy, fairness and objectivity – indeed with what you might call high journalistic standards?*

FRENCH: *They've put some members of my profession to shame, no doubt about it, Peter. Some members, I stress. Doddsy's right, there are certain people who, I would say, need to go away and have a look at the journalistic code, and maybe start taking their jobs a wee bit more seriously in the future. Because we do live in a different age now. Citizen journalism is here to stay. Anyone with a mobile phone camera and a Twitter account can become a journalist now. But whether this episode represents a potential sea change in how sports journalism is conducted in this country, I have my doubts. Call me cynical if you like but I don't think too much will change in that regard, I'm sorry to say. Certainly not in the short to medium term anyway.*

PETER: *One thing will change for sure, there'll be no more succulent lamb on the menu, that cosiness between the media and Rangers is over now, surely?*

FRENCH: *Time will tell, won't it? The story isn't going to go away anytime soon, we'll see what happens with the Newco.*

PETER: *That would be unforgivable surely, if lessons weren't learned after all that has happened. Doddsy, I'll give you the last word this week, and I suppose this must sound like a strange question, given the fact that Rangers are now dead. But I have to ask you nevertheless, where do you think Rangers go from here?*

DODDSY: *The fans need clarity going forward, we need to know what happens next. In the end we all need to get behind the new company and the new owners, despite the misgivings we may have about them. There'll always be a Glasgow Rangers in my opinion, so let's support the new club.*

PETER: *OK, on that note we have to leave it for another week. I hope you can join us next week when, if there's time in amongst all these off-field shenanigans, we'll be previewing the European Championships to be held in Poland and the Czech Republic. So make sure you stay with us over the summer, because one thing's for sure, we won't be short of things to talk about. Until next time then, goodnight and keep enjoying your football.*

— Roll credits. And we're out.

16. INTERFERENCE AND RECEPTION

— Malcolm will be joining us today, Helen informed the room. — I'm under strict instructions not to begin the meeting until he has arrived. Would anyone like a coffee while we're waiting? Doddsy, Alison and myself all put in orders for hot drinks and we sat there in the spartan, third-floor meeting room with its whiteboards and its powerpoints and its uncomfortable office furniture for what seemed like an interminably long period ay time, waiting for the big boss' arrival, before Helen finally returned, accompanied by both Gus McGregor and Malcolm Munroe. A staffer from the canteen wheeled in a drinks trolley and Helen began pouring the coffees.

— Gus has some good news for us, it would appear, she remarked as all the eyes in the room fixed on the executive.

— We're going to the Czech Republic in the summer, he announced. — One programme, a series finale set against the backdrop of the European Championships, which as you all know, are being jointly hosted by the country this year. We'll be in Prague, Peter, on the eve of the tournament, he nodded in my direction as he conveyed this information. — Hopefully we can set up an OB from the venue of the opening match.

— We're gony be up at Letná? I was elated at McGregor's revelation. This was potentially the most significant news I'd been given in the last two years because to take the show out of the studio and be trusted with an outside broadcast in a foreign location was no small thing, and the emotional relevance of the destination to me in particular was lost on no-one. We were all firing off questions for the next five minutes or so, which Gus was doing his best to answer, but he was mostly straight-batting our various inquiries back at us with his customary unruffled professionalism. Eventually, when he could offer us no more answers, he left the room, but Munroe stayed. It took a while for the general delight and appreciation in the room to start seeping away, as we began to realise that something else seemed to be going on, although at this stage it wasn't clear what.

— Any particular reason you're joining us today, Malcolm? I eventually asked.

— I just wanted to share this happy moment with you, he remarked smugly.

— It's great news. I can't wait to tell my wife, but we'll be starting our editorial meeting soon. Not only had McGregor indicated that Lenka would be welcome along, but he had hinted that they would be willing to use her as a translator on the trip, and I was dying to let her know what was happening and talk through the implications with her.

— I'll be staying for your EM this afternoon, Munroe announced.

— Really?

— Yes, I like to sit in on these meetings from time to time, he mused. — Especially now that this programme appears to be showing so well in the ratings. I'm keen to see for myself the talent that lies behind what we're doing here.

— We've been showing well in the ratings since we started out Malcolm, Alison pointed out. — Are you sure your presence today has nothing to do with the fact that this is such a hot week for news? she echoed my thoughts exactly.

— You poor cynical soul, Munroe chastised her. — It's true there are certain issues which are high profile and current, and yes, it is a particularly sensitive time at the moment. We need to get the show right this week, lads and lassies, both in its tone and in its pitch, and in its content as well of course.

— Let's kick off, shall we? Helen had apparently absorbed this unusual and, at least as far as I was concerned, highly alarming development quicker than the rest of us. — Who wants to start? she asked.

— Well I think the obvious topic to lead with would be the continuing saga of the liquidation of Rangers, I eventually suggested. — There have been a host of new revelations and developments in the last week and I think we should bring the viewers up to date with everything that's been going on since our last edition.

— What's your line and how are you selling it? Munroe asked. I was slightly confused by the question, not because I wasn't used to Munroe's tiresome use of such sportsdesk jargon, although we had done a pretty good job ourselves to steer clear of that kind ay pretentious language in our two years on the show, but because the answer should have been obvious to anyone with a passing acquaintance of how this programme worked.

— I thought we might lead off with it straight from the top, run with it strongly all the way through, and conclude with the fallout and the potential consequences, I proposed.

— So you want to devote another entire show to this subject?

— Of course, that's our tried and tested format, Malcolm. We select one particular topic and stick with it, and we've barely even scratched the surface here with these unfolding events, I explained. — As some of my colleagues are fond of saying, it's the story that keeps on giving. There's always next week or next month or next year to come back and talk about something else.

— This week is an exception.

— What do you mean, Malcolm? Sorry Helen, what's going on here? I put down my pen and closed my notebook. — This kind of interference has never happened before on our show, I pointed out.

— Your show? Listen to the man! What's never happened before? A senior manager taking an interest in what it is you do up here? Well, perish the thought.

— Malcolm, the reason this programme is showing so well in the ratings, as we've just mentioned, is in my opinion largely due to our editorial independence and the license we've been given to determine our own content. As I'm sure you know, David and Gus leave us to it for the most part. They've learned to trust our judgment in terms of discretion and sensitivity and in managing our audience's expectations. We know what we're doing here. Suggestions are welcome, as are criticisms and observations, but don't try and interfere with our editorial judgment. That's not how this show works. We've never even had an Exec Producer looking over Helen's shoulder, David trusts her implicitly and lets her get on with it. The result is a dynamic, vibrant and lively programme, slightly controversial but only so far as we're able to give people more insight and analysis into what's actually happening. That's been our remit from the start and that's why we've been able to deliver on ratings and exert a bit of influence in high places here and there.

— Influence, huh?

— Come on, Malcolm, I've been here two years, I know influence is what it's all about, much more so these days than ratings or circulation even. The two tend to go hand in hand most of the time, but if it comes to the crunch most newspapers and broadcasters will slash their prices and take a hit financially if they think there's some other advantage to be gained in the corridors of power.

—Two years eh? A veteran! You certainly talk like one! he remarked caustically. — You can't devote the entire programme to Rangers. Our rivals are going large on it and indeed we've been covering the story ourselves in every possible outlet. You've devoted one show to the subject already, this time we have to offer something else, confound those audience expectations once more, just as we've done so successfully in the past.

— Malcolm, I protested, — our rivals are going large on it as you say, but they're not grappling with the full implications. For the most part they seem to be skirting around the main issues. All we've heard from them is 'Rangers will never enter administration', then when the bailiffs turned up at the door it shifted to 'it's inconceivable that Rangers will be liquidated', now the club is dead and buried all we're hearing is 'new Rangers are just the same as old Rangers and they'll be back in the SPL next season' etc., etc., ad infinitum. Folk are sick ay aw this bullshit, they look to us to tell them the truth and that's what we intend to do.

— The truth? The awful truth, wherever it leads? The truth, the whole truth and nothing but the truth? *Mea culpa, mea culpa!* Is that what you're saying?

I was gony chastise the cunt for breaking into Latin, poor Doddsy wouldny know what the hell he was talking about, but then I realised that I'd started it two seconds earlier. — Something like that, Malcolm, yeah, I offered simply instead.

— And I suppose that truth involves Rangers being punished incessantly for the heinous crimes against humanity they have committed in the name of sport? It occurred to me, possibly the first time since I'd known him, that Malcolm Munroe was losing his cool. However it wasn't the first time since I started working in this business that I found myself wondering what it was that Rangers did to have friends like these in such high places.

— Well I happen to think that the offences they have committed, which we all but know to be true, are extremely grave, Malcolm yes. Doddsy disagrees as to the seriousness of the allegations. He wants to offer the club's fans a bit of perspective, and some hope for the future, and we fully intend to argue it out on tomorrow's show.

— Not this time, I'm afraid.

— Malcolm, please … I looked round the room in

exasperation, searching for support. — Doddsy, what do you make ay this, mate?

— Gets me aff the hook anyroad, Doddsy shrugged. — There doesny seem to be much hope or perspective out there at the minute. I could dae the old singing fae the same hymn sheet, morale boosting, rallying cry sort ay nonsense, but that's usually in the context ay a deflating defeat or being knocked out ay Europe a wee bit too early. We're aff the fuckin chart here but, nae cunt knows whit you're supposed to dae when you've been fuckin liquidated.

— What do your pals at the club think? Helen asked.

— They're aw fuckin scoobied an aw, he revealed. — But they'll be workin on something, I promise you that. The PR firms are gony be making hay oot ay aw this, that's for fuckin sure.

— Tell me what you think we should be talking about tomorrow then, I asked Malcolm.

— Well, he considered, — we have this interesting segment on women's football that we could peg to the upcoming Women's European Championships, which are talking place in Belarus next month.

— Are they indeed?

— Oh yes sir, they surely are. Weren't you aware that the UEFA Women's European Championships were taking place later this summer?

— No, Malcolm, I wasn't. Who the hell is interested in women's football?

— A large number of women, I should imagine. Women make up fifty percent of the population, you know, and a sizeable proportion of your audience as well, I shouldn't have to remind you.

— Yes, that's because the majority of women who are

interested in football are interested primarily in the men's game. The research is quite clear on that, just ask Alison. I'm not knocking minority sports, but as I said a minute ago, that's not what we do here. It's beyond the scope of our remit, especially when the biggest story in the history of Scottish football has landed on our doorstep. We should be following up and expanding on the whole Rangers situation, examining it from every angle until we're blue in the face hearing about it if necessary, because that's what the punters want.

— I wouldny know what to say about women's football, Malcolm, Doddsy eventually managed to find his voice to back me up. — It's like butter and jam together on your toast, I just cany hack it.

— How is it like butter and jam on your toast? I asked incredulously.

— Well, I like them separate, Doddsy expounded, — toast and butter is fine, toast and jam is fine, but put them thegether and it's just a mess.

— What the fuck are you talking about, mate?

— It's the same hing wi women's fitba, sure it is? It should work, I mean, I like women … and I like fitba …

— But women's football just confuses you? I finally caught on to the semblance of logic in Doddsy's argument.

— Exactly right. When you put them thegether, I just cany hack it, honestly.

— Alison, what do the stats tell us about coverage of women's football? I indicated. Alison had been playing about on her laptop for much of the duration of this discussion, and I hoped that a ratings warning might help Munroe see sense.

— The audience for it is limited in the extreme, she pointed out. — The numbers are right down there with shinty and handball, I'm afraid. Coverage would usually be limited to an add-on segment at the end of a mainstream broadcast.

286

— Fine, we'll do that then, Munroe announced.

— How do you mean, Malcolm? Helen ventured.

— We can lead on Rangers, no more than ten or fifteen minutes, then it's the piece on the women's game. If we cover it properly tomorrow, then we probably won't have to mention women's football ever again. Which between you, me and the four walls would be no bad thing. But there you go, that's showbusiness for you.

— Here was me thinking you had a genuine interest in the women's game, Malcolm, I observed.

— So, Munroe coughed, — Rangers? Game me through it.

— The run through is not until tomorrow, Malcolm.

— I know and I'll be there. In the meantime, show me what you have.

— Peter has some thoughts on how Rangers landed themselves in this situation, Helen disclosed. — That would seem to be a good place to start.

— OK, let's hear it.

— Well, I sighed, opening my notebook again, — Rangers were advised by this dodgy pornographer guy that the EBT scheme was a legal way to avoid paying tax on high earnings. The problem was that the payments had to be discretionary. No self-respecting foreign mercenary is going to play for Rangers on the promise of a discretionary payment, so there had to be a secondary, undisclosed contract. This is a key factor in the club's current difficulties, because secondary contracts represent a violation of the governing body's rules, which state that all payments received for playing football have to be properly registered and fully disclosed.

— So they fell between two stools.

— Exactly. They could either pay their players in a standard contract, in which case they would have to pay top rate tax on their earnings; or they could use EBTs, which would mean the amounts would have to be assured with a secret agreement. Rangers maintain it was an administrative error, and the payments were there in their annual accounts, but nobody at the SFA bothered to check. Now it's finally all being examined closely and as you say, in the end it looks like they fell between two stools; they neither satisfied the tax authorities nor the governing bodies.

— All this is still sub judice of course.

— Rangers have appealed the verdict of the tax tribunal yes, although they've already admitted liability in several cases, and the governing bodies' investigations continue. But we've seen the evidence and we're satisfied there's been wrong-doing.

— So am I, Munroe concurred.

— We talked about this last week, Doddsy remarked.

— We mentioned it last week with Michael French, but we can follow up and expand on it here.

— Agreed. If we never went back to something we'd already covered, most of you lot would be out of a job in about a fortnight, Munroe pointed out.

— Right enough.

— Would anyone like more tea or coffee? Helen, it seemed, had been reduced to the status of a tea lady in this particular meeting, in place of her usual role as chair and final arbiter on all editorial matters.

— No thanks.

— No thanks, Helen.

— OK, I'm happy with that. Martin, do you have anything to offer at this stage?

— I'll just counter wi the usual. None of the current

allegations have been proved, Rangers are still ...

— Rangers are innocent until proven guilty, blah blah blah, bullshit bullshit. Yes, OK, I'm happy with that. Where do we go from there?

— I want to focus on the serious implications of the whole scandal, the unprecedented nature and the extent of the offences.

— Where are you going with this?

— Well, if proven, I believe this would represent one of the biggest and longest corruptions in the history of sport. The allegations are that Rangers spent at least ten years fielding improperly registered players, avoiding taxes, beating small provincial clubs who were desperately trying to live within their means, after one or two high profile administration events had cleared out most of the cowboys ... and all this at a time when financial fair play was the buzz issue of European football and corporate tax avoidance was a major scandal in domestic politics. Rangers were signing players they couldn't afford and paying them wages with money that wasn't rightfully theirs. It was an artificial way of increasing their footballing budget, which I will contend was akin to cheating, or financial doping as it's sometimes known. The evidence shows these practices go back at least a decade, but who knows how long it's really been going on? I can only think that the widespread use of drugs amongst East German athletes in the 1970s and 80s constitutes a more prolonged and sustained period of cheating in sport.

— Scratch all of that.

— What?

— We won't be going there. I'm sorry, but this is not the appropriate outlet for such hyperbole.

— I'm afraid I have to disagree with your characterisation, Malcolm. Every outlet in Scotland agrees this is one of the biggest stories in sport. It's leading the national news for Christ's sake.

— It is, which is why I think enough has been said about it already. We can do some of the analysis stuff with the EBTs and the dual contracts, then we move on to the women's game.

— I want to include something about Rangers' history, I asserted. — I have it on reliable advice that Newco Rangers are perpetrating a fraud by claiming to be the same club, wearing the same livery, laying claim to the old club's history et cetera, while the company has gone bust owing tens of millions of pounds. If that's the case, and the tax authorities hear about it, then we could be heading into a whole new cycle of this story. The liquidators won't stand for it, the taxman will quite justifiably object and the acquisition of the liquidated club's assets could be struck down in court. In which case the new club's problems could be only just beginning, they might end up dwarfing the troubles of the old club.

— Sorry, we won't be going there either. Not tomorrow anyway.

— Why? I demanded to know, the exasperation in my voice by this time surprising even me. — Look, Malcolm, this is the first time you've ever come down here, I pointed out. — It's the first time anyone in fact has tried to influence or limit content on this show since the first few weeks of the programme, when we were just finding our feet and we appreciated a wee bit of assistance at the time because of our inexperience. But we know what we're doing now. And I'm telling you, this edition is going to tank. We have a right good programme here, Malcolm, with a dedicated, appreciative and growing audience, and we want to keep it going. It's like you're deliberately ruining the magic we have, and all for what? You've still not explained to us the purpose of this intervention.

— All I can say to you is that it has been discussed at a

very high level, and that this is the decision which has been arrived at.

— I can't help thinking, Malcolm that your presence here is a result of the documentary that was aired on another channel earlier in the week, which revealed the extent of what Rangers have been up to, ever since God knows when. There could be waves and waves of this for months to come, years even. We're only just starting to get to grips with the implications here. The mainstream media have barely scratched the surface yet, in terms of the fallout and the ...

— THIS IS THE MAINSTREAM FUCKING MEDIA! Munroe suddenly exploded. — When are you people going to fucking realise that? This. Is. The. Mainstream. Fucking. Media. He repeated, more quietly this time, jamming his finger on the table in staccato rhythm to accentuate his every word. — This! he gestured at the scenery. — What do you think all this is? This building, look at it. Do you think all this fancy architecture was put up here just for show? This is the mainstream fucking media, it's fucking heart and soul, and the sooner that fact starts to sink into your tiny minds then the sooner we'll all get along a fuck of a lot easier.

It was an astonishing moment, for everyone. I wished there was a camera crew hovering nearby who had captured the moment in passing, or perhaps could come in and film it and preserve the reaction for posterity, revealing the true Munroe in all his company man badness. The outburst had shorn him of every aspect of front and pretence and cast him clearly in all his dubious, Machiavellian, control-freak, media man glory. Very quickly though a dawning realisation began to wash over me. It started in the pit of my stomach but moved rapidly into my brain and struck me with the force of a blow to the head. I saw in one indescribable moment the futility and pointlessness, not only of the discussion we'd just been participating in, but of every discussion we'd ever had on the show, and of all the hard work we'd put in over the last two years. The idealism and the joyful naïvety of everything we'd been attempting to achieve up to that point passed out of me at that moment and was lost forever.

My mobile phone began to ring, with its muffled but identifiable tone interrupting the stony silence which had fallen over the room.

— I thought you were supposed to switch those things off during these meetings, Munroe observed dryly.

— It's my family phone, I pointed out flatly. — It's my wife calling, she only uses it if it's very important so I better take the call. Excuse me, I stepped outside and answered the phone, — Hello Lenka, what's up darlin?

— Peter, are you free?

— I'm actually in a meeting just now, can I call you back?

— Erm yes OK, but I am coming into your office.

— Why? What's the matter?

— Don't worry, I need to see you.

— Alright, I'll call you back shortly.

— No. I will arrive in ten minutes, so please meet me at the reception.

— OK, I'll do that, bye, I hung up. — She's on her way in, I informed the room when I returned. There didn't seem to be much discussion going on in my absence.

— What for? Helen asked.

— I don't know, she wouldn't say.

— I believe we're pretty much done here, Munroe declared.

— Are you sure everything's OK? Helen looked at me.

— There doesn't seem to be a problem, but she's coming in. There are a few things I need to talk through with her anyway, pertaining to the news about Prague and this discussion we've just been having.

— Our discussion? What does your wife know about how the media works?

— Not much, luckily for her, I answered Munroe.

— OK, meeting adjourned, I'll see everyone tomorrow at two o'clock, Helen announced.

— I hope your wife is OK, Munroe told me as we slowly left the room. — I apologise for my outburst, Peter, I shouldn't have lost my cool like that. It's not like me. But I don't have to remind you, do I, that this is a public service broadcaster? Covering minority sports is an important part of our charter for the community.

— You're right, it's not like you, Malcolm. It must just be the effect I have on some people. And no you don't have to remind me of our wider responsibilities. I'm just confused and pretty stunned as a matter of fact. I thought you trusted us to put together an independently produced, in-house, edgy programme that viewers can relate to. Either that or you can interfere as and when it suits you, in which case we can make some other sort of programme altogether. This sort of editorial pressure from above is against the spirit of this show and our audience will pick up on it, I assure you. They'll detect it, I know they will. They'll figure out that something, somewhere is not as it should be. They're a very discerning, media savvy bunch of people, and they'll know they're watching something other than what they're used to seeing.

— It's your job to ensure that nothing seems amiss, that's what we pay you for. I'm sure you'll bring all your broadcasting skills to bear on the programme tomorrow in your usual way.

— I'll do my job to the best of my ability, Malcolm, I can assure you of that, but like I say, I need to talk this through with my wife.

— You do that, Munroe told me as he turned on his heels and departed along the corridor.

Alison looked at me all doey-eyed and expectant.

— Yes please, Ali, women's football. All the help you can give me, I told her.

*

— Peter, I'm pregnant.

— What?

— I'm pregnant.

— What?

— I'm pregnant.

— What?

— *Milačku*, I'm pregnant.

— What?

— Please stop saying what.

— What? I mean, erm, how do you know?

— I did an examination.

— You mean a test?

— A test, yes.

— What did the test say?

— It said that I am pregnant.

— Right.

— Are you happy?

— Of course, yes, I embrace my wife although it's a

strange moment, in which temporarily, I hardly seem to know that she's there. — Sorry, I'm just surprised, I eventually smile at her.

— Why? We are married nearly four years.

— Right enough … Sit down over here, I tell her and I sit down myself on a plastic green seat, before I fall down. I barely notice the cheesy, smiling two metre sized image of my face towering over us on a lime-green billboard.

— So we are going to make here a little Czech boy, I reach my hand towards her belly.

— Or maybe a wee Scottish girl, she responds, playing out the scenario we had often rehearsed together in some of our more tender moments. This time though, it was for real.

— Let's go home, I indicated.

— Are you finished here at work?

— Yes.

— OK.

— We can go home and make sure, I suggested with a glint in my eye, hoping that Lenka would pick up on my amorous intentions, as we left the reception area and departed the building.

— I am sure, she answered and for a moment it seemed that the subtlety of my suggestion had failed to penetrate the language barrier. But then I thought I detected a slight smile growing in the corner of my wife's mouth.

— You'll never guess where we're going next month, I remarked.

17. THE LAST EPISODE

PETER: *Hello and welcome to another edition of the Scottish football debate, the last in the present series unfortunately, because it seems we could go on talking and talking all summer about what's been happening in our game recently and still not fully exhaust the subject. We're joined this week by Shona McGovern, the captain of the Scotland Ladies team, and we'll be hearing more about the exploits of Shona and her teammates at the Women's European Championships later in the programme. I'm also joined by my customary sidekick Martin Dodds. Doddsy, you ready, mate? Let's jump right in from where we left off last week, shall we? It's the biggest story in the history of Scottish football – the liquidation of Rangers, discuss!*

DODDSY: *I'm not sure we're any further down the line this week than we were last week, are we, Peter? It's a tragedy we're witnessing, unfolding day by day in front of our very eyes, an absolute tragedy. This is Glasgow Rangers we're talking about, it's a tragedy when it happens to a small club, like Gretna, or Clydebank or whoever ...*

PETER: *Third Lanark?*

DODDSY: *Exactly, but no to Glasgow Rangers. This cany be happening, honestly I still cany believe it, Peter, that we're here today talking about this, I've just no come to terms wi it yet, I've got to be honest.*

PETER: *I think that sense of unreality has maybe hindered Rangers themselves Doddsy, would you not agree? Because perhaps people all the while believed that the club would somehow extricate itself from this situation by whatever means. All the time they were sinking deeper and deeper into financial difficulty, it was always assumed that they would somehow be OK in the end, and now reality has dawned, and the club is no more.*

DODDSY: *You could well be right, Peter, I just ..., I just .... I'm sorry, I don't know what to say.*

PETER: *I understand. Never mind, let's try and concentrate this week on some of the fallout, if we can. We know a bit more now about the allegations Rangers will face after another explosive documentary in midweek, which revealed further evidence of the scale of their misuse of the dual contracts. Rangers are bang to rights here, aren't they, Shona? At a time when financial fair play is the talk of European football, financial doping as it's known, I know you're in a delicate state of mind, Doddsy, so I'll choose my words carefully, Rangers have been caught cheating here, have they not?*

— Careful, Peter, we've been over this, Helen whispered in my earpiece. — Don't go too far with the language, we don't want Malcolm breathing down our necks, she warned.

DODDSY: *I think cheating is too strong a word, Peter ...*

PETER: *Let's hear from Shona, can we?*

SHONA: *I don't know if cheating is the right word, Peter, that's for other people to decide when the evidence is presented and the various inquiries have run their course, but I think it's becoming increasingly clear to everyone that Rangers were up to no good. The most damning thing for me is that it was all borrowed money, I couldn't believe that when I watched the documentary. It appears that the banks just gave the club absolute free rein to build up mountains of debt. We thought it was David Murray's fortune that was bankrolling Rangers, because that's what we were led to believe by the press, but it seems he hardly put a penny of his own money in. In fact he was taking money out the club through the EBT scheme, so he certainly has questions to answer as well.*

PETER: *It was David Murray's stated intention to ensure there was as wide a gap as possible between Rangers and Celtic. Well it seems he's achieved that now, Doddsy, only not quite, I suspect, in the way he intended.*

DODDSY: *You can say what you like about David Murray and I'm no gony defend the guy. The worst thing he done, as far as I'm concerned, was gie the club to Craig Whyte, but that's another story. Like I said though, Peter, I think this use of the word cheating is inappropriate here, certainly as far as the players were concerned. They were paid to play football and that's what they done. They turned up to training every day, turned up on matchday every week and gave their all for Rangers. How is that cheating? Players areny financial experts, they won those games, won those titles fair and square, there's no question of any wrongdoing as far as the players are concerned.*

PETER: *I don't think anyone's suggesting that the players were wilfully involved in anything untoward. If the EBTs turn out to be illegal, I don't believe there will be too many people lining up to have a go at the players on that score, because as you say, they have representatives that deal with all their financial affairs. But proper financial governance is the responsibility of the corporate entity, is it not? The corporate entity that has now been liquidated, I might add. If the club had been administered properly and was acting within the rules then most of these players would never have been at Rangers in the first place, surely? Rangers were winning games and winning trophies with players that they couldn't actually afford because they were using taxpayers money to artificially increase their player budget, which seems to me a pretty clear case of financial doping, Doddsy. On top of that, most of the players it seems were improperly registered, and I think we've seen enough documentary evidence now to know that these allegations are real and substantial, and have to be answered.*

DODDSY: *We have. And I can see where you're coming from fae that point of view. Rangers would have gained a small sporting advantage by virtue of the unpaid tax on players' earnings, I can see the argument there.*

PETER: *A small sporting advantage? I surely don't need to remind you, Doddsy, that during this period Rangers won one title by a single point, and another by a single goal. It begs the question does it not, should Rangers be stripped of these titles and other trophies that they won while these schemes were in operation?*

DODDSY: *No, I don't think so.*

PETER: *Why not?*

DODDSY: *Because nothing's been proved yet, Peter. These are all just allegations we're talking about just now, this is all still sub judice.*

PETER: *You're perfectly correct, these matters are still under official investigation. Let me rephrase the questions. If these allegations are shown to be true, and I think now we've been presented with enough evidence to suggest that there is at the very least a case to be answered, then should the club be stripped of those titles that were won improperly, if the verdict goes against them?*

SHONA: *What difference does it make if they're gony be liquidated anyway?*

Laughter in the gallery.

DODDSY: *It makes a lot ay difference, sweetcheeks, I'll tell you. You just hang fire there, darling, you'll get your turn in a wee second, we'll come to the ladies' game in just a wee minute. Sorry what were you saying, Peter? Stripping ay titles? No, I don't think there should be any talk of that nature if I'm honest with you, Peter. That would mean depriving the players of honours that they won fairly and squarely. What are you gony do, ask them to hand the medals back? That's just not practical, and it's never gony happen in a million years anyway. Can you see lads like Richard Gough or Iain Ferguson or Stuart McCall handing back their medals just because some judge says they didny win them fairly and squarely. I'd like to be there when they go chapping on Archie Knox's door, asking for his 'medal back.*

PETER: *I think those guys had left the club by the time the EBT scheme was put in place, but in theory at least, why not? Why shouldn't the medals be handed back, it happens in athletics.*

DODDSY: *That's when competitors have willfully cheated, we've agreed the players didny do that.*

PETER: *I'm just pointing out, there's a precedent for handing medals back. But let's talk about the club. If the club is proved to have cheated,*

— Careful, Peter, that word is toxic. Please have a mind for what Malcolm is making of all this.

if the club is found guilty of wrongdoing, should the trophies be taken back? Let the players keep their medals if they want.

DODDSY: *No.*

PETER: *Why not?*

DODDSY: *Because Rangers have been punished enough.*

PETER: *Doddsy, you're an intelligent guy, you must know that's a pile ay nonsense. They haven't been punished at all yet. All that's happened so far is that Rangers have suffered the consequences of their own actions. You go into administration, you're deducted ten points; you allow yourself to be liquidated and you want to reform? You start again at the bottom. Those are the rules, you might as well complain about not being awarded any points if you suffer a defeat. That's just what happens. All this 'we've been punished enough' nonsense is like saying, I've been caught embezzling from the company, I've lost my job and my wife has left me, so please don't send me to jail. In fact, call off all the prosecutions and investigations into my erroneous activities, why don't you, because I've been punished enough and I have my reputation to think of.*

— That's enough on this, more than enough. Wrap it up and move on to the women's segment.

DODDSY: *I think we'll have to agree to disagree there, Peter.*

PETER: *Not for the first time! OK, well in case you were unaware, the women's European Championships will take place in Belarus over the summer and last month Scotland's ladies secured their qualification for this prestigious event. We'll talk more with Shona about it in a moment, but first our intrepid reporter Dougie Laird went to find out the secret of their success. Let's have a look at his report.*

I'd seen Munroe in the corner of my eye loitering about the set while we were recording, but now we had gone to Laird's piece, he wandered out in front of the cameras.

— This is nothing like the run through from this afternoon, he complained.

—Yes it is, Malcolm. It may not be word for word, but it's going according to plan. This is how we do this, we run through a rough version in the afternoon just to put us in the mood for the evening. It's all going well as far as I can see, I looked for Doddsy to back me up but I think he was still too shell-shocked from the discussion and from seeing his club being put out of business to offer much help. Munroe was a strict SBC by the book man and expected his programmes to run like clockwork. Our looser, more anarchic style seemed to go against everything he stood for. — Relax, Malcolm, we know what we're doing here, I assured him. — You better get off the set, mate, this is a pretty short piece. He's barely had a day to put it together.

— Back in thirty seconds, Helen confirmed audibly, at which point Munroe reluctantly removed himself from the set, like a thwarted predator retreating to its lair. I was pleased with Shona's contribution so far, she seemed bright and engaged and that gave me confidence to treat the segment with the

301

respect it was due. In addition Alison had come up trumps again with some great research, and as a result I had a few questions up my sleeve that I was keen to hear her views on.

— And we're back, Peter.

PETER: *Shona, you must be looking forward to the tournament in a few months. Can you tell me, what do you think of Scotland's chances overall?*

SHONA*: I think we're in with a shout. We won't be the favourites of course, the usual suspects, Germany, Sweden and possibly the French will be the most highly fancied teams, but we're going there to compete, that's for sure. And of course, just like in Argentina '78, 'England cany dae it, cause they didny qualify!'*

PETER: *Brilliant! I feel a wee song coming on there, Shona. Doddsy, women's football – discuss!*

DODDSY*: It's no for me, Peter, I must admit, although I might tune in at the end just to see them swap shirts.*

SHONA: *That's outrageous! You see, these are the prejudices and the preconceived ideas that we have to overcome in the women's game. You like football, don't you Martin? You should give these girls a chance, there's a high level of skill and quality on display at the Euros, it's a very high standard. It can be more technical and tactically based, because there isn't the same level of physicality as you find in the men's game.*

DODDSY: *Darlin, it's just no for me, I'm sorry. Best ay luck over in Belarus, but I'll be on my holidays by then. It should work, should it no, women's football? But I'm afraid it doesny, it's like butter and jam on your toast.*

PETER: *How is it like butter and jam on your toast, Doddsy?*

— Don't set him up for that line, please! Oh God …

DODDSY: *Well, I like butter on my toast and I like jam on my toast but the two just don't go thegether. Similarly, I like women and I like football, but women's fitba just confuses me.*

Laughter.

SHONA: *You do seem quite a confused individual, Doddsy, in more ways than one.*

PETER: *On a more serious note though Shona, I'd like to ask you, leaving Doddsy's concerns aside for a minute, is there a problem of perception generally towards women's football? If so, what would you say to those people who are maybe a bit sceptical?*

— Nice, Peter, like it. Keep running with that.

SHONA: *I think there is a problem, yes. The views we've heard expressed by your colleague there are not untypical, particularly within the sometimes macho or false male bravado world of the men's game. But I repeat to anyone who maybe has doubts about what I just stated, the women's game is full of quality. It's technically and tactically sophisticated and is maybe easier on the eye than some games you might see in a physically dominated men's league like ours in Scotland.*

PETER: *And of course, women's football has only just turned professional, so it's not necessarily fair to compare it to the men's game, because it has a hundred years of catching up to do. Whereas if you compare it with Junior football or the highest level of the amateur game, you're actually already well ahead of the curve in terms of development.*

SHONA: *We absolutely are, Peter, that's right. We want to arrive at a situation that you see in other sports like tennis, where the women's game is very similar to the men's, with the obvious exception that it's less physical and powerful. But we can match the men on the football field in terms of skill and finesse, and therefore we hope to offer an alternative version of the sport that many people might find more appealing.*

303

PETER: *So do you think the women's game will ever be as popular as the men's then?*

SHONA: *I don't see why not, I mentioned tennis and that has to be the model for us. Women's tennis is just as popular as men's.*

DODDSY: *I wonder why that is ...*

PETER: *Hang on Shona, that's not strictly true, is it? The men's game is more popular, even in tennis, which has a long tradition of women's competition. Can women's football really compete with men's, given that, as we've agreed, it's more or less starting from scratch here in Scotland?*

SHONA: *You're right, women's tennis doesn't draw the same ratings as men's, but crucially women are paid the same amount in tennis as their male equivalents. This is a really huge step in the right direction for women's sport.*

PETER: *Do you think female footballers should be paid as much as men?*

DODDSY: *Never in a million years, don't be ridiculous, Peter.*

PETER: *Doddsy, gony do us a favour a wee minute. Shut up and don't say another word until we go off the air. Would you do that please, mate?*

— Oh Jesus, Peter, please, we have five minutes to go. There's no way you can stretch this out for another five minutes without Martin, you've no right to speak to him like that anyway. You're holding this together great, please don't go rogue on us now, for fuck's sake!

SHONA: *Thank you. Yes I don't see why women shouldn't earn as much as men in football. It's certainly something to aspire to. Tennis has shown us that sport isn't all about market forces, because women's prize money is equal with men's, even though as you point out, more people watch men's tennis.*

304

PETER: *See, isn't this the crux of the matter though, Shona? Who's going to pay for it? Male footballers are already paid vastly over the odds, but it can be justified in only one way – market forces. With all the billionaires and media egos floating about, the game can apparently afford these outrageous salaries, unless you play for Rangers of course but we'll leave that aside for now. Can you tell me, who is going to pay you and your colleagues upwards of ten, twenty, thirty thousand pounds a week to play football in front of a few hundred people?*

SHONA: *I'm not suggesting that, Peter.*

PETER: *Don't get me wrong, I don't know and I don't want to know how much money you earn from playing the game, Shona, but let me pick up on the tennis analogy that you referred to, if I may. In that sport, when the two great dominating ideologies our modern society collided, namely women's issues and market forces, it was women who won through, and consequently female tennis players are now paid as much as their male counterparts, even though their game is less popular and they play fewer sets in grand slam events. How do women in general justify this and indeed how would you apply that justification to football?*

SHONA: *I'm sorry, Peter, you've lost me, I don't understand the question.*

— Get it back. Bring Doddsy in. Apologise to Doddsy, bring him in again and get it back. This is retrievable, Peter, please!

PETER: *Come on Shona, you've demonstrated already on this programme that you're an articulate and intelligent person. Don't be coy now, you understand me perfectly well. There was a direct conflict of interest in the game of tennis between women and their associated issues and market forces, and it was women who won. What implications does this have for other sports, including football, and indeed for society in general?*

— This is going to be the end of my career, your career, every fucker in here's career.

SHONA: *I'm sorry, Peter, I can't answer that, I disagree with the premise of your question.*

PETER: *Which premise? That women triumphed over market forces? That men's tennis is more popular than women's? Which premise do you not agree with?*

SHONA: *All of them, I should imagine.*

PETER: *Well OK, then, we'll move on because it's clear you don't want to answer the question, Shona.*

DODDSY: *Can I just say something here, Peter?*

PETER: *No, Doddsy, you can't, shut up. I think we'll leave it there, as far as tonight's discussion goes.*

— You can't leave it there, we still have three minutes left on the clock. Get it back before I have kittens.

PETER: *We still have a moment or two left of the programme tonight folks and I'd like to take this time to make a short announcement.*

— What fucking announcement?

PETER: *I've been presenting this programme for almost two years now, and I have to say that it's been a wonderful experience. I have been very privileged to have met and worked with some extraordinarily talented and dedicated people, it's been a roller-coaster ride and for the most part an absolute joy, but this period in my life, I have decided, is coming to an end. We live in a world in which people are defined by the jobs they do, our occupations determine our income, our social status, our perception of ourselves and of one other, and for the last two years this programme has defined me in more ways than I can begin to explain. But now it's all over.*

— Oh my God, it's a Dave Lee Travis moment.

PETER: *Ever since I first pitched the idea of this show to the good people here at the SBC, I made it clear that I wanted us to be an independent voice. I wanted to go out on a limb and bring you, the viewers, a level of discussion which I believed you deserved on all matters relating to our national game. I wanted to eschew the gratuitous negativity that pervades our game and to put the tabloids and the commercial broadcasters in their place, because I believed that we could have a more intelligent debate on all matters relating to football here in Scotland. And for the most part I reckon we've succeeded, in a small but significant way; we haven't revolutionised the domestic game or ushered in an era where Scotland is able to put an international team on the park to compare with the Austrian* Wunderteam *of the thirties, the Hungarian 'Golden Squad' of the fifties or even the Dutch masters of total football from the seventies; but we have, I believe, in our two short years on the air intervened in the culture in a positive and productive way. And if nothing else we've hopefully kept you entertained for half an hour every week and given you something to think about concerning the wonderful diversion from the mundane details of everyday life that is the beautiful game of football. Lately however, I've been unable to discuss the important matters pertinent to arguably the biggest story in the history of British sport, namely the liquidation of Rangers football club, in a way that I would like, and that I believe you, the viewer, would appreciate. Let me freely admit first of all that I am unambiguously not a Rangers supporter, and I never will be. I don't like the club, in fact I consider them broadly speaking to be a disreputable institution, with demonstrably little concept of, or regard for, what sport should stand for in our society, namely respect and fair play. Doddsy disagrees, he thinks they're wonderful! Yet we're still friends because, despite the odd moment, we respect each other's opinions and our right to hold and express them. Regardless of my own personal views, I have no interest whatsoever in pursuing a witch-hunt against the former club, I simply want to see them subject to the same justice that the rest of us would face, and at the moment I feel quite strongly that we're falling well short of those standards. Our society is based on justice and the rule of law and at the moment these principles are not being applied in a way that I feel they should be. I considered that Rangers transgressions were in a sporting context almost as serious as the systematic drugs cheating practised behind the Iron Curtain over a sustained period in the nineteen seventies and eighties. Doddsy disagreed, I wanted to discuss it, but we were told at yesterday's editorial meeting that it was not an appropriate subject for tonight's show, despite the fact that no managerial censorship or interference has ever been applied to this programme before. They trusted us, the big bosses, at least they used to before now; clearly they don't trust us anymore, and certainly not with this issue in particular. I wanted to bring into the spotlight the fact that Rangers may well be in further trouble with the tax authorities for their continued use of the name Rangers, and their insistence on trying to hold onto the old, liquidated club's history, and indeed laying claim to be the very same institution as the one which has recently been wound up. Doddsy would have argued that this was perfectly reasonable, and I would have disagreed; again we were not allowed to discuss it. I wanted to question Rangers boast that they will return to the top flight in a few short years, debt free; despite the fact that the old company still owes money all over town. And indeed I wished to assert my opinion that Rangers so far seem to have escaped relatively lightly from the whole affair and shown a shocking lack of remorse, contrition or sense of shame; I wanted to consider the possibility that the club may in the fullness of time be stripped of prizes that were won illegally, and other related issues, all of which and more is already being widely discussed on the internet, but we didn't even get that far in yesterday's meeting. This is the biggest story in the history of Scottish sport and the mainstream media are, I believe, with very few exceptions, misinforming you as to its significance and manipulating the information that is being conveyed to you about it. For the last two years I have made it my role to point out such inaccuracies and inconsistencies but now it seems that my hands are tied, so what's the point? From the start I always maintained that I would not allow myself to become just another talking head or another rent-a-quote, agenda driven pundit, and I promised myself that if at any point I was in danger of turning into another media lackey then I would do the honourable thing, and regrettably it appears that such a moment has arrived. Besides, my wife is pregnant. As every man and his dog already seems to know, she is from the Czech Republic and we want to go home and start our new family in that country. Coincidentally, this summer's European Championships are being jointly held in Poland and the Czech Republic and I am contractually obliged to present a special edition of the programme, the last of the summer, live from Prague immediately preceding the opening game of the tournament in a little over three weeks time. Following that broadcast however, me and my wife will almost certainly be remaining in the country and we won't be returning to Scotland. So this is goodbye. So long, and thanks for all the fish. I'm certain the show will go on, the audience response to it has been nothing short of fantastic, and I'd like to thank you all for watching and for caring. I'd also like to thank the people who you don't see at home, who work tirelessly on the show, there are too many to mention but I'd like to single out Alison, my trusty assistant and researcher without whom I wouldn't sound half as smart or as well-informed as I appear on this show, and Helen, my Producer, who is currently having a cow in the gallery over there, just off set.*

— You're not fucking wrong, pal. Ten seconds, get us out of here.

PETER: *Doddsy, it's been a riot, mate. You have a tendency to disappear up your own arsehole from time to time, which I've particularly noticed in the last few months or so, but you're a good bloke and I wish you well.*

DODDSY: *Thanks a million, Peter, it's been superb, honestly, pal.*

— Jesus Christ, he's tearing up.

— What? Camera two on, Doddsy.

— He's fucking greetin, look!

PETER: *Shona, thanks for being tonight's guest and good luck to you and your teammates over in Belarus.*

SHONA: *You're welcome, Peter, and thank you.*

PETER: *That's it from me for tonight, for the series and indeed forever. We'll see you one last time over in Prague, then it's goodbye. Thanks for watching, and goodnight.*

Spontaneous outbreak of applause.

— Roll credits, and we're out.

It was just as well that I was mobbed with well-wishers, most of them congratulating me on the happy news about Lenka and the baby, because Munroe was still hovering about, just off set, but he was frustrated by the crowd in his efforts to try and huckle me. I hung about long enough to shake a few more hands and indulge some of the more shocked expressions for a wee while, but then I was off. As soon as I could, I jumped in the car and went home to my wife.

18. THE DOG HOUSE

Here I am, sitting with my agent in a Byres Road coffee shop, which I suppose is where a lot ay people in ma line of work end up. Or ma former line ay work, I probably should say. They call this place The Bean House, although as far as my career in the mainstream media is concerned, it might as well have been called The Dog House. We've taken an alfresco seat out in the late afternoon, early summer sunshine, but for some reason Agent Wonga doesn't seem particularly keen on the surroundings, despite the fact that he's the cunt who arranged for us to meet here in the first place.

— It never ceases to amaze me, he's been waiting a while, but now he finally begins to pontificate, — how folk would want to leave their house to pay four pound for a cup ay coffee, when they can sit at home and drink as many as they fuckin well like for a fraction ay the price.

— I suppose for the same reason that people go to pubs, I suggest, — to be sociable. You can consume as much alcohol as you want in your own home as well, and save yourself a fortune, but people like to go out. I'm no sure what he makes of my reply, as he doesn't immediately respond, but I doubt I've convinced him because so far he still hasny managed to remove the same contemptuous scowl fae his face which I've been forced to look at ever since he first showed up here.

— Fitter women in pubs, he eventually remarks, which leaves me wondering exactly what pubs he drinks in.

— So, Mark, where do we go from here? I sit up and clear my throat. — Have you had any luck, any joy so far with looking into some ay the things we talked about? I cautiously try to get things started.

— It's been difficult, bud, he states flatly. — That was some fuckin stunt you pulled the other night. Naebidy in television wants to work wi you ever again, it seems.

— I'm still popular wi the supporters though, I point out. — I've been wading through my inbox for the last six days. The Tartan Army want to make me an honorary vice president, apparently.

— A fat lot ay good that's gony dae you, Nimmo considers. — And you're no the only one who's been receiving messages. A number ay ma colleagues are telling me that I ought to win some kind ay award, if I can manage to find you any sort ay work in this business ever again.

— I never even knew they had presidents and vice presidents, I ponder. — You'd have thought the Tartan Army would have colonels and brigadiers to go along wi the ordinary foot-soldiers, would you no?

— Peter, fucking pay attention, would you? This is a serious situation I'm in here. My friends are aw telling me that I've got one, which in agentspeak means that I'm stuck wi a rogue client, who I cany get rid ay and who I cany find work for either. I'm perfectly within my rights to dump you fae high heaven, pal, you know that don't you, and have nothing to do wi you ever again. Do you hear what I'm saying?

— At least I made a bit ay a splash, did I no? I'm a Youtube sensation now, you know. Just what I always wanted.

— You are a fuckin tube an aw pal, I'll grant you that.

— It's no just the internet though, is it? They've been playing that clip from the end ay the last edition of the programme on official news and entertainment outlets the length and breadth ay the country. If they wanted, the SBC could have pulled the broadcast, but they never, they put it out there. What does that tell you?

— What does it tell you? Nimmo bats my question back to me.

— What you've said to me many times, I shrug, — there's no such thing as bad publicity, no in this line ay work anyway.

— Exactly, Peter. Now if you gie me the green light here, I'm sure there'll be endless opportunities to take advantage ay this situation, Nimmo seemed to be warming to the task in hand at last, after I'd repeated his jejune mantra. — If we play this right, things could really open up for us here, because between you me and the gatepost, I'm hoping this might be the chance that I've been looking for as well. Treat every challenge as an opportunity, that's always been ma philosophy. We could really be going places on the back ay this, but we have to strike while the iron is hot now, don't we, son? I've already been fielding quite a number ay calls just this morning alone.

— Who's been in touch then?

— I've had Hat Trick productions on the phone.

— Oh aye? What did they want?

— They want you to be a guest presenter on *Have I Got News For You.*

— Seriously?

— Well, to be honest wi you, he hesitated, — it was me that was on the phone to them. But there's possibilities there.

— What did you say to them?

— I couldny get through, I just left them a voicemail, but there's a chance they'll have you on.

— A chance?

— Was worth a try, you never know your luck.

— Whether you're a guest presenter or just a pundit on that show, it's a couple ay days work at most. I'm looking for something on a slightly more permanent basis, mate. Can we get back to reality here, what about some ay the ideas we talked about during the week? Have you made any inquiries there? Have you had any joy wi any ay them?

— So, you're looking at politics, are you? It's no really a

313

very sexy subject, Peter, and to be honest, I didny think it was something you were particularly interested in, he tells me as he slurps his cappuccino.

— It isny really, but we might be able to make something work, I explain. — If it was the right programme and we could approach the subject from a similar point of view as the last show, try and discuss issues honestly and intelligently et cetera, then it could be worthwhile. We could play my erstwhile disinterest and perceived neutrality as a kind ay virtue, the guests have to convince me of the points they're making, and my apparent apathy works as a kind of bullshit alert mechanism. Once they start waffling, or giein us the party line, I cut them off and steer them away fae aw the usual rhetoric back in the direction of saying something interesting and honest.

— OK, here's what I've come up wi. Forget aw that perceived neutrality nonsense, you get to quiz politicians fae your own left-wing perspective. Ask them anything you want, debate them, push your opinions on them, argue it out, have an absolute field day. You'd be great at that, you could bring aw your fearsome talents to bear on these MPs and MSPs. Gie them aw your commie bullshit. Then a right wing blogger, or whoever they can find who has an opposing opinion to yourself, gets to do the same. So it's a political debate wi a difference, aw that lofty BBC Jeremy Paxman impartiality crap is oot the windae. You get to be as partisan as you like, but both perspectives are aired, because there's another cunt there giein it aw fuckin Mussolini just to balance things out. What dae you think?

— Why does there have to be balance?

— Eh? I'm no sure what you mean, Peter. Nobody's gony gie you airtime to spout your agenda all over the airwaves, this isny the United States, you know. The media here have to gie the audience both sides ay the story.

— This is the most instinctively Socialist country in Western Europe and ma moderately left-wing views have got to be balanced out by some fuckin foaming at the mouth fuckin right-wing maniac? Is that what you're telling me, Mark?

— Let me work on it, we could get someone from a different ideological headspace than yourself. It wouldny have to be Genghis Khan.

— Have you heard some ay these Tory bloggers, Mark? Forget it, mate, I don't think I'm equipped to go toe to toe wi some erstwhile elected representative of the people over issues that he's inevitably gony know a lot more about, and sure as fuck care a lot more about, than me. I can argue wi your Doddsys aw day long about football, I'm no sure I could do the same wi politicians.

— You'd be fully briefed, there'd be a couple ay tidy wee researchers doing aw the donkey work on your behalf. Aw you'd need to dae is swat it up before every show.

— Just out ay interest, what channel would this be on?

— Scottish Television are showing a definite interest.

— Jesus Christ, Mark, you really know how to scrape the fuckin barrel, don't you? What else you got?

— Nothing. That's it pal, as far as politics goes. If you want to be the next Jonathan Dimbleby, then this is the best I can do for you.

— What about independence? In the run-up to the referendum there's gony be a spate ay these discussion programmes, is there no? Obviously it'll be the same old faces most ay the time, but surely there has to be some level of interest in an alternative format. That would certainly get ma attention, if we could come up wi something along those lines, even back at the SBC.

— It's no gony happen, Peter.

— How no?

— You've burnt your bridges there, mate, I'm afraid.

— Says who? You don't seem to realise, I'm still quite highly regarded back in the old organisation. There's still a lot ay folk back at Specific Key who appreciated what I was doing over there and plenty of sympathy for how I reacted when it all fell apart at the end. Come on, you should be tellin me this. I shouldny have to blow ma own trumpet here, that's your job.

— I'm tellin you, Peter, forget it. It's no gony happen.

— How no?

— Because you'd never get it by Ballantyne and Munroe. You can have as much sympathy amongst the rank and file as you like, it's no gony make a blind bit ay difference when it comes to the people who matter. Here, let me ask you something. Did they ever quiz you about your views on independence at any point during the two years that you worked at the SBC?

— I cany say that they did, I pondered. — No wait, that's no quite right in actual fact. It was one ay the subjects that was brought up during that whole induction grilling I had wi Malcolm before they offered me the gig. He asked me about my views on independence, sectarianism, my political orientation and so on. But that was it, they never mentioned anything like that to me ever again.

— Well, your views were noted, let's just leave it at that.

— No they wereny, it was just a shakedown, Mark. They were just testing the water wi me, like they would wi any new employee, checking me out, making sure I wasny some sort ay zealot, who was gony turn up on their doorstep and start … how did you put it? … Spouting his own agenda all over their airwaves. Honestly, it was all very routine, nothing more than that.

— Really? And what exactly did you say to them?

316

— On what subject?

— On independence! What answer did you give them, when they asked you your view on whether Scotland should remain part of the United Kingdom?

— I think I said something like, Scotland has benefited from the Union at times in the past, but what self-respecting country in this day and age wouldny want to govern its own affairs.

— Did you no mention something along the lines ay, what characteristics did Unionists believe the Scottish people were lacking, that would prevent them from running their own affairs in a competent and capable manner?

— That's right, that's more or less what I said word for word, if I remember right. How did you know that?

— What else did you tell them?

— Nothing, that was it. Honestly, it was a very brief discussion.

— So you indicated to them that you were pro-independence?

— I guess I did, aye. I figured that in the Scottish national broadcaster there might be some leeway for views that were sympathetic towards Scottish self-determination.

— The SBC is pro-union.

— Really.

— Yes.

— Come off it. I'm no naïve, Mark, I know that broadcasters have their agendas, they like to set the tone and content of a particular discussion and maintain control of the narrative, but that's a bit ay a bold statement, is it no? The SBC is pro-Union?

— There are a million and one reasons why it suits the SBC

for Scotland to maintain the status quo. Where do you think they get their funding from for a start?

— Hold on a minute, that doesny make sense. If what you say is true, why did they employ me then? I told them right from the get-go, don't forget, that I was pro-independence.

— They needed someone like you in order to refute the suggestion that they were all a bunch of gun toting Unionists.

— I'm sorry, I don't believe that. You're saying that the only reason they commissioned my programme in the first place was because they needed a fall guy for the pro-independence lobby?

— It wasny the only reason. You had other qualities which they admired and who's to say they wereny right to go wi you? You're a talented guy, and you made a success ay the gig they offered you. At least until the other day you did. It's complicated, Peter, you cany just point to one factor and say that's the reason everything happened the way that it did. This is what the paranoiacs and the media haters cany understand, nothing ever happens in this business for one reason and one reason alone. It's a murky old world we're living in, you don't need me to tell you that, do you? You came along wi this fresh new idea, it was right for the time, everything was aligned right in the media firmament at that particular moment and you seized the opportunity to make a success ay it.

— It doesny make any sense, I shake my head. — Now that I've made a success ay it, as you say, what was to stop me from giein it laldy, and shouting my pro-independence agenda from the rooftops during their airtime, or in whatever other outlet is prepared to give me the time ay day? Surely that was the whole point of the compliance scrutiny, to make sure that any views I held were broadly conforming to the party line, and if not then at least to establish that I was sensible and moderate and could be trusted wi a television camera and a microphone pointing in ma direction.

— They wouldny have gied two fucks if you'd started shouting on about independence. Support for the Yes campaign is still languishing in the mid to high 30s in percentage terms. You can go out and join up wi them if you want, Peter, nobody's gony care.

— How no?

— This is where it gets ugly, I'm afraid, Nimmo hesitates.

— Get to the fuckin point, would you, Mark.

— They were happy to employ you as someone they could point to with pro-independence views, he explains slowly, — but it was felt that, as a sports broadcaster, any opinions you expressed on the subject would lack credibility and gravitas.

— So they win two nil, I concede, as the reality of the situation finally starts to dawn on me. — I see it now, it's beginning to add up. Most sports broadcasters, generally speaking, haveny got two brain cells to rub thegether, have they?

— The penny starting to drop now, is it?

— What a fuckin slow-witted cunt I am, I lament.

— Back ay the net.

— Jesus Christ, I think I'd prefer you to keep me away fae politics awthegether, Mark, if you don't mind. I've no got the stomach for it, what else you got?

— Good, cause there's no money in it anyway.

— What else you got, Mark?

— Don't be too down about it, Peter, that's how things work. They may have used you to suit their needs at the time, but they gave you a career. Do you think you'd be sitting here wi me otherwise, discussing your next move in television and your celebrity status? Try and be philosophical about it, you had a good run at it wi the SBC, sure you did? Be grateful for that.

— What else you got?

— Celtic TV? He rummages through his folder. — You could do a piece for them once a week. Forget aw the neutrality bullshit once and for all, you can shed those particular robes and just come out as a Celtic man. Be a relief, I'd imagine.

— Fuckin would an aw. Just once a week, you say?

— That's aw they were prepared to discuss.

— Any drawbacks?

— Shite money.

— Might have known.

He flicks through a few more documents. — There's always this.

— What?

— Don't suppose you fancy Kids TV?

— What, you gony put me in a Teletubbies outfit?

— Good money, he shrugs.

— Come on, Mark, be serious for a minute, would you?

— I was being serious, but we'll gloss over that then. Do you want to be a presenter on Sky Sports News? You can sit there in your best Tory boy outfit next to the girlfriend you *wished* you had.

— No I don't, Mark. What else you got?

— Actually that looks like it's pretty much it as far as the offers and inquiries are concerned.

— That's it?

— Fraid so, he closes his folder.

— I have to tell you, Mark, in all seriousness, I'm a wee bit disappointed in you if that's aw you have for me. I was hoping for something a wee bit more concrete than what you've showed me so far.

— That's the end, mate, I'm sorry. I'm out ay ideas.

— I suppose it's my own fault, I reflect. — Being a freelancer, I was never really much of a media insider. I never attended any high power meetings, or went to any award shows, did I? I should have made more ay an effort to get in wi the in crowd, should I no? Do you agree?

— You were never nominated for any fuckin awards, that's how you never went to any award shows, the bastard correctly points out.

— That's true. But still, do you understand what I'm saying? I'm actually quite a boring person when it comes to the crunch. I don't particularly enjoy going to drug-fuelled parties or hanging out wi dull, egotistical celebrities. Happily married, drinks in moderation, keeps himself to himself, the odd puff of ganja every now and then, but that's aboot the size ay it. I blame masel, I'm a boring cunt really at the end ay the day.

— I know, I always wondered what was the matter wi you.

— I wonder the same thing.

— We'd have had mair ay a chance if you were a cokeheid like Dougie Laird.

— Right enough. My bad, I suppose.

— What is it you want to do, Peter? Nimmo eventually asks me. — Just tell me, in an ideal world, if you could do anything you wanted, what would it be?

I'm struck by how difficult it is to provide an answer to this question and I have to think about my reply for a while, because although it seems an obvious line of inquiry, it's one that I seem to be unprepared for.

— I'd like to make football documentaries, I eventually offer. — Films about the history of football and the social impact of the game. You know there was a guy called Johnny Madden who played in Celtic's first ever match. He went out to Prague and coached there for twenty odd years. I'd love someone to give me a camera crew and a couple ay researchers, because I think he would make a fascinating subject for a short film or a documentary.

— I'll look into it for you.

— Would you?

— Sure. It's no gony happen, I'll tell you that now, but I promise I'll make a few inquiries for you.

— Right. Cheers.

— How's it going, Peter Fitzpatrick? It is you, is it no? Some random punter has approached our table, and I'm already nodding my appreciations at him in the usual, slightly forced manner. — Really enjoy the show, mate, that was some exit the other night there! Fucking brilliant by the way, I pure loved it.

— Cheers for watching, mate, means a lot, I tell the guy.

I see a second figure approaching as well, out of the corner of my eye. This guy's obviously just been made aware of my presence, because even while I'm still shaking the other boy's hand he makes a move on me. He picks up a glass of mineral water that's been standing on the table next to us ever since we sat down, and before I even have time to react, he's tipped it over me.

— You're lucky they only have plastic glasses here, ya dirty Fenian fucker! The guy tells me. — Fuck off back to Bulgaria and take yir fuckin gypsy whoor ay a wife wi you, he adds and then scarpers, with my erstwhile admirer tearing after him in hot pursuit, eager to extract his surrogate revenge on my behalf.

I'm left sitting there in stunned silence, drenched to the bone and looking like I've pished my pants. Nimmo isny exactly overflowing wi sympathy, for some reason he seems to find the whole situation remarkably funny.

— Could have been worse, he laughs as I try to dry masel off. — Goes wi the territory, I'm afraid, in this town.

— Well it shouldny! I protest.

— Bulgaria, what was he talking about?

— He meant the Czech Republic.

— Hey, I hope you're no seriously considering going back there. You cany give in to these bastards for a start, you have to stand up to people like that.

— Whatever I do, Mark, people like that won't come into my thinking one way or the other, I promise him. — Come on, let's go and sit inside, can we? I'm fuckin soaked here.

— Er, I think we're pretty much done here, pal, Nimmo tells me.

— I see. Is that you off then?

— That's me away the now, aye, he looks at his watch. — I have another meeting in half an hour or so. You need to have a right good think about what you want to do here, Peter. When you've done that, you can give me a shout, he advises me as he stands up and offers me his hand.

— I'll do that, Mark, I reply, but I cany help smiling as I watch him get into his car and drive away, because I know, as certainly as a man can know anything, that I'll never set eyes on the cunt again as long as I live.

19. HOMEWARD BOUND

When Kevin McGarry first arrived in Prague about five or six years ago now, in a car with a bunch of mates to see Celtic play Sparta in a Champions League group match, it was me who persuaded him no to go home after the game, but to stay and start a new life for himself in this city and to send his pals back to Scotland in the motor without him. Now the tables seem to have been turned; I'm flying into Prague with the rest of the production crew - all the boys and girls are here, Doddsy, Helen, Alison and although he's not on the flight with us I'm delighted that Davie Keane has promised to join us later on for what is going to be my final edition of 'The Scottish Football Debate'. After which, I shall once again find myself without a source of steady income, self-unemployed, floating in a jobless limbo, left to fend for myself again like so many other members of the massed ranks of Thatcher's lower middle classes.

I know what no longer appeals to me, financial services and the media, the two sectors, and I still cany quite figure out how this all happened, that I've so far found myself gainfully employed in; I'm far less certain right now however when it comes to identifying areas that I could potentially see myself involved with in the future, but one thing's for sure - I'll need to figure something out soon because there's a wean on the way and I have a family to look after. But these are concerns that will have to wait for another occasion, because right now we're here and there's work to be done. We have a programme to make, which we're hoping is going to be broadcast live from the venue of the opening match of this summer's European Championships, Prague's Letná Stadium, or as it appears to have been rechristened during my relatively short absence from the city, the AXA Arena. As soon as we're done here, and the show is behind me once and for all, then I can maybe turn my attention to trying to sort out my future and considering where I go from here because, as I say, I have a wife and child to support and right now I'm no even sure what country we'll be living in this time next month.

So much for my own precarious situation; Kevin McGarry on the other hand is very much the Prague resident these days, signed up by local side Slavia and working up at Strahov, coaching a bunch of their most talented young footballers. He was a football player himself, was Garra, but through a combination of injury and disillusionment wi the game in Scotland, he never managed more than a handful of games for Airdrie and then a few more for the mighty Smash and Grabs of Kirkintilloch, before he had to call time on his playing career. He ended up working as a joiner in Glasgow and he took a big risk to give that up as well, but he seems to have found a way back into football and I'm pleased to see the success and enjoyment that it's bringing him. I'd have felt guilty if it hadny worked out for Kevin over here, after me persuading him that abandoning his friends and family and his job back in Scotland, and starting a new life for himself in a foreign country that he knew next to nothing about, was a good career move for him at the time.

We touch down in the newly renamed Vaclav Havel airport, and after collecting our luggage and equipment, we're whisked through the passport and security checkpoints out to our waiting convoy of vans, trucks and taxis. Lenka and I have supposedly been put in charge of all communications and discussions of a local nature, but so far we've not been required and by the time we've made it to the Hilton at Massarykovo Nádraží and checked ourselves in, I've still not heard a word of Czech spoken since I arrived back in the country. I immediately ring Garra from the hotel room and tell him we've arrived. There's an editorial meeting later this evening which I'd like him to be involved with, and ideally I'd want him to participate in the show in some way. If we can persuade him to appear live in front of the cameras, or even do a recorded, 'in the can' piece, Garra could provide a real, first hand flavour of Czech football, and it would offer an

325

interesting slant on the issues we'll be discussing if he could share his knowledge and experience with us.

I meet him in the lobby and we spend an hour or two catching up over a few beers. He's invited his Irish girlfriend over and the four of us take a meal in the restaurant, on expenses of course, until it's time to head back down to the foyer where already folk are gathering in advance of our EM. I introduce him to Davie Keane and we settle into our seats for the meeting. Lenka and Garra's girlfriend Roisin sit up at the bar, with Lenka still redundant in her role as our erstwhile interpreter. There's another meeting tomorrow on the logistical issues with the local crew and the Letná administrative staff in which, I imagine, she will be less underemployed because I don't think Tam the cameraman or Jimmy the sound man speak too much Czech.

Following some more introductions Garra seems to be well acquainted with everyone by the time we sit down to the meeting.

— What are your thoughts on Czech football, Kevin? Helen immediately asks him. — How do things out here compare to your experiences back in Scotland?

— The first thing I should say is that I love it out here, Garra answers. — It was a real eye opener for me moving to a new country. My own experiences of trying to break through as a youngster in Scotland is a part of my life that I'd rather no recall to be honest with yous. Let's just say, youth development back in the day was a pretty haphazard affair, I found, although I understand things are changing and people like Mr. Keane are now able to bring their experience to bear at a club like Celtic, which is great to see. Out here though, the approach is totally different from what I was used to at home. Everything is done correctly in this country, every aspect of the game is coached and taught in a proper, methodical manner with an eye for every minute detail. I would say that the approach could be described as scientific almost. All the skills and techniques are coached and demonstrated to the players, so that they can be copied and learnt. Likewise, the physical aspect of the game is taught through training, every player receives speed coaching for example, so that even if a player isny the quickest, he's at least as quick as he can be. Similarly the mental side of the game is assessed and every player's attributes are noted, and they receive training on that as well. Their intelligence and psychological capabilities are tested and calibrated, and this information is all fed into the coaching database so that every player's strengths and weaknesses can be analysed and assessed. Altogether I'd say it's pretty different to what I experienced when I was a youngster trying to make the breakthrough at Airdrie.

— Do you think these are aspects that we need to take on board in Scotland? Helen is performing a kind of mock interview on Garra to assess his credibility and his suitability as a guest on the show.

— Definitely, aye. I would have loved to have had this kind ay set-up back home when I was sixteen, seventeen, Garra answers. — There's certainly things we can learn, like I say, I'm not entirely up to date with what Davie's doing at Celtic these days, but there's definitely aspects that can be incorporated.

— Would you agree, Davie? I ask.

— I would on the whole, yes. We've been trying to implement similar elements of the game as well with our youngsters. It's different when they get a bit older but for the thirteen and fourteen year olds, we kid on with them that football is a subject on the school curriculum, which has to be learned, assessed, tested and improved upon. It should be their favourite subject of course, what would they rather be doing, we like to ask them, studying maths and French or learning how to play football. We've had a lot ay success with this approach but I have a question for Kevin. I played against Central and Eastern European teams at club and international level and I found that their play could be quite stodgy at times. They had talent, they were ferociously competitive footballers and well-organised sides, but as I say they maybe lacked a wee bit of inspiration at times. So I'd like to ask you, Kevin, if you don't mind, if we adopted these training methods that you employ here back home, how do you think they would work in Scotland? We're very open to new ideas but the question always comes back to one concern, how do you ensure that imported methods don't stifle the instincts that young Scottish footballers acquire as they grow up. Aspects that suit players in one country might no work quite as well in another and you have to guard against simply importing foreign methods wholesale, and then sitting back fat, dumb and happy and assuming that everything will be hunky-dory from there on in. Do you follow me?

— I do, Mr Keane and you're a hundred percent correct, Garra agrees. — I always felt that I had an excellent start in the game just by being surrounded by football the whole time while I was growing up, and by learning not just the skillset required to be a good player, but the mentality required to want to succeed. Contrary to popular opinion, that doesny necessarily come from a burning desire to win games of football, at least not at a young age anyway; it comes from a love of the game, and from an understanding of the emotions you inspire in people when you beat a defender with a clever turn for example. I felt that really strongly when I was playing the game, unfortunately not at as high a level as you Davie, but in some ways the level didny matter, it always gave me a buzz to be recognised as a good player. And that buzz, rather than the competitive instinct to win games, is what inspired me to play well and to be recognised as an important member ay the team. The best players of course understand that out here too, but probably no to the same extent. I would say you're right to caution against trying to import whole chunks of one country's methods and just assuming they'll be effective somewhere else, even if they've already been used successfully. It has to be tailored to meet the needs of the culture and the mentality of the young players you're working with, and you need the right personnel to be involved as well. I think that's maybe why Slavia were so keen to employ me, they were looking for that extra something that maybe Northern European players and teams like Scotland have, and they're no so good at here. Because they're wanting to learn from other countries as well. These days we're all watching each other's football on television and asking ourselves, how can we add these wee elements that we see being practised abroad to our domestic game, without losing our strengths or compromising our unique identity. This is what we're talking about here at Slavia, and as I say, it's night and day compared to what I experienced as a young player in Scotland.

— Kevin, how would you fancy appearing on the programme and talking about these things? Helen asks.

— No, I don't think so, Garra reflects. — I'm no really sure that I want to get involved to that extent.

— Why not? You'd be paid.

— Aye, that'd be great, he laughs momentarily. — No sorry, it's just no my scene really, Helen. I'd just like to keep my heid down and concentrate on ma coaching, if you don't mind.

— What about a recorded piece, I suggest? — Maybe we could come out to your training ground, Kevin, and do a wee segment out there, maybe ask you a few questions?

— We'd have to figure out how to peg it to an issue we were discussing, Helen points out. — It can't just be a random interview with an old pal of yours, Peter.

— What about the Johnny Madden thing? Garra reminds me. I'd been discussing this possibility with him when we were having dinner earlier, and I'm glad we've had the opportunity to raise it in the meeting.

— That's right, aye. Come on Helen, we need to do this. Johnny Madden played in Celtic's first ever game in 1888, then he came out here and coached Slavia Prague for thirty odd years. He was part of the whole movement of Scots who took football out into foreign countries and taught the world how to play the game. We'd have no problem pegging it to any other discussion we were having, and Kevin can either present or introduce the piece.

— No, Peter, you would present it. I can help you out with the club, introduce you to the relevant persons, if you want to talk to anyone at Slavia.

— Could you do that, Kevin? Helen asks.

— Of course, aye. It works for me too, because it's an important part of Slavia's history we're talking about, so I know for a fact that they'd be only too happy to help you out.

— We could start the piece out at his grave, I suggest. — I'll take everyone out to Olšanské hřbitovy tomorrow and we can have a wee look around. Lenka can deal with any permissions we need and act as our go-between. We can get something scripted overnight and I can start the piece from out there: how Scots invented the modern game.

The discussion continues in this vein for another half an hour or so. I'm pleased that Garra is gony be helping us out, even though I was hoping he would do something to camera. At the same time though I totally respect his decision and his wishes, because if I could turn back the clock, there's a fair chance I'd never want to look down a television camera either, if I could possibly avoid it. For one tantalising moment, I'm intensely jealous of my old mate and I envy him his anonymity even more than I covet Davie's popularity and status as an idol of the Scottish game. After the meeting I hear the two footballers in discussion about a possible role at Celtic Park. Apparently there's a vacancy for a suitable coach in the same age group that Garra's currently working with and Davie appears to more or less offer him the job on the spot. I'm no sure what Garra's intentions are, I think he's a bit surprised to be seemingly recruited in this way by the club he's always supported, but I hear him promise Davie that he'll consider it carefully.

The next day we take a trip out to the cemetery and I'm lauding Johnny Madden by his graveside as one of the unheralded pioneers of Scottish football and waxing lyrical on camera about Scotland's close connections with the early development of the game in Central Europe. I mention John Dick who coached at Sparta, and Jimmy Hogan, whose lessons in Austria and Hungary on the short Scottish passing game helped lead to the growth and subsequent development of outstanding teams in those respective countries. It's a new departure for me, we usually have Dougie Laird or a host of other wannabe reporters queuing up to do this sort of thing for the show, while I'm sitting in my comfy presenter's seat and never leaving the studio. It's not quite the kind of full scale football documentary that I was recently discussing with my erstwhile agent Mark Nimmo, as it's only a five minute film, but who knows, maybe I'll be able to approach one or two production companies about a more in-depth piece, or maybe even a whole series ay them.

After the programme is aired, we're gony head out into the town for my leaving party and everyone's invited. I reckon I can still put my local knowledge to good use, and with Lenka and Garra's help of course, hopefully manage to show these boys and girls a good time in this city.

On the day of recording we set ourselves up for the show in a hotel overlooking Wenceslas Square. Our attempts to broadcast the programme live from Letná stadium itself, on the eve of the tournament's opening match, have unfortunately been thwarted. We were latterly informed that all the studio space at the ground was fully booked up in advance by television companies and broadcasters from all across Europe looking to transmit their coverage of the game the next day, and despite Lenka's best Slavonic entreaties, we wereny able to be accommodated. Priority was given to media from those countries whose national team had managed to qualify for the event, she was informed, so that ruled us out.

At my suggestion we've abandoned the idea of a footballing backdrop altogether and instead moved ourselves across town to the city's most iconic, well-known square, where thousands of Czechs gathered during the Prague Spring to protest against the cultural oppression of the Communist government. In the background of our set is the balcony where Havel and Dubček appeared in 1989 to announce to another gathering of thousands that the government had resigned en masse and that Communism in Czechoslovakia had effectively ended. I've always wondered, ever since I first came to this town the best part of a decade ago now, what happens the day after a revolution? The building is now occupied by a Jewish department store, and it's immediately obvious everywhere you look in this city that the country has changed beyond all recognition in the last twenty odd years. But that's on a very different timescale, and the question still fascinates me, I must admit, what the hell happens the day after a revolution?

By the time we're ready to go to air I've been fully briefed, and with all the info that I'll need at my fingertips I run through the customary soundcheck in our makeshift studio. Ever since I saw him again, I've been plugging Garra for more information on the Czech game, and we've had a few more meetings and informal discussions in the last day or two, with Alison playing her role as key researcher as well, particularly on the subject of the 'Scotch professors', that select group of men who taught the world how to play football. Of course I fully intend to pass off Alison and Garra's combined knowledge and research as my own during the programme, and in the process I'll be trying to make myself look good on television. There are people who spend a lifetime in this line ay work, building a career and earning a reputation for themselves on the back of other people's endeavours like this, but for me two years of pretending to be cleverer than I really am is enough. If only I was a wee bit sharper, I might have realised sooner that I'm in the wrong business.

— Cue, Peter, Helen finally announces in my ear.

It feels good to be home.

THE END

Some other books from Ringwood Publishing

All titles are available from the Ringwood website (including
first edition signed copies) and from usual outlets.
Also available in Kindle, Kobo and Nook.
www.ringwoodpublishing.com

Ringwood Publishing, 7 Kirklee Quadrant, Glasgow, G12 0TS
mail@ringwoodpublishing.com
0141 357-6872

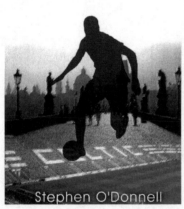

Paradise Road

Stephen O'Donnell
Paradise Road is the story of
Kevin McGarry, who through
a combination of injury and
disillusionment is forced to
abandon any thoughts of playing
football professionally. Instead he
settles for following his favourite
team, Glasgow Celtic, whilst trying
to eke out a living as a joiner.
It considers the role of young
working-class men in our post-
industrial society; the road Kevin
travels towards self discovery leads
him to Prague, where he develops
a more detached view of the
Scotland that formed him and the
Europe that beckons him.

*"A spectacular debut novel packed with social insight but all captured in
real world dialogue that flows superbly"* - **Bella Caledonia**-

ISBN: 978-1-901514-07-0   £9.99

Silent Thunder

Archie MacPherson

Silent Thunder is set in Glasgow and Fife and follows the progress of two young Glaswegians as they stand up for what they believe in.

They find themselves thrust headlong into a fast moving and highly dangerous adventure involving a Scots radio broadcaster, Latvian gangsters, a computer genius and secret service agencies.

Archie MacPherson is well known and loved throughout Scotland as a premier sports commentator.

"An excellent tale told with pace and wit"

Hugh Macdonald -The Herald

ISBN: 978-1-901514-11-7   £9.99

A Subtle Sadness

Sandy Jamieson

A Subtle Sadness follows the life of Frank Hunter and is an exploration of Scottish Identity and the impact on it of politics, football, religion, sex and alcohol.

It covers a century of Scottish social, cultural and political highlights culminating in Glasgow's emergence in 1990 as European City of Culture.

It is not a political polemic but it puts the current social, cultural and political debates in a recent historical context.

ISBN: 978-1-901514-04-9   £9.99

Torn Edges

Brian McHugh

Torn Edges is a mystery story linking modern day Glasgow with 1920's Ireland and takes a family back to the tumultuous days of the Irish Civil War.

They soon learn that many more Irishman were killed, murdered or assassinated during the very short Civil War than in the War of Independence and that gruesome atrocities were committed by both sides.

The evidence begins to suggest that their own relatives might have been involved

ISBN: 978-1-901514-05-6   £9.99

The Malta Job

Alwyn James

John Smith, a young Scottish journalist with literary aspirations, is sent to Malta to complete a sequel to the very successful MacMurder, a round-up of Scotland's more infamous homicides. The original author had died just before completing the planned sequel MacAbre, a follow-up tale of other gruesome Scottish crimes.

Once on Malta, with the dead author's notes, he gets involved in gripping events involving high romance, exciting adventure and a bank heist crime worthy of inclusion in either book

ISBN: 978-1-901514-17-9 ....£9.99

Yellow Submarine
Sandy Jamieson

Yellow Submarine explains how a small football club from a town of just 50,000 inhabitants became a major force not just in Spain but in Europe, including becoming Semi-Finalists in the Champions League, the UEFA Cup and the Europa League and 2nd in La Liga.

The success of Villareal offers supporters a model of how they too might live the dream, without having to rely on Russian or American billionaires or Arab dynasties.

ISBN: 978-1-901514-02-5   £11.99

Celtic Submari
Sandy Jamieson

Celtic Submari explains how an invasion of Vilarreal by 10,000 Celtic supporters in 2004 created a set of circumstances that has led to a lasting friendship between supporters of Villarreal and Celtic. This friendship is unique in football and offers the wider football world a model of camaraderie and togetherness that shows how football can be a force for good.

Rivals for 90 minutes, Friends for Always

ISBN: 978-1-901514-03-2   £9.99

Black Rigg
Mary Easson

Black Rigg is set in a Scottish mining village in the year 1910 in a period of social and economic change. Working men and women began to challenge the status quo but landowners, the church and the justice system resisted. Issues such as class, power, injustice, poverty and community are raised by the narrative in powerful and dramatic style.

ISBN: 978-1-901514-15-5   £9.99

Dark Loch
Charles P. Sharkey

Dark Loch is an epic tale of the effects of the First World War on the lives of the residents of a small Scottish rural community. The main characters are the tenant crofters who work the land leased to them by the Laird. The crofters live a harsh existence in harmony with the land and the changing seasons, unaware of the devastating war that is soon to engulf the continent of Europe.

The book vividly and dramatically explores the impact of that war on all the main characters and how their lives are drastically altered forever.

ISBN: 978-1-901514-14-8   £9.99

Calling Cards
Gordon Johnston

Calling Cards is a psychological crime thriller set in Glasgow about stress, trauma, addiction, recovery, denial and corruption.

Following an anonymous email Journalist Frank Gallen and DI Adam Ralston unravel a web of corruption within the City Council with links to campaign against a new housing development in Kelvingrove Park and the frenzied attacks of a serial killer. They then engage in a desperate chase to identify a serial killer from the clues he is sending them.

ISBN: 978-1-901514-09-4   £9.99

Good Deed
Steve Christie

Good Deed introduces a new Scottish detective hero, DI Ronnie Buchanan.

It was described by one reviewer as *"Christopher Brookmyre on speed, with more thrills and less farce"*.

The events take Buchanan on a frantic journey around Scotland as his increasingly deadly pursuit of a mysterious criminal master mind known only as Vince comes to a climax back in Aberdeen.

ISBN: 978-1-901514-06-3   £9.99